*New York Times* and *USA Today*
bestselling author
TERESA MEDEIROS
is one of a kind!

"One of my all-time favorite authors."
—SHERRILYN KENYON

"Few authors have Medeiros's storytelling talents."
—*RT BOOK REVIEWS*

"Try a novel by Teresa Medeiros and you will
swear it was written just for you."
—LISA KLEYPAS, *New York Times* bestselling author

"A superb storyteller.... Medeiros can pull every
last emotion from the reader with tear-inducing
scenes and laugh-out-loud dialogue."
—*BOOKLIST*

"Medeiros is a premier novelist!"
—*SINGLE TITLES*

"Medeiros is magic!"
—CHRISTINA DODD

**Turn the page for more critical acclaim for
Medeiros's charming romantic adventures!**

"From the first page to the last, she holds you enthralled with an enchanting plot, charismatic characters, and strong sensuality. It's another deep-sigh keeper from a master!" —*RT Book Reviews* (Top Pick!)

"Both primary and secondary characters are vividly three-dimensional; her plot is full of tasty twists."

—*Booklist* (starred review)

"Charming. . . . Readers will enjoy the appealing, self-reliant heroine. . . . Quick-paced, clever dialogue lightly sprinkled with Scottish slang moves things along."

—*Publishers Weekly*

"[A] funny, gently poignant historical that revitalizes the well-worn feuding families plot with wit, sizzle, and twists that turn expectations on their heads. A delightful diversion that deserves a sequel." —*Library Journal*

"An entertaining historical love story which mesmerizes by keeping the surprises and humor continuously coming."

—*Single Titles*

"A beautifully written historical romance with all the right ingredients for a passionate, thrilling story."

—*Fresh Fiction*

"An adventure ride through the Scottish Highlands, with plenty of twists and turns, secrets, surprises, laughter, and sighs along the way. . . . I read it in one day, then turned around and read it all over again the next. It's Teresa Medeiros at her finest!" —*The Romance Dish*

## ALSO BY TERESA MEDEIROS

*The Devil Wears Plaid*
*Goodnight Tweetheart*
*The Pleasure of Your Kiss*

# TERESA MEDEIROS

## *The* Temptation of Your Touch

POCKET BOOKS

New York   London   Toronto   Sydney   New Delhi

Pocket Books
A Division of Simon & Schuster, Inc.
1230 Avenue of the Americas
New York, NY 10020

This book is a work of fiction. Names, characters, places, and incidents either are products of the author's imagination or are used fictitiously. Any resemblance to actual events or locales or persons, living or dead, is entirely coincidental.

First Pocket Books paperback edition February 2013

POCKET and colophon are registered trademarks of Simon & Schuster, Inc.

For information about special discounts for bulk purchases, please contact Simon & Schuster Special Sales at 1-866-506-1949 or business@simonandschuster.com.

The Simon & Schuster Speakers Bureau can bring authors to your live event. For more information or to book an event, contact the Simon & Schuster Speakers Bureau at 1-866-248-3049 or visit our website at www.simonspeakers.com.

Manufactured in the United States of America

10  9  8  7  6  5  4  3  2  1

ISBN  978-1-4391-5790-9
ISBN  978-1-4391-7074-8 (ebook)

To Luanne, my sweet sister of the soul.

And for Michael, the man who made all of my dreams come true.

# Acknowledgments

I'd like to thank Garnet Scott, Stephanie Carter, Tina Holder, Gloria Staples, Veronica Barbee, Diane Alder, Richard Wimsatt, Janine Cundiff, Ethel Gilkey, Nadine Engler, Nancy Scott, Elliott Cunningham, Tim Autrey, and all of my tennis buddies for keeping me smiling (even when I'm on deadline).

And my heartfelt thanks to the city of Metropolis, Illinois, for keeping the dreams of Superman alive and for being my home away from home whenever I need to rediscover my creative soul.

# ⇌ *Chapter One*

MAXIMILLIAN BURKE WAS A very bad man.

He watched a tendril of smoke rise from the mouth of the pistol in his hand, trying to figure out exactly when he had embraced the role of villain in the farce his life had become. He had always been the honorable one, the dependable one, the one who chose each step he took with the utmost care to avoid even the possibility of a stumble. He had spent his entire life striving to be the son every father would be proud to claim as his own. The man any mother would want her daughter to marry.

At least that's what everyone had believed.

It was his younger brother, Ashton, who had gone around getting into brawls, challenging drunken loudmouths to duels, and facing the occasional firing squad after stealing some priceless relic—or woman—from a Middle Eastern potentate. But now Ash was comfortably settled in the family's ancestral home of Dryden Hall with his adoring wife and their chattering moppet of a daughter. A daughter, according to gossip, who had been blessed with her mother's flaxen hair and laughing green eyes. A daughter who should have been his.

Maximillian briefly closed his eyes, as if by doing so he could blot out the image of the niece he would never see.

While Ash enjoyed the domestic bliss that should have been Max's with the woman Max had loved for most of his life, Max stood in a chilly Hyde Park meadow at dawn, his expensive boots coated in wet grass and the man he had just shot groaning on the ground twenty paces away. Ash would have laughed at Max's predicament, even if a drunken slur cast on Max's sister-in-law's good name had prompted it.

Max could not seem to remember Clarinda's honor was no longer his to defend.

When he opened his gray eyes, they were as steely as flints. "Get up and stop whining, you fool!" he told the man still writhing about in the grass. "The wound isn't mortal. I only winged your shoulder."

Clutching his upper arm with bloodstained fingers, the young swell eyed Max reproachfully, his ragged sniff and quivering bottom lip making Max fear he was about to burst into tears. "You needn't be so unkind, my lord. It still hurts like the devil."

Blowing out an impatient sigh, Max handed the pistol to the East India Company lieutenant he had bullied into being his second and stalked across the grass.

He helped the wounded man to his feet, gentling his grip with tremendous effort. "It's going to hurt more if you lie there whimpering until a constable comes to toss us both into Newgate for dueling. It will probably fester in that filth and you'll lose the arm altogether."

As they crossed the damp grass, the young man leaned heavily on Max. "It wasn't my intention to give offense, my lord. I would have thought you'd have thanked me instead of shooting me for being bold enough to say aloud what everyone else has been whispering behind your back. The *lady* in question did jilt you at the altar. And for your own brother, no less!"

Max deliberately stripped his voice of emotion, knowing only too well the chilling effect that always had on his subordinates. "My sister-in-law is a *lady* of extraordinary courage and exceptional moral fiber. If I should hear you've been speaking ill of her again, even in so much as a whisper, I will hunt you down and finish what we started here today." The lad subsided into a sulky silence. Max handed him off to his white-faced second and the hovering surgeon, relieved to be rid of him. Resting his hands on his hips, Max watched them load the young fool into his rented carriage.

If Max hadn't been so deep in his cups when he had overheard his unfortunate dueling opponent loudly tell his friends that legendary adventurer Ashton Burke had married a sultan's whore, Max would never have challenged the silly lad to a duel. What the boy really needed was a sound thrashing before being sent to bed without supper.

Despite his regrets, Max had to admit that relinquishing his heroic mantle was almost liberating. When you were a villain, no one looked at you askance if you frequented seedy gambling hells, drank too much brandy, or neglected to tie your cravat in a flawless bow. No one whispered behind their hands if your untrimmed hair curled over the edge of your collar or it had been three days since your last shave.

Max gave the sooty stubble shadowing his jaw a rueful stroke, remembering a time when he would have discharged his valet without a letter of recommendation for letting him appear in public in such a disreputable state.

Since resigning his coveted chair on the Court of Directors of the East India Company in the aftermath of the scandal that had sent the society gossips into a feeding frenzy for months, he was no longer forced to make painfully polite conversation with those who sought his favor. Nor did he have to suffer fools graciously, if not gladly. Instead, everyone scurried out of his path to avoid the caustic lash of his tongue and the contempt smoldering in his smoky gray eyes. They had no way of knowing his contempt wasn't for them but for the man he had become—the man he had always secretly been behind the mask of respectability he wore in public.

He would rather have people fear him than pity him. His ferocious demeanor also discouraged the well-meaning women who found it unthinkable that a man who had been one of the most eligible catches in England for over a decade should have been so unceremoniously thrown over by his chosen bride. They were only too eager to cast him in the role of wounded hero, a man who might welcome their clucks of sympathy and fawning attempts to comfort him, both on the ballroom floor and between the sheets of their beds.

Shaking his head in disgust, Max turned on his heel and went striding toward his own carriage. He needed to get out of London before he cast an even greater stain over his family's good name and his own title by killing someone. Most likely himself.

The lieutenant returned the pistol to its mahogany case before trotting after Max. "M-m-my lord?" he asked, his stammer betraying his nervousness. "W-where are you going?"

"Probably hell," Max snapped without breaking his stride. "All that remains to be seen is how long it will take me to get there."

# ⇥ *Chapter Two*

"*A*NNIE! ANNIE! I'VE SOMETHING you must see!"

Anne Spencer withdrew her head from the cast-iron oven as young Dickon came racing into the kitchen of Cadgwyck Manor, all gangly limbs and boundless enthusiasm. With its low ceiling, exposed rafters, massive stone hearth, and scattering of faded rag rugs, the kitchen was by far the most cozy chamber in the drafty, old manor and the one where its residents chose to spend most of their free time.

"Mind your tongue, lad," Anne scolded as she slid a large wooden paddle from the stove and swung it toward the sturdy pine table, depositing two loaves of freshly baked bread topped with buttery, golden crusts on the table's scarred top.

Having never dreamed she would excel at such a domestic pursuit, she could not resist sparing a moment to admire her handiwork. Most of her early efforts at baking had resulted in the ancient stove's belching black clouds of smoke before it coughed up something that looked more like a smoldering lump of suet than anything fit to be consumed by humans.

By the time she returned her attention to Dickon, he was bouncing up and down on his heels with excitement. "How many times have I told you how important it is to stay in the habit of addressing me as Mrs. Spencer?"

"Even when there's no one around to hear?"

"Beer? There's no beer, lad, and if there was, you'd be too young to drink it."

They both turned to look at the old woman rocking in a chair in the corner of the kitchen. Nana squinted at them through her rheumy eyes, the merry click of her knitting needles never faltering despite her gnarled fingers and swollen knuckles. They had long ago stopped trying to guess what she could be knitting. It might have started out as a stocking or a scarf, but now it trailed behind her wherever she shuffled, growing longer each time Anne scraped aside a few pennies to buy another skein of wool at the market.

Anne exchanged an amused look with Dickon before saying loudly, "Don't fret, Nana. Our young Dickon here has always preferred brandy to beer."

Harrumphing her amusement at Anne's jest,

Nana returned to her knitting. Her hearing might be failing her, but her mind was still sharp as the proverbial tack.

Setting aside the paddle and dusting the flour from her hands, Anne nodded toward the rotund pooch napping on the rug closest to the hearth. "Nana might be too deaf to hear you, but what about dear old Piddles over there? He's always been an insatiable gossip." Piddles, the rather ill-favored and ill-tempered result of a sordid tryst between a pug and a bulldog, lifted his grizzled head just long enough to give them a disdainful snuffle through his flattened nose before curling himself back into a ball. Anne pointed at the calico cat who was treating the threadbare cushion of the other rocking chair as if it were his own private throne. "And then there's Sir Fluffytoes. Who knows what secrets the rascal might reveal to his numerous ladyloves to coax them out of their drawers?"

Dickon wrinkled his sun-freckled nose at her. "Now you're just being silly. Everyone knows cats don't wear drawers—only bibs, boots, and mittens."

Laughing, Anne gave Dickon's already hopelessly tousled tawny hair an affectionate rumple. "So what treasure have you brought for me today? Another dinosaur egg perhaps or the mummified corpse of a shrew that met its tragic fate at the merciless claws of Sir Fluffytoes?"

Dickon gave her a reproachful look. "I never said that was a dinosaur egg. I said dinosaurs had a right number of things in common with birds."

As the lad reached into his jacket, Anne recoiled out of habit. She had learned from bitter experience to check his pockets for snakes, frogs, mice, or any other reptile or rodent likely to send Lisbeth or one of the more squeamish housemaids into a fit of shrieking hysterics. Her smile faded as Dickon's freckled hand emerged with an expensive-looking square of vellum sealed with a daub of scarlet wax. "It was waiting for us in the village."

Anne took the letter from his hand, almost wishing it *were* a snake.

In her experience, the post rarely brought good news. A quick perusal of the exclusive Bond Street address on the outside of the missive confirmed today was going to be no exception to that rule.

Just as she had expected, the letter wasn't addressed to her but to Mr. Horatio Hodges, the butler and de facto head of the household whenever the manor's current master was not in residence.

Ignoring that small fact, Anne slipped one chipped fingernail beneath the wax seal and unfolded the cream-colored sheet of paper. As she scanned the letter's contents, her face must have revealed far more than she intended for Dickon immediately snatched the missive from her unsteady hands, his lips moving as he struggled to decipher the elegant handwriting. Anne had patiently been working with him on his letters, no easy feat when he much preferred to be out roaming the moors or scouring the steep cliffs for long-forgotten smugglers' caves or cormorant nests.

Even with his limited reading skills, it didn't take Dickon long to understand the gravity of their situation. When he lifted his eyes to her face, dismay had darkened their caramel-colored depths. "We're getting a new master?"

"Disaster?" Nana echoed loudly, her needles still clicking. "Is there a disaster?"

"So it seems," Anne replied grimly, swiping a smudge of flour from her flushed cheek. Given that she had sworn no man would ever be her master, the irony of their predicament did not escape her. "I was so hoping they would leave us to our own devices for a while."

"Don't look so worried, Annie—I mean, *Mrs. Spencer*." At the exalted age of twelve, Dickon considered himself a man full grown and more than capable of looking after them all. Anne wondered if she was to blame for forcing him to grow up too fast. "I doubt the gent will be here long enough to trouble any of us. We made short enough work of the last one, didn't we?"

A reluctant smile canted Anne's lips as she remembered the sight of their former *master* bolting over the hill toward the village as if the Beast of Bodmin Moor were snapping at his heels. Since he had publicly sworn he would never again set foot on the property, she had anticipated he might sell the manor or foist it off on some unsuspecting relative. She just hadn't expected it to be so soon.

"And then there was the one before that," Dickon reminded her.

They'd barely avoided an official inquiry over that one. The village constable still looked at Anne askance when she did her shopping at market on Fridays, forcing her to don her most guileless smile.

"That one wasn't precisely our doing," she reminded Dickon. "And I thought we all agreed we would speak of him no more. God rest his lascivious soul," she muttered beneath her breath.

"Well, if you ask me," Dickon said darkly, "the rotter got just what he deserved."

"No one asked you." Anne plucked the note from Dickon's hand to give it a more thorough reading. "It seems our new master is to be a Lord Dravenwood."

Something about the very name sent a shiver of foreboding down Anne's spine. Once, she might have recognized the name, would have known exactly who the gentleman's mother, father, and second cousins thrice removed were. But the noble lineages immortalized between the covers of *De-brett's Peerage* had long ago given way in her brain to more practical information, like how to beat a gen-eration of dust out of a drawing-room rug or how to dress a single brace of scrawny partridges so they would feed ten hungry servants.

She squinted, trying to read between the lines, but nothing in the letter from the earl's solicitor gave a clue as to their new master's character or whether the man would be arriving with a wife and half a dozen pampered bratlings in tow. With any luck he'd be some potbellied, gout-ridden sot in his dotage, already half-addled from decades of overin-dulging in too many overly rich plum puddings and after-dinner brandies.

"Oh, no," she whispered, dread pooling low and heavy in her breast as her gaze fell on the date neatly inscribed at the top of the page. A date she'd over-looked in her haste to read the rest of the letter.

"What is it?" Dickon was beginning to look wor-ried again.

Anne lifted her stricken eyes to his face. "This let-ter is dated nearly a month ago. The post must have been delayed in reaching the village. Lord Draven-wood isn't scheduled to arrive at the manor a week from today. He's scheduled to arrive . . . *tonight!*"

"Bloody hell," Dickon muttered. Anne might have

chided him for swearing if his words hadn't echoed her own feelings so precisely. "What are we going to do?" the boy asked.

Gathering her scattered composure, Anne tucked the letter into the pocket of her apron, her mind working frantically. "Fetch Pippa and the others immediately. We haven't a second to squander if we hope to give our new master the welcome he deserves."

## Chapter Three

THE JOURNEY TO HELL was much shorter than Max had anticipated. It seemed the abode of the damned wasn't located in the stygian depths of the underworld but on the southwest coast of England in a wild and windswept place the unbelievers had christened Cornwall.

As his hired carriage jolted its way across the stony sweep of Bodmin Moor, rain lashed at the conveyance's windows while thunder growled in the distance. Max drew back the velvet curtain veiling the window, narrowing his eyes to peer into the night beyond. He caught a brief glimpse of his own scowling reflection before a violent flash of lightning threw the bleak landscape into stark relief. The lightning vanished as quickly as it had come, plunging the moor back into a darkness as thick and oppressive as death. Given how ridiculously overwrought the entire scene was, Max wouldn't have been surprised to hear the ghostly hoofbeats of King Arthur and his knights as a spectral Mordred pursued them or to see the Bodmin Beast, the phantom creature who was said to haunt these parts, loping along beside the carriage, eyes glowing red and teeth bared.

Letting the curtain fall, he settled back on the plush squabs, feeling an unexpected rush of exhilaration. The rugged terrain and ferocious weather perfectly suited his current temper. If he had sought to banish himself from the comforts and charms of civilization, he had chosen well. The bone-rattling journey from London alone would have been penance enough for a less sinful man.

There had been a time when his father might have tried to talk him out of leaving London. But when the gossip about Max's duel had reached the duke's ears—and the society pages of the more sordid scandal sheets—the duke had been forced to admit it might be in everyone's best interests if Max took a brief *respite* from polite company. His father still hadn't recovered from the blow of Max's resigning his prestigious position with the East India Company. Even Max's mother, who had yet to give up on her cherished hope that Max would find a new—and far more suitable—bride, had managed no more than a token protest when informed of his plan to manage the most remote property in the family's extensive holdings.

If it had been within his power, Max would gladly have relinquished his title along with his career. Ash had ended up with everything else Max had ever wanted. Why not just hand him the earldom and make him heir to their father's dukedom as well?

As his parents had bid him an affectionate farewell in the drawing room of their London mansion, neither of them had been able to meet his eyes, plainly fearing he might recognize the relief within their own. Since his past transgressions had come to light on the day his bride had jilted him, proving he wasn't the perfect son they had always believed him to be, Max had become a stranger to them both—dangerous and unpredictable.

Despite his determination to embrace the rigors of his exile, he felt a flare of relief when his carriage traded the rutted road for a cobbled courtyard. He wasn't immune to the temptation of stretching his long legs after being confined to the cage of the vehicle for hours—and days—on end.

He was gathering his hat, gloves, and walking stick when the coachman flung open the carriage door. Rain dripped steadily from the drooping brim of the man's slouch hat.

"Have we arrived at our destination?" Max was forced to practically shout to be heard over the rhythmic slap of the rain against the cobblestones.

"I have," the man said shortly, his long face looking

as if it would shatter completely if it dared to crack in a smile. "'Tis as far as I'll go. You'll have to hire one o' the locals to take you the rest o' the way."

"Pardon? I was under the impression you'd been engaged to take me to Cadgwyck Manor."

"I was hired to take you to the *village* of Cadgwyck," the man insisted.

Max sighed. His diplomatic skills had once been the stuff of legend, but of late the reserves of his patience had been all but exhausted. "If this is the village, surely the manor can't be that much farther. Wouldn't it make more sense to press on than to go to all the trouble of unloading my baggage just so it can be reloaded into another conveyance? Especially in this weather."

"'Tis as far as I'll go. I'll go no farther."

Max wasn't accustomed to having his will defied, but it was rapidly becoming clear the taciturn coachman was not to be swayed, either by logic or threats. Since Max didn't have a stockade, a firing squad, or even a dueling pistol at his immediate disposal, he found himself with no recourse but to exit the man's carriage.

"Very well," he said stiffly, yanking on his gloves.

He climbed down from the carriage, tugging the brim of his hat forward to shield his face from the wind-tossed gusts of rain. He straightened to find himself standing in the cobbled courtyard of a ramshackle inn. He half-expected the inn to be named Purgatory, but a splintery sign suspended on creaking chains over the door proclaimed it the Cat and Rat. Max could only hope it was a tribute to the faded black cat with a rat hanging out of its mouth painted on the sign and not what they served for supper.

The establishment had plainly seen better days, but the cozy glow of the lamplight spilling through the windows promised a haven for the weary—and wet—traveler.

Max watched as the coachman's outriders piled his trunks beneath the overhang of the inn's roof, where they would at least be out of the worst of the weather. He supposed he should be grateful the lunatic hadn't dumped him and his baggage in the middle of the moor.

The coachman scrambled back up into the driver's seat, drawing an oilcloth hood up over his hat to shelter his dour countenance. *He must be in a great hurry to escape this place,* Max thought. He wasn't even lingering long enough to change out his team or allow his outriders a bit of refreshment.

As the man gazed down at Max, shadows hid everything but the sharp glint of his eyes. "God be with you, m'lord," he said before muttering beneath his breath, "You'll have need o' Him where you're goin'."

With that enigmatic farewell, the coachman

snapped the reins on his team's backs, sending the carriage rocking away into the darkness.

Max stood there in the rain gazing after him, not realizing until that moment just how weary he was. This weariness had little to do with the hardships of his journey and everything to do with the thirty-three years that had preceded it. Years spent chasing a single dream only to have it slip through his fingers like a woman's sleek blond hair just when it was finally within his grasp.

Max's expression hardened. He wasn't deserving of anyone's pity, especially his own. Forcing himself to shake off his ennui along with the droplets of rain clinging to the shoulder cape of his greatcoat, he went striding toward the door of the inn.

MAX ENTERED THE INN on a tumultuous swirl of wind, rain, and damp leaves. The common room was far more crowded than he had anticipated on such an inhospitable night. Well over a dozen patrons were scattered among the mismatched tables, most of them nursing pewter tankards of ale. Max hadn't seen any other coaches in the courtyard. Since it was the only establishment of its kind in these parts, the local villagers probably assembled there nightly to indulge in a pint—or three—before seeking out the comfort of their own beds.

A thick haze of pipe smoke hung over the room. A cheery fire crackled on the grate of the stone hearth, making Max wish he were an ordinary man who could afford the luxury of drawing off his damp gloves and warming his hands by its flames before settling in to enjoy a pint and some companionable conversation with his mates.

He tugged the door shut behind him. The wind howled a protest as it was forced to retreat. An awkward silence fell over the room as the gaze of every man and woman in the place settled on him.

Max returned their gazes coolly and without a trace of self-consciousness. He had always cut an imposing figure. For most of his life, he had only to enter a room to command it, a trait that had served him well when negotiating peace treaties between warring factions in Burma or assuring Parliament the interests of the East India Company were also the interests of the Crown. He could feel the curious stares lingering on the plush wool of his greatcoat with its multilayered shoulder capes and brass buttons, the ivory handle of the walking stick gripped in his white-gloved hand, the brushed beaver of his top hat. The last thing the patrons of the tavern had expected to blow through their door on this night—or any other—was probably a gentleman of means.

He gave them ample time to take his measure before announcing, "I'm looking for someone to transport me to Cadgwyck Manor."

Suddenly, no one would look at him. Instead, they exchanged furtive glances with one another, lifted their mugs to their lips to hide their faces, or gazed into the steaming depths of their mutton stew as if the answers to the mysteries of the universe could be found there.

Baffled by their odd behavior, Max cleared his throat forcefully. "Perhaps you misunderstood me." His voice rang with an authority honed by years of snapping out orders to brash young lieutenants and chairing board meetings attended by some of the wealthiest and most powerful men in England. "I'm seeking to engage someone to carry me and my baggage the rest of the way to Cadgwyck Manor. I'm willing to pay. And pay well."

The silence grew even more tense, broken only by an ominous rumble of thunder. Now the villagers wouldn't even look at each other. Max studied their drawn profiles and hunched shoulders, fascinated against his will. He could easily have dismissed them as a provincial and unfriendly lot with an instinctive mistrust of strangers. But as a man well acquainted with battle fatigue in all of its incarnations, he recognized that their nervous twitching and averted gazes were not a result of hostility but fear.

A woman Max assumed must be the innkeeper's

wife came bustling out from behind the bar, wiping her hands on her ale-stained apron. Judging by the fetching dimples in the dumplings of her cheeks and the alarming way her heavy breasts threatened to overflow the front lacings of her bodice, she had probably been quite the buxom beauty in her day.

"Now, m'lord," she crooned, her smile a shade too friendly, "why would ye want to go back out on such a foul night as this? Especially when ye've got everything you need right here. Why, we've even a mattress ye can let in a private room!" Her smile deepened to a leer. "Unless, of course, ye'd like someone to share it with ye."

The woman seized a scraggly-haired young barmaid by the elbow and thrust her in Max's general direction. The girl gave him a flirtatious smile, which might have been more alluring if both her front teeth hadn't been missing.

Suppressing a shudder at the thought of sharing some flea-infested mattress with a barmaid who probably also had fleas—or worse—Max offered both women a polite bow. "I appreciate the hospitality of your fine establishment, madam, but I've already come all the way from London. I've no desire to waste another night on the road, not when I'm this close to my destination."

The woman cast the man polishing a pewter tankard behind the bar a desperate glance. "Please, sir, if ye'll just wait till morning, we'll have our boy Ennor take ye up to the manor. And I won't let him charge ye so much as a ha'penny for his trouble."

Ignoring her offer, Max swept his gaze over the room, assessing its occupants with a jaded eye. "You there!" he finally said, settling on a hulking giant of a man with a shiny melon of a head and a homespun shirt stretched taut over the slabs of muscle in his shoulders. The man was hunched over a bowl of stew and did not look up as Max strode over to his table. "You look a strapping sort, not inclined to let a little rain or a bit of thunder and lightning keep you from making a tidy profit. Have you a conveyance?"

"Won't go." The man spooned another heaping mouthful of stew into his mouth. "Not afore the sun comes up. She wouldn't like it."

"She?" Max cast the innkeeper's wife a bewildered glance. Although the woman looked perfectly capable of wielding a mean rolling pin, she hardly looked menacing enough to hold an entire village hostage.

"*Her.*" The man finally lifted his head to meet Max's gaze, his voice a rumble even deeper than the thunder. "The White Lady o' Cadgwyck Manor."

## Chapter Four

AN AUDIBLE GASP WENT up from the other patrons of the inn. Catholicism had fallen out of favor in these parts over three centuries ago, after King Henry VIII had decided it would be simpler to divorce Catherine of Aragon than to behead her, but from the corner of his eye, Max saw a man sketch the sign of a cross on his breast.

As understanding slowly dawned, an emotion he hardly recognized came bubbling up inside of him. Throwing back his head, Max did something he hadn't done for months and had suspected he might never do again.

He laughed.

It was a deep, ripe, full-bodied laugh, as out of place in the tense atmosphere of the tavern as a baby's cry would have been at the undertaker's.

"She won't like that, either," the bald man warned dourly before returning to his stew.

Max shook his head, still grinning. "I can't believe all of this nonsense is over a ghost! Although I don't know why I should be so surprised. It's not as if I'm a stranger to native superstitions. In India it was the *bhoot* who wear their feet backward and cast no shadow. In Arabia, the cunning *efreet* who can possess a man's body and then trick others into doing its will. And what crumbling manor or castle in England doesn't come equipped with its own spectral hellhound or Gray Ghost? I did a fair bit of reading after I decided to come here, and it seems Cornwall is so rife with spirits of the dead it's a miracle they aren't stumbling over each other's chains." He began to tick them off on his fingers. "There's the Bodmin Beast, of course, along with the shades of all the sailors lured into dashing their ships on the rocks by unscrupulous wreckers out to salvage their cargo. Then there are the ghosts of the wreckers and smugglers themselves, doomed to wander the mist as flickering lights for all eternity as punishment for their terrible crimes."

He shook his head ruefully. "But if I'm to have a ghost, naturally it would be a White Lady. Because God knows I haven't already wasted enough of my life being haunted by a woman!"

The villagers were beginning to eye him askance, as if he were the one making mad assertions. Even to his own ears, his voice had a wild edge to it, just shy of violence.

The innkeeper's wife planted her hands on her generous hips, her disapproving scowl warning him just how quickly the villagers could turn on him. "Ye might not be so quick to dismiss our words as a bunch o' rubbish—or be so bloody smug—if ye'd have seen the face o' the last master o' the house on the night he came runnin' into the village a little after midnight, half-dead from fleein' whatever evil lurks in that place."

"Why, he wouldn't even speak o' the things he saw!" the barmaid added, her face growing even paler beneath its curtain of lank, lemon-colored hair.

"Aye," said an old man with leathery skin and a patch over one eye. "Unspeakable they were."

The other villagers began to chime in, growing bolder with each word. "He swore he'd never set foot in that cursed place again, not for all the money in the world."

"At least he escaped with his life. The one before him weren't so lucky."

"Took a tumble out a fourth-floor window, he did. Found him in the courtyard, his head twisted clean round on his neck."

A hush fell over the common room once again.

The rain had subsided, and for a long moment there was no sound at all except for the eerie whistle of the wind around the eaves.

When Max finally spoke, his voice was soft, but edged with an authority that dared anyone within earshot to defy him. "I've spent the last twelve years of my life journeying to places most of you will never see, not even in your darkest dreams. I have seen men do unspeakable things to each other, both on the battlefield and off. I can assure you ample evil lurks in the hearts of men without conjuring up phantoms and monsters from the shadows of our imaginations. Now," he said briskly, "I've no intention of squandering any more of my time or yours." He reached into an inner pocket of his greatcoat and withdrew a leather pouch. He tossed it toward the nearest table, where it landed with an impressive clunk. "Twenty pounds to the man who possesses the backbone to get me to Cadgwyck Manor before the rain sets in again."

The eyes of the inn's patrons gleamed with avarice as they gazed upon the pouch.

Max wasn't playing fair. But if he hadn't tried to play fair for most of his life to atone for the one time he hadn't, he wouldn't have ended up stranded in this miserable tavern at the mercy of a bunch of overly superstitious rustics. The men in the tavern were fishermen, shepherds, and farmers living a hardscrabble life on whatever scraps the sea and the land deigned to toss them. Twenty pounds was more than most of them could hope to earn in a year.

Still, no one moved to accept his offer.

Until a scrawny young man rose slowly to his feet. Ignoring the dismayed gasps of his companions, he drew off his cap in a gesture of deference before wadding it up in his tense hands. "Derrick Hammett, sir. I'm yer man."

Max eyed him thoughtfully, taking in the sunken hollows of his cheeks and the way his clothes hung loosely on his rawboned frame, before retrieving the pouch and tossing it to him. "Very well, lad. Let's make haste then, shall we? I'm sure this White Lady of yours is only too eager to meet the man who will be her new master."

MAX HAD ENVISIONED ARRIVING at the gates of his new home in the dry, cozy comfort of a carriage, not while perched stiffly on the bench of a rattle-trap cart with chill rivulets of rain trickling beneath his collar and down the back of his neck. Despite his young driver's best intentions, the lad had been unable to make good on his promise to get Max to Cadgwyck Manor before the rain returned.

As they passed between two stone gateposts, one

of them leaning crazily to the left, the other to the right, the sky hurled violent gusts of rain at them, rendering the brim of Max's hat utterly useless. Twice during their journey up the long, twisting drive he was forced to climb down from the cart to help the boy dislodge its wheels from jagged ruts carved by the rushing water, an exercise that ruined his expensive gloves and left both his boots and his temper much the worse for wear.

The weather in this place was as perverse as its people. Just as they reached the top of the hill and the promise of shelter, the wind gathered speed, whipping away the last of the rain. It carried on its breath the salt-tinged scent of the sea and the muted roar of angry waves breaking against the cliffs on the far side of the house.

Setting his jaw in a rigid line to keep his teeth from chattering, Max peered through the gloom, struggling to catch his first glimpse of his new home.

A pale splinter of a moon materialized from behind a wisp of cloud, and there it was, perched at the edge of the towering cliffs like some great hulking dragon.

Max's father had informed him he had picked up the property from a distant cousin for a song. *If that were so,* Max thought grimly, *it must have been a very sad song indeed. Perhaps even a dirge.*

It was difficult to believe the manor had seen

better days, although he might be convinced it had seen better centuries. An abandoned stone tower crowned one corner of the structure, complete with crumbling parapets and a lopsided turret. A glistening curtain of ivy had clawed its way up the weathered stones and through the gaping black holes of the windows, making it look like a place where Sleeping Beauty might dream away the years while waiting for a prince's kiss that would never come.

The front door was set like a rotting wooden tooth in the mouth of an ancient gatehouse that must have been part of the original castle charged with the duty of guarding these cliffs. The various descendants of that castle's lord had haphazardly slapped Elizabethan wings on each side of the gatehouse, then adorned the entire monstrosity with several deliciously droll Gothic touches—gables pitched at dizzying angles, lancet windows set with cracked panes of jewel-toned glass, impish gargoyles spitting streams of rainwater on the unsuspecting heads of anyone reckless enough to pass below them.

A tragic air of neglect hung over the place. Shutters hung at awkward angles over the grimy windows. The roof sported several bald spots, where slate shingles had been hurled into the night by the gleeful fingers of the wind and never replaced.

Had the village lad not been with him to confirm

this was indeed their destination, Max might have mistaken the manor for a ruin. The house looked as if it would do them all a great favor—especially Max—by completing its inevitable slide over the edge of the cliff and into the sea.

Despite its dilapidated state—or perhaps because of it—Max felt a curious kinship with the structure. The two of them might just suit after all. The manor looked less like a home and more like a lair where a beast might go to lick its self-inflicted wounds in privacy and peace.

The wind sent a fresh veil of clouds scudding across the moon. Darkness reared up to cast its shadow over the house once more.

That was when Max saw it—a faint flicker of white in the window of the crumbling tower, gone as quickly as it had appeared. He frowned. Perhaps he had been wrong about the tower being abandoned. Or perhaps a broken pane of glass still clung to a splintered window frame, just large enough to pick up a reflection.

But a reflection of what?

With the moon cowering behind the clouds, there was nothing but an endless stretch of moor on one side of the manor, and jagged cliffs and churning sea on the other. The flash of white came again, no more substantial than a will-o'-the-wisp against that solid wall of blackness.

Max glanced over to see if his companion had noticed it, but Hammett was using every ounce of his attention to keep his team from bolting back down the hill. Both horses were tossing their heads and whinnying nervously, as if they were as eager to depart this place as their young master. By the time Hammett got them under control and brought the cart to a lurching halt, the tower was once again shrouded in darkness.

Max gave his eyes a furtive rub with the palms of his hands. He was hardly a man given to fancy. Those spectral flashes must simply be a symptom of his own exhaustion—a trick of his weary eyes after the grueling journey. Due to the run-down state of the house, a man was more likely to be murdered by a loose chimney pot or a rotted banister than a vengeful ghost.

"Are ye sure they're expecting ye, m'lord?" Max's young driver blinked the last of the rain from his ginger lashes as he gazed anxiously up the hill toward the manor's forbidding edifice.

"Of course I'm sure," Max replied firmly. "My solicitor sent word over a month ago. The household staff has had ample time to prepare for my arrival."

Despite Max's insistence, he couldn't blame the young man for his skepticism. Except for that mysterious flash of white, the house looked as deserted and unwelcoming as a tomb.

Max gathered the single portmanteau he had salvaged from his baggage and climbed down from the cart. He had decided to leave the rest of his bags at the inn and risk the villagers picking through them rather than transport them in the back of the cart, where they would have been soaked through in minutes.

"It's nearly ten o'clock," he pointed out. "The lateness of the hour must be taken into account. And I can hardly expect even the most devoted of servants to be lined up in an orderly row on the front steps to greet their new master in this foul weather."

Although Hammett still looked dubious, he managed an encouraging nod. "I'll bring the rest o' your baggage at first light, m'lord. I swear I will."

Reaching into his coat, Max drew out a second purse and tossed it to him. "In my years with the East India Company, I came to believe a young man should always be rewarded for both his bravery and his gallantry."

"Oh, sir!" Hammett gaped down at the purse, a disbelieving grin splitting his gaunt face. "Why, thank you, sir! Me mum and me sisters thank you, too. Or at least they will once they see this!" Although he was plainly itching to go, he shot the house another reluctant glance. "Would ye like me to wait until ye're safely in?"

"I appreciate the offer but that won't be—"

Just like that, Hammett snapped the reins, wheeled the cart around, and went careening down the hill.

"—necessary," Max finished on a whisper heard only by his ears. The rattle of the cart wheels quickly faded, leaving him all alone with the desolate wail of the wind.

Gripping his portmanteau in one hand and his walking stick in the other, he turned toward the house. Once, he had imagined returning from some long journey to a far different scenario. One where a loving wife ran out to greet him, trailed perhaps by a towheaded moppet or two, all eager to leap into his arms, smother his face in kisses, and welcome him home.

Squaring his shoulders, Max went striding toward the door, ruthlessly banishing that vision from both his imagination and his hopes. As he climbed the stone stairs leading up to the makeshift portico tacked onto the gatehouse, the wind tossed a few fresh droplets of rain into his face.

Drawing off his hat, he hesitated at the top of the stairs. He was at a complete loss as to how he should proceed. He was accustomed to being greeted with deference wherever he went, not left standing outside a closed door like some beggar at the gates of heaven.

Should he use the tarnished brass knocker to alert

the servants to his arrival? Should he test the door-knob himself? Or should he just go striding into the place as if he owned it?

Which, of course, he bloody well did.

He was lifting his walking stick to give the door a firm rap when it began to swing slowly inward, its unoiled hinges creaking in protest.

## ✢ Chapter Five

Max stood his ground, half-expecting to be greeted by a swirl of mist or some chain-clanking ghoul. A stocky, stoop-shouldered man with a snowy white mane of hair appeared in the doorway, bearing a single silver candlestick. The candle's flame cast wavering shadows over the man's downcast face, a victim of his unsteady hand.

Without a word of explanation or greeting, the man turned toward the interior of the house, as if it were of no particular import to him whether Max chose to follow.

Max cocked a questioning eyebrow but didn't hesitate for long. While the musty smell and flickering candlelight could hardly be called cozy, it was a definite improvement over the darkness and damp of the night.

The two-story entrance hall of the manor was covered in some sort of burgundy velvet-flocked paper. Sections of it had peeled away in moldering strips to reveal the unpainted plaster beneath. Max suspected some valuable wainscoting was buried beneath it as well. Despite enduring the abuses of more recent centuries, the ancient gatehouse had sound structural bones.

His gaze drifted upward as they passed beneath a grand chandelier. Cobwebs draped the fixture's tarnished brass arms, and its once-graceful tapers were melted down to beeswax nubs. On the far side of the entrance hall, a broad staircase climbed up to a second-story gallery shrouded in shadows. A handsome longcase clock hugged the wall at the foot of the stairs, its pendulum hanging still and silent. Its gilded hands were frozen, seemingly forever, at a quarter past midnight.

Max's silent escort led him through a pair of open pocket doors and into the drawing room. A handful of oil lamps scattered on various tables battled the gloom. Despite their valiant efforts, it wasn't difficult to see why the manor had looked so dark and inhospitable from the drive. The house had been graced with ample windows, but dusty velvet drapes guarded every one of them.

Remembering with a pang of longing the crackling good cheer of the fire at the Cat and Rat, Max noted that a fire hadn't even been laid on the drawing room's marble hearth to welcome him. Could the manor's staff be so provincial they were ignorant of even that basic courtesy? He lowered his portmanteau to the faded Turkish carpet. The butler— or at least Max assumed it was the butler, given that there had still been no proper introduction—set his candlestick on a low-slung pier table, shuffled over to the wall, and gave an unraveling bellpull a feeble yank. A cloud of dust spilled down upon his head, sending him into a violent fit of sneezing.

The man was still snuffling and dabbing at his eyes with the cuff of his shirt when the door at the far end of the drawing room swung open. It seemed Max had done his staff a disservice. They had turned out to greet their new master after all.

They paraded into the drawing room, only managing to arrange themselves in a proper row after a fair amount of elbowing, giggling, muttering beneath their breath, and treading on each other's feet. Max felt his anger melting to dismay. No wonder the manor was in such sorry neglect. There wasn't nearly enough staff for a house of this size. Why, his town house on Belgrave Square had twice the number of servants!

It hardly strained his advanced mathematical skills to count the still wheezing butler, five housemaids, and a lad wearing footman's livery plainly tailored for a grown man. A powdered wig that looked as if it had been rescued from the head of some unfortunate French aristocrat just *after* his trek to the guillotine sat askew on his head. Max blinked as a moth emerged from the wig and fluttered toward one of the oil lamps.

While the maids quickly averted their gazes to their feet, the lad settled back on his heels and gave Max a look rife with insolence.

There was no sign of a cook, a wine steward, or a groom of the chambers. Max was already beginning to regret not forcing his valet to share his exile. He had just assumed there would be a manservant in the house he could recruit for the position.

Just when he had given up any hope of receiving a proper welcome, a woman glided through the door and took her place at the end of the row, her lips curved in a dutiful smile. "Good evening, my lord. I am Mrs. Spencer, the housekeeper of this establishment. Please allow me to welcome you to Cadgwyck Manor."

In Max's experience, the butler customarily did the welcoming when one was needed. But his new butler was currently occupied with plucking bits of dust from his moth-eaten coat, the faint tremor in his hands even more pronounced now that he'd divested them of the heavy candlestick.

Max inclined his head in a curt bow. "Mrs. Spencer."

Despite the rather motley appearance of the rest of the staff, Mrs. Spencer appeared to be all that was proper in an English housekeeper. Her posture was impeccable, her spine more ramrod straight than that of most military men of Max's acquaintance. A crisp white apron offset her stern black dress.

Her brown hair had been drawn back from her face and confined in a woven net at her nape with a severity that looked almost painful. Her pale skin was smooth and unlined, making it difficult to determine her age. Max judged her to be close to his own thirty-three years, if not older.

She was a plain woman with nothing striking or unique about her features to draw a man's eye. Her chin was pointed, her cheekbones high, her nose slender and straight, though a shade too long to be called delicate. She smiled with her mouth closed as if her lips were accustomed to holding back as many words as they spoke. Or perhaps she was simply seeking to hide bad teeth.

The only feature that might tempt a man to take a second look were her eyes. Their dark-green depths sparkled with an intelligence that could easily have been mistaken for mischief in a less guarded woman. Her sole concessions to vanity were the delicate tatting peeping out of her collar and the thin chain of braided silver that disappeared beneath it. Max's natural curiosity made him wonder what dangled at the end of it. A cheaply painted miniature of Mr. Spencer perhaps?

"I trust you had a pleasant journey," she said, lifting one delicately arched brow in an inquiring manner.

Max glanced down. Water was still dripping from the hem of his greatcoat to soak the carpet beneath his feet, and fresh mud was caked on the once-supple calfskin of his favorite pair of Wellingtons. He returned his gaze to her face. "Oh, it was simply divine."

Just as he had expected, his sarcasm was wasted on her. "I'm so very pleased to hear that. I'm afraid there are some who find our climate less than hospitable."

"Indeed," he said drily, his words underscored by a fresh rumble of thunder. "That's certainly difficult to imagine."

"If you'll allow me, I shall introduce you to the rest of the staff."

If he hadn't been distracted by the velvety timbre of her voice, Max would have informed the housekeeper the only thing he was interested in being introduced to at that moment was a tumbler of brandy and a warm bed. The cultured note in her speech shouldn't have surprised him. The upper servants of a household might hail from the local villages, but they commonly affected the accents of the ladies and gentlemen they'd been hired to serve. Most were talented mimics. It seemed his new housekeeper was no exception.

"These are the housemaids," she informed him, gesturing toward the row of young women. "Beth, Bess, Lisbeth, Betsy, and Lizzie." Mrs. Spencer had just reached the end of the row when a sixth maid came racing into the drawing room, skidding to a halt at the far end of the row. "And Pippa," Mrs. Spencer added with somewhat less enthusiasm.

While her fellow maids had at least taken the time to pin up their hair and don aprons and caps, young Pippa looked as if she had just stumbled out of bed. Her gown was rumpled, its collar gaping open at the throat, and she hadn't even bothered to hook the buttons on her scuffed half boots.

The other maids bobbed dutiful curtsies; Pippa yawned and scratched at her wild, dark tangle of hair before mumbling, "Your grace."

"*My lord* will be sufficient," Max said. "I won't be *your grace* until my father dies, and the man is in such vigorous health he may very well outlive me."

"If we're lucky," the young footman muttered beneath his breath.

"Pardon?" Max shifted his frown to the boy.

Mrs. Spencer's smile tightened as she reached to give the lad's ear a fond tweak. "Our head footman, Dickon, was just saying how fortunate we are to have a new master here at Cadgwyck Manor. We've been quite adrift since the last one took his leave in such haste."

"Aye," Dickon muttered, rubbing his ear and giving her a resentful look from beneath his tawny lashes. "I was just saying that, I was." As far as Max could tell, the lad wasn't just the head footman. He was the *only* footman.

"Called back to London on some urgent bit of business, was he?" Max was not yet willing to let on that he knew the last master of the house had fled the premises in terror, pursued by some dread specter from his own imagination.

"We can only assume," Mrs. Spencer replied, calling his bluff with an unruffled stare of her own. "I'm afraid he didn't linger long enough to give us any reason for his abrupt departure." She turned away from Max, her voice softening. "I would be quite remiss in my introductions if I left off the captain of this fine ship we call Cadgwyck Manor—our esteemed butler, Mr. Hodges."

A muffled snore greeted her words. Max craned his neck to discover the man who had let him in the door had slumped into a faded Hepplewhite chair and dozed off. His chin was tucked against his chest like a plump pigeon resting its beak in the feathers of its breast.

"*Mr. Hodges,*" the housekeeper repeated, much louder this time.

The butler started violently, shaking himself awake. "Teatime, is it? I'll just go fetch the cart." He sprang to his feet and went bolting from the room, leaving the rest of them staring after him.

Max arched one brow. Apparently the man wasn't a mute as he had first feared, but simply a garden-variety lunatic.

In the time it took for Mrs. Spencer to turn back to Max, she had recovered both her composure and her smile. Folding her hands in front of her like some sort of beatific Buddha, she said, "You must be terribly weary after such a long journey, my lord. Dickon would be delighted to show you to the master chamber."

Judging by his sullen scowl, the young footman would be even more delighted to shove Max over the nearest cliff. Or out the nearest open window.

"That won't be necessary, Mrs. Spencer," Max said. "I'd prefer that *you* escort me to my chamber."

Although Max would have thought it impossible, Dickon's scowl darkened.

Mrs. Spencer's expression remained carefully bland. "I can assure you young Dickon is perfectly capable of—"

Max took a step toward her, using the advantage of his size and his physical presence to underscore his words. "I insist."

The housekeeper's crisp smile wavered. Although Max could tell it displeased her, she had no choice but to respect his wishes or risk defying him in front of the other servants, which would set a poor example indeed.

Her smile returned. As her lips parted, he was reminded of a cornered creature baring its teeth at him. Teeth that weren't bad after all, but were small and white and impressively even except for the winsome gap between the two in the front.

"Very well, my lord," she said stiffly, retrieving from the pier table the heavy candlestick the butler had abandoned. For some reason, Max had a sudden image of it coming down on the back of his head.

She started toward the entrance hall, tossing a look over her shoulder that could easily have been mistaken for a challenge had they met as equals instead of master and servant. "Shall we proceed?"


MAX FOLLOWED HIS NEW housekeeper up the shadowy staircase toward the deeper gloom of the second story. He knew he ought to be ashamed of himself. He had always had his autocratic tendencies, but he had never been a bully. So why was he taking such mean-spirited pleasure in baiting a stranger—and an inferior at that?

He could hardly fault Mrs. Spencer for trying to foist him off on Dickon. Max had been a willing slave to propriety for most of his life. He was well aware there was nothing proper about a lone woman escorting a man to his bedchamber, especially a man she had just met. Perhaps he had simply wanted to see if the composure the woman wore like a suit of armor had any chinks.

Judging by the stiff angle of her neck, the rigid set of her shoulders, and the almost-military cadence of her half boots on each tread of the stairs, it did not. Her determination was so unyielding she might have been marching along behind Hannibal and his elephants as they crossed the Alps during the Second Punic War.

Max's gaze strayed lower, finding a vulnerability he had not anticipated in the subtle sway and roll of her hips. Something unsettling lay in imagining any hint of womanly softness beneath those crisp layers of starched linen. She stole a glance over her shoulder at him; he jerked his gaze back to her face. He was also not in the habit of ogling women's derrieres, especially women in his employ.

"Am I to assume that was the entire staff on display down there?" he asked, hoping to remind them both of his new role as lord of the manor.

"I should say not!" Mrs. Spencer exclaimed, as if the very notion was nonsense. But her next words quenched Max's swell of relief. "There's also Nana the cook. I saw no need to disturb her since she has to rise so early to prepare breakfast. And on the second Tuesday of every month, Mrs. Beedle comes up from the village to assist with the laundering of the linens. I believe you'll discover we run a very efficient household here at Cadgwyck, my lord. One that is quite beyond reproach."

Max trailed his fingertips through the thick layer of dust furring the banister, wondering if she might not be as mad as his new butler.

During that awkward silence he noticed a most peculiar trait—his housekeeper jingled when she walked. It took his weary brain a minute to trace the musical sound to the formidable ring of keys she wore at her waist.

"That's quite a collection of keys you have there," he commented as they approached the second-story landing.

Without missing a beat, she replied, "Someone has to mind the dungeons as well as the pantry."

"Must be a challenge for you to sneak up on people. Rather like a cat wearing a collar with a bell on it."

"*Au contraire,* my lord," she purred, surprising Max anew with the graceful way the Gallic syllables rolled off her tongue. "When one expects a cat to wear a bell, removing the bell only makes the cat that much more dangerous."

This time the smile she cast over her shoulder at him was sweetly feline. When she returned her attention to the stairs, Max narrowed his eyes at her slender back, imagining her slinking through the halls of the manor in the dead of night, up to any manner of mischief. He would be wise not to underestimate her. This kitty might yet have claws.

The swish of her hips beneath her staid skirts seemed even more pronounced now, as if she were deliberately baiting him. As they reached the second-story gallery, the wavering shadows fled before the gentle glow of her candle. A halo of light climbed the wall, illuminating the portrait hanging directly across from the top of the stairs.

Max's gaze followed it, as irresistibly drawn as a hapless moth might be to a deadly flame.

His breath caught in his throat. Mrs. Spencer was forgotten. His desperate desire to collapse onto a warm, dry mattress was forgotten.

Everything was forgotten except for the vision floating before his eyes.

## *Chapter Six*

"My God," Max whispered, taking the candlestick from Mrs. Spencer's hand and holding it aloft.

The housekeeper did not protest. Her sigh was resigned, almost as if she had been anticipating such a reaction.

Max had been entertained in some of the finest homes in England, had toured countless museums in Florence and Venice during his grand tour, and seen hundreds of such portraits in his day, including many painted by masters such as Gainsborough, Fragonard, and Sir Joshua Reynolds. Dryden Hall, the house in which he had grown up, was home to an entire gallery of his own stern-faced ancestors. But he'd never before been tempted to forget they were anything but flecks of dried paint on canvas.

The artist of this portrait, however, had captured

not just a likeness, but a soul. To even the most in-
sensitive eye, he had obviously been madly in love
with his subject, and his intention was to make
every man who laid eyes on her fall in love with
her, too.

He somehow conveyed the illusion that he had
caught her in the wink of time just before a smile.
One corner of her lips was quirked upward, leaving
one to wait in breathless anticipation for the dimple
that would surely follow. Those ripe, coral lips might
tease with the promise of a smile, but her sherry-
colored eyes were openly laughing as they gazed
boldly down at Max beneath the graceful wings of
her brows. They were the eyes of a young woman
tasting her power over men for the first time and
savoring every morsel of it.

Her curls were piled loosely atop her head, held in
place by a single ribbon of Prussian blue. A few tendrils had escaped to frame full cheeks tinted with a
beguiling blush no amount of expensive rouge could
duplicate. Her hair was no ordinary brown but a
rich, glossy mink. She wore a dress the sumptuous
yellow of buttercups in the spring—a marked con-
trast to the gloom of the gallery. The pale globes of
her generous breasts swelled over the square-cut
bodice of her high-waisted gown.

Something about both her beauty and her manner of dress was timeless. She might have been im-

prisoned in the faded gilt frame for a decade or a century. It was impossible to tell.

"And just who would you be?" he murmured. A brief glance down the gallery confirmed that the rest of the portraits had been removed, leaving darkened squares on the wallpaper where they had once resided.

The housekeeper sniffed, reminding Max of her presence. "The rest of the artwork was sold, but *she* comes with the house. It's a stipulation of the sale agreement. No matter how many hands the property passes through, the portrait must remain."

Max could easily understand why the house's past masters might not have grumbled about such an eccentric entailment. Most men would be happy to pass the portrait every day and pretend such an enchanting creature were his wife.

Or his mistress.

"Who is she?" he asked, oddly reluctant to relegate the woman in the portrait to the past, where she undoubtedly belonged.

"Another time perhaps, my lord. It's late and I know you're exhausted. I wouldn't wish to bore you."

As Mrs. Spencer started to turn away, Max's hand shot out to close around her forearm. "Bore me."

She froze in her tracks at his imperious command, her startled gaze flying to his face. Only seconds before he had nearly forgotten her existence. Now he was keenly aware of how near she was to him in the flickering candlelight. Of each shuddering breath that passed through her parted lips. Of the uneven rise and fall of her breasts beneath the starched linen of her bodice. Of the faint, clean scent of laundry soap and freshly baked bread that clung to her the way expensive perfumes clung to other women.

Her bones felt almost delicate beneath the tensile strength of his hand. He had wrongly assumed she would be forged from something cold and unbreakable, like granite or steel. His gaze lingered on her lips. When not curved into a closemouthed smile that was no smile at all, they looked surprisingly soft and moist and inviting. . . .

The candlestick in his other hand had listed, and the steady drip of the melted candle wax against the toe of his poor beleaguered boot finally broke the peculiar spell that had fallen over them.

Removing his hand from her person as if it belonged to someone else, he said gruffly, "It wasn't a request, Mrs. Spencer. It was an order."

Mrs. Spencer smoothed her wrinkled sleeve; the look she gave him from beneath her fawn-colored fringe of lashes made it clear exactly what she thought of his order. "Her name is . . . *was* Angelica Cadgwyck."

*Angelica.*

Max's gaze strayed back to the woman in the portrait. The name suited her. Despite her impish charms, she certainly had the face of an angel. "I gather her family was the namesake for both the manor and the village?"

"Up until little more than a decade ago, they were the closest thing the county had to royalty. And from what I understand, Angelica was their crown princess. Her mother died when she was born, and her father, Lord Cadgwyck, doted upon her."

"Who could blame him?" Max muttered beneath his breath, bewitched anew by the sensual promise in those sparkling brown eyes. "What happened to her?"

Mrs. Spencer's elbow brushed the sleeve of his coat as she joined him in front of the portrait, gazing up at it with a distaste equal to his fascination. "The same thing that always happens when a young woman is raised to believe her every whim should be satisfied without giving any thought whatsoever to the consequences. Scandal. Disaster. Ruin."

Intrigued by the note of scorn in her voice, Max stole a sidelong glance at the housekeeper's disapproving profile. He should have known such a woman would have no sympathy for those who fell prey to temptations of the flesh. She had probably never experienced even the most harmless of them.

"What manner of scandal?" he asked, although he could probably guess.

"At a fete given in her honor on her eighteenth birthday, she was caught in a compromising position with a young man. The artist of this very portrait, I believe." The housekeeper shrugged. "I don't hail from Cadgwyck so I wasn't privy to all the sordid details. All I know is that her brother was rumored to have shot and killed the young man without even the benefit of a duel. Her father suffered an apoplexy and went mad with grief. The brother was carted off to prison—"

"Prison?" Max interrupted, engaged against his will by the lurid tale. "I thought murder was a hanging offense."

"The Cadgwyck name was still a powerful influence in these parts, so the young man managed to escape the gallows and was deported to Australia. Apparently, her father had made some ill-advised investments prior to all this. Scenting blood in the water, the creditors descended and the family lost everything—their fortune, their good name . . . even this house, which had been in Cadgwyck hands since the original castle was built five centuries ago."

Max returned his gaze to the portrait. "What became of her?"

Mrs. Spencer shrugged, as if the fate of one foolish girl was of little to no import to her. "What was there left for her to do after bringing ruin upon everyone she loved? On the night before they were to vacate the premises, she flung herself over the cliff and into the sea."

Since losing Clarinda to Ash, Max had grown accustomed to the dull, heavy ache in his heart. The piercing pang he felt in that moment caught him off guard. He had no reason to grieve for a girl he had never met. Perhaps it was simply impossible for him to imagine that such a vivacious young creature would surrender her life without a fight.

"Was there an investigation? Any suspicion of foul play?"

"None whatsoever," Mrs. Spencer said flatly. "The girl left behind a note that made her intentions quite clear."

"Notes can be forged."

The housekeeper slanted him a wry look. "In overwrought theatricals and gothic novels perhaps. But we are not so clever or diabolical here in Cornwall. I suspect her suicide was simply the impulsive action of a rash young girl steeped in a morass of guilt and self-pity."

Max gazed up at the portrait, in danger of forgetting the housekeeper's presence once again. "I should have liked to have made her acquaintance."

"Don't despair, my lord. You may yet get your chance."

Mrs. Spencer retrieved her candlestick from his hand and went sweeping away toward the staircase on the opposite end of the gallery, leaving Max with no choice but to follow or be left behind in the darkness.

As the full import of her words sank in, he could not resist stealing one last look over his shoulder to watch the portrait of the irrepressible Miss Cadgwyck melt back into the shadows.

AT THE FAR END of the third-floor corridor of the east wing, Mrs. Spencer used one of the keys from her expansive collection to unlock the master suite. As she pushed open the door, Max felt his spirits sink. The spacious chamber still bore traces of its former splendor, but the marble hearth was just as dark and dusty as the one in the drawing room. Nor was any supper laid before it.

A single lamp burned on the side table next to the canopied four-poster, casting more shadows than it dispelled.

Had Max known he was going to receive such an inhospitable welcome, he might have at least lingered at the inn for a bowl of stew. Apparently, he was expected to content himself with the maddening aroma of bread wafting from Mrs. Spencer's hair. As savagely hungry as he suddenly was, it was all he could do not to lean down and gobble her right up.

She had stepped aside to let him pass, making it clear she had no intention of placing so much as the pointy little toe of her half boot across the threshold of his bedchamber. Did she truly believe herself in danger of being ravished? Did he appear so desperate for female companionship that he would toss the first female domestic who crossed his path down on the musty mattress and force himself upon her?

Max could feel his temper rising. He had spent so much of his life holding it in rigid control he almost didn't recognize the danger signs until it was too late.

When he finally spoke, his jaw was clenched so tightly his lips barely moved. "Would a fire in the hearth be too much to ask? And perhaps a bite of supper as well?"

His housekeeper's smile lost none of its infuriating serenity. "Of course not. I'll send Dickon up right away with a tray and your portmanteau." She started to turn away, then looked back at him. "Have no fear, my lord. We'll be here to see to your every need."

The woman's husky voice, completely at odds with her starched appearance, played over Max's strained nerves like crushed velvet. Her innocent promise sent an image flitting through his mind, an image more shocking than any other he had contemplated on this night . . . or perhaps for a long time.

Still smiling, she gently drew the door shut in his face, leaving him to wonder if he had chosen a punishment even he did not deserve.

ANNE MADE IT AS far as the second-story gallery before collapsing against the balcony rail, her breath coming quick and hard. She felt as if she'd just run up a dozen flights of stairs instead of walking down one. She lifted a hand to smooth her hair, the tremor of her fingers betraying her. The unflappable Mrs. Spencer had vanished, leaving Anne to pay the price for her composure.

"I daresay his lordship is not quite what you expected."

The mocking voice came out of the darkness, making Anne jump and grab at her heart. It might not have startled her so badly if the sentiment hadn't echoed her own thoughts with such eerie accuracy.

Pippa came gliding out of the shadows, grinning at her. "What's wrong? Did you think I was a ghost?"

Still clutching her heart, Anne glared at the girl. "Keep springing out at me like that and you'll be one before your time. Why aren't you back in bed?

I barely managed to rouse you out of it to greet our illustrious new master."

Pippa had just turned sixteen, but when she wrinkled her pert little nose at Anne, she looked as if she were seven again. "Don't be such a scold. I was just making sure His-High-and-Mighty didn't try to take any liberties with his new housekeeper."

"And just what were you going to do if he did?"

"Hit him over the head with a poker."

Anyone else would have assumed Pippa was joking, but Anne wasn't even surprised when the girl's slender hand emerged from the folds of her skirts to reveal the implement in question. Given the bloodthirsty glint in her eye, Pippa might have undertaken the task with more relish than was strictly necessary.

"Dear Lord, Pippa!" Anne exclaimed. "You're going to get us all hanged for murder. There's no need for you to play knight in shining armor to my damsel in distress. I'm quite capable of looking after myself."

"And Lord Scowlywood looks quite capable of ravishing a housekeeper and perhaps a scullery maid or two, all without removing his greatcoat or wrinkling his cravat."

Remembering how his powerful hand had closed over her arm with such startling intimacy and how close that simple touch had come to undoing her, Anne blew out a disheartened sigh, conceding Pippa's point. "He's certainly no doddering old fool inclined to drink too much port and mistake a sheet on a broom handle for a shrieking portent of doom."

Pippa's observation also forced Anne to relive the shock of walking into the drawing room to find him standing there, glowering beneath those heavy, dark brows and dripping all over the Turkish carpet brought back to the original castle by some marauding Cadgwyck ancestor after the final Crusade. As she had gazed upon his forbidding visage for the first time, it had been all she could do to keep Mrs. Spencer's congenial smile pasted on her lips.

The earl stood well over six feet, but it wasn't his height—or even the intimidating breadth of his shoulders beneath the shoulder capes of his greatcoat—that was so imposing. It was his effortless command of the room and all who were in it. Another man might have looked ridiculous standing there with hat in hand and mud-caked boots, but Dravenwood looked more inclined to bellow "Off with their heads!" while the potential victims scurried away to fetch him an ax.

Perhaps both his barber and his valet had met with just such a fate. The thick, sooty waves of his hair weren't artfully trimmed as was the current fashion but were long enough to brush the collar of his greatcoat. Striking threads of silver burnished the hair at his temples, and his beautifully sculpted jaw was shadowed with at least two days' worth of stubble.

His dark-lashed eyes were gray, as gray as the mist that swirled over the moors. Anne had always thought gray to be an ordinary color, but his eyes had the disconcerting habit of flashing like summer lightning when he was displeased.

The greatest threat to them was the glint of intelligence in those eyes. He was not a man who missed much, and that, more than anything else, could prove to be their downfall if they weren't careful. When she had introduced herself, his gaze had flickered over Anne, taken her measure, then dismissed her for what she was—a menial, an underling, his inferior. He didn't find her wanting; he simply found her beneath his notice.

Which was exactly where she needed to stay.

"Well, you have to admit dispatching him with a poker would have solved most of our problems," Pippa suggested cheerfully. "Or at least bought us a bit more time to continue our search before the next master arrived."

"Not if we all ended up in the village jail, awaiting a visit from the hangman. But you are right about one thing: the sooner Lord Scowly—Lord *Draven-wood*," Anne corrected herself, "is in a carriage and on his way back to London, the sooner things can go back to normal around here."

"Normal? We've spent the last four years combing the manor from the cellars to the attics for a treasure that may not even exist. I'm not even sure I remember what normal is."

Hoping to hide her own misgivings from Pippa's bright, dark eyes, Anne said firmly, "The treasure exists and it's only a matter of time before we find it. Once we do, we can leave this place forever and make a home of our own far away from here."

"But what if it's nothing more than a family legend? A fairy tale trotted out to entertain children and stir the imaginations of dreamers? Dreamers have been searching for Captain Kidd's buried plunder for over a century now and not a single coin has been found."

Anne touched her fingertips to the familiar shape of the locket that always hid beneath her bodice, and never strayed far from her heart, reminding them both of why they had no choice but to keep searching. "I stopped being a dreamer a long time ago. Which is why I know the treasure is real and that we're going to find it. We simply have to send Lord Dravenwood on his way as quickly as possible so we can get back to the business at hand. Preferably without the assistance of any hearth tools." Sweeping the makeshift weapon from Pippa's hand,

Anne started down the gallery, her steps once more brisk with confidence. "The earl may appear to be invincible, but he's already proved he has the exact same weakness as any other man."

Pippa trotted along behind her. "And just what would that be?"

Anne stopped in front of the portrait that faced the descending staircase, holding her candle aloft. "*Her.*"

Angelica Cadgwyck gazed down upon them from her exalted perch, her lush lips quirked as if she were hiding some delightful secret that could only be coaxed from her with a kiss.

"Ah," Pippa said softly. "So our lady has already added another heart to her collection. Her appetites really are insatiable, aren't they?"

"Up until the moment Lord Dravenwood saw the portrait, I would have sworn the man didn't have a heart."

Anne had seen the look on the earl's face often enough on the faces of other men. Men who stopped in their tracks and gaped at the woman in the portrait as if they had been struck both mute and blind to everything but the beauty before them.

As Anne had watched their new master succumb to that same old spell, she had felt herself disappear, winking out like a star at the approach of dawn. She should have been pleased her efforts to make herself invisible had met with such success.

Instead, she had felt a sharp twinge of disappointment.

For the briefest blink of time, she had allowed herself to believe this one might be different. That he might be immune to such superficial charms. She couldn't imagine what had prompted her to entertain such an absurd and dangerous notion. Perhaps it was the cynical curl to his lip, his droll sarcasm, or the way the grooves bracketing his mouth deepened when other men might have smiled.

But the second she'd seen him surrender his heart—and his wits—into Angelica's lily-white hands, she had known he was no different from any other man.

As she gazed up into Angelica's knowing eyes, she felt a pang of something even sharper than disappointment, something more akin to jealousy. Now she was being truly ridiculous. Angelica would serve them well, just as she always had.

"Come, Pippa. I need to send Dickon up with some supper for our new master. The sooner he takes himself off to bed, the sooner he can make the acquaintance of the woman of his dreams." She lowered the candle, robbing Angelica of her halo of light. As she herded Pippa toward the stairs, Anne stole one last glance over her shoulder at the portrait, barely resisting the childish urge to poke her tongue out at Angelica's smug visage. "And his night-mares."

ANGELICA CADGWYCK STOOD GAZING down at the stranger who had invaded her home. Even with his unshaven jaw and unruly hair, there was no deny-ing he was a beautiful man. But she had learned the hard way that a beautiful face could hide a dark and destructive heart.

She had hoped to catch a glimpse into that heart by coming here tonight, but he was no less guarded in sleep than he had been in wakefulness. His lips were pressed into a forbidding line, and the faint furrow between his brows made it look as if he were still scowling, even in his dreams. She was seized by a peculiar urge to touch him, to see if she could soothe that furrow away with the tender caress of her fingertip.

But he was flesh and she was nothing more than a dream, deliberately fashioned to haunt the hearts of men.

She was already beginning to suspect this man was no stranger to ghosts. He muttered something beneath his breath, then gritted his teeth and stirred restlessly, sending a lock of dark hair tumbling over his brow.

Angelica reached out a pale hand toward him, yearning only to touch something warm and solid and surging with life before she had to go drifting back into the cold, lonely night.

MAX HAD NEVER BEEN a man who dreamed. When he had confessed that to his fiancée, Clarinda had looked up at him with her dazzling green eyes and exclaimed, "Don't be ridiculous! Of course you dream. All men do. You just don't remember what you dreamed."

He'd given little credence to the notion until late that night in his bed at Cadgwyck Manor when he felt a woman's cool fingers tenderly brush the hair from his heated brow. He groaned and shifted restlessly in the bed. That simple touch was somehow both soothing and arousing, stirring his body and his soul. He longed to capture her slender wrist in his hand, to bring those fingertips to his mouth and kiss them one by one as a prelude to tasting the softness of her lips.

Determined to do just that, he reached for her. But his hand closed on empty air. He opened his eyes and gazed up into the shadows gathered beneath the canopy of the unfamiliar bed, finding himself exactly as he had expected to.

*Alone.*

How was it that such a simple dream could seem more vivid and real to him than the waking fog he'd been wading through in recent months? Even if he willed himself to do so, he didn't think he would be able to forget it.

It might have been easier to do so if he weren't still fully aroused and aching for a woman's touch on some far more provocative spot than his brow.

Despite the cool façade he presented to the world, Max's appetites were stronger and more driving than those of most men. That was exactly why he had vowed never to lose control of them. If his brother had taught him anything, it was just how much damage a man could do when he self- ishly indulged his lusts without stopping to count the cost to those around him.

Of course, Max hadn't exactly lived as a monk, either. He had always been too much of a gentle- man to pay for his pleasures, but he was not above satisfying his baser needs with some discreet widow looking for a bliss more transitory than matrimo- nial.

All of that had ended when Clarinda had finally accepted his suit. Temptations were far less difficult to resist when he was anticipating sharing a mar- riage bed with the woman he had adored for most of his life. He had been confident marriage to Clarinda would fulfill his every desire, both emotional and carnal.

*Bloody fool,* he thought, kicking away the tangle of bedclothes and throwing his long legs over the side of the bed. As he emerged from the bed curtains, shoving them aside as he did so, the damp chill hanging in the air struck his overheated flesh like a dash of icy water.

The fire the surly little footman had laid still languished on the grate, its soft glow bathing the ancient mahogany armoire crouched in the corner and the tray of nearly untouched food on the Pembroke table. After the tray had been delivered, Max had discovered he was too exhausted to eat after all. He had listlessly pushed the bland bits of beef and potato around on the plate until tossing down his fork in disgust and taking himself off to bed.

An unexpected draft played over the crisp hairs furring his naked chest. With its chill caress stirring gooseflesh wherever it touched, Max slowly turned his head to find the French windows leading to the balcony standing wide open, as if to invite in whatever the night had in store for him.

# ❖ Chapter Seven

HE LACE PANELS ADORNING the French windows fluttered in the breeze like a bride's tattered veil. Max's scowl deepened along with his bewilderment. Those windows had been closed when he had retreated behind the musty velvet curtains of the bed. He would be willing to swear his life on it.

He reached to the foot of the bed to retrieve his dressing gown, thankful he'd had the foresight to pack it in his portmanteau since the rest of his baggage wouldn't be arriving until morning. Knotting the robe's silk belt around his waist, he rose and padded over to the windows.

The rain had stopped but the moon was still huddled behind a towering bank of clouds, leaving the night beyond the balcony shrouded in darkness. Thinking that perhaps the windows had blown open, Max examined both the latches and their moorings. They seemed perfectly sound, but that didn't mean they were strong enough to withstand a particularly violent gust of wind.

Accepting the irrefutable logic of his own deduction, he reached to close the windows and return the night to its proper place. But before he could, an unexpected scent drifted to his nose. A scent quite distinct from the clean fragrance of the rain and the briny tang of the sea.

A scent that was delicate and floral and unmistakably feminine.

Max's nostrils flared as he drew the heady elixir into his lungs. It stirred long-buried memories of sultry summer nights and velvety, white petals too shy to bloom while the sun was still up.

*Jasmine.*

Lured by the irresistible aroma, he stepped out onto the balcony, barely feeling the chill of the rain-soaked tiles beneath his bare feet. Had it not been the wrong time of year for such a tender and fragrant flower to bloom, he might have been able to convince himself that a pergola or a trellis was nearby beneath his balcony. With the wind whipping his hair from his eyes and snatching at his dressing gown with greedy fingers, he found it difficult to believe anything but the hardiest of plants could survive this harsh climate.

The wind also dispelled the lingering hint of perfume, leaving him to wonder if he had imagined it. Shrugging off the scent's intoxicating effects, he started for the balcony windows. He might as well return to the dubious comfort of his bed, where he could blame any other such ridiculous fancies on dreams he would not remember in the morning.

That was when he heard it—the distant tinkling of a music box playing a melody that was hauntingly beautiful and yet just off-key enough to make the tiny hairs on the back of his neck shiver to life.

He slowly pivoted on his heel, his narrowed eyes searching the night. The east wing had been built at just enough of an angle to the gatehouse to give him an unobstructed view of the tower standing sentinel over the far side of the manor. Without the moon to give it an air of tragic romance, the structure was nothing more than a crumbling ruin—a darker shadow against a sea of turbulent clouds. The tower's windows were vacant eyes with no mysterious flashes of light to bring them to life.

Yet Max would have sworn the eerie waltz wafting to his ears on the wings of the wind was coming from that direction. He drifted to the edge of the balcony, his hands closing around the damp iron of the balustrade.

The music ceased abruptly, almost as if spectral hands had slammed the lid of the music box.

Max released a breath he hadn't even realized he

had been holding. He stood there for a long time but there was no repeat performance, no sound at all except for the muted roar of the wind and the distant crash of the waves against the rocks.

Another man might have doubted his senses, but a mocking smile tugged at one corner of Max's mouth. "I've been haunted by the best," he murmured. "If you want to be rid of me, sweetheart, you'll have to do better than that."

Leaving his challenge hanging in the air, he turned his back on the night and returned to the master chamber, gently but firmly drawing the French windows shut and latching them behind him.

SINCE THEIR PREVIOUS MASTER had rarely risen before noon, Anne fully expected Lord Dravenwood to spend most of the morning languishing in bed. She was caught off guard by the staccato tap of his bootheels crossing the second-floor gallery at only half past eight. She tossed the broom she'd been using to judiciously apply fresh cobwebs to the entrance hall chandelier behind a rusting suit of armor and scurried over to the wall to give the ancient bellpull a hearty yank. She could only hope someone was on the other end to hear its jangle of warning.

She smoothed her hair out of habit as she hurried back across the floor. She had risen before dawn to choose her garments with deliberate care—no easy feat when faced with a cast-off armoire containing only a handful of black and gray gowns, all cut from serviceable linens and wools. She had finally settled upon a sturdy merino the same misty-gray shade as Lord Dravenwood's eyes. A freshly starched apron completed her ensemble. The apron was the identifying badge of the domestic, its purpose to ensure none would embarrass themselves by mistaking her for a lady of the house.

Anne checked to make sure her locket was tucked safely into the bodice of her gown. She knew she would have an extra second or two to prepare as Lord Dravenwood approached the painting at the end of the gallery. No man had ever made it past Angelica Cadgwyck without slowing to pay homage. Still, she couldn't resist rolling her eyes when his footsteps paused at the top of the stairs. He was doubtlessly searching Angelica's exquisite face, trying to determine if the arrival of dawn had broken the spell she had cast over him in the night.

By the time he started down the last flight of stairs, Anne was standing at the foot of them, her hands clasped in front of her as she dutifully awaited her master's pleasure.

Or displeasure, it would seem, judging by the way he was glowering at her from beneath his thick, dark brows. Shadows brooded beneath his eyes, making it look as if he'd slept little. Or perhaps not at all. Anne pressed her lips together to suppress a smirk of triumph.

Perhaps only one night at Cadgwyck was enough to make him realize his mistake in coming here. With any luck, he was coming down to inquire just how quickly she could arrange for his passage back to London. That would be one order she would hasten to obey.

Stepping off the last stair, he scowled at the frozen hands of the longcase clock. "How is one ever supposed to know what time it is around here? Make a note to get the bloody thing fixed." He must have seen her eyes widen for he shifted his scowl to her. "I hope you're not easily offended by the occasional oath. I'm afraid I spent more of my career with the East India Company in the presence of ruffians than ladies."

"Ah, but I'm no lady," she gently reminded him. "I'm your housekeeper. And I do believe the clock is quite beyond repair. From what I understand, it hasn't worked since the night . . ."

As she trailed off, he arched one eyebrow in a silent demand for her to continue.

She sighed sadly, seeking only to whet his curiosity. "For a *very* long time."

His thoughtful grunt warned her he wasn't satisfied with her answer, but was willing to content himself with it. For now.

"I trust you slept well?" she offered, watching his face carefully.

"As well as can be expected in an unfamiliar bed. Although you'd think by now I would be accustomed to sleeping in strange beds."

Now it was her turn to arch an eyebrow at him.

A glimmer of unexpected amusement warmed his cool gray eyes. "My position on the Court of Directors of the Company required a great deal of travel. To climes far more inhospitable than this one." He peered around the drafty entrance hall, the lines bracketing his mouth deepening a degree. "Although that might be hard to imagine."

"How very fortunate you were! Most people around here will go their entire lives without ever traveling more than a league away from the patch of ground where they were born."

"I never cared for it. I've always been a man who preferred the simple charms of hearth and home to the unpredictability of the unknown."

"So will your lady be joining us at Cadgwyck Manor after you're properly settled in?" Anne carefully inquired.

A fresh shadow crossed his face. She didn't realize she was holding her breath until he said shortly,

"I have no lady." He reached up to give the stubble darkening his jaw a rueful stroke. "At the moment I find myself more in need of a valet."

His current appearance certainly lacked the polished edges expected of a gentleman. His wavy, dark hair was tousled as if he'd raked his fingers through it instead of a brush. He had taken enough care to don a claret waistcoat of watered silk and a black coat, but he wore no cravat. His shirt was laid open at the collar to reveal the strong masculine lines of his throat.

Something about his artless disarray made Anne suddenly feel as if her own collar were choking her. She touched a hand to her throat to make sure one of her buttons wasn't about to spring free of its mooring without her leave. "Perhaps Dickon could—"

Lord Dravenwood's glower returned. "I have no intention of letting that surly little brat near my throat with a straight razor. Is there no one else in the household who could assist me for a time in the morning and evening? The butler perhaps?"

"Oh, no," Anne said swiftly. "I'm afraid Hodges's duties are far too demanding. We couldn't possibly spare him."

Another skeptical grunt. "What about that lad from the village who brought me up here last night? He wouldn't have any formal training, of course, but he seemed the sort who would be quick to learn and eager to please."

"Derrick Hammett?" She nodded toward the leatherbound trunks piled up in a corner of the entrance hall. "He delivered the rest of your baggage to the front stoop shortly after sunrise and departed before anyone could so much as thank him or offer him a shilling for his trouble. I sincerely doubt he'd be interested in the position. Most of the villagers won't come within shouting distance of the manor. Even Mrs. Beedle, the laundress who comes once a month, won't set foot in the house, but insists we carry all of the soiled linens out to her kettle in the courtyard."

Scorn laced the earl's deep, resonant baritone. "I suppose it's because of that superstitious twaddle about the ghost."

"I gather you don't believe in such apparitions?"

He lifted one broad shoulder in an indifferent shrug. "We're all haunted in one way or another, are we not? If not by spirits, then by our own demons and regrets."

"Are you speaking from experience, my lord?" Anne could not resist asking.

The chill returned to his eyes, giving them a frosty glint. "What I am doing, Mrs. Spencer, is speaking out of turn. If the local villagers refuse to serve at Cadgwyck Manor, where did you find the staff you have? Such as they are," he added, eyeing the chandelier, which appeared to be in imminent danger of collapsing beneath the weight of the cobwebs drifting from its spindly arms.

"They were engaged from other areas. With Mr. Hodges's expert assistance, of course."

This time he didn't even bother with a grunt. He simply studied her face through narrowed eyes, his penetrating gaze threatening to breach all of her defenses. Anne had forgotten how it felt to have a man look at her that way. She honestly wasn't sure *any* man had ever looked at her that way.

She couldn't help but wonder what a man like Lord Dravenwood saw when he looked at her. She had no Milk of Roses to smooth out her complexion, no rice powder to dull the faint sheen of her nose, no paste mixed with lampblack to darken her lashes to a sooty hue. The greatest luxury she allowed herself these days was tooth powder, which she used to polish her teeth upon rising and before bed each night.

Did he even realize a woman's heart beat beneath the cloth-covered buttons of her staid bodice? Did he suspect that some nights she woke up tangled in her sheets, her body aching with a yearning she could not name? A yearning that was beginning to bloom again beneath his steady gaze.

Reverting to the stiff formality that always served her so well when dealing with his kind, Anne said, "I've already rung for your breakfast, my lord. If you'll allow me to escort you to the dining room, I'll see to it that you are served immediately."

She was turning away from him, seeking to escape that dangerous gaze, when his hand closed over her arm. It was the second time he had touched her, but that didn't lessen the delicious little shock that danced along her nerves. She hadn't felt delicate or feminine for a long time, but it was difficult not to with Lord Dravenwood's dark form looming over her, his large hand easily encompassing her slender forearm. The back of his hand was roped with veins and lightly dusted with crisp, dark hair. Drawing an uneven breath through her parted lips, she reluctantly lifted her gaze to his face, half-afraid of what she might find there. "My lord?"

"Your eyes . . ." he murmured, his harsh expression softened by bewilderment as he gazed down into them.

# *Chapter Eight*

ANNE HAD TO USE every ounce of self-control she possessed not to lower her lashes, but to continue to boldly meet Lord Dravenwood's gaze. She had never expected him to be *that* observant. "Pardon?"

"Your eyes," he repeated more forcefully. "Last night I would have sworn they were green, but now they seem to be brown."

She offered him her most soothing smile. "My eyes are a quite ordinary hazel, my lord. They can appear different colors in different light—sometimes brown, sometimes green, sometimes a mixture of both."

This time she didn't wait for him to relinquish his hold on her. She simply slid her arm neatly out of his grasp and started toward the dining room. She didn't even spare a glance over her shoulder to make sure he was following. Her only desire was to escape before the bewilderment in his eyes could harden into suspicion.

MAX SAT ALL ALONE at the head of a long mahogany table that could easily have accommodated thirty guests, feeling more than a little ridiculous. The only other furniture in the room was a dusty sideboard sporting a silver tea set in desperate need of a sound polishing.

The moldering velvet drapes had been drawn back from the impressive wall of windows overlooking the cliffs, inviting in the meager rays of what passed for daylight in this place. The wavy panes of glass were nearly as grimy as the curtains, making the choppy, gray sea beyond the cliffs look even grayer.

As he awaited the arrival of his breakfast, Max caught himself cocking his head to listen for the telltale jingle of Mrs. Spencer's keys. The merry sound that accompanied her every step was completely at odds with her oh-so-proper appearance. When he had found her waiting for him at the foot of the stairs, her every button and hair had been in place, as if secured with the same starch she used on her collar and apron.

Apparently, the only thing unpredictable about the infernal woman was the color of her eyes.

He was already regretting that awkward moment when he had seized her arm. He couldn't imagine what had possessed him to put his hands on her not once, but twice, since his arrival at the manor. He'd never been inclined toward manhandling the help. Of course, nor was he in the habit of engaging in personal conversation with them. In his father's household, and later in his own, servants had always been treated as if they were of no more consequence than the furniture—necessary, but hardly worthy of notice.

But who else was he supposed to talk to in this accursed place? Himself? The ghost? A derisive snort escaped him. A few more lonely nights in this mausoleum and he might find himself doing just that.

There was no reason why he shouldn't be perfectly content with his situation. After all, hadn't he come here to the ends of the earth because he wanted to be left alone?

As the dining room door came swinging open, he sat up eagerly. The tantalizing aroma of freshly baked bread drifted through the doorway, making his stomach quicken with anticipation.

The young footman ducked through the door, a tray balanced in his hands. His scrawny chest was swallowed by the oversize coat of his faded blue livery. The legs of his trousers had been pinned up at the ankles so they wouldn't trip him. His powdered wig was canted at an even more precarious angle than it had been the previous night.

The boy slapped the tray down on the table in front of Max, rattling the china dishes, then with a grudging flourish whipped away the silver lid shielding Max's meal.

Although Max's disappointment was keen, he could find nothing to complain about. It was standard English breakfast fare—a pair of poached eggs, a bowl of watery porridge, a limp kipper, three rashers of overcooked bacon, a piece of underdone toast. The food looked every bit as tasteless as it did colorless. There was no sign of the buttery, golden loaf that had haunted his culinary fantasies ever since he had caught the aroma of it clinging to Mrs. Spencer's hair.

Without a word, the footman took his place next to the sideboard, staring straight ahead like one of the king's guards.

The boy's truculent silence was going to make for a long meal. A *very* long meal. Max took a sip of his lukewarm tea, wishing it were something much stronger, before asking, "Have you any newspapers I might peruse while I breakfast?"

The boy blew out a disgusted huff, as if Max had requested the Holy Grail be located without delay so his tea could be served in it. "I'll see what I can find."

Max had finished his bacon and was poking listlessly at his eggs with his fork when Dickon returned with a yellowing broadsheet tucked beneath his arm. Max unfolded the brittle pages to discover it was a copy of the *Times* . . . dated October 1820. Since Max had no desire to read what Queen Caroline had been wearing at her husband's coronation sixteen years ago, he tossed the useless thing aside. It seemed he had escaped not only London but the modern world altogether.

He managed to choke down a few spoonfuls of the lumpy porridge before a combination of boredom and curiosity prompted him to speak again. "Dickon? It is Dickon, is it not?"

The boy shot him a suspicious glance. "Aye, sir . . . um . . . m'lord."

"How long have you been in service at Cadgwyck?"

"Nearly five years now, m'lord."

Max frowned. "Just how old are you?"

"I'm seventeen," the boy said staunchly.

*What you are,* Max thought, *is lying through your teeth.* The boy didn't look to be more than a day over thirteen. And that was a generous estimation. "Were you hired by Mr. Hodges?"

"No, it was An—Mrs. Spencer what gave me my place here."

"Your Mrs. Spencer seems to wield an uncommon amount of influence for a mere housekeeper," Max remarked thoughtfully.

"She's not *my* Mrs. Spencer. She belongs to no man."

"Not even Mr. Spencer?" Max asked, amused against his will by the unmistakable note of pride in the lad's voice.

"Oh, there is no Mr. Spencer," the lad blurted out. When he saw Max's eyebrow shoot up, a flicker of alarm danced over his face. "At least not anymore. Mr. Spencer died in an unfortunate . . . um . . . accident. Crushed by a . . . a wagon, he was. A very large, very heavy wagon."

"How tragic," Max murmured, wondering just how long the unflappable Mrs. Spencer had been a widow. Based on the way her breath had quickened and her lips had parted both times he had put his hand on her arm, it must have been a long time indeed. If the mere touch of his hand had stirred such a response, he couldn't help but wonder how she would react if a man actually tried to kiss her. Shaking off the absurd and dangerous notion, he said, "It's no wonder she ended up as a domestic. There are very few avenues open to a woman who must make her own way in the world without the protection of a man."

Dickon didn't even try to disguise his snort. "If

any man crosses Mrs. Spencer, he'll be the one in need of protection."

Before Max could stop himself, he had returned the boy's cheeky grin, making them compatriots for the briefest of seconds. Then, as if realizing he was guilty of consorting with the enemy, Dickon jerked himself back to attention, staring straight ahead with his face set in even more sullen lines than before.

Sighing, Max returned his attention to his breakfast. Since he had no idea if anything more nourishing—or flavorful—would be forthcoming for lunch, he forced himself to finish every bite of the pallid fare before rising and leaving the boy to clear his place.

When he emerged from the dining room, he nearly collided with his stalwart housekeeper, who was hovering over a potted ficus tree just outside the door, watering can in hand. She might have been more convincing in her task if the tree had sported a single living leaf. Or if her watering can had so much as a drop of water in it.

Had she been lurking outside the door all along listening to every word of his conversation with young Dickon? Perhaps Max should have paid more heed to her warning about the cat and the bell. As long as she was relatively still, her ring of keys would not betray her.

Determined not to be drawn into yet another inappropriate exchange, he offered her a curt nod and continued on his way.

She fell into step behind him, her dogged pursuit shredding what was left of his frayed temper. "I wasn't sure what you had planned for your first morning at Cadgwyck, my lord. If you'd like, I could take some time out of my duties to go over the household schedule and accounts with you."

"That won't be necessary," he said without slowing his strides. "You've managed this long without me. Just continue doing whatever it is you're doing."

If she was taken aback by his words or the dismissive wave he aimed in her direction, the cheery jingle of her keys did not betray her. "I trust you found breakfast to your satisfaction, my lord. Will you be requiring—"

He wheeled around to face her, forcing her to bring herself up short or risk colliding with the immovable expanse of his chest. "What I require, Mrs. Spencer, is some decent coffee with my breakfast and a newspaper published in the current decade. Beyond that, all that I require is to be left to my own devices. If I'd have wanted to have my every need anticipated by some well-intentioned, yet interfering, female, I would have remained in London."

With that, he turned on his heel and went stalking toward the nearest set of French windows, de-

termined to escape both the house and his meddling housekeeper.

Behind him, he heard nothing but silence.

IT TOOK MAX ONLY a brief turn about the grounds of Cadgwyck Manor to discover they were as neglected and unkempt as the interior of the house. Clumps of weeds had sprung up between the cracked flagstones of the terraces, while scraggly, untrimmed shrubs and dangling vines transformed every walkway into a shadowy maze. The lawn had long ago surrendered to the same rambling ivy that had clawed its way up the walls of the crumbling tower. An ornate bronze birdbath crowned by a mossy statue of Botticelli's *Venus* sat in the center of what must once have been a handsome garden, its basin choked with stagnant water. An air of deserted melancholy hung over it all.

Although he stalked from one end of the grounds surrounding the house to the other, Max encountered no gamekeeper, no gardeners, no stable boys. Of course, why would stable boys be required to tend a stable populated only by rustling mice and the swallows that had darted in through the gaping holes in the roof to build their nests in its sagging rafters? For the first time, it occurred to him he was practically a prisoner in this place.

His restless ramblings finally led him to the edge of the cliffs. Savage gusts of wind tore open his coat and whipped his hair away from his face. Propping one booted foot on a rock, he leaned into its battering force, grateful to finally find a worthy opponent with whom he could do battle. Someone besides himself.

At the foot of the cliffs far below, the wind churned the peaks of the waves into foaming whitecaps before driving them to their death against the jagged rocks. The ceaseless roar of the sea was much louder here. A towering wall of clouds brooded on the horizon, their ever-present threat sharpening the very air with the scent of danger.

Despite his growing misgivings about coming to Cornwall, Max had to admit the landscape had a raw, seductive beauty, a wildness that was as stirring to the blood as a swallow of fine whiskey or a beautiful woman. It was as if he were standing on the edge of a storm that could break at any minute, sweeping away everything in its path and making all things new.

Off to the left, he could see a shallow cove cut into the cliffs, where the rocks grudgingly gave way to a half circle of sandy beach. When he was a boy, such a sight would have sent his imagination soaring with dreams of smugglers and the shuttered glow of lanterns dancing along the beach beneath a moonless sky, of secret passageways winding their way deep into the stony recesses of the cliffs, and heaps of shimmering treasure buried in long-forgotten caves. But those dreams had long ago been replaced with ledgers full of endless columns of figures and long, dull board meetings where he presided over a bunch of gouty old men more interested in fattening their own coffers than in steering their company—and their country—toward the future.

The back of Max's neck prickled. Even with his gaze fixed on the sea, he could feel the inescapable shadow of the manor behind him, its windows gazing down upon him like watchful eyes. He wondered if other eyes were watching him as well—mercurial eyes with a maddening tendency to shift when a man least expected it from the glossy green of leaves in deep summer to the rich brown of burled walnut.

He hadn't lingered long enough to see if his curt rebuke had made those eyes darken with hurt.

Seized by a fresh restlessness, Max turned away from the sea and began to stalk along the edge of the cliffs. As he studiously banished his housekeeper from his thoughts, another woman intruded. And not the woman he had expected—the woman who was now happily wed to his brother.

No, this was a mocking little minx, her lustrous brown hair piled carelessly atop her head, her lightly blushed cheek poised on the verge of dimpling. Max slowed his steps as he picked his way over the rocks, wondering just how many times Angelica Cadgwyck's dainty feet might have trod this very path.

And at precisely which spot she had chosen to end her life.

As he reached the very tip of the rugged promontory that jutted out over the sea, his question was answered as surely as if he'd spoken it aloud. Here, the wind was even more relentless. Nearly staggering against its force, Max drew close enough to the edge of the cliff to watch the roiling sea break over the jagged, glistening blades of the rocks below.

Had moonlight glinted off those same rocks on the night Angelica died? Or had clouds shrouded the moon and tricked her into believing that if she took flight off the bluff, she would drift gently down into the arms of the sea?

Max lifted his eyes to the distant horizon. He could almost see her standing there—a young woman blinded by tears, about to be cast out of the only home she had ever known. The ruthless wind would have stripped the pins from her hair like the fingers of a jealous lover until it danced in a cloud around her beautiful, tearstained face.

Her lover was dead, her brother carted off to prison, then banished from these shores, never to return, and her father driven mad by grief. Which one of them had she mourned the most in that moment? Had she given the brash young artist both her body and her heart or held one in reserve for some future love? A love she would never live long enough to meet.

In the fraction of time before she had stepped off the edge of that promontory, had she been fleeing her destiny or rushing forward to embrace it with open arms?

Without warning, the thin shelf of rock beneath Max's feet began to crumble. He jumped backward just in time to watch what was left of the shelf tumble toward the sea in a dizzying spiral before shattering against the rocks below like so many grains of sand.

# ❧ Chapter Nine

As Max watched the swirling sea swallow the pulverized rocks just as it must have swallowed Angelica Cadgwyck's broken body all those years ago, his chest heaved with delayed reaction. Despite the violent pounding of his heart—or perhaps because of it—he hadn't felt this alive for a long time.

When he had arrived at Cadgwyck last night, he had foolishly assumed the chief dangers a man might encounter in such a place were a loose chimney pot or a rotted banister. He had never dreamed the cliffs themselves might try to lure him to his doom. Had he been possessed of a more suspicious—and less practical—nature, he might even have suspected foul play. But common sense told him the shelf of rock at the tip of the promontory had simply been weakened by time and the elements. He had no one to blame for his near fatal plunge into the sea but himself. He should never have wandered so close to the cliff's edge.

Shaking his head, Max turned to give the windows of the house a rueful look, wondering if anyone else had witnessed his folly.

He half-expected to see Angelica herself laughing merrily down at him from some shadowy attic dormer, but there was nothing ghostly about the flicker of movement he glimpsed in a second-story window.


As Lord Dravenwood's sharp-eyed gaze swept the back of the manor, then returned with eerie precision to the exact window where she was standing, Anne ducked behind the velvet draperies. Her mouth was dry, her heart still racing madly beneath the palm that had flown to her chest when he had stumbled back from the edge of the cliff, only inches away from a plunge into nothingness.

She fought to steady her breathing before peeping around the edge of the curtain again. To her keen relief, Dravenwood had already turned away from the house and was beginning to make his way farther along the cliffs, this time remaining a safe distance from their treacherous edge.

"This one's going to be trouble, isn't he?" Pippa observed, setting down her ash bucket to join Anne at the window of the cozy second-floor study.

Pippa had made a more concerted effort to embrace her role of maidservant on this day, taming her flyaway dark curls into two proper braids coiled neatly above her ears and donning an apron with only a few faded chocolate stains marring its snowy-white surface.

Anne watched their new master pick his way over the rocks, unaccountably angry at him for frightening her so badly. "They're all trouble, dearest," she said darkly. "It's just a matter of degree."

Despite her reassurances, Anne knew Pippa was right. Trouble was written in every line of Lord Dravenwood's bearing—in the stiffness of his broad shoulders, the way he carried himself as if he were nursing some mortal wound no one else could see. It was etched in the shadows that brooded beneath his eyes and in the way his coat hung loosely on his tall, rangy frame, as if it had been tailored for a different man.

A man who hadn't forgotten how to smile.

But those were just warning signs. Even without them, he was the sort of man who could cause trouble for a woman with little more than a smoldering glance from beneath the thick, sooty lashes veiling his quicksilver eyes or the casual brush of his hand against the small of her back. And if such a man should choose to employ the full range of his seductive skills, he could easily go from being trouble to being a full-fledged disaster. At least for the woman foolish enough to grant him access to her vulnerable heart—or her body.

Anne could feel Pippa's worried gaze lingering on her face. "Whatever is the matter with you, Annie? Why, you're as white as a ghost yourself!"

"And why wouldn't I be?" Anne replied with a lightness she was far from feeling. "I was afraid the careless fool was going to tumble headlong over the cliff, leaving us to explain yet another unfortunate *accident* to the constable."

"What do you suppose ails the man?" Pippa's smooth brow puckered in a quizzical frown as she watched Lord Dravenwood stalk along the edge of the cliffs, the tails of his coat blowing out behind him. "Do you think he's recovering from some terrible illness? A brain fever or some exotic malady he picked up on one of his journeys perhaps?"

Anne would have wagered Lord Dravenwood was suffering from a sickness of the heart, not the body. She knew its signs only too well, having nearly died from it herself once.

"Whatever ails him, it's none of our concern." As the earl turned and began to make his way back toward the manor, she yanked the drapes shut. "If

I have anything to say about it, he'll be gone soon enough, just like all the others."

Pippa hauled her bucket over to the hearth and dumped its contents on the pristine iron grate. A dark cloud of ash shot up into the air, forcing her to wave it away from her watering eyes. "If we succeed in driving him away, won't they just send another pompous nobleman in his place?"

"Perhaps," Anne said firmly, hoping to hide her own doubts. "But thanks to our diligent efforts, the infamy of the White Lady of Cadgwyck is beginning to spread beyond the borders of Cornwall. If her legend continues to flourish, it's going to grow ever more difficult for them to find a buyer or overseer for the property. With any luck, they'll leave us to our own devices just long enough for us to find what we've been looking for."

"What if they should decide to close down the house altogether? *Before* we can find the treasure?"

"I don't believe they'll do that as long as they have a household of loyal servants willing to remain in this cursed place. After all, we're the only ones standing between the manor and utter ruin." Anne wagged her eyebrows at Pippa. "At least that's what we're allowing them to believe."

Pippa set aside the bucket. "Just what manner of mischief are you proposing this time?"

"Nothing too extreme. I suspect all his lordship really needs is a little nudge toward the door."

"A nudge or a shove?"

Anne lifted her shoulders in a noncommittal shrug. "Whatever will serve us best."

"Promise me you'll take care, won't you?" Pippa urged, her dark eyes absent their usual teasing spark. "I fear he might be more dangerous than the others."

Anne wanted to dismiss the warning. But she knew far more about the dangers a man such as Dravenwood could present to a woman than Pippa did. Dangers lurking behind longing looks and stolen caresses and pretty promises never intended to be kept.

Mustering up a reassuring smile, she marched past Pippa and to the fireplace. Kneeling on the hearth, she reached up into the chimney and fumbled blindly about until she located the grimy iron key that controlled the flue.

She gave it a sharp twist, then rose, briskly dusting ash from her hands. "Try not to fret so much, my dear. Lord Dravenwood might be a threat to me, but I can assure you Angelica is more than his match."

"MRS. SPENCER!"

To Anne's credit, she didn't even flinch when that thunderous shout came echoing through the halls of Cadgwyck Manor later that night. The convivial conversation she and her staff had been enjoying around the long pine table in the kitchen ceased abruptly. Lisbeth seized Betsy's hand in a white-knuckled grip while the other maids exchanged wide-eyed glances of alarm over their steaming bowls of bisque prepared with lobsters Dickon had trapped for them just that morning.

Hodges lurched halfway to his feet, snatching up the wicked-looking knife they'd used to cut the bread. Dickon clapped a hand on the old man's shoulder, easing Hodges back into his chair before gently removing the knife from his clenched fist and sliding it out of harm's reach. Pippa buried her pert nose even deeper in the dog-eared copy of *The Castle of Otranto* she had filched from the manor's library.

In an ominous silence broken only by the cheery click of Nana's knitting needles and Piddles's snoring, Anne took one more sip of the succulent soup before laying down her spoon. She dabbed delicately at her lips with her napkin, then rose from her chair. "If you'll excuse me, it seems the master is in need of my services."

As she started for the door, the rest of them eyed her as if she were marching off to the gallows. She forced herself to maintain her even pace as she climbed the stairs and crossed the second-story gallery, keenly aware of Angelica Cadgwyck's mocking gaze following her every step. Her composure wasn't tested until she passed the third-floor staircase at the far end of the gallery and saw the man barreling down the long corridor. Heading straight for her.

Lord Dravenwood looked as if he'd just marched out of the gates of hell. Soot blackened his face, making the whites of his eyes gleam that much more vividly. His hair was wild and his coat missing entirely. Each of his furious strides left a blackened footprint on the shabby carpet runner. A billowing cloud of smoke trailed behind him.

Another man in his predicament might have looked comical. But perhaps one had to have a sense of humor to look comical. He just looked murderous.

Ignoring her instinctive urge to snatch up the hem of her skirts and flee in the opposite direction, Anne donned her most unflappable expression as he halted in front of her. His broad chest was still heaving, although whether with rage or from exertion she could not tell.

Given the sparks of unholy wrath shooting from his eyes, it seemed only fitting that he smelled of fire and brimstone as well. His ash-smudged shirtsleeves had been shoved up to reveal muscular forearms generously dusted with curling, dark hair.

"You bellowed, my lord?" she inquired, jerking

her gaze away from that rather riveting sight and its unanticipated effects on her composure and back up to his face.

His sharp eyes missed nothing. "I do hope you'll forgive my shocking state of undress, Mrs. Spencer," he said with scathing courtesy. "I had to use my coat to fan the smoke out of the study before it choked me to death." His eyes narrowed in an accusing gaze. "When you informed me the study would be a pleasant place to enjoy an after-dinner brandy, you neglected to mention it would turn into a death trap the minute I lit the fire that had been laid upon the hearth."

"Oh, dear." Anne touched a hand to her throat in what she hoped was a convincing display of dismay. "Are you quite all right?"

"Fortunately, I was able to smother the flames and wrestle the windows open before being overcome by the smoke. When was the last time that chimney was cleaned? Seventeen ninety-eight?"

Anne shook her head, heaving a bewildered sigh. "I don't understand what could have happened. Why, I checked the damper myself only this morning when Pippa and I were airing out the room! I would have sworn the flue was—" She stopped abruptly, lowering her eyes before casting him an uneasy glance from beneath her lashes.

Dravenwood folded his arms over his chest, an

expression far too cynical to be called a smile quirking one corner of his lips. "Let me guess. You think the ghost was the one who tampered with the flue."

"Don't be ridiculous, my lord! You said yourself there was no such thing as ghosts."

His jaw tightened. "What I said was that men are perfectly capable of creating things to haunt them without the aid of the supernatural."

"And quite right you are about that, I'm sure. Perhaps it was simply a malfunction of some sort. I'll send the maids to clean up the study and have Dickon check the flue right away."

"Very well. Then you can send Hodges to my chambers. As you can see, I'll be requiring some assistance with my bath."

A flutter of panic stirred in Anne's throat. She had not anticipated this complication. "Perhaps Dickon can check the flue in the morning. I'm sure he'd be more than happy to assist you in the bath if you'll just give me a moment to—"

"Send Hodges," Dravenwood commanded. "Unless, of course"—he leaned toward her in an unmistakably menacing manner, his stern voice betraying not so much as a hint of humor—"*you'd* rather assist me."

Unfortunately, the earl's raw masculinity was made even more potent by his savage appearance. With his gray eyes smoldering with a fire of their own, his hair tousled as if by a lover's fingers, and his bared teeth dazzling white against the soot-darkened planes of his face, he looked like a man capable of anything. Anything at all.

A dangerous little flame uncurled low in Anne's belly, bringing a kindred rush of heat to her cheeks. She wouldn't have been surprised to see smoke rising from her own flesh.

She took an awkward half step backward before saying stiffly, "I'll have Lisbeth and Betsy draw a bath and send Hodges up to assist you."

"Thank you," he replied with exaggerated formality.

Through narrowed eyes Anne watched him stride away from her, almost wishing she had armed herself with Pippa's poker.

MAX SANK DEEPER INTO the copper hip bath, resting the back of his head against its rim. He had to cock his knees up at an awkward angle just to partially submerge his long legs, but the warm water lapping at the muscled planes of his chest almost made up for the inconvenience. He made a mental note to have Mrs. Spencer order a tub more suited to a man his size.

A reluctant half smile curved his lips at the memory of his housekeeper's outraged expression when he had suggested she attend him in his bath. He didn't know why he took such delight in taunting the stiff-necked woman, but there was no denying it gave him a naughty little thrill of satisfaction. One he hadn't felt for a long time.

For a brief time as boys, he and Ashton had endured a tyrant of a German nanny they had taken equal delight in tormenting. He could still remember her guttural screams on the night she had rolled over on the hapless lizard they had slipped into her bed. Max's smile slowly faded. That was when he and Ash had been inseparable, long before their love for the same girl had torn them apart.

The German nanny and Mrs. Spencer were probably equally deserving of his scorn. He was beginning to suspect the White Lady of Cadgwyck Manor was nothing more than an imaginative attempt to excuse the incompetence of her staff. He had a good mind to dismiss the lot of them and replace them with a capable household of servants summoned directly from London. Servants who would never dare to challenge his authority or gaze up at him with a faintly mocking sparkle in their fine hazel eyes.

Somehow, the thought didn't hold as much appeal as it should have. If he sent for his London staff, they might know nothing about the house or its resident ghost, but they would know everything about him.

He had come to this place to escape the prying eyes he could feel following him every time he entered a drawing room, the whispers he could hear even when they thought he wasn't listening. Mrs. Spencer and her motley little crew might tax his patience, but at least they didn't scurry out of his way as if he were some sort of ill-tempered monster or, worse yet, shoot him pitying glances behind his back.

He retrieved the cake of bayberry soap floating in the water and ran it lazily over his chest to wash away the lingering taint of the soot. What would he have done if Mrs. Spencer had called his bluff and taken him up on his offer to assist him with his bath?

As he closed his eyes, he could almost feel her pale, cool hands gliding over the heat of his damp flesh. Could imagine himself reaching up to pluck the pins from her hair one by one until it came tumbling around her face to reveal its mysteries. Could see himself wrapping his hand in that silky skein and tipping back his head as she leaned over and touched her parted lips to his, enticing him to run the very tip of his tongue over the winsome gap between her teeth before plunging it deep into the hot, wet softness of her—

"Holy hell!" Max swore, shooting straight up out of the water and shaking off the dangerous daydream along with the droplets of water beading in his hair.

Where in the bloody hell had *that* come from? He'd never once entertained such naughty notions about the German nanny. Of course the German nanny had been shaped like the bulwark of a warship and had a deeper voice and a more impressive pair of mustaches than Max's father. Still, the very thought of his prickly housekeeper welcoming his kiss or his advances was beyond ludicrous. She was far more likely to grab him by the scruff of the neck and shove his head under the water until the bubbles stopped rising.

A timid knock sounded on the door. Had he somehow succeeded in summoning up the object of his unseemly fantasies?

"Enter," he commanded gruffly, sinking back into the water to disguise the telltale heaviness of his groin.

The door creaked open, the soft glow of the lamplight revealing Hodges's snowy-white head. The butler minced gingerly into the room, his gaze darting from side to side as if to search for potential assailants. He had a thick towel draped over one forearm.

At first Max feared Hodges had been struck mute again, but after an awkward silence the butler said, "Mrs. Spencer sent me, my lord. She said you had need of assistance with your bath."

"You have excellent timing, Hodges. The water was just beginning to cool."

Hodges hesitated for a second, as if confused about what should happen next, then dutifully hastened to the side of the tub. Spreading the towel until it formed a curtain between them, the butler politely fixed his gaze elsewhere while Max climbed out of the bath.

Max took the towel and began to rub it briskly over his head and chest, as unself-conscious in his nakedness as any man who had been dressed by someone else for as long as he could remember. "My apologies for the inconvenience, Hodges. I realize this task is beneath your position. We really must look into finding me a proper valet."

"I'm sure Mrs. Spencer will see to it."

Max wrapped the towel around his waist, eyeing Hodges's broad, blank face thoughtfully. The man's cheeks and nose were a little ruddy, as if he'd done his share of drinking in his day. "You're the butler of this household, are you not? Don't you have any concerns about Mrs. Spencer usurping your authority?"

"Mrs. Spencer is quite good at what she does." Hodges's words had a stilted quality, almost as if he were some Drury Lane actor practicing his lines for a Saturday matinee. "I am more than happy to defer to her wishes."

Max snorted. "A sentiment Mr. Spencer shared, no doubt. At least if he knew what was good for him."

"Mr. Spencer?" Hodges echoed, the glazed look returning to his eyes.

"Mrs. Spencer's dearly departed husband? Dickon told me all about the tragic accident that claimed the man's life."

Hodges blinked several times as if striving to remember something he'd been told long ago. "Ah, yes!" Relief brightened his face. "The wagon!"

"From what Dickon said, it sounded like a terrible tragedy. I daresay the good widow was prostrate with grief."

"From what I hear, she was inconsolable! She was devoted to the man, you know. Utterly devoted."

While Max digested that bit of information, Hodges retrieved Max's dressing gown from the hulking armoire in the corner and held it open so Max could step into it.

Max let the damp towel fall to the carpet and accepted the butler's invitation, knotting the sash of the dressing gown around his waist.

Hodges beamed at him, plainly proud his efforts had been so well received. "Will that be all, my lord?"

"I do believe it will." Taking Hodges by the elbow, Max gently steered him toward the door.

Before the butler's hand could close on the doorknob, Max snatched the door open himself, half-expecting his housekeeper to come tumbling headfirst into the room. But the shadowy corridor was deserted. Max poked his head out the door and looked both ways. Not a soul was in sight—either living or dead.

"Your services have been very much appreciated," he assured Hodges. "You have no idea how helpful you've been."

As the butler went bobbing off down the corridor, humming cheerfully beneath his breath, Max closed the door behind him and leaned his back against it. Pondering everything he was learning about his rather enigmatic housekeeper, Max murmured, "Very helpful indeed."

THAT NIGHT MAX DREAMED again.

Despite his many trips to China, Max had never visited an opium den. But he had always imagined it would feel something like this—his limbs weighted to a bed or a couch in a pleasant stupor while his mind drifted away, unfettered by the chains that bound it during his waking hours. Chains he had forged himself with his single-minded devotion to duty and his slavish adoration of a woman whose heart had always belonged to another man.

Leaving his body behind, he soared through the open French windows of his bedchamber and into the night. The wings of the wind carried him straight to the dizzying height of the cliffs. A woman stood at the very tip of the promontory, her back to him. She wore the same dress she had worn in the portrait, its voluminous skirts rippling in the wind. The dress was the color of buttercups ripe with the promise of spring.

A spring that would never come if she took one more step.

Max ached to gather her shivering body into the warmth of his arms, stroke her wind-tossed hair, and tell her that, although it seemed impossible now, her broken heart would mend. He would see to it himself, even if he had to gather the scattered shards of it with his bare hands and piece them together one by one.

But he'd left his body paralyzed on the bed. All he could do was watch in helpless horror as she spread her graceful arms into wings and disappeared over the edge of the cliff.

Max sat straight up in the bed, his breathing a harsh, painful rasp in the darkness. Only seconds ago he would have sworn he wouldn't be able to budge if someone set a lit match to his mattress, but now a terrible restlessness seized him. He threw back the sweat-dampened sheets and shoved open the bed curtains, desperate to escape their smothering confines.

His dream was no less vivid to his waking eyes. He could still see that forlorn figure standing at the edge of the cliffs. Could feel his own helpless anguish as he watched her make a decision she would never be able to take back. He swung his legs over the edge of the bed and stared at the shadowy outline of his own hands in the darkness, despising how powerful they looked, yet how powerless they felt in that moment.

Cool night air spilled over his heated flesh. He slowly lifted his head. For a dazed moment, he thought he must surely still be dreaming because the windows leading to his balcony were standing wide open.

An icy chill danced down Max's spine. He had secured the windows himself before retiring, checking and double-checking their latches, then giving their handles a stern shake to test them. He had even locked his bedchamber door to ensure none with mischief on their minds could sneak into the room while he slept. A quick glance confirmed the door was still closed, the brass key still visible in its lock.

As he turned his gaze back to the windows, a gentle breeze caressed the frozen planes of his face. There was no storm on this night, no violent gusts of wind he could blame for wrenching the windows open. They had either opened of their own accord or been opened by some unseen hand.

As he watched, a ribbon of mist came drifting

into the room, bringing with it the haunting fragrance of jasmine—dense and sweet and seductive enough to drive a man's senses wild. For the briefest instant, the mist seemed to coalesce into something more substantial—a human form with long, flowing hair, a rippling, white gown, and gently rounded curves. Max blinked and the illusion vanished as quickly as it had appeared.

Biting off an oath, he reached to the end of the bed for his dressing gown. He yanked on the garment, then strode through the open windows and onto the balcony. The fragrance of jasmine was weaker there but still potent enough to make his groin tighten with longing.

Gripping the balustrade, he turned his fierce gaze toward the abandoned tower, half-expecting to see a spectral flash of light or hear the tinkling notes of a music box. The tower remained dark and all he heard were the waves breaking over the distant rocks, a wistful murmur on this peaceful night instead of a roar.

The tension slowly seeped from his body. Hadn't he accused the last master of Cadgwyck of being chased from the premises by his own imagination? Yet he was no different. He had allowed an overwrought dream and melodramatic tales of an old tragedy to stir his fancies in a way they hadn't been stirred since he was a boy.

Angelica Cadgwyck was nothing more than a stranger to him. No matter how wretched her fate, he had no reason to give her a foothold in his imagination . . . or his heart. There was probably some perfectly sound explanation for why the windows kept slipping their latches. Come morning, aided by the bright light of day and his refreshed wits, he would find it.

Shaking his head at his own folly, he rubbed a hand over his tousled hair and padded back inside. The scent of jasmine had completely dissipated, making him wonder if he had conjured that up from some long-buried memory as well.

He had slipped out of his dressing gown and was poised to climb back into the bed when he glanced over his shoulder and saw the door to his bedchamber standing open.

## ❧ Chapter Ten

THE BRASS KEY WAS still in its keyhole, right where Max had left it, but the door stood ajar. The corridor beyond was as dark as an underground tunnel.

Max stood there in a misty wash of moonlight, his every sense tingling with awareness. Then he heard a sound even more disconcerting than an off-key tune ground out by the rusty gears of a music box—a rippling echo of laughter, feminine and sweet.

He might have been able to dismiss some maudlin specter weeping into her invisible handkerchief. But something about that girlish giggle was irresistible. It was like the taunting laughter of a child playing hide-and-seek while actually longing to be found.

His lips twisted in a grim smile as he tossed aside the dressing gown, strode over to the wardrobe, and yanked out a pair of trousers and a shirt. He donned the trousers and tugged the shirt over his head but didn't waste time securing it at the throat. His hands were unnaturally steady as he located the tinderbox and lit the candle sitting on the side table. Taking up the brass candlestick, he headed for the corridor.

The wavering flame of the candle did little to penetrate the darkness. Max hesitated just outside his chamber, cocking his head to listen. All he heard was the peaceful hush of the sleeping house. He was beginning to wonder if he had imagined the laughter just as he had the scent of jasmine, but then it came again, faint but unmistakable.

Now that he was actually in the corridor, the ghostly echo seemed to be coming from even farther away, as if it were traveling not just through the shadowy passageways of the house but through the corridors of time itself. Dismissing the absurd notion, Max moved toward the sound with the fleet grace of a born hunter.

He slipped silently down the stairs to the second floor, his senses heightened by a strange elation. He had felt the same way standing on the edge of the cliff earlier in the day, only seconds before the world had crumbled beneath his feet. Perhaps it wasn't Angelica Cadgwyck's intention to drive him away, but to drive him mad. Or perhaps he was already mad. Most men would flee from a ghost, yet here he was, eagerly pursuing one.

He crossed the second-floor portrait gallery, his candle casting flickering shadows over the empty walls where the Cadgwyck ancestors had once resided. By the time he reached Angelica's portrait, he wouldn't have been surprised to find the ornate gilt frame empty and its occupant romping gleefully through the entrance hall below. But when he lifted the candlestick, Angelica was still gazing down her slender nose at him, her eyes knowing, her lips poised on the verge of a smile, as if she were about to reveal some terribly amusing secret she could only share with him.

A draft as warm and sweet as a woman's breath breezed right past him. The candle's flame guttered once, then went out, leaving him alone in the darkness with her. He stood there, inhaling the acrid smell of snuffed wick, and waited for his eyes to adjust to the meager moonlight drifting through the grimy arched window above the front door.

A new sound penetrated the gloom. It took a minute for Max to place the rhythmic ticking, to recognize it as the sound of a pendulum swinging back and forth in a graceful arc, measuring each second as if it would be his last. Max slowly turned, a fresh chill dancing down his spine. It was the long-case clock at the foot of the stairs, the clock with its hands frozen at a quarter past midnight. The hollow ticktock seemed to echo each heavy thud of his heart.

The warning of the innkeeper's wife echoed through his memory: *Ye might not be so quick to dismiss our words as a bunch o' rubbish if ye'd have seen the face o' the last master o' the house on the night he came runnin' into the village a little after midnight, half-dead from fleein' whatever evil lurks in that place.*

If Max had thought to check his pocket watch before he left his bedchamber, what would he have found? That it was rapidly approaching the moment when something so terrible had happened in this house even time had stopped to mourn it?

He *had* ordered Mrs. Spencer to have the clock fixed. Perhaps in her eagerness to please him, she had done just that.

A skeptical snort escaped him as he dropped the useless candlestick and went speeding down the stairs, rounding the ornately carved newel at the bottom of the staircase to bring himself face-to-face with the clock.

The ticking had ceased. Wan moonlight bathed the clock's impassive face, revealing its motionless hands dutifully stationed at the twelve and the three. Max's heart was left to beat on all alone.

Curling his hands into fists, he swung away from the clock and swept his gaze over the entrance hall.

He was shocked to realize he wasn't the least bit afraid. He was angry. He didn't care for being toyed with, not by any man or woman and certainly not by some chit of a ghost who still fancied herself mistress of *his* house.

As if to taunt him, a sweet ripple of girlish laughter danced through the entrance hall. Max strode to the center of the hall, then slowly turned, holding his breath to listen. Too many rooms and corridors led off the hall to determine from which direction the laughter was coming.

The moon drifted behind a wisp of a cloud, bathing the hall in shadows. That was when he saw it—the briefest flash of white down a darkened corridor, like the trailing skirts of a woman's gown as she darted around a corner.

Spurred on by the thrill of the hunt, Max broke into long strides. As he rounded the corner where he had seen the flash of white, he sensed a presence in the darkness ahead of him, moving quickly.

But not quickly enough.

Another corner loomed at the end of the corridor. He quickened his pace. He had no intention of letting his prey escape, not when he was this close to getting his hands on it. As he swung around the corner, his arms shot out to seize whatever they found in front of him.

He was half-expecting them to close on empty

air. Which was why it was such a shock to his senses when the bundle he hauled against his chest turned out to be warm, soft, and ever so human.

As his captive squirmed against him, panting with frustration, it wasn't the haunting scent of jasmine that tickled his nose but another aroma— one that made his stomach clench with hunger and reminded him just how bland his supper of over- cooked beef and underdone potatoes had been. Puzzled, he wrinkled his nose. Could a ghost smell of something as mundane, yet irresistible to a man's appetites, as freshly baked bread and cinnamon bis- cuits?

The bundle in his arms abruptly stopped squirm- ing. After a moment of silence, an acerbic voice came out of the darkness. "The next time you need something in the middle of the night, my lord, you might try simply ringing the bell."

# ⤞ *Chapter Eleven*

ANNE HELD HER BREATH as she awaited Lord Dravenwood's response, resisting the dangerous urge to relax against the broad expanse of his chest. For such a cold man, he was incredibly warm. He radiated heat like a cookstove on a blustery December day.

Once he had seized her, it hadn't taken her long to realize her struggles against his unyielding arms were futile. He seemed to be exceptionally well formed for a man who had probably spent much of his career seated behind a desk.

Despite holding herself as stiffly as she could, there could be no denying the shocking intimacy of his makeshift embrace. One of his muscular arms was cinched around her waist while the other was wrapped firmly around her shoulders, just above the swell of her breasts. He'd planted his feet apart to balance them both, leaving her legs to dangle between his splayed thighs, the tips of her toes barely brushing the floor. His hips cradled the softness of her rump as if they'd been designed by their Maker for just such a provocative purpose.

The awkward silence only made the rasp of his ragged breathing more obvious. His chest hitched unevenly against her back while his heated breath caressed the back of her neck. A helpless shiver of reaction danced over her flesh. Anne almost wished she'd left her hair unbound to protect her vulnerable nape from that tantalizing assault instead of dividing it into two precise braids.

She had assumed identifying herself would win her freedom.

She had assumed wrong. Although Lord Dravenwood's grip had softened a nearly imperceptible degree, his arms showed no sign of relinquishing their prize. He lowered his head next to hers in the darkness, his brandy-scented breath grazing the side of her throat.

Her eyes drifted shut as if even the darkness was too much for them to bear. She could feel both her muscles and her will softening of their own accord. Could feel her head listing to the side to expose the tingling curve of her throat to his lips.

It had been so long since a man had touched her … kissed her yearning lips. If he turned her in his arms and used his weight to bear her back against the nearest wall, would she have the strength to resist him? Or would she twine her arms around his neck and draw his warm, seeking lips down to hers?

"Honey. Sugar," he murmured, his husky baritone a seduction all its own. His breath danced over the delicate swath of skin behind her ear. "Cinnamon. Nutmeg. Vanilla. Fresh cream."

His words slowly penetrated the languorous haze threatening to overcome her. She frowned in bewilderment. He wasn't whispering endearments but ingredients. And it wasn't his lips gliding toward the curve between her throat and shoulder but his nose.

Her eyes flew open. The man wasn't trying to seduce her; he was *sniffing* her!

"My lord," she snapped, having no difficulty whatsoever striking just the right note of exasperation, "have you any intention of unhanding me before morning?"

This time her words had the desired effect. Dravenwood released her so abruptly she stumbled and nearly fell. She was surprised by how chilly the air felt without his arms to shield her from it.

She slowly turned to face him. He loomed over her, a faceless silhouette against the deeper shadows.

"Why do you always smell like that?" he demanded, his voice deepening to a near growl.

"Like what?"

"Like something that just came out of the oven. Something warm and freshly baked."

Although it certainly wasn't the accusation she had expected, Anne still felt oddly guilty. "As housekeeper, I spend a fair amount of my day in the kitchen planning the weekly menus and overseeing the cook."

"I've yet to see anything emerge from the kitchen of *this* house that smells like *that*. Except for you, that is."

"Is that what drove you to accost me? You mistook me for a warm cross bun?"

"I mistook you for"—he hesitated—"an intruder. It's a risk you run when you wander about the manor in the dead of night ... without your clothes," he added pointedly.

Anne could almost feel the heat of his gaze sweeping over her. Apparently, his night vision was much keener than hers. She touched a hand to her throat, reassuring herself there was no need to stammer or blush in embarrassment. Her modest nightdress shrouded her from throat to ankle. Of course, now he knew exactly what it was shrouding. He had felt the softness of her curves mold to the hardness of his own body, had felt the wild patter of her heart as she writhed against him.

"I thought I heard a noise so I came to investigate," she said primly.

"Without a lamp? Or even so much as a candle?"

"I would think you'd be more in need of a candle than I would. I'm far more familiar with the house and less likely to bark my shins or tumble down a flight of stairs."

"Or out a fourth-floor window," he said coolly, reminding them both of the fate another, less fortunate, master of the house had met.

Anne's mouth fell open, then snapped shut. She could feel him studying her again, but was grateful she couldn't see his expression. She would do well to guard her sharp tongue. If she goaded him into dismissing her, all was lost.

"I left my chamber with a candle," he finally admitted. "But it was lost to a draft."

"Old houses do tend to have an abundance of those."

"Among other things. Aren't you the least bit concerned about roaming around the manor in the dark yourself when it's been rumored there's a vengeful ghost on the loose?"

Anne shrugged. "We seem to have reached a mutual agreement with our White Lady. We don't trouble her and she doesn't trouble us."

"Aha!" He drew a step closer to her, bringing his

triumphant features into focus. "So you do believe in ghosts!"

"It's impossible to live in this house and not believe in spirits of some sort. The past can be a very powerful influence on the present."

"Only for those who insist on dwelling in it." His words had a bitter edge, as if he had recognized the irony in them even before they were out of his mouth. "You claimed you heard a noise. Just what did you hear?"

"Nothing of consequence. Probably just a loose shutter banging against a window."

"I heard a woman laughing."

His stark confession hung between them, a shimmering thread of truth cutting through the darkness.

It pained her to neatly sever that thread with her next words. "What you most likely heard was a pair of housemaids giggling over some nonsense in their beds. The girls rise early and work hard during the day. I try not to deny them their simple pleasures."

He was silent for so long Anne knew he hadn't believed a word of her explanation. But he'd been a diplomat long enough to recognize a standoff when he saw one. "What of yourself, Mrs. Spencer?"

"Pardon?" she asked, confused by his question.

"Do you deny yourself your simple pleasures? Or do you prefer the more complicated ones?"

For a long moment Anne found it difficult to breathe, much less formulate a coherent answer. When she finally did, the arid formality had been restored to her tone. "I trust you can find your way back to your bed, my lord. I'll strive to see you pass the rest of your night undisturbed."

As she turned away from him, she would have almost sworn she heard him mutter beneath his breath, "Pity, that."

She started down the darkened corridor, still feeling the prick of his suspicious gaze against her back. She forced herself to measure each step, though she was nearly overcome by the absurd notion that he was going to seize her again. That he was only a breath away from closing the distance between them so he could wrap a powerful arm around her waist and draw her back against the seductive heat of his body. She'd resisted the temptation to melt against all of that enticing masculine strength once, but she wasn't sure she'd have the fortitude to do it again.

She waited until she'd reached the shelter of the servants' staircase before giving in to the overpowering impulse to flee.

BY THE TIME ANNE reached her attic room, she had a stitch in her side and was gasping for breath. She slipped inside the room and closed the door, twisting the key in the lock with trembling fingers.

Pippa and Dickon had helped her install the lock before their last master had arrived. The three of them had laughingly celebrated their efforts, knowing all the while it would be a feeble defense against a powerful shoulder or a booted foot.

Anne pressed her ear to the door but heard no sign of pursuit. She sagged against it, going limp with relief. She had certainly never intended to end her evening in her employer's arms. She had only her own carelessness to blame. She knew every cranny and nook of this house. If she had anticipated his pursuit, she could easily have eluded him.

She'd grown accustomed to men fleeing her company, not seeking it. She certainly hadn't expected Lord Dravenwood to plunge headlong into the darkness, turning the hunter into the hunted.

She pushed herself away from the door. She'd left a candle burning on the washstand, and as she crossed the floor, she caught a glimpse of her reflection in the looking glass that hung over it.

Mesmerized against her will, she drew closer to the mirror. She expected to see what she saw every morning when she arose—an ordinary face, not unpleasing, but certainly not worthy of praise or adulation. But tonight her breasts were rising and falling unsteadily beneath the plain, white linen bodice of her nightdress. Her eyes were sparkling, her cheeks flushed a soft rose, her lips slightly parted as if awaiting a lover's kiss. She lifted her hands as if they belonged to someone else and raked her fingers through her braids, releasing her aching head from their pressure. Taming the thick mass was a constant struggle, usually requiring a wealth of pins that stabbed her scalp every time she turned her head. Her hair spilled around her shoulders in a rippling cloud, and she was left staring into the face of a stranger.

Her lips tightened. No, not a stranger at all but a face she knew only too well, a face she had hoped never to see again except as a distorted reflection in the eyes of those too foolish to recognize it had never been anything more than an illusion.

Leaning forward, she blew out the candle, banishing that creature to the past where she belonged.

# ❧ Chapter Twelve

$\mathscr{A}$NNE STOOD AT THE head of the long pine table in the kitchen the next morning, her gaze traveling the circle of faces turned expectantly toward her. Each of those faces was desperately dear to her, but she still felt the burden of their need weighing down her heart. Sometimes she didn't know if her heart would be strong enough to bear it.

Nana had already finished her porridge and retreated to her rocking chair in front of the hearth to rescue Sir Fluffytoes from the hopeless tangle the cat had made of her yarn. Hodges was rocking back and forth in his chair and humming the singsong notes of a nursery rhyme beneath his breath, the front of his white waistcoat already dappled with various food stains.

Anne sighed. She had hoped to send Hodges back to the cellar to do some more excavating while Lord Dravenwood was occupied elsewhere, but in his current condition, Hodges probably wouldn't be able to find the cellar, much less any treasures that might be hiding there.

Pippa and Dickon sat directly across from the maids, who had managed to stop giggling and chattering just long enough to give Anne their attention.

Anne had found the five young maids on the streets of London, living from one crust of bread to the next. They shared one thing in common with her—they had all been left to fend for themselves after being betrayed by a man. Or in some of their cases, by many men.

When Anne had first brought them to Cadgwyck, they had slunk around the manor like a pack of feral cats, shying away from every sudden movement and loud noise. Their hair had been stringy and dull, their features pinched by a combination of hunger and mistrust.

Now their hair was shiny, their faces full and glowing with good health and good humor in the cozy light from the kitchen fire. To them, Cadgwyck Manor wasn't a pile of crumbling stones, but the only true home they'd ever known.

Anne had deliberately chosen the window of time before the earl would rise to address them all.

"I don't wish to alarm any of you," she said, pitching her words at a volume even Nana could hear over the steady creak of her rocking chair, "but I'm afraid we're going to have to endure Lord Dravenwood's company for a little longer than we anticipated."

"And just why is that?" Pippa demanded, looking alarmed.

Anne bit her bottom lip. "I fear I have only myself to blame. In my haste to be rid of the man, I may have overplayed my hand last night."

"Oh, dear!" Betsy's cheerful little pumpkin of a face went as pale as the starched folds of the mobcap perched atop her yellow curls. "He didn't catch you, did he?"

If she closed her eyes, Anne could still feel Dravenwood's arms enfolding her, hauling her against the hard, ruthless planes of his body as if she weighed no more than a feather from one of his pillows. "In a manner of speaking, yes. But I told him I'd left my bed to investigate a mysterious noise myself."

"And he believed you?" Lizzie asked hopefully.

Anne could still see the skeptical gleam of the earl's eyes shining down at her out of the darkness. "I'm not sure Lord Dravenwood believes in much of anything. Since his suspicions have already been stirred, I think it would be best if we try a more subtle approach from this day forward."

Pippa blew an errant curl out of her eyes, her expression sulky. "Just how long must we put up with the insufferable man?"

Anne took a deep breath. "A fortnight at least. Perhaps as much as a month."

Dickon groaned. "I can't wear that silly wig for a fortnight. It itches something fierce!"

"You're just going to have to bear up. He'll be gone soon enough, just like all the rest," Anne assured the boy. "We don't want to make him *too* comfortable, of course, or he might stop pining for his London luxuries and decide he fancies it here. We'll keep feeding him uninspiring meals and making sure the house is as inhospitable as possible. But for the time being there will be no more peculiar noises in the night or mysteriously closed chimney flues. I think it would be best if Angelica didn't put in any more appearances for a while."

"She won't care for that," Pippa warned. "You know what a brat she can be when it comes to getting what she wants."

"I've often thought the two of you were kindred spirits in that respect," Anne shot back, earning an appreciative chuckle from Dickon. Pippa made a face at him.

"Angelica has always been a good girl," Hodges said softly to the remains of his porridge. "If she is overly indulged, it is only because she deserves to be."

Anne gazed down at his snowy-white head, forced to swallow around the sudden tightness in her throat. "Yes, darling. Angelica *is* a good girl. If not for her, none of us would be here right now."

Dickon still didn't look convinced. "How are we supposed to keep hunting for the treasure if he's always lurking about, ordering us to fetch his gloves or lick his boots clean or glowering at us as if we'd accidentally gelded his favorite stallion?"

"We'll simply have to take more care," Anne replied. "Once the earl has relaxed his guard a bit, we'll have a much better chance of—"

"Mrs. Spencer!"

## ❧ Chapter Thirteen

ANNE FROZE RIGHT ALONG with the rest of them as the echo of that familiar roar slowly faded. After a stark moment of silence, one of the rusty bells strung over the door began to jangle with undeniable violence.

"Do you hear the cathedral bells?" Hodges clapped his pudgy hands, his eyes shining like a child's. "Why, it must be Christmas morning!"

Lizzie gazed up the inscription above the bell, her eyes as round as saucers. "'Tis the master's bedchamber."

Pippa gave Anne a wide-eyed look, but Anne shook her head in answer to the girl's unspoken question. Neither Anne nor Angelica had had a hand in this bit of mischief. Anne was as bewildered as the rest of them by their master's abrupt summons. Keenly aware of their anxious gazes following her every move, Anne forced herself to walk calmly from the kitchen. She waited until she was out of their sight to quicken her steps to a run.

WHEN ANNE ARRIVED AT the east wing, Dravenwood was pacing back and forth in the corridor outside his bedchamber in shirtsleeves and trousers, his untied cravat hanging loose around his throat. He wasn't trailing smoke or reeking of fire and brimstone, but he did appear to be in a devil of a temper.

As she approached, he wheeled around and stabbed a finger toward the closed door. "There is a creature in my room!"

To Anne's credit, she managed to keep a straight face. "What is it this time, my lord? A ghost? A bogey? Or perhaps a werewolf?"

Scowling at her from beneath a brow as dark and forbidding as a thundercloud, he reached down and flung open the door. Anne gingerly peered around the door frame, unsure of what she would find.

Piddles was curled up right in the middle of his lordship's bed, chewing on a piece of mangled leather. As they crept into the room, the dog bared his pronounced underbite and let out a low growl, as if to warn them away from attempting to wrest his prize from him so they might chew on it themselves.

A smile slowly spread across Anne's face. "That is

not a creature, my lord. *That* is a dog." She squinted at the shiny leather tassel dangling from one corner of the dog's mouth. "And what is that? Is it . . ."

"It *was* one of my very best boots," Dravenwood said morosely. Piddles gulped, then swallowed. The tassel disappeared.

As the dog went back to gnawing on what was left of the boot, the earl glared at him. "I discovered him when I came out of the dressing room. How do you suppose the little wretch got in here?"

"Was the door secured?"

Dravenwood snorted. "Why should that matter in this house? He probably just walked right through it."

"If it wasn't locked, he may have nudged it open with his nose."

"Such as it is." Dravenwood eyed a squashed black button disparagingly, as if it couldn't possibly have any useful purpose.

"I'm afraid it's a long-standing habit of his."

"Along with ingesting wildly expensive footwear?"

Sighing, Anne nodded. "As well as stockings, straw bonnets, and the occasional parasol. I'm terribly sorry, my lord. I'll be more than happy to remove the dog from your chamber, but I fear your boot is quite beyond repair." She marched over to the bed and snapped her fingers. "Piddles, down!"

The dog uncurled himself and obediently descended the bed stairs, landing on his stocky legs with a decided thump. He sank down on his squat haunches, the remains of the boot still hanging from his mouth, and looked up at her expectantly.

Dravenwood frowned. "Every time I got anywhere near the bed, the beast snapped at me like a baby dragon. I was afraid I was going to lose a finger, if not an entire hand."

"Dickon is the one who trained him."

"Well, that explains it. Why do you call him—"

As if anticipating the question, Piddles strolled to the foot of the bed, hiked up his leg, and proceeded to ruin the earl's other boot.

Anne held her breath. Their last master would probably have kicked the cantankerous little dog out the nearest window for such a slight.

But after a short pause, Lord Dravenwood simply sighed. "Well, it wasn't as if I was going to have need of one boot."

Unmindful of his narrow escape, Piddles trotted from the room, his stub of a tail wagging proudly as he displayed his trophy for all the world to see.

"Did you never have a pup when you were a boy, my lord?" Anne could not resist asking.

Dravenwood shook his head. "My father had hunting hounds, of course, but he believed such beasts were for sport, not for pleasure."

"And what did you believe?"

He frowned as if no one had ever asked him such a thing before. "One winter, when I was a very small lad, I found a litter of kittens that had been abandoned by their mother in a corner of the hayloft. They were tiny, mewling creatures . . . so very helpless. I wrapped them up in my woolen muffler and carried them back to the house, thinking I might be able to coax my father into letting me keep them in my bedchamber until they grew old enough to thrive on their own. He informed me that animals had no place in a house and I must give them to one of the footmen for safekeeping." Dravenwood's voice remained almost painfully expressionless. "I found out later he ordered the footman to drown them in a bucket."

Anne gasped. "How unspeakably cruel! How could he do such a wretched thing to those poor, innocent creatures?" *And to his own child,* she thought, her heart going out to that eager little boy who had hurried back to the house in the cold with his precious bundle.

"I'm sure he thought he was teaching me a valuable lesson about life."

"What? Not to trust a footman?"

"That only the strong are worthy of survival." Judging by the cool look he gave her, it was a lesson he had learned only too well.

Effectively reminded of her place, Anne smoothed

her apron and said stiffly, "I'll send someone to tidy up right away, my lord."

Eyeing the puddle spreading around his remaining boot, Dravenwood's eyes narrowed to silvery slits. "Dickon. *Send Dickon.*"

HAVING LEFT DICKON ON hands and knees, muttering beneath his breath as he grudgingly scrubbed the floor of the master bedchamber, Max sat all alone at the head of the massive dining-room table. He was wearing his *second* favorite pair of boots and feeling no less ridiculous than he had the day before.

As he waited for his breakfast to arrive, he was forced to smother a yawn. His midnight encounter with both the ghost and his housekeeper had kept him tossing in his bedclothes until the wee hours of the morning.

He should never have mentioned hearing the ghostly laughter to Mrs. Spencer. She and the other servants were probably gathered in the kitchen at that very moment, having a hearty laugh at his expense.

The dining-room door swung open and two of the maids came bustling in. One of them made a beeline for the sideboard, while the other came around the table and set a plate in front of him. His breakfast appeared to be identical to the one he'd suffered through yesterday, except today the toast was burned to a blackened crisp and the rashers of bacon limp and undercooked.

The girl stepped back and beamed at him, plainly awaiting some sign of his approval.

"Thank you, Lizzie," he said wanly.

"You're welcome, m'lord," she replied, blinking at him with her big brown eyes. "But I'm Beth."

"Well, then, thank you, Beth."

The girl's smile began to falter. "I'm not Beth. I'm *Beth*."

Max blinked at her, utterly confounded.

The girl at the sideboard cast a glance over her shoulder. "She's Bess, my lord, but she has a slight lisp. Beth is the scullery maid."

He scowled at the second girl, mainly because she had been arranging extra dishes on the sideboard just in case—God forbid—he would care for more of the unappetizing fare on his plate. "Then I suppose you must be Lizzie."

The girl blushed so furiously the smattering of freckles across her snub nose disappeared. "Oh, no, m'lord, I'm Lisbeth. Lizzie is the upstairs maid."

"A hopeless endeavor," Max muttered beneath his breath. "Suppose I just call you all Elizabeth and be done with it."

"Very good, sir," the two maids said in unison, bobbing curtsies in such perfect synchronization they might have been choreographed.

As Beth... *Bess* joined her companion at the sideboard, Mrs. Spencer appeared with a tall Sèvres pot. Max hadn't thought it possible for her to smell any more enticing than she had when he had held her in his arms last night, but that was before a whiff of rich, dark coffee drifted to his nostrils. As he inhaled the bracing aroma, he was tempted to jump up and press a lusty kiss to her tightly pursed lips out of pure gratitude. He couldn't help smiling to himself as he imagined her reaction to *that*.

"My lord," she murmured in way of greeting as she leaned over his shoulder to fill his cup.

He took a sip of the potent brew, closing his eyes for a moment to savor its bitter smoothness. Although he had dutifully hosted tea every afternoon for his commanders and their wives during his time in India, it was this irresistible concoction he craved.

"I wouldn't drink too much if I were you," Mrs. Spencer whispered, her velvety voice dangerously close to his ear. "I've heard it can deprive a man of his sleep."

He whipped his head around to give her a suspicious look, but she had already retreated to the sideboard, where she was placing the pot next to the chafing dishes, her profile a study in innocence. Before he could catch her eye, Hodges came marching into the room and dutifully placed a folded newspaper next to Max's plate.

Max glanced at the date inscribed at the top of the *Times*. The edition had been published a fortnight before he had left London for Cornwall. He had already lazily perused its pages over a delicious breakfast in the plush comfort of his dining room in Mayfair.

But, per his request, the newspaper *was* from the current decade, so he had no choice but to accept the small token with grace. "Thank you, Hodges."

As Max unfolded the newspaper, his nostrils recoiled from another, far more unpleasant, smell—the stench of scorched paper.

"I took the liberty of pressing the paper for you," Hodges explained.

Max held up the newspaper, peering at the butler through the iron-shaped hole in the middle of the financial page. "Yes," he said drily. "I can see that." He snapped the paper shut, sending a cloud of crisp ash fluttering through the air to settle over the top of his poached eggs like flakes of pepper. "I do appreciate the effort, Hodges, but you might try using a slightly cooler iron next time."

"Very good, sir." Looking quite pleased with himself, Hodges marched back out of the room, adding an odd little skip just as he reached the door. Max slanted a glance at the sideboard, but Mrs. Spencer had slipped out as well when he wasn't looking. She must not have been wearing her infernal ring of keys.

Backing out of the room and bobbing curtsies all the way, the Elizabeths quickly followed suit, leaving Max all alone with his singed newspaper and his bland breakfast, the coffee his only comfort.

AFTER BREAKFAST MAX WENT up to the second-floor library, where he hoped to find a book to while away the long, dreary morning. But when he entered the gloomy chamber, he found the little dark-haired maid perched on a stool in front of the towering floor-to-ceiling bookshelf on the far wall, her back to the door.

Although the room looked as if it hadn't been properly cleaned since Elizabeth sat on the throne, Max assumed she must be working. But as he watched, she tugged a single book forward to the edge of the shelf, then slid it back into its place. She repeated the process with the next book and then the next, until she was teetering for balance on the stool. Each time she slid a book out, she would cock her head to listen, almost as if she was waiting for some sort of resulting reaction. When she reached the end of the shelf, a dejected sigh escaped her.

Max leaned one shoulder against the door frame and drawled, "Looking for something?"

She swung around so quickly she nearly went tumbling headfirst off the stool. With her bright, dark eyes and pointed chin, she had the face of a charming little fox, and as Max watched, it flushed a dusky pink. "Oh, no, my lord. I was just dusting."

He gave the feather duster protruding from her apron pocket a pointed look. The duster's glossy feathers looked as if they'd just been plucked from the fowl that morning.

If he expected the girl to express remorse at being caught in such a blatant lie, he was doomed to disappointment. Instead, she heaved a martyr's sigh as she descended from the stool. "I suppose you'll be wanting the truth now."

"Please don't trouble yourself on my account," he said, his voice dripping sarcasm.

"If you must know, I was searching for something I might read in my bed tonight. After all of the drudgery of the day, it's such a pleasure to curl up beneath the blankets with a rousing story." As if to prove her point, she snatched a book from the nearest shelf and cradled it to her chest.

Max strode over and plucked the book from her hands, turning it so he could peruse the cover. "Ah, *The Mechanization of Plowing in an Agrarian Society.*

Yes, I can see how that might make for rousing bed-time reading after a vigorous day of not dusting."

Pippa snatched the book back, returned it to the shelf, and grabbed another one, taking the time to read the title first as she did so. She held the clothbound book up to reveal the title—*A Sicilian Romance*. "Have you read any of Mrs. Radcliffe's work?" she asked, inching her way around him and toward the door. "This one is absolutely thrilling! My favorite scene is the one where poor Julia finds her presumed-dead mother imprisoned in the haunted dungeons of the Mazzini castle while flee-ing the debauched overtures of the dastardly Duke de Luovo!"

Before Max could open his mouth to point out that it was *his* library and *his* book she was steal-ing while she was supposed to be working, she was gone. He stood blinking at the empty doorway for a minute, feeling a bit like the dastardly Duke de Luovo himself, then turned toward the bookshelf.

After casting a look over his shoulder to make sure he was still alone, he drew a book to the very edge of the shelf, then quickly pushed it back into its slot. He waited expectantly, but the hearth didn't swing open to reveal a secret passageway, nor did a trapdoor open up beneath his feet to swallow him.

He shook his head, a rueful snort escaping him.

If he didn't get a grip on his imagination, he would soon be as dotty as the rest of the inhabitants of this house.

MAX QUICKLY DISCOVERED *The Mechanization of Plowing in an Agrarian Society* made for equally dry reading during the daylight hours. Which is how he found himself back on the second-story landing later that morning, gazing up at the mysterious Miss Cadgwyck's portrait. She seemed determined to haunt his waking hours as well as his dreams. He still couldn't understand why a stranger would stir such sympathy in his heart.

She had chosen her fate just as surely as he had chosen his.

He locked his hands at the small of his back, striving to view her through dispassionate eyes. There was no denying her face was striking enough to drive a man to all manner of folly. To win the favor of such a woman, a man might lie, steal, cheat, duel, or even murder.

He'd spent most of his life believing Clarinda to be the most beautiful woman he would ever lay eyes on. But even when the two of them were at their closest, hers had been a beauty as cool and unattainable as the moon. Angelica's charms were far more warm and approachable.

"Shall I fetch you a chair, my lord, so you'll be able to make calf's eyes at Miss Cadgwyck in comfort?"

That dry, familiar voice jolted him out of his reverie. Was that a hint of pity he heard in it? Or contempt?

He turned to find his housekeeper climbing the stairs, a pile of clean linens in her arms. In another time, another place, he might have chided her for not using the servants' staircase. But he was oddly glad to see another face. Especially a living one. "Should I be embarrassed to be caught mooning over a portrait of a girl long dead?"

Mrs. Spencer joined him on the landing. "I wouldn't waste the effort if I were you. You're certainly not the first gentleman to be ensnared by her spell."

His housekeeper was garbed all in black on this day, and as she tilted back her head to give the portrait a jaded look, she resembled nothing so much as a drab crow gazing up at a vibrant canary. There was no sign of the warm, soft woman Max had held against his body in the dark. The woman who had stirred him with her scent and the provocative press of her curvy little bottom against his groin.

Trying desperately to forget that woman, he returned his attention to the portrait. "What became of Miss Cadgwyck after the . . . accident? Does she rest in the family crypt or is she buried somewhere else on the property?" Max knew that some zealots would never stomach a suicide being interred with their esteemed ancestors, many of whom had probably committed far more damning sins.

"Her body was never recovered. All they found was her yellow shawl tangled around one of the rocks."

The housekeeper's words struck Max's heart a fresh blow. As he scowled up into Angelica's laughing eyes, it was nearly impossible for him to imagine all of that vitality, all of that charm, reduced to bones at the bottom of the sea—stripped of their flesh by tide and time.

He almost welcomed the anger that surged through him. "I can't help but think her story might have had a different ending if there had been even one person who cared enough to follow her out onto that promontory. Someone who could have wrapped their arms around her and pulled her back from the brink."

He must have imagined Mrs. Spencer's sharply indrawn breath, for when she spoke, her voice was flatter than he had ever heard it. "There was no one to save her. She was all alone."

Max gave her a sharp look. "If there were no witnesses, how do you know that?"

"Servants' gossip. Whenever a scandal rocks the nobility, tongues will wag, you know."

"Was it those wagging tongues who resurrected the unfortunate young lady from her watery grave to terrorize the future masters of Cadgwyck?" As he remembered the haunting hint of jasmine that had made his groin ache with longing, his scowl deepened. "Although I suppose there are some shades a man might welcome into his bedchamber in the lonely hours between midnight and dawn." He slanted his housekeeper a mocking glance. "Why, Mrs. Spencer, I do believe I've managed to shock you. You're blushing."

"Don't be ridiculous," she said tartly, the flush of rose tinting her delicate cheekbones giving proof to his words. "I'm not some green girl who blushes and simpers at the mere mention of romantic entanglements."

"Ah, yes, I forgot that as a widow you're no stranger to what takes place between a man and a woman in the privacy of their bedchamber."

Their eyes met, giving Max a jolt he hadn't expected and a reason to regret his mockery. Especially when he was assailed by a vivid image of what would never happen with *this* woman in the privacy of *his* bedchamber.

Still, she was the first to look away. "That may be true, but that doesn't mean I wish to discuss it with my employer." Brushing past him, she continued down the gallery, her steps crisp with purpose.

"What do you think she desires?" he called after her.

Mrs. Spencer stopped and slowly turned to face him, her expression even more wary than usual. "Pardon?"

"Isn't that the popular notion? That souls who have been somehow wronged are doomed to roam the earthly plane in death until they find what they were denied in life? If Angelica *has* returned to this house, what could she be searching for? What do you think she wants?"

"Perhaps, Lord Dravenwood, she simply wants to be left alone." Clutching the pile of linens to her breast like a shield, Mrs. Spencer turned and left him there in front of the portrait, her impertinent rump twitching beneath the black linen of her dress.

Max watched her go, Angelica's spell momentarily broken.

IN THE DAYS THAT followed, Max had no more visits to his bedchamber from Angelica, Piddles, his housekeeper, or anyone else. Oddly enough, the long, peaceful nights made him feel *more* restless instead of less. After tossing and turning in the tangle of his sheets for what felt like hours, he would throw open the French windows and stride out onto his balcony, his nostrils flared to detect any lingering hint of jasmine. He would stand gazing across the courtyard at the crumbling tower on the far side of the manor until the night's chill sank deep into his bones. But no matter how long or how patiently he waited, he heard no off-key tinkling of a music box or haunting echoes of girlish laughter. The muffled roar of the sea was the only sound to reach his ears.

The days were even longer than the nights. When he had fled London, he had dreamed only of escape, not of what he might do to occupy his mind and his hands during the interminable hours between dawn and dusk. Until he had resigned from the Company, his every waking hour had been consumed by board meetings, appointments, teas, balls, delicate treaty negotiations, and speeches before Parliament. Even during the longest, dullest sea voyages, there had been figures to study, memorandums to dictate to his secretary, languages to master, and business ledgers to fill with his precise scrawl.

Now he spent his days stalking along the cliffs, trying to convince himself it wasn't too late for the salt-edged wildness of the wind to blow the cobwebs from his brain. He would walk for hours only to find himself standing once again on the very spot where Angelica had taken flight, gazing down at the churning whitecaps and the sea crashing against the rocks below.

After nearly a week of such aimless ramblings, he made a rather startling discovery. For the first time since losing Clarinda, he was hungry. No, not just hungry . . . he was bloody well famished. Yet whenever he returned to the house for lunch or supper, he was met with fare even more bland and tasteless than what he had endured for breakfast.

It wouldn't have been so galling if his house-keeper didn't walk around smelling like a bakery. Mrs. Spencer might be cool and distant, but the aroma clinging to her was warm and irresistible.

Max was seated at the head of the dining-room table one night when Dickon lurched clumsily through the door, a silver tray rattling in his hand. Max took a sip of sherry to hide his disappointment. If Mrs. Spencer had delivered his supper, he might at least have been able to steal a whiff of something that smelled like actual food.

As Dickon leaned over to place a plate in front of him, Max caught himself staring at the boy's powdered wig. No . . . it wasn't his imagination. The wig was most definitely on backward.

Max waved a hand toward it. "Do you like wearing that ridiculous thing?"

Dickon straightened, eyeing him mistrustfully. "No, m'lord."

"Then why do you?"

"Because Annie . . . um . . . Mrs. Spencer says if I'm to be a proper footman, I have to wear the proper attire. It's only proper."

Hunger had sharpened Max's temper to a dangerous edge. "From this day forward, I'm the one who will decide what's proper around here, not your Mrs. Spencer. Please remove it. At once."

"Very good, sir." Dickon dragged off the wig, looking so relieved he forgot to scowl for a minute. His hair was a tawny brown, plastered to his head by sweat except for an irrepressible cowlick at the crown.

The boy bowed his way from the room, leaving Max all alone with a plate containing a few shriveled potatoes and a kidney pie. Max pierced the pie's crust with his knife. Not a single enticing tendril of steam emerged. Why should it when everything in this accursed house was served at a lukewarm temperature that was somehow less appetizing than if it had been served cold?

Max had yet to lay eyes on the mysterious Nana. He was beginning to wonder if he had inadvertently done something to offend the cook—like defiling her daughter or murdering her firstborn offspring. Why else would the infernal woman torture him day in and day out with her appalling dishes? Or perhaps they were all in cahoots and had decided that slowly starving him would leave less evidence for the constable than shoving him out a window.

Max picked at the pie's dry crust with his fork, growing both hungrier and angrier by the moment. He finally summoned up the courage to try a forkful of the meat but was forced to spit it out with his next breath—not because of its taste but because it had none.

Deciding it was far past time for Nana to make the acquaintance of her new master, he tossed down his napkin and went storming from the room.

MAX HAD NO TROUBLE locating the basement kitchen. All he had to do was follow the cheerful clink of silver against earthenware and the sound of voices raised in happy chatter. As he approached the doorway, a husky ripple of female laughter assailed his ears, infectious and irresistible.

"Oh, do go on, Dickon!" someone else cried, clapping her hands in anticipation.

Max arrived in the doorway of the kitchen to find his staff gathered on benches around a crude pine table. Mrs. Spencer sat on the far side of the table, a genuine smile exposing that fetching little gap between her front teeth, making her hazel eyes sparkle, and erasing a decade from her age. As another throaty giggle escaped her, he realized with an all-too-pleasant shock that it had been her laughter he had heard.

He made no attempt to disguise his presence, but they were all too engrossed in the proceedings taking place in front of the stone hearth to take notice of him.

Dickon was holding court there, his powdered wig once again perched precariously on top of his head. Piddles sat at the boy's feet, gazing up at the boy as if equally mesmerized by his performance.

"So then he said"—Dickon fixed his face in a ferocious scowl and deepened his voice to a menacing upper-crust drawl—"'Do you like wearing that ridiculous thing?' to which I replied, 'Of course I like wearing it, my lord. Who wouldn't want to wear a deceased hedgehog on their head?'"

Two of the Elizabeths collapsed in fresh titters while another was forced to wipe a mirthful tear from her eye with the hem of her apron. Hodges pounded his open palms on the table, chortling like some great overgrown baby.

"What happened next?" Pippa demanded. "Did he insist that you be carted off to the dungeons or thrown to the dogs?"

Tucking his thumbs in the waistband of his breeches, Dickon puffed out his scrawny chest to a ridiculous degree. "That was when he said, 'From this day forward, *I'm* the one who will decide what's proper around here, not your precious Mrs. Spencer. Please remove it. At once!' "

With that, Dickon swept the wig from his head with a flourish and dropped it on Piddles's head. The dog endured the indignity with grace, looking exactly like a jowly barrister Max had once debated in Parliament.

Max waited until the fresh round of laughter had died out before putting his own hands together in a slow round of applause. "A creditable impersonation, young master Dickon. Your talents are obviously wasted here. You should be treading the boards at the Theatre Royal."

# ❧ *Chapter Fourteen*

$\mathcal{M}$AX'S STAFF WHIPPED THEIR heads around as one, their faces reflecting a mixture of horror and alarm at finding their employer leaning against the door frame, surveying them through dispassionate eyes.

Dickon immediately snatched the wig off Piddles and thrust it behind his back, ducking his head sheepishly. The only one who seemed unfazed by his appearance was an ancient woman rocking to and fro in a cane-backed chair in the corner. Judging by the heaps of multicolored yarn piled at her feet, she had spent the last hundred years knitting a scarf for a giant. Since Max had never laid eyes on her before tonight, he could only assume she must be the elusive Nana, the author of all his culinary misfortune since arriving at Cadgwyck.

Mrs. Spencer rose, her charming smile replaced by the tight-lipped expression he was coming to hate. The smile that wasn't a smile at all, but something designed solely to placate others. "Why, Lord Dravenwood, is there something you require?" She gave the row of rusting bells over his head an accusing look. "We didn't hear you ring."

As Max's gaze traveled the circle of wary faces, he recognized his staff for the first time for what they truly were—a family. When his own family had gathered for supper, it had been in a formal dining room much like the one he had just left. Conversation had been limited to his father's bombastic pronouncements on whatever politician had most recently provoked his ire and their mother's sympathetic murmurs. Most meals were eaten in a tense silence broken only by the clink of silverware and the muted breathing of a battalion of servants standing behind their chairs, waiting to attend to their every need.

Occasionally, when their father would turn red and start to sputter, Ash would kick Max under the table and pull a funny face, but Max would keep his eyes carefully fixed on his plate, knowing he would be the one to suffer for their insolence should the duke take notice of it.

Max had vowed to himself that when he was master of his own house, his family would gather around a table much like this one to eat and talk and laugh and savor the pleasure of one another's company. But that dream was done now. He might be master of this house, but he would never be anything more than an outsider in the eyes of those gathered around this table—an intruder on their happiness.

The bench across from Mrs. Spencer had an empty place, and for one crazy moment Max wanted nothing more than to ask if he could join them. But he simply straightened and said stiffly, "I was wondering if you might have some salt."

"I'll have Lisbeth bring it to you," Mrs. Spencer promised, relief evident on her face. Apparently, she thought him heartless enough to sack them all just for having a bit of fun at his expense.

He was about to beat a less than graceful retreat when he spotted it—a loaf of freshly baked bread sitting in the middle of the table. The golden loaf must have emerged from the oven right before his arrival. Steam was still rising from its crusty, perfectly browned top, taunting him with the very scent that had been driving him mad since his arrival at Cadgwyck. A small earthenware crock of freshly churned butter sat next to it, just waiting to be slathered over all of that warm, yeasty goodness.

It was nothing but a humble loaf, perfectly suited to a tenant's cottage, not the master's table. Yet the mere sight of it made Max feel savage with want.

His hands curled into fists. He was the master of

this house. The bread belonged to him. He slowly lifted his eyes to meet his housekeeper's wide-eyed gaze.

*Everything* in this house belonged to him.

Something dangerous must have been in his expression. Her lips parted as if she was suddenly having difficulty drawing breath. One of her pale hands fluttered nervously to the scrap of lace at her throat.

If he hadn't had a lifetime of practice denying himself the very thing he wanted the most, Max might not have been able to muster up the fortitude to turn his back on both her and her damned bread.

But after taking only two steps, he stopped. Without a word, he pivoted on his heel, marched straight back to the table, and snatched up the enormous carving knife resting next to the bread. One of the Elizabeths squeaked in alarm, and another shrank back in her chair as if he were going to murder them all. Giving his housekeeper the same look Hades had probably given Persephone before sweeping her away to his underworld lair to have his way with her, he brought the blade of the knife down in a shining arc, impaling the loaf of bread with a single savage motion.

He made it as far as the door with his prize before returning for the butter and a plump sausage. The servants were all gaping at him as if he'd gone stark raving mad, but in that moment he didn't care what anyone thought of him as long as his appetites were satisfied.

He paused in the doorway just long enough to give his housekeeper a curt nod. "Thank you, Mrs. Spencer. That will be all."

IN THE MONTHS SINCE Clarinda had jilted him at the altar, Max had grown accustomed to paying the price for embracing dissipation. He would wake at midday with a pounding head and unsteady hands, his gullet still burning from all the brandy he'd poured down it the night before. He would stagger out of bed and to the convenience, one hand raised to shield his bleary eyes from the merciless rays of the sun. Then he would crawl back into the bed and wait for dark to fall so he could do it all over again.

What he was not accustomed to was waking at dawn with a full belly and a smile curling his lips. He rolled to his back and stretched like a tomcat after a night of successful prowling, a satisfied groan escaping him.

After sitting at the dining-room table all by himself and gorging himself on bread, butter, and sausage, he had retired early and slept like a babe. During his years with the Company, he had dined at the tables of both lords and princes, but none of their exotic delicacies could compare to the hearty goodness of that simple meal.

Hoping to steal a few more hours of sleep, he drew in a deep, contented breath redolent with the scent of baking bread. At first he thought the enticing aroma had clung to him, but as the haze of sleep faded, he shot to a sitting position, yanked open the bed curtains, and poked his head out, sniffing at the air.

Five minutes later, Max was hastening down the stairs, tying his cravat as he went. He soon found himself leaning against the kitchen door frame, his gaze drinking in all the details he'd been too hungry and angry to notice the night before.

The kitchen was tucked away in the basement of the manor, but a high row of windows along the far wall welcomed in the hushed glow of the dawn light. Here, there was no sign of the dust and decay that seemed to plague the rest of the manor. A cheerful fire crackled on the grate, its warmth smoothing the edge off the morning chill. Gleaming copper pots and bunches of dried herbs tied up with frayed ribbons hung from iron hooks set in the exposed rafters. The flagstone floor and low ceiling made the room feel like a large, cozy cave.

Piddles was curled up on a faded rag rug in front of the stone hearth, his chin resting on his paws while a plump calico cat with tufted, white feet dozed in the cushion of the rocking chair in the corner.

It wasn't his cook but his housekeeper bending over to peer into the open door of the cast-iron oven. Max sincerely doubted Nana's rump had ever been that shapely. For once Mrs. Spencer didn't look as if she'd been dipped into a vat of starch. A large white apron protected her skirts, and her face was flushed pink from the heat of the stove. Several strands of hair had escaped the net binding her chignon and tumbled down to frame her face. Max watched in reluctant fascination as one of them began to curl in the moist heat.

Despite her dishevelment, she looked happier than Max had ever seen her. She was even humming some tuneless ditty beneath her breath.

Just as she closed the door of the oven with a rag-wrapped hand, he said, "An early riser, are we, Mrs. Spencer?"

Straightening so fast she nearly bumped her head on a copper stew pot, she spun around to face him. She looked as guilty as if he'd caught her in flagrante delicto on the kitchen table with some strapping young gardener, an image that gave Max more pause than he had planned.

The rag slithered to the floor. Her hand darted up to tuck a strand of hair back into the net, but met with little success. "My lord, even in London I'm sure it is customary to ring when you need something, not creep up on your servants and frighten them half out of their wits."

"What do you think you're doing?" he asked flatly.

She glanced at the table. It was covered from end to end with sacks of meal and flour, crocks of butter and lard, a basket of brown-speckled eggs, bottles of spices, stoneware bowls, and a slew of other utensils and ingredients, many of them unidentifiable to Max's untrained eye.

Her mouth took on a faintly insolent cast. "Cooking."

Max advanced on her. "I was under the impression that Nana did the cooking for the household."

"Nana is feeling a bit under the weather today." As if to remind him someone was within screaming distance, Mrs. Spencer nodded toward the door. "She can't manage the stairs any longer so she sleeps in a room just down the corridor instead of in the servants' quarters."

Max moved around the end of the table. She turned with him as he stalked her, following him warily with her eyes as if he were a snarling hound and she a wounded fox. "And just how many days of the week is Nana under the weather?" he asked. "Four? Six? *Seven?*"

"She is getting on a bit in years. We don't mind lending a hand when we can."

*"We?"* Max looked around the kitchen pointedly. *"You* seem to be the only one here."

Mrs. Spencer lifted her stubborn little chin. "I've discovered that if I rise early, I can work undisturbed for a while before the others awaken."

Max could almost feel her exasperation with him growing. He might be master of the house, but this was *her* kitchen. *Her* territory. He was the interloper here. She would probably like nothing more than to pick up the flour-dusted rolling pin from the table and chase him from the room.

"Is there something you need?" she asked.

As he gazed upon her proud visage, Max was surprised to feel a dangerous surge of desire uncoil within him. He needed many things, none of which she could supply.

"If not," she said, turning away from him with a defiant flounce of her apron, "I have other matters to—*Ow! Damn it all!"*

He'd gotten her so flustered she had forgotten all about the fallen rag and seized the stove door's handle with her bare fingers. As she cradled her wounded hand to her breast, gritting her teeth to keep another cry from escaping, Max quickly closed the distance between them. Helpless tears sparkled in her hazel eyes, making them look larger and more luminous.

Cursing himself for distracting her, he gently tugged

her hand into his own. "Let me see," he urged when she kept her fingers tightly curled.

Her breath escaped in a near sob. "There's no need. I don't require a nursemaid."

"It wasn't a request. It was an order."

She sniffed. "That's very high-handed of you. I hope you know I plan to mock you mercilessly over supper tonight, and my impressions are even more spot-on than Dickon's."

"Make sure and include the part where I sack you for disobeying a direct order."

Still glaring at him, she reluctantly unfolded her hand. Each of her slender fingers had an angry red mark on it.

"Fortunately, you let go of the stove before the skin could blister. But it must hurt like the very devil." He glanced up to catch her biting her lower lip. "You may cry if you like."

"How very magnanimous of you. Must I seek your permission for that as well?"

Despite her sullen expression, she didn't protest when he led her over to the basin resting on the long table beneath the row of windows. He cranked the pump, then gently guided her wounded hand beneath the spigot. As the cool water cascaded over her fingers, she moaned. Her eyes fluttered shut, her face going slack with relief.

Max was strangely transfixed by the sight. Her

mink-colored lashes weren't particularly long but they were lush and curled lightly at their tips. She didn't appear to be wearing a trace of powder, yet her skin had the smooth purity of fresh cream. His gaze strayed to her lips. When not flattened into a dutiful smile or puckered into a disapproving moue, they were surprisingly ripe and rosy with an enticingly kissable little Cupid's bow at their top. She opened her eyes and he yanked his gaze back to her hand before she could catch him staring.

"Come," he said gruffly, tugging her over to one of the benches flanking the table. He eased her into a sitting position, then straddled the bench and sank down in front of her. "I've just the thing for your burns."

Thankful he hadn't gobbled down every bit of butter in the house during his culinary orgy, he dipped his fingertips into an earthenware crock and began to dab a bit of the stuff onto each of her wounds. Most women of his acquaintance wouldn't leave the house without elbow-length gloves to protect their lily-white skin. But her hands were lightly tanned with fingertips that sported a callus and shallow nick or two. They were the hands of a woman who was no stranger to hard work.

"How did you know the butter would help?" she asked, casting him a shy glance from beneath her lashes.

"I had a baby brother who used to get into a great deal of mischief as a lad. He was always knocking down beehives or swiping hot mincemeat pies out from under Cook's nose and scorching his fingers. I had to play nursemaid to his wounds more than once so our parents wouldn't find out what havoc he'd been wreaking and give him a sound thrashing."

"*Had* a baby brother?" she echoed softly, plainly fearing the worst.

Max couldn't quite keep the bitter edge from his tone. "He's no longer a baby."

"What about you? Didn't you get into any mischief of your own?"

A rueful snort escaped him. "Very little. But only because I didn't dare. Before I could stand up in my cradle, it was drummed into my head that I was the eldest son, my father's heir, and the hope of all who worshipped at the Burke altar. Mischief was a pleasure afforded to lesser mortals, not to solemn little boys in short pants who would someday be dukes."

"It sounds like a heavy burden for a child to bear."

"I'm not sure I ever was a child."

"Did your father approve of your career with the East India Company? I thought noblemen were expected to do little more than lounge about at their clubs with other gentlemen of means, sipping brandy and discussing their tailors and their triumphs at the faro tables."

Max shuddered. "A pursuit for which I was singularly ill suited. My father nearly had an apoplexy when I announced my intention to join the Company. But once he saw that my influence would imbue the Burke name with even more prestige and power, he embraced my choice as if it had been his fondest ambition for me."

"Didn't you ever tire of being the perfect son? Didn't you ever want to escape the shackles of duty and do something really . . . wicked?"

A reluctant half smile canted his lips as he lifted his eyes to meet her inquisitive gaze. "With my every breath."

Only then did he realize he had finished smoothing the butter over her burns, but was still cradling her hand. His thumb was absently stroking the center of her palm, tracing lazy circles over the satiny skin he found there.

His smile faded. This was an impossible situation. She was an impossible woman. Yet in that moment, with her hand cupped trustingly in his and the sweetness of her peppermint-scented breath fanning his lips, the world seemed ripe with possibility.

It suddenly occurred to him that this might be his chance to break the chains of duty. What could be more wicked than stealing a kiss from the lips of his housekeeper? Why, it was practically a rite of passage, wasn't it? Nefarious gentlemen had been seducing their housekeepers and parlor maids for centuries.

Max's body had already hardened in anticipation, urging him to do something wild and impractical for once in his life, consequences be damned.

He lifted his other hand toward her face, half-expecting her to flinch away from his touch. But when he brushed his thumb over the softness of her cheek, she held as steady as her gaze. One of her stray curls tickled the backs of his fingers as his thumb strayed into even more dangerous territory, grazing the velvety warmth of lips no longer pressed together, but parted in invitation. Testing the softness of those lips with the firmness of his thumb only deepened his hunger until all he could think about was how sweet they would taste beneath his own.

As Max leaned forward, Mrs. Spencer's lashes swept down to veil her luminous eyes, almost as if to deny what was about to happen. Their lips were a breath away from meeting when the first tendril of smoke came wafting between them.

## ⁂ Chapter Fifteen

OTH ANNE'S AND DRAVENWOOD'S gazes flew
to the stove to discover thick, acrid clouds of
smoke billowing around the cracks in the cast-iron
door. Crying out with dismay, Anne sprang to her
feet and rushed for the stove. This time she remembered to grab both a rag and a wooden paddle before throwing open the door. Her rescue effort came
too late. The paddle emerged from the oven topped
with a smoldering lump.

She dumped it on the table. Dravenwood joined
her, gazing down at the blackened bread with a dismay equal to, if not greater than, her own.

"Forgive me," he said, his voice still husky with an
emotion that could have been either chagrin or desire. "I should never have distracted you."

"The blame is entirely mine," she replied, her fingertips absently straying to the familiar shape of the
locket beneath her bodice. "I allowed myself to for-

get that only a few careless seconds of inattention can ruin everything."

He nodded curtly, then strode from the room without another word.

Anne watched his broad shoulders disappear through the door, recognizing with a treacherous stab of regret that neither of them would be foolish enough to make that mistake again.

"THE MASTER WISHES TO see you in his study."

Anne glanced up from her task of halfheartedly grinding some fresh garden dirt into the drawing room carpet with the heel of her boot to find Lizzie standing in the doorway. The young maid was wringing the hem of her apron in her hands, looking nearly as anxious as Anne felt.

Anne had been halfway expecting this summons since her encounter with Lord Dravenwood in the kitchen that morning. She had hoped finally receiving it might loosen the knot of dread in her stomach, not tighten it into an inescapable vise.

She had spent the past ten years desperately trying to prove she was no longer the same girl she had been. But all it had taken was a tender caress and the tantalizing promise of a kiss from Dravenwood's beautifully sculpted lips to shatter that illusion. What might she have done if their lips had actually touched? Wrapped her arms around his neck and climbed into his lap? Would he have stolen her heart as deftly as he stole her kiss? Was she even capable of giving one without the other?

"Thank you, Lizzie." Tucking a flowerpot half-full of dirt beneath the ruffled skirt of a chaise longue, she managed an encouraging smile for the girl before climbing the stairs to meet her fate.

The door to the study had been left open a crack. Anne slipped into the room to find Lord Dravenwood seated behind the dusty cherrywood desk, surrounded by towering stacks of ledgers with mildewed covers and yellowing pages. He was making notations in one of the open ones, his concentration absolute.

She stood there, waiting for him to acknowledge her presence. That morning in the kitchen she had discovered just how intoxicating—and how dangerous—it could be to have his attention focused on her with such intensity.

A wavy, dark lock of hair had fallen over his eyes. He brushed it back impatiently, his pen still flying across the page. Something about the boyish gesture unleashed an odd tenderness in Anne's heart. Knowing it was wrong to spy on him in such a craven manner, she cleared her throat.

He glanced up immediately, his pen ceasing its motion. He didn't say anything but simply took her measure from beneath the thick, dark wings of his brows. She was no longer the vulnerable woman who had allowed him to nurse her wounds and nearly steal a kiss. Her apron was freshly starched, her hair neatly dressed and confined to its tidy little net.

They were once again master and housekeeper, each knowing their places and which boundaries were not to be crossed.

Ever.

Striving to keep her expression as free of emotion as possible, Anne returned his gaze evenly. "You had need of me, my lord?"

His eyes narrowed ever so briefly before he closed the ledger with an audible snap, making it clear *she* was now the business at hand. "I believe it is you who have need of me, Mrs. Spencer. After our *discussion* this morning, I realized I was being completely remiss in my duties."

"You? Remiss? In *your* duties?"

"If I hadn't been remiss, you wouldn't have been attempting to do the work of an entire day before the sun had so much as crested the horizon."

"I am the housekeeper of this establishment. It's my job to make sure everything runs smoothly."

"That may be true, but it's not your job to do everyone else's job." He leaned back in his chair, steepling his fingers beneath his chin.

His hands were everything a man's hands should be—strong, powerful-looking, with a light dusting of dark hair on their backs and long, elegantly tapered fingers. They were the sort of hands a woman could easily imagine caressing . . . gliding . . . stroking . . . Anne jerked her gaze back to his face, horrified by the wayward direction of her thoughts.

"From what I've observed since I've been here, you're saddled with a daft butler, an ancient cook, several affable but supremely incompetent maids, and an ill-tempered footman who doesn't know a silver salver from a dormouse. If you keep trying to compensate for the shortcomings of your staff, all you'll succeed in doing is working yourself into an early grave."

Before Anne could stop it, a bitter laugh bubbled from her lips. "Perhaps I'm simply trying to work my way *out* of an early grave."

"I'm confident you're doing the best you can, but one woman can only do so much. It was evident to me from the first night I arrived that the manor's staff wasn't adequate to care for an estate this size. Yet I did nothing to rectify the situation. Which is why I've decided to send to London for some help."

Anne felt her lips go numb at the thought of a horde of strangers traipsing about the manor, digging into things that were none of their concern. Things long buried that desperately needed to stay that way. And other things that must only be unearthed by her and her staff.

"I can assure you that won't be necessary," she said, fighting to keep a note of hysteria from creeping into her voice. "I'm the one who allowed the other servants to grow lax in their duties when there was no master in residence. Once I explain what's required of them, they'll work harder. I swear it."

"I might be able to believe that of the younger ones, but what about Hodges? And Nana? You're supposed to be running a household here, Mrs. Spencer, not a home for the elderly and the mentally infirm."

"Nana and Hodges would be devastated if deprived of their positions. Neither of them have any family left to look after them. They have nowhere else to go. Hodges has only recently started exhibiting signs of a mental decline," she lied. "I fear it's the result of an injury he suffered in the war."

Dravenwood scowled suspiciously at her. "Which war?"

"The one with Napoléon," Anne replied, hoping that would cover most wars of the past several decades. "It would hardly be sporting to shunt him aside after he so valiantly served his country and king."

Dravenwood grunted. "And what of Nana? Was she a gunner in the Royal Navy?"

"Nana faithfully served a local family for most of her life," Anne said, hoping a morsel of truth would placate him. "But when she started losing her hearing, they insisted she be replaced and gave her notice. Her only desire now is to live out the rest of her years here at Cadgwyck—in the place she has come to call home." Anne drew close enough to lay her palms on the desk, willing to sacrifice her stiff-necked pride on the altar of his mercy. "Please, my lord. If the others agree to work harder to lighten my load, may Nana and Hodges stay?"

"Of course they may stay." He frowned up at her, looking genuinely insulted. "What did you think I was going to do? Cast them into the hedgerows to fend for themselves?"

She straightened, sighing with relief since that was exactly what she had feared. "Thank you, my lord. Will there be anything else?"

"There is *one* more thing." The lascivious glint in his eyes made Anne's stomach tighten all over again.

"Yes, my lord?"

"I don't care what other slop you feed me, but I want some of that bread you bake on my table. Every day. For breakfast." After a moment of thought, he added, "And supper."

Anne could feel a smile flirting with her lips. "I believe that can be arranged. Will *that* be all, my lord?"

"For now." The innocent words sounded oddly provocative on his beautifully chiseled lips. Lips that had been a breath away from claiming hers just that morning.

She had almost reached the door when he said, "Mrs. Spencer?"

She turned, eyeing him warily.

"Has it ever occurred to you that I may not be the heartless ogre you believe me to be?"

"No, my lord," she said solemnly. "I'm afraid it hasn't." But just before she slipped out the door, she flashed him a genuine smile, not her usual tight-lipped one.

"Impossible woman," she heard him mutter beneath his breath as he returned to his ledgers.

"I DEMAND AN INCREASE in my wages!" Pippa exclaimed as she and Dickon struggled to wrestle a rolled-up Turkish rug out of the drawing room and through the entrance hall the following afternoon.

"You don't receive any wages," Anne reminded her. Anne was perched on a rickety ladder in the middle of the hall, using a broom to swipe the thick veil of cobwebs from the tarnished brass arms of the chandelier. Every twinge and throb of her muscles only served to remind her that she was the one who put them there.

"All the more reason to demand an increase." Heaving an exhausted sigh, Pippa dropped her end of the carpet and plopped down on it. She'd covered her dark curls with a linen kerchief to keep the dust out of them.

Dickon rolled his eyes. "I don't know why *you're* in such a foul temper." The boy gave the open front door a longing glance. "I could be out on the moor right now hunting for supper or catching a wild pony to ride. Instead, I'm stuck in this miserable house doing women's work with the likes of you."

"Don't grumble, dear," Anne chided from her swaying perch. "You'll get plenty of fresh air when you're out in the courtyard beating a decade of dust from that rug."

Muttering something beneath his breath that would doubtlessly have gotten his ears boxed if Anne could reach them, Dickon gave his end of the rug a hard yank, dumping Pippa in the floor. As she sprang to her feet, rubbing her rump and glaring after him, he dragged the rug the rest of the way out the door.

Anne tossed down the broom, then descended from the ladder. She dusted off her grimy hands, surveying the results of their handiwork with a satisfied smile.

She'd wasted no time in fulfilling her promise to Lord Dravenwood. A sneezing Beth and Bess had spent most of the morning dragging the moldering draperies down from the tall, arched windows and were now diligently scrubbing years of grime from the wavy panes of glass. Betsy was slopping a mop around the floors, while Lisbeth dipped her rag in a container of linseed oil and beeswax to buff the mahogany of the banister to a rich luster. Lizzie was upstairs whisking old sheets off the furniture and stuffing handfuls of fresh feathers purchased from the local goose girl into all of the mattresses. Even Hodges and Nana had insisted on doing their part. Hodges was gleefully collecting every bit of tarnished silver in the house and dragging it to the kitchen so Nana could her set her gnarled hands to the task of polishing it.

With their limited resources, there was no way for them to restore the house to its former glory. All they could do was hold up a dim mirror to reflect what once had been. But even those modest efforts had stirred up more than just dust. If Anne tilted her head just right, she could almost hear the graceful notes of a waltz drifting out from the deserted ballroom, the merry clink of champagne flutes hefted in a teasing toast, the muted murmur of conversation, and laughter from voices long gone. Angelica gazed down upon them from her haughty perch at the top of the stairs. It was impossible to tell from her cryptic smile if she approved of their efforts or was mocking their foolishness.

Pippa followed the direction of Anne's gaze. "Our White Lady hasn't made an appearance in almost a fortnight. And now you're making the manor so comfortable Lord Imperious won't ever want to leave. I'm beginning to suspect you're not in as great of a hurry to be rid of the man as you'd like us to believe."

"Don't be absurd," Anne replied, her voice sounding oddly unconvincing even to her own ears. "Of course I am. But I thought we agreed it would be in all of our best interests to tread carefully with this one. He's no fool like the rest."

"I wasn't implying *he* was a fool," Pippa replied, giving Anne an arch look before heading out the side door to join Dickon in the courtyard.

"Saucy little baggage," Anne muttered, knowing it was probably only a matter of time before Pippa and Dickon stopped using their paddles to whack the rug and started whacking each other.

Despite what Pippa believed, the last thing she wanted was for Dravenwood to linger at Cadgwyck. They were wasting precious time that could better be spent looking for the treasure. Plus, the longer he stayed, the harder it was going to be to dislodge him. All Anne was doing now was humoring the man, allaying his suspicions and waiting for him to relax his guard. Once he did, she would gladly step aside and let Angelica have her way with him.

She was assailed by a shocking image of Dravenwood sprawled on his freshly stuffed mattress beneath the canopy of his bed, wearing little more than a silk sheet draped low on his narrow hips and a come-hither smile.

"Mrs. Spencer!"

Had Anne still been atop the ladder when that deep, masculine voice interrupted her wicked little fantasy, she would probably have tumbled off and broken her neck. Drawing a handkerchief from the pocket of her apron and dabbing at her flushed cheeks, she hastened toward the stairs. How had her wayward imagination produced such a ridiculous notion? She'd never seen the earl wear a genuine smile, much less a come-hither one.

She arrived at the corridor outside Lord Dravenwood's chamber to find it deserted. She gave the door a tentative knock.

"Enter," he commanded gruffly.

Anne cautiously eased open the door, half-expecting to find Piddles devouring another pair of boots or Sir Fluffytoes tangled up in the earl's finest cravat. But the earl was all alone, sitting on a stool in front of his dressing table, glowering at his reflection in its beveled looking glass.

He shifted his gaze, his smoky gray eyes meeting hers in the looking glass. "I'm sorry to pull you away from your duties, but I have need of you."

*I have need of you.*

That bold confession made Anne wonder what it would be like to be truly needed by such a man. To hear those same words whispered in her ear in the dark of night in a lover's hoarse tones.

She stepped forward, deliberately sharpening the brisk edge of her voice. "How may I be of service, my lord?"

He swiveled on the stool, revealing the flash of the shears in his hands and the handful of glossy, dark locks littering the hardwood floor around him.

"Oh, no!" she exclaimed, unaccountably dismayed by the sight. "What have you done?"

"I was starting to look like a savage. Or an American. I've become much more adept at looking after myself since arriving at Cadgwyck, but I need you to help me trim my hair. As you can see, I'm making quite the muddle of it."

Anne's gaze flew back to his hair. She felt a ridiculous surge of relief. He hadn't yet done irretrievable damage to it, although the right side was decidedly longer than the left.

She took another step into the room, then hesitated. An intimate task like cutting a man's hair was far more suited to his valet or barber. Or his wife.

"Why don't you let me summon Dickon, my lord?"

"If I'm not going to let the lad near my throat

with a straight razor, what makes you think I'd trust him with a pair of shears?"

Growing ever more desperate, she said, "Then Hodges perhaps . . ."

He cocked his head and gave her a reproachful look.

She huffed out a sigh. "Very well, then. If you insist . . ."

Donning her most imperturbable air, she marched across the room to his side. She brushed the fallen hair from his shoulders, that simple contact making her fingertips tingle with awareness. Her hands lingered of their own volition, measuring the impressive breadth of his shoulders until she realized what she was doing and jerked them out of harm's way.

As she removed her apron and swept it around his shoulders to protect his coat from further insult, she could not resist asking, "Are you certain you should let *me* near your throat with a sharp instrument?"

"Not entirely. But convincing the local magistrate I tripped and fell directly onto the blades of a pair of shears would no doubt tax even your considerable resources." Casting her a darkly amused look, he offered her the shears, handles first.

She accepted them, her lips compressed to a thin line. As she leaned over him to assess the damage he'd already done, the warm, masculine spice of bayberry soap drifted to her nostrils. An answering warmth purled low in her belly.

He held himself as still as a marble statue beneath her hands as she captured a thick lock of his hair between her fingers and gave it a tentative snip. She was clever enough to realize her power over him in that moment was nothing but an illusion, easily shattered by nothing more than a look or a touch.

"Was this the sort of task you once performed for Mr. Spencer?"

She glanced down to find him surveying her face, his expression inscrutable. "On occasion," she replied, her hands slowly gaining in confidence as she moved around him.

"And was yours a happy union?"

"For a time. As are most."

"Just how long have you been on your own?"

*Forever,* she almost blurted out before remembering it only felt that way. "Nearly a decade."

A frown touched his brow. "That's a very long time for a woman to make her own way in this world. Was there no one to look after you after you lost your husband?"

"I'm quite capable of looking after myself, and I've found all the family I need right here at Cadgwyck. What of you, my lord?" she asked, hoping to shift the attention away from herself. "How long have you been *on your own?*"

She expected him to chide her for her impertinence, but he simply shrugged and said, "All my life, it seems."

Their eyes met for the briefest of seconds, then she continued snipping gently away at the right side of his hair until its length matched that of the left. She shied away from cutting it any shorter than the rugged line of his jaw. His sooty locks tended to wave and curl even more without the extra weight bearing them down.

"There," she said when she had finished, guiding him around on the stool so they could both admire her handiwork in the looking glass. "I believe that should do it. At least until you get to a proper barber."

Without thinking, she reached down and feathered his freshly trimmed hair between her fingers, much as she would have done Dickon's. Their gazes met in the looking glass and her hand froze in midmotion. No matter what duty he required of her, she had no right to touch him in such a familiar manner.

She moved to jerk her hand back, but he caught it in his own, his powerful fingers curling around hers, steadying the faint tremble she found there. He held both her gaze and her hand captive, and for a breathless moment she thought he would bring her hand to his lips or use it to inexorably tug her into the warm shelter of his lap.

Instead, he gave it a gentle squeeze. "Thank you, Mrs. Spencer."

Assailed by a curious mixture of relief and disappointment, she slid her hand from his, then whisked her apron from his shoulders. "Will there be anything else, my lord?"

Still watching her in the looking glass through hooded eyes, he opened his mouth, then closed it again before saying softly, "No, Mrs. Spencer. I believe that will be all."

Anne drew the door shut behind her, then sagged against it, her breath escaping her in a wistful sigh. Pippa had been right all along. Their new master *was* more dangerous than all the rest.

But for all the wrong reasons.

# ❧ *Chapter Sixteen*

"**P**LEASE, DEAREST . . . I HAVE faith in you. I just know you could remember if you'd only try a bit harder."

Max was crossing the entrance hall the next morning when he recognized his housekeeper's voice drifting out of the drawing room. He froze in his tracks. He'd never been given to eavesdropping, but something about the soft, coaxing note in her voice—a voice that was usually crisp and edged with pride—was riveting.

"I tell you, I can't remember!" Max recognized Hodges's voice as well, though he'd never heard the butler sound quite so petulant. "I've wracked my brain until my head aches but it won't come to me!"

"Perhaps if you gave it just one more go?" Mrs. Spencer urged.

Max eased close enough to the arched doorway to peer into the room.

Hodges was seated in a Sheraton chair that had one splintered leg propped on a book. Mrs. Spencer was kneeling beside him with a hand resting on his thigh. She was peering up into his red-rimmed eyes, hope and desperation mingled in her expression. "You mustn't give up. You're our only hope and we're running out of time. Oh, please, darling . . ."

Max stiffened. If she begged him like that, he wasn't sure he could refuse her anything.

"It's just not there! Can't you see I'm doing the best I can?" Hodges wailed, burying his ruddy face in his hands.

"Of course you are." She gently patted the old man's leg, her shoulders slumping in defeat. "There, there, dear. It's all right. I'm so terribly sorry. I shouldn't have pushed you so hard."

Max cleared his throat.

Hodges jerked up his head, and both of their gazes flew to Max's face. The sheen of tears in the butler's eyes was unmistakable, just as was the frustration and guilt on the housekeeper's wary face.

"Is there something amiss?" Max asked. "Perhaps I can be of assistance."

Mrs. Spencer rose to her feet, her shoulders once again ramrod straight. "Dear Mr. Hodges has simply forgotten where he put the key to the wine cellar. I'm sure he'll remember before we have need of it."

Max glanced at her waist, where her ever-present

ring of keys still hung. She was lying to him. Her gaze might be bold, even challenging, but all that meant was that she had been lying for so long she had become fluent in the language. Max had lived a lie himself for almost a decade. He knew just how easily that could happen.

Hodges had averted his eyes and was gripping the carved arms of the chair in a futile effort to hide the palsied trembling of his hands.

Aside from threatening to dismiss the both of them, Max had little recourse. And if he did that, he might never learn what they were hiding. "Don't overtax yourself, Hodges," he said, returning his thoughtful gaze to Mrs. Spencer's face. "Sometimes things that go missing have a way of turning up where you least expect them."

MAX AWOKE THE FOLLOWING morning to the patter of rain against the French windows of his bedchamber. He considered braving the cliffs for his usual morning walk, but by the time he finished breakfast, the rain was falling in relentless gray sheets past the wall of windows in the dining room, obscuring even the tempestuous tossing of the sea.

Another man might have found the hushed gloom and the steady drumming of the rain on the roof cozy. It would have been a perfect opportunity to return to the study, light a fire to burn off the damp, and continue to review the account ledgers and correspondence left by the former masters of Cadgwyck Manor. He had come here ostensibly to manage the estate, not haunt it himself. But the very idea of spending the day trapped behind a desk, devoting himself to the same inconsequential drivel that had consumed his attention for most of his life, suddenly seemed unbearable.

He was passing a window in the stairwell after breakfast when the rain abated just enough to allow him to catch a glimpse of the tower standing sentinel on the other side of the courtyard. He ducked his head, peering through the curtain of gloom. The mere sight of the tower quickened his senses in a way no dusty ledger ever could. He hadn't realized until that moment just how much he had missed Angelica's visits.

An unexpected smile tugged at one corner of his mouth. If his White Lady wouldn't come to him, then perhaps it was time to go to her.

IT TOOK MAX NEARLY half an hour to make his way across the house to the west wing. He could simply have thrown on an overcoat and hat, slipped out one of the terrace doors, and crossed the wet cobblestones of the courtyard, but he wanted to avoid the prying eyes of the servants. Their efforts to set the house to rights hadn't yet progressed this far. Along the way he passed darkened rooms crowded with furniture slumbering beneath ghostly white sheets. A pair of towering doors decorated with peeling gilt opened onto a cavernous ballroom where Angelica Cadgwyck must once have danced in the arms of her adoring suitors. After Max was forced to detour around his third locked door, he began to regret not bringing his housekeeper's ring of keys with him.

Or perhaps his housekeeper herself.

He finally reached a windowless corridor with rotting floorboards that groaned ominously beneath his boots. The gloom grew so thick he was forced to feel his way along the walls for the last few steps of his journey until the corridor ended in a door.

After fumbling about for a minute, cursing himself for not having the forethought to bring a candle, he finally located an iron handle and gave the door a shove. It resisted for a moment, as if reluctant to yield its secrets, then surrendered with a gusty sigh.

Max found himself standing on the first floor of the tower, blinking with relief to discover he was no longer in darkness. Just as he had suspected, the tower had most likely been the keep of the original castle. Murky light stole through arrow slits set at intervals in the stone walls. The winding stairs hugging the exterior wall were crumbling in spots and slick with the rain blowing through the arrow slits and trickling through the cracks in the wall. Despite that it would be only too easy to slip, break his neck, and remain undiscovered for days, Max's steps were strangely confident as he started up the stairs.

They wound their way up to an iron-banded, oaken door that looked far older than anything else Max had encountered in the house. Unlike the door at the foot of the stairs, this one gave easily beneath the cautious push of Max's hand.

Before he had a chance to get his bearings, a white shape flew directly at his face.

# ❧ Chapter Seventeen

$\mathcal{L}$ETTING OUT A GUTTURAL cry, Max instinctively threw up his hands to protect his eyes. From the frantic beating of the wings about his head, he quickly realized it was not some wailing banshee accosting him but a confused egret that had darted in through one of the broken windowpanes. Once the bird realized Max wasn't a threat, it quickly lost interest in him and went soaring up to land on one of the rafters, where it sat prettily preening its feathers.

Bemused by his own reaction, Max shook his head, thankful his acerbic housekeeper hadn't been around to see *that*.

As his surroundings reclaimed his attention, he turned in a slow circle, gazing about him in rapt fascination. Because of its dilapidated state, he had assumed the tower would have been unoccupied for generations. Instead, it was as if he'd stumbled upon the abandoned abode of some fairy-tale princess who had just stepped out for a decade or two and would soon return in a flourish of satin and silk and a cloud of perfume. Max moved deeper into the room, beguiled against his will by the romance of it all.

The round chamber occupied the entire top floor of the tower. Dirt and mold stained the stone walls, but at some point they had been whitewashed and decorated with an intricate pattern of ivy eerily similar to the real ivy now creeping through the shattered windows.

A tarnished brass bed sat between two of the lancet windows, the rotting lace adorning its half-tester drifting in the rain-scented breeze. A delicate cherrywood harpsichord sat nearby. Max could easily imagine a young girl's graceful fingers tripping lightly along its keys, charming forth some timeless melody from Bach or Handel. He wandered over and touched a finger to one of its yellowing keys, striking a wheezing note that made him wince.

A tall, oval looking glass with a jagged crack down the middle of it hung in a frame designed so it could be tilted to reveal the one gazing into it at the most flattering angle. As Max reached up and adjusted it, he almost expected to see another face gazing back at him. But all he saw was his own countenance split in two by that crack, expressionless and draped in shadow.

Turning his back on the looking glass, he wandered over to one of the windows overlooking the cliffs and the sea. The cushions of the window seat had rotted away long ago, but Max could still see a young woman curled up on them with a book in her hand, while the rain beat against the diamond-paned windows on a day just like this, as cozy and secure as the egret would be when she returned to her nest.

A skirted dressing table sat directly across from the bed with a broken stool sprawled on the floor in front of it. Max's steps slowed as he approached it. He was already trespassing, but somehow invading the sacred domain of a young woman's dressing table made him feel even more like a marauder.

There was something irresistibly feminine about the dusty items scattered across the marble top of the dressing table—an ivory-backed mirror with a silver handle; a pair of amber hair combs; a cachou box of lip salve; an assortment of bottles labeled with promising names like *Milk of Roses, Olympian Dew,* and *Bloom of Ninon*; a faded ribbon rosette that might have been plucked from an elaborate coiffure and carelessly tossed on the table in the wee morning hours after dancing the night away at some magnificent ball.

And a single bottle of perfume.

Max drew the cut-crystal stopper from the elegant bottle, then lifted the bottle to his nose, already knowing what he would find. Its contents had dried up long ago, but as he inhaled, the subtle notes of jasmine filled his lungs—sultry, erotic, yet strangely innocent. He was carefully returning the bottle to its place when he saw the heart-shaped silver box adorned with pearl plating sitting on the corner of the table.

He hesitated, knowing just how Pandora must have felt when presented with such an enticing temptation. He picked up the box, cradling it in a hand that suddenly seemed far too large and clumsy to be entrusted with such a treasure.

Fighting a mixture of dread and anticipation, he gently lifted the hinged lid to reveal an empty interior lined in ruby velvet. A handful of familiar, slightly off-key, notes drifted through the room just as they had drifted through his balcony door on his first night at the manor.

Unable to bear their piercing sweetness, he slammed down the lid. If anything could summon up a spirit that wished only to be left alone, then surely it was that haunting melody. Restoring the music box to its rightful place, he turned to survey the rest of the room, growing ever more desperate to find some clue to the mystery that was Angelica Cadgwyck.

He was facing a tall mahogany armoire almost

identical to the one in his room. He crossed the timber floor with a determined stride, hesitating only when his hands closed over the ivory knobs on the twin doors. One of the doors hung askew on its hinges, leaving a narrow crack between door and frame. Bracing himself for some grinning skeleton to come tumbling into his arms, he threw open both doors at once.

All he saw were the remains of an extravagant wardrobe that had gone unprotected from the elements for years—shredded satin, shattered silk, moth-eaten merino. The floor of the armoire was littered with delicate slippers in faded pastel shades with frayed ribbon laces and curling toes. When he nudged one of them with his boot, a squeak of protest warned him a family of baby mice had taken up residence there.

Leaving the doors of the armoire hanging open, he swung back around to face the room, finally forced to admit that his was a fool's errand. If Angelica was guarding any secrets, she had taken them over the edge of that cliff with her.

A row of dolls gazed down their noses at him from a shelf carved into the stone wall itself. Hairline cracks marred their pale porcelain faces, but did nothing to detract from their haughty demeanors. Even their daintily pursed lips looked disapproving. Oddly riveted by the sight, Max drifted across the tower toward them. Their satin skirts were stained with mildew but still arranged in precise folds. They had obviously been placed there with tender care by the hand of a girl too old to play with them any longer but too young to relinquish their cherished place in her heart.

He reached up to draw one of the dolls from the shelf. She didn't resemble her young mistress, yet something was oddly familiar about her. Her painted lips didn't seem to be pursed in disapproval, but to hide a smile. Her brown eyes were lit with a mocking twinkle. Unable to place the resemblance, Max shook his head ruefully, wondering if he was losing his wits completely. He was starting to see ghosts everywhere he looked.

He was returning the doll to her perch when he noticed something odd. He had believed her to be sitting on a Prussian-blue velvet cushion befitting her exalted station, but closer inspection revealed it wasn't a cushion at all but a velvet-bound book. Max shoved the doll carelessly into the corner of the shelf and drew the book into his hands.

A gentle ruffle through the fragile pages confirmed that it was a journal—the sort a young girl might use to preserve her musings and dreams.

*And her secrets.*

Still holding the journal, Max wandered over to one of the windows, where the light was marginally better. He gazed blindly out over the rain-slicked cobblestones of the courtyard. Despite his romantic fancies, Angelica hadn't been some captive princess abiding in this tower. And even if she had been, he had come too late to rescue her. If he had even an ounce of integrity left in his soul, he would return the journal to its hiding place and do what Mrs. Spencer had suggested—leave Miss Cadgwyck to rest in whatever peace she had managed to find.

Before Clarinda had walked away from him and back into his brother's arms, that's exactly what he would have done.

Propping one boot on the splintered remains of the window seat, Max opened the journal to its first page. It began with the usual mundane meanderings of any child enchanted with dolls and ponies and fairy cakes. But between the lines of those simple yet charming sketches of daily life at Cadgwyck, a portrait far clearer than the one on the landing began to emerge.

Angelica had been overly indulged perhaps, but still keenly aware of those around her. She was the first to notice when her childhood nurse was suffering from a toothache and required a poultice to relieve it. Nor was she above mourning when the young son of one of her father's grooms suffered a fatal injury after being kicked by an ill-tempered horse. The ink on the page where she recounted that incident was splotched and the paper wrinkled, as if it had been forced to absorb more than one tear.

She clearly adored her father and looked up to her older brother, Theo, even as she despaired of his constant teasing and tweaking of her curls. She envied him the freedoms he enjoyed as a boy and seized every opportunity she could find to sneak out and run wild on the moors alongside him, even if it meant risking a stern scolding from her papa when she returned. But apparently the man couldn't stay angry at her for long because he would relent every time she crawled into his lap and fixed her small arms around his neck.

Max skimmed through the pages, discovering long gaps between the dates as she grew older. She'd probably been too busy living life to record it. As the years danced past, the script grew more flowery, the clumsy blots of ink replaced with the elegant penmanship of an educated young lady.

After a drought of several months, he found this entry:

*March 14, 1826*

> *Papa has decided to commission a portrait of me for my eighteenth birthday. Although I know it will please him, I am dreading the prospect of sitting for hours on end for some stuffy old artist*

*without twitching so much as an eyelash. However shall I survive such torture?!*

A smile touched Max's lips. Like any girl of seventeen, she was prone to fits of drama and overembellishment. But as he read her next words, his smile faded.

*April 3, 1826*

*I can be silent no longer. I must now make a confession fit for no other ears but yours: I am in love! It has come upon me like a storm, a fever, a sweet, yet terrible, madness! Upon our very first meeting, he brought my hand to his lips and pressed a kiss upon it as if I were already the sophisticated young lady I so often pretend to be for my other suitors. I fear sitting for this portrait may prove to be a sort of torture I had not anticipated.*

*April 14, 1826*

*You cannot know how difficult it is for me to strive to appear calm and collected as he arranges me for his pleasure, commands me to tilt my head this way or that, scolds me ever so gently when I fidget or fail to smother a yawn. The merest touch* of his fingertips against my cheek makes me a stranger even to myself. As he leans over me to correct the angle of a curl or a ribbon, I am terrified he will hear my heart beating like the wings of a captive bird in my breast and discover all. It is almost as if those piercing blue eyes of his are peering into my very soul. I dare not be so bold as to hope for his affection, but in those moments I fear I would do anything to win the slightest crumb of his approval. Anything at all.

April 28, 1826

Oh, woeful day! The portrait is finished! Where once I was counting the seconds until my birthday ball with joyful anticipation, now I dread the day of its arrival. Every tick of the clock brings me closer to the moment when he will be gone from here, taking my still-beating heart with him.

May 3, 1826

He is teasing me mercilessly by refusing to let me see the portrait until its public unveiling at the ball. I tremble at the prospect. What if it should reveal the besotted creature I have become? Would *he be so cruel as to expose the deepest yearnings of my heart to the mockery of the world?*

*May 6, 1826*

*All is not yet lost! He sent me a note, begging me to meet him in the tower after the unveiling of the portrait. What if he should try to steal a kiss? He cannot know he would not have to steal it for I would give it freely. How could I do any less when he already has my heart?*

Max's brow furrowed in a thoughtful frown. So Angelica and her beloved artist had not yet been lovers when she agreed to meet him in the tower that night. She had still been an innocent, yet ripe for seduction. Especially by some cunning lothario whose every word, smile, and touch had been calculated to lay bare the heart of a young woman undone by the joy and anguish of first love.

Even as he felt his frown deepening to a scowl, Max knew he was being unfair. If the portrait was any indication, the artist had been just as enamored of Angelica as she was of him.

He was about to turn the page when another realization struck him. If their final rendezvous had taken place in the tower, then chances were that this was where the man had died. Max studied the timber floor, every stain and shadow now suspect. Angelica's lover might have breathed his last right beneath Max's very boots. For some reason, Max abhorred the notion of Angelica's nest, her charming refuge from the harsh realities of the world, being forever tainted by such violence.

The next page of the journal had no date, just six stark words, absent of dramatic flourishes and exclamation marks:

*I am ruined. All is lost.*

Dread uncurled low in his gut as Max slowly turned the page. He already knew what he would find—blank pages, all that remained of a life unlived. He began to frantically flip through them, almost as if he could will the words to appear. Words that would reassure him Angelica had given herself enough time to realize that as long as she could draw breath, all was *not* lost. There was still hope.

But her voice had fallen silent, leaving him with nothing but empty pages and the hushed whisper of the rain.

The journal fell shut in his hands. He was still gazing down at it, dazed by his journey into the past, when a furious female voice cut through the quiet.

*"What in the devil do you think you're doing?"*

# ❧ Chapter Eighteen

$\mathcal{F}$OR AN ELUSIVE MOMENT, Lord Dravenwood looked so guilty Anne thought he was going to tuck Angelica's journal behind his back like a schoolboy caught perusing a book of naughty etchings. Before she could fully appreciate just how oddly beguiling that was, the expression vanished, leaving his eyes hooded and his face as inscrutable as always.

*He* was the last thing she had expected to find when she'd climbed the stairs to the tower. None of the former masters had been bold enough to beard the White Lady in her lair.

She had been standing there paralyzed in the doorway for what felt like an eternity, watching him handle the journal with a touch so tender it was almost reverent. The sight of his strong, masculine hands ruffling through those fragile pages had sent a delicious little shiver through her, almost as if he were touching *her*.

Desperate to shake off the lingering sensation, she stormed across the tower and snatched the journal from his hands, earning a raised eyebrow for her trouble. "Men! Always interfering where they're not welcome or wanted! I suppose you thought you could just march up here and begin rifling through things that are none of your concern as if you hadn't been taught any better. Why, you ought to be ashamed of yourself!"

He continued to survey her with infuriating calm.

"Why are you looking at me like that?" she demanded when she realized he was not responding to her fit of pique.

A grave smile slowly spread across his face. It was the first smile he had given her that didn't contain so much as a hint of mockery. The smile transformed his face, deepening the grooves around his mouth and making her heart stutter. "I was just thinking that I haven't been scolded like that since I was in short pants. Actually, I was so eager to please as a child I'm not sure I've *ever* been given such a magnificent setdown. Except by my little brother, of course."

For a dangerous moment, Anne had allowed herself to forget this man was not her equal but her employer. Seeking to escape the havoc his smile was still playing with her heart, she turned toward the window, absently hugging the journal to her breast as she gazed out at the falling rain. "Forgive me. I shouldn't have been so passionate in my protest. It's just that the young lady in question has been the subject of sordid gossip for over a decade now. She's had her life dissected and her honor impugned by complete strangers who would denounce her as a strumpet just so they might appear more virtuous." She could feel her temper rising again. "I'm not saying the girl is without blame, but it's far more difficult for women who are embroiled in scandals than men. The women's reputations are destroyed, while the men get to go off scot-free to seduce the next innocent they encounter, boasting about all their conquests along the way."

"From what you told me," he gently reminded her, "the man who seduced Angelica didn't exactly walk away unscathed."

"Well, he proved to be the exception to the rule," she admitted, thankful Dravenwood couldn't see how hard her face must have looked in that moment. "All I'm saying is that the girl doesn't deserve to have her belongings pawed through by strangers. She already lost so much. Couldn't we at least leave her some small measure of privacy and dignity?"

She sensed rather than saw Dravenwood come up behind her. He was standing so close she could feel his warmth, could smell the scent of the bayberry soap that clung to his freshly shaven throat and jaw.

Could remember how warm and safe she had felt when he had held her against his body in the dark and how she had shuddered with anticipation when she had believed he was going to kiss her.

Reaching over her shoulder, he gently but firmly tugged the journal from her grip. She turned to face him, deeply disappointed that he would so callously dismiss her wishes.

He was already crossing the tower. As she watched, hugging herself with her now empty arms, he tucked the book back into its hiding place, then placed the doll on top of it. He even took the time to fan the doll's mildewed skirts out in precise folds so they would shield Angelica's secrets from any other prying eyes.

"There." He turned back to face her. "Satisfied?"

She nodded, although watching his capable hands handle the doll with the same tenderness he had used when handling the journal had stirred such a deep yearning in her she wasn't sure she would ever be satisfied again.

More to distract herself than him, she wandered over to the bed and trailed a hand over the tattered lace hanging from the canopy. It drifted through her fingers like cobwebs. "After seeing this chamber, it's probably not difficult for you to understand how Angelica grew up to be such a brat. According to local lore, her father sent to Paris to have all of those ridiculous dolls specially commissioned just for her."

"Sounds like your ordinary doting papa to me." A corner of the earl's mouth curled in a droll smile. "If ever I was blessed with a daughter, I'd probably be tempted to do the same thing."

Trying not to imagine a laughing Dravenwood with a little girl with sooty-dark curls and misty-gray eyes perched high on his shoulder, Anne said, "From what I've heard, the tower hadn't been fit for habitation for centuries, so Angelica charmed her father into bringing in an army of workmen and spending a fortune renovating it just so she could preside over her own little kingdom. She probably fancied herself some sort of long-lost princess." Anne shook her head, a helpless, little laugh escaping her. "And who could blame her, given how hopelessly indulged she was?"

"Some children can be spoiled without being ruined. I suspect she was one of those."

Anne gaped at him, unable to hide her surprise. "Why would you say such a thing?"

Dravenwood jerked his head toward the journal. "Because when she was only seven years old, she already understood her birthday was also the anniversary of her mother's death and sought to cheer her father by doing a watercolor of her mother with a harp and angel wings as a gift to him. Because when she was eleven and several of her father's tenants were stricken with cholera, she defied his express wishes and slipped out of the house to deliver baskets of food to their cottages. Food she'd been scavenging from her own plate by skipping dinner and going to bed hungry for nearly a week."

Unable to bear any further recitation of Angelica's virtues, Anne snapped, "It's easy to be generous when you lack for nothing yourself."

"You're being rather hard on the young woman, aren't you? Especially after making such a passionate plea on her behalf."

"I was defending her privacy, not her character."

Dravenwood's eyes narrowed to smoky slits as he studied her. "Perhaps your own staunch moral character makes it difficult for you to sympathize with the failings of mere mortals."

Anne would almost have sworn he was mocking her. His penetrating gaze seemed to peel away her thin veneer of respectability, to see straight through to all of the subterfuge, all of the lies she'd told to accomplish her aims.

He'd already given her a taste of just how persuasive he could be. How he might tempt a woman to spill her secrets just by drawing her into his arms and brushing his mouth ever so lightly against her lips.

Armoring her heart against the power of that gaze, she said, "And are you including yourself among the mortals or the gods?"

His harsh bark of laughter was edged with bitterness. "It probably won't surprise you to learn that I've spent most of my life sitting high upon Mount Olympus, gazing down my nose at those I considered less virtuous than myself." His expression darkened. "But I can assure you it's a very long fall from Mount Olympus. And a *very* hard landing."

*Not if you have someone waiting to catch you in their arms.*

The thought sprang unbidden to Anne's mind. She inclined her head, hoping the shadows would hide her blush. Unfortunately, her reticence only fueled Dravenwood's curiosity.

"You chided me for invading Miss Cadgwyck's *kingdom,* as you call it, but just what were *you* doing here?"

Anne couldn't very well tell him she'd come here intent upon doing the same thing she'd been doing for the past four years whenever she had a free moment—searching, always searching, wracking her brain and the chamber for any clue to the location of the only key with the power to free her from this tower forever.

So instead she told him the closest thing to the truth she could manage. "Sometimes I come here to be alone. To escape. To think." The cozy patter of the rain only seemed to confirm her words. "But I should get back before the others miss me." She gestured toward the door, inviting him to precede her.

Visibly amused by her high-handedness, he started for the door. She followed, but just as they reached the landing, he turned back, eyeing her thoughtfully. "Since you found me here, you haven't once addressed me as 'my lord.' I rather like that."

"What would you prefer I call you? *Master?*"

As their gazes met, some infinitesimal shift in his expression gave her reason to regret those mocking words. A dangerous ember smoldered deep in those cool gray eyes of his, threatening to make her *staunch moral character* go up in a poof of smoke. "My Christian name is Maximillian."

Trying not to imagine how satisfying the name would sound rolling off her tongue, she blinked innocently at him. "Very good, my lord."

"Do you have a Christian name? Or is *Mrs.* your Christian name?"

"Anne. My name is Anne." Even though his face revealed nothing, it wasn't difficult to imagine what he was thinking—a plain name for a plain woman. "Do watch your step on the stairs, my lord," she cautioned. "Yet another reason for you to stay clear of this place. The stairs are crumbling and could be quite dangerous to anyone not familiar with them. Why, you might have fallen and—"

"Broken my neck?" he volunteered helpfully.

"Turned your ankle," she said stiffly.

He pondered her warning for a minute, then

stepped aside. This time there was no mistaking the challenge in his mocking smile as he graciously extended a hand toward the stairs. "After you, Mrs. Spencer."

LATE THAT NIGHT MAX found himself once again standing before Angelica's portrait. He lifted his candle higher, bathing the portrait in its loving light. He might never know the woman she would have become, but his trip to the tower had enabled him to steal a glimpse of the girl she had been.

He leaned closer to the portrait. He'd been too busy mooning over Angelica's winsome face to pay any heed to the signature scrawled in the corner of the canvas. So *this* was the man whose merest touch had set her heart to "beating like the wings of a captive bird" in her breast. Max's eyes narrowed. He was certainly no stranger to the gnawing pangs of jealousy; he just hadn't expected to suffer them over a woman who had died a decade ago.

Committing the artist's name to memory, he straightened. Now that he'd read Angelica's diary, he was even more curious about what exactly had happened on the night the portrait was unveiled. Perhaps he had been looking for answers in the wrong places. Tomorrow he would send Dickon to the village with a dispatch for London. If answers were available within the annals of London society gossip, he knew just the man to find them.

ANNE WOVE HER WAY through the market, paying little heed to the cacophony of voices and noise drifting around her. She'd already nabbed a handsome goose, freshly plucked, and a new skein of yarn for Nana from one of the traveling vendors who set up rickety wooden stalls along the main street of the village each Friday morning. She always kept a large store of supplies at the manor, but before she made the long walk home that afternoon, the basket hooked over her arm would be laden with any extras they would require for the week to come.

As she passed the fox-faced magistrate, she spared him a cool nod. She could feel his beady little eyes following her as she moved on to the next stall. Once, such scrutiny might have tempted her to tug the brim of her homely black bonnet a few inches lower in the hope its shadow might hide her face. But now she held her head high, having learned that most people in the world saw only what they expected to see. And what they expected to see when she strolled by was the plain and pious visage of Cadgwyck Manor's housekeeper.

The brisk autumn air was redolent with the

aroma of roasted chestnuts. Unable to resist the enticing scent, Anne stopped at the next stall to purchase a bag for Dickon from her own pin money.

"Nearly shot the poor fellow dead, he did. That's what me cousin Molly heard. Had to flee London before they arrested him for duelin'."

As Anne moved on to the next booth, toying with some pretty silk ribbons she knew Pippa would adore, she paid little heed to the nasal tones of Mrs. Beedle, the village laundress. The woman was a notorious busybody. Anne had little patience for such gossip herself, having discovered firsthand just how much havoc it could wreak on a life.

"I thought he had the look of a rogue about him—marchin' into *my* Ollie's tavern, tossin' 'round purses of gold in that high-handed manner o' his and orderin' everyone about as if he owned the place."

Anne jerked up her head, a lavender ribbon slipping through her fingers. There could be no mistaking the braying voice of Avigail Penberthy, the innkeeper's buxom missus. Nor could there be any mistaking the identity of the high-handed rogue who went marching about as if he owned every inch of land beneath his shiny leather boots.

Unable to resist the temptation, Anne sidled closer to the two women, adding eavesdropping to her burgeoning catalog of sins.

Mrs. Beedle lowered her voice. "Molly heard he was the perfect gent till his fiancée threw him over. Jilted him at the altar and ran off to marry another just as they was about to say their I do's!"

As both women sighed in chorus, their sympathies shifting, Anne felt a stab of empathy in the vicinity of her own heart. She could only imagine what a terrible blow such a slight must have been to a man of Dravenwood's unyielding pride. Now she understood why he had arrived at Cadgwyck looking as if he were haunted by his own ghosts. He must have loved his fiancée very much for her abandonment to have cut him so deeply.

"I didn't think he'd last a night at the manor, much less more than a fortnight. He must have made a deal with the devil hisself to survive livin' in that tomb," Mrs. Penberthy suggested, a shudder rippling through her voice.

"The devil?" Mrs. Beedle whispered. "Or the devil's mistress?"

Normally Anne would have been thrilled to hear evidence that Angelica's legend was growing, but on this day, the women's nonsense was grating on her nerves. Refusing to listen to another word of it, she brushed past them, giving Mrs. Penberthy's ample bottom a hearty bump with her basket as she did so. "Pardon me," she murmured.

Both women started, then exchanged a guilty glance. "Why, Mrs. Spencer, we didn't see you there!"

"No, I gather you didn't." Anne fixed the laundress with an icy stare. "Mrs. Beedle, I expect we'll be seeing you at the manor next week?"

The laundress gave her a lukewarm smile. "Aye, Mrs. Spencer. I'll be there."

Leaving them with a cool nod, Anne continued on her way, feeling their eyes follow her all the way to the end of the street.

"MY LORD?" ANNE TENTATIVELY poked her head around the door frame of the library later that afternoon to find her employer reclining in a leather wing chair, his long, lean legs in their skintight trousers propped on an ottoman and crossed at the ankles.

"Hmmm?" he said absently, turning a page of the book he was perusing.

Anne barely resisted the urge to roll her eyes when she saw it was *An Inquiry into the Nature and Causes of the Wealth of Nations* by Adam Smith. She allowed herself a moment to covertly study the clean, masculine lines of his profile, the inky sweep of his lashes, the hint of beard darkening his jaw, even though he'd shaved only that morning. Remembering the gossip she'd heard in the village, she could not help but wonder what sort of woman could break the heart of such a man.

"I checked the post while I was in the village today. This was waiting for you." Crossing to him, she dutifully held out the missive.

Laying aside the book, he sat up and eagerly took the square of folded vellum from her hand. But it was apparently not the piece of correspondence he had been hoping for. He made a sound beneath his breath that sounded suspiciously like a *harrumph* before sliding his thumb beneath the wax seal. As he unfolded the vellum and began to read the letter, his face went pale beneath his tan.

"What is it?" Anne asked, her heart stuttering with alarm. The last letter that had arrived at Cadgwyck Manor had delivered *him* to her doorstep.

As he slowly lifted his head, his expression dazed, she drew closer to him without realizing it. The letter slipped through his long, aristocratic fingers and floated to the floor. "It's my brother."

Anne felt a pang of dread in her own heart at his words. "Is it ill tidings? Has something terrible happened to him?"

"No. Something terrible has happened to me." Dravenwood raised his stricken eyes to her face. "He's coming here. With his family."

# ❖ Chapter Nineteen

ANNE FOUGHT TO SWALLOW back her own dismay. The last thing she needed was more meddlesome Burkes running around the manor, snapping out orders and poking their handsome aristocratic noses into matters that were none of their concern. "I suppose we can make ready some more rooms," she said reluctantly.

The earl shot to his feet, forcing her to take a stumbling step backward. Raking a hand through his unruly hair, he began to pace back and forth across the room like a caged tiger. "You don't understand. We have to write him back immediately. We have to stop them."

"And just how do you propose to do that?"

"I don't care how we do it. We'll tell them the manor isn't fit for habitation. We'll tell them there's a daft butler. And a surly footman. And a ghost. And an incontinent dog!"

Anne took advantage of his frenzied pacing to rescue the letter from the floor. As she scanned the remainder of it, she almost wished she had left it there. Hoping to soften the blow, she gently said, "I'm afraid it's too late for that, my lord. As we learned when we received word that you were scheduled to arrive at the manor, the post is notoriously slow in getting to Cadgwyck. According to this letter, your brother and his family left Dryden Hall nearly a week ago. They're scheduled to arrive here in less than two days."

Dravenwood groaned. "Two days?" He abruptly changed direction, forcing her to quickly nudge the ottoman out of his path before he fell over it. "Damn him," he muttered through clenched teeth. "Damn them both."

"I take it you don't welcome their arrival?" she ventured cautiously.

"Of course I do," he drawled with scathing sarcasm. "The same way I would welcome taking afternoon tea with Attila the Hun. Or a recurrence of the Black Plague." He began to mutter again, more to himself than to her. "It's just like him, isn't it? Believing he can come here and somehow charm his way back into my good graces." Dravenwood stopped in his tracks, as if struck by a new thought. "He may very well be coming here to kill me."

"Have you done something that warrants killing?"

He gave her a sharp look. "You don't look as if that would surprise you very much."

Anne kept her face carefully blank. "What would you have me do, my lord?"

Rubbing the back of his neck, he sighed. "Your job, I suppose. Make ready their chambers," he ordered, his dismay hardening into grim resignation. "As much as I'd like to, we can't very well turn them away. I wouldn't give him that much satisfaction." His face brightened. "Perhaps if we feed them some of that slop you feed me, they won't linger very long. But whatever you do"—he gave her such a threatening look she took an involuntary step backward—"do *not* give them any of your bread."

ANNE HESITATED OUTSIDE THE closed study door. She had been dreading this moment all day, but there was no longer any way to put it off. She dried her damp palms on her apron before giving the door a gentle rap.

"Enter."

Obeying the clipped command, she eased open the door and slipped into the room. Lord Dravenwood was seated behind the massive cherrywood desk. The ledgers containing the household accounts, both past and present, were no longer scattered haphazardly across the desk but had been organized into neat stacks. One of them lay open on the leather blotter. As she watched, he dipped his pen into a bottle of ink, turned the page, and began to make a fresh notation.

She had never before seen him look quite so composed. One would have sworn he'd been dressed and groomed by the most competent valet in London. His jaw was freshly shaven, his silver-and-gray-striped waistcoat buttoned beneath his coat, his snowy-white cravat neatly tied. His hair was the only thing that had resisted taming, its sooty ends still curling in open rebellion around his starched collar. Anne sensed that this was her first glimpse of the real Maximillian Burke, the cool and contained man who had ruled his own private empire for years from behind a desk much like this one.

When the tip of his pen continued to scratch its way across the page, she cleared her throat awkwardly. "I'm sorry to disturb you, my lord, but Dickon has spotted a private conveyance crossing the moor. I believe it can only be your brother."

He glanced up, giving her a look so mildly pleasant it made her stomach curdle with alarm. She would have much preferred one of his ferocious scowls. "And just what would you have me do about it?"

"Aren't you going to come greet them?" she asked tentatively.

"I shall leave that to you." He returned his attention to the ledger, dipping his pen in the inkwell once more. "As I recall, you rose to the task with admirable aplomb the night I arrived at Cadgwyck Manor."

"But, my lord, he's your *brother*." As both her bewilderment and her dismay deepened, Anne sought comfort by tracing the familiar shape of the locket beneath her bodice. "If you haven't seen each other for a time, I thought you might want to—"

"I don't pay you to think, Mrs. Spencer," Dravenwood said without looking up.

Anne stiffened as if he had slapped her. "No, my lord," she replied, her tone edged with frost. "I don't suppose you do."

Refusing to give him the satisfaction of asking if she could be dismissed, she turned on her heel and started for the door.

"Mrs. Spencer?"

She turned back, eyeing him warily.

"Once they arrive, my brother will doubtlessly want to see me. You may send him in after he and his family have dined. *Alone.*"

"As you wish, my lord."

Anne left him there with his ledgers, forcing herself to gently draw the door shut behind her when all she wanted to do was slam it hard enough to rattle both the door frame and him.

ANNE STOOD UNDER THE portico at the top of the crumbling stairs, watching the coach jolt its way up the rutted drive. This was a private coach, not a rented conveyance, with a handsome team of six matched grays, four liveried outriders, and a scarlet-and-gold ducal crest emblazoned on its shiny lac-quered door. For the first time, she stopped to wonder why her employer—the current Earl of Dravenwood and future Duke of Dryden—hadn't arrived in such regal splendor.

Dickon waited beside the drive in his own ragged livery, but no wig, playing the roles of both foot-man and groom. The afternoon wasn't exactly fair, but nor was it as damp and chill as recent days had been. The balmy wind threatened to tease a few stray tendrils of hair from Anne's chignon.

As the coach rolled to a halt, Dickon shot her an uncertain look over his shoulder. She made a subtle shooing motion. He hurried over to the coach to whisk open the door.

Anne had no idea what to expect, but the man who descended from the coach was as fair as their master was dark. He was the same height as Dravenwood and had equally broad shoulders, but he was slightly leaner. His caramel-colored hair was straight and cropped close to his head.

His boots had barely hit the ground when he was forced to spin around and catch a flaxen-haired toddler before she went tumbling out of the coach headfirst like an exuberant puppy.

"Whoa, there, Charlotte!" he called out, a dazzling grin splitting his sun-bronzed face. "You do love to keep Papa's reflexes honed, don't you, sweetheart?"

Holding the squirming little girl in the crook of his arm, he offered a hand to his wife. Tucking her gloved hand in his, a woman emerged from the coach, all but the graceful curve of one cheek hidden beneath the shadow of her beribboned hat brim.

Dickon directed the coachman and outriders toward the tumbledown stables as the trio started up the broad stone stairs. The adorable moppet tucked a thumb in her little pink rosebud of a mouth and laid her head on her father's breast, suddenly overcome with shyness. She had been dressed with all the care of one of the dolls in the tower, but a smudge of dirt darkened the knee of one ivory stocking, and sugary biscuit crumbs were scattered across the bib of her pinafore.

As Lord Dravenwood's brother reached the top of the stairs, Anne pasted a dutiful smile on her lips just as she had done on the night her new master had arrived. "I'm Mrs. Spencer, the housekeeper of this establishment. Welcome to Cadgwyck Manor, my lord."

The man's brow furrowed in a mock scowl that was an impeccable imitation of his brother's real one. "*Mr. Burke* or *sir* will do, Mrs. Spencer. Didn't Max warn you?" He leaned down, lowering his voice to a conspiratorial whisper. "I'm one of those ill-mannered commoners he so disdains."

Anne had to bite back a genuine smile. The man's lazy grin and the mischievous sparkle dancing in his amber eyes were nearly irresistible. Those eyes crinkled when he smiled, as if he had spent much of his life squinting into the bright sun.

A rich ripple of laughter escaped his wife. "Don't let my husband fool you, Mrs. Spencer. There's nothing common about Ashton Burke. He's as unconventional as they come."

As Mrs. Burke tipped back her head to reveal one of the most beautiful faces Anne had ever seen, Anne felt a curious twinge in the region of her heart. She had never felt so plain or so envied another woman her potions and powders and curling tongs.

The icy edges of the woman's Nordic blondness were softened by the irresistible warmth of her smile. Her green eyes were tilted upward at their outer corners like the eyes of some exotic cat.

She surprised Anne by taking her hand. "Thank you so very much for your hospitality, Mrs. Spencer.

It was rather impulsive of us to come here. I do hope we haven't put your staff to any extra trouble."

"None whatsoever," Anne lied. She'd had the maids working nearly around the clock ever since she had learned of their impending visit. Even a grumbling Pippa had pitched in. For some unfathomable reason, Anne didn't want Dravenwood's brother to find him living in a pigsty.

Mr. Burke looked around, his expression going from playful to cautious. "So where is that devoted brother of mine?"

Anne had been dreading the question. "I'm afraid Lord Dravenwood is otherwise occupied at the moment."

Burke exchanged a knowing glance with his wife. "That's just about what I would have expected of dear old Max. So how does he occupy his time these days? Counting his gold? Conducting mock battles with his tin soldiers as he used to do with me when we were lads?" Burke wagged his eyebrows at Anne. "Flogging the peasants?"

Anne had even more difficulty hiding her smile this time. "I can assure you Cadgwyck Manor has no shortage of pursuits to keep your brother's attentions engaged. Now, if you'll allow me to show you to your rooms . . ."

She turned only to run smack-dab into the door. *Bloody hell,* she thought. Hodges must have locked it behind her as soon as she exited the house. She reached to her waist for her ring of keys only to discover she must have left them on the kitchen table.

Casting an apologetic look over her shoulder at their guests, she called out cheerfully, "Hodges! I seem to have accidentally locked the door. Would you mind unlocking it?" When her gracious request met with only silence, she leaned closer to the door and hissed, "*Hodges! Open the door this minute!*"

After a muffled "Very good, ma'am," the door swung open to admit them.

Hodges stood there, beaming at them like a demented cherub, his hair nearly as wild as his eyes. Praying their guests wouldn't notice his odd demeanor, or would at least be too polite to comment upon it, Anne ushered them through the entrance hall.

As she led them up the stairs and past Angelica's portrait, she stole a glance at Mr. Burke, curious to see if his reaction would mirror his brother's and that of every other man who had ever laid eyes on it.

Strangely enough, Mrs. Burke noticed the portrait first. "Oh my! What an enchanting creature she is!"

Her husband cast the portrait a brief, disinterested glance before slipping an arm around his wife's waist and murmuring something in her ear. She laughed aloud and smacked him playfully on the arm. Apparently, the earl's brother only had eyes for his wife, a realization that left Anne with a strangely wistful ache in her heart.

"MY LORD, MR. BURKE is here to see you." Anne stood in the doorway of the study, fully prepared to duck should her employer hurl a ledger, an inkwell, or perhaps a globe of the world at her head.

She had done exactly as instructed—seen to it that the earl's brother and his family were served a mediocre supper, sans bread—shown Mrs. Burke and her daughter to their rooms, and then informed Mr. Burke his brother would see him in the study.

"Very well. Show him in," Dravenwood said without looking up, his tone clipped but civil. He was still seated behind the desk, surrounded by his moat of ledgers. Anne was beginning to suspect he used the desk as a barrier to keep everyone at arm's length.

She ushered Mr. Burke into the room, then turned to go.

"Stay."

Caught off guard by his command, Anne turned back to find Dravenwood glowering at her from beneath the raven wings of his eyebrows. She didn't dare defy him, not with his looking at her as if she were a peasant who might just require a sound flogging as soon as they were left alone.

Fascinated against her will by his desire to keep her close, she moved to stand dutifully in the corner of the room. The earl's brother gave her a curious look before sinking into the worn leather wing chair situated at an angle to the front of the desk with a negligent grace that had probably always escaped his more formal brother. With the two men facing each other across the desk, both their similarities and their differences stood out in stark relief.

Dravenwood surveyed Burke through eyes as cool as Anne had ever seen them. "So to what do I owe the dubious honor of this visit?"

To Mr. Burke's credit, he didn't waste time on pleasantries that would neither be appreciated nor returned. "We came to inform you that we're leaving England. We decided early on that we didn't belong at Dryden Hall, but were waiting for Charlotte to grow old enough to travel. It probably won't surprise you to learn the life of a country lord and his lady doesn't suit either one of us."

Although the earl struggled to hide it, he appeared to be more surprised than his brother had anticipated. "But where will you go?"

"To Morocco first to visit Farouk and Poppy. Poppy is expecting their first child and would like Clarinda to remain with her until the babe is born. Then it's on to Egypt. Now that I've somehow managed to convince Father I'm not a *complete* wastrel, he's expressed interest in funding an archaeological expedition just outside of Giza."

"And just what will Clarinda do while you're out digging for buried treasure? Do you really believe that to be a suitable environment for a wife and child?"

"Clarinda wouldn't have it any other way. I'm afraid she developed quite a taste for adventure and the exotic while a *guest* in Farouk's harem. And besides, I don't think she ever intends to let me out of her sight again." Burke's crooked smile freely admitted he wasn't entirely displeased with that development.

Dravenwood leaned back in his chair, surveying his brother through hooded eyes. "Why did you really come here, Ash? To rub my nose in your wedded bliss? I know I deserve it—and far worse—but if you're seeking to punish me for what I did to the two of you, I can promise you there's no need. I'm quite capable of punishing myself."

Anne frowned, wondering what transgression Dravenwood could possibly have committed against his brother and his brother's wife.

All traces of humor fled Burke's face, leaving it uncharacteristically somber. "We didn't come here to gloat, Max. We came here to say good-bye. We have no way of knowing how long we'll be gone from these shores. And Clarinda had some sentimental notion that you might want to meet your niece before we left. She could very well be a woman grown before you'll have another chance to see her." When his brother continued to survey him through dispassionate eyes, Burke sat up on the edge of his seat. "I have to confess that I also wanted to make my own good-byes. I realize things between us have been a little . . . um . . . *strained* in the past few years, but I can still remember a time when it was you and me doing battle with the rest of the world. Our swords may have been nothing but a pair of tree branches, but I always knew I could depend on you to protect my back. No matter what has transpired since then, you're still my brother. You'll always be my brother." As Burke extended his hand across the desk, inviting Dravenwood to take it, Anne held her breath without realizing it.

Leaving his brother's hand hanging in midair, Dravenwood asked, "When will you be leaving Cadgwyck?"

"Early tomorrow morning. Our ship departs from Falmouth on Thursday."

"Very well, then. I wish you Godspeed." With that, Dravenwood went back to jotting down figures in his ledger, rejecting his brother's offer of reconciliation with no further fanfare.

Yanking back his hand, Burke surged to his feet, looking even more like his older brother now that he was angry. He stood there, glaring at the top of his brother's head. "I had hoped time might have softened your heart, but I can see you're still the same intractable ass that you always were."

With that, Burke turned and stormed out of the room, slamming the door behind him with satisfying force. Dravenwood lifted his head to stare at the door for a moment, his face curiously blank, then rose from the desk and moved to gaze into the leaping flames on the hearth, his broad back to Anne.

She crept out of her corner, beset by an almost overwhelming urge to ease the stiffness of his stance with a comforting word or a smile. After all, there must have been some reason he'd asked her to stay and witness such a painfully private exchange.

"My lord?" she said softly. "I may be speaking out of turn, but I hate to see you at such painful odds with your own brother." She cleared her throat, choosing her words with care. "I had a brother once, you see. He used to drive me mad with his bossiness and his teasing. But I always knew in my heart that if anyone dared to wrong me, he would knock them flat. I never thanked him for that or told him how much he meant to me. I just assumed that if I reached out, he would always be there." She swallowed, a familiar heaviness weighting down her heart. "Until the day he wasn't."

Dravenwood continued to contemplate the flames,

showing no sign that he was considering her words, or even that he had heard them.

"I'd give anything to have my brother back, to hear his laughter or be able to take his hand in mine." Anne crept closer, addressing that unyielding back. "What I'm trying to say is that you shouldn't let pride make you wait until it's too late to reconcile with Mr. Burke. We can never know what the morrow might bring."

Dravenwood was silent for a long moment before finally saying, "You're right, Mrs. Spencer." Anne's heart surged with warmth. She was about to ask him if he wanted her to fetch his brother back when he continued, "You *are* speaking out of turn, and in the future I'd appreciate it if you would strive to remember your place. That will be all," he added, making it clear he had no further need of her or anyone else.

ANNE WAS STANDING BENEATH the portico the next morning, watching Mr. Burke and his family prepare to climb into their waiting coach, when her employer emerged from the house and stalked right past her, his handsome face grim with determination. The shadows beneath his eyes bespoke of a sleepless night, much like Anne's own had been.

"Where are you going?" she called after him, too

startled to add *my lord* or to remember his affairs were none of her concern. He had made that abundantly clear last night in the study.

"To bid my brother and his family a proper farewell," he growled, starting down the stairs at a rapid clip. "I would hardly be a gracious host if I didn't." He shot her a virulent look over one shoulder. "And as you were so kind to remind me, we never know what the morrow might bring."

Anne picked up the hem of her skirts and hurried down the stairs after him, fearful it wasn't reconciliation but murder that was about to be done. As the earl's long strides carried him toward the coach, his brother froze while offering his wife a hand to assist her into the vehicle. Mr. and Mrs. Burke exchanged a cautious glance, but before either of them could react, their little girl wiggled her way out of her mother's grip and slid to the ground.

"Charlotte!" her mother cried out.

It was too late. Charlotte was already barreling her way back up the drive on her fat, little legs, shrieking, "Unca Max! Unca Max!" at the top of her lungs.

Dravenwood stopped in his tracks, looking like a man about to be crushed beneath the hooves of a team of runaway horses. The little girl skidded to a halt and began to bounce up and down on her heels, holding her arms up to him. She was obviously accustomed to being greeted with open arms wherever she went. Much like Angelica Cadgwyck must have been.

Anne had never seen such a powerful man look so helpless. She held her breath, fearing for a moment that he wasn't even going to acknowledge the child's presence. But he slowly bent down, folding his tall frame to scoop her up into his arms.

As he straightened back to his full height, Charlotte wrapped her arms around his neck, clinging to him like a baby spider monkey for a minute before leaning back and giving him a chiding look from green eyes that were a mirror of her mother's. "Don't look so sad, Unca Max. We be back soon." She pressed a noisy kiss to his cheek, then rested her head on his shoulder, her silvery-blond hair looking even fairer next to the darkness of his own.

By that time, her parents had caught up with her.

Burke held out his arms for the child, but Dravenwood showed no sign of relinquishing her. "I don't understand," Dravenwood said, the bewilderment reflected in his eyes tugging at Anne's heart. "How does the child know who I am?"

"Oh, I told her *all* about you," his sister-in-law confessed, a smile touching her lips. "How you used to help me with my sums when I was a little girl so my governess wouldn't rap my knuckles with her ruler. How you bandaged up my stuffed bear after he lost an eye because I had left him out in the rain all night. How you rescued me from that feral dog when I was twelve and carried me all the way home in your arms."

Burke folded his arms over his chest, looking dangerously sulky. "And I told her how your toy soldiers always bested mine in battle when we were lads and how you used to sink my wooden battleships in the tub while that awful German nurse was making me wash behind my ears."

The earl glanced down at the flaxen head resting so comfortably against his shoulder before lifting his eyes to his sister-in-law's face. "You're as shameless as ever, aren't you, Clarinda?" he said softly. "You knew that if I ever laid eyes on her, I'd be helpless to resist her charms."

"Come, Charlotte," Burke said gently, holding out his arms to his daughter. "It's time for us to go."

Dravenwood cradled the child close for a moment, burying his face in her sleek hair, before reluctantly surrendering her to his brother.

Before Burke could turn away, Dravenwood awkwardly thrust a hand toward him. Burke gazed warily down at it, then lifted his eyes to his brother's face. Although Dravenwood's scowl was as ferocious as ever, Anne would have sworn she saw a flicker of uncertainty in his eyes.

She was afraid Burke was going to reject his brother's offer just as his brother had rejected his. But Burke shifted Charlotte to the crook of his other arm and seized Dravenwood's hand in a hearty grasp. Then Burke turned and carried his daughter toward the waiting coach, leaving his wife and his brother facing each other in the drive. For some reason she could not fathom, Anne began to feel like even more of an intruder. But it was too late to creep back up to the portico without attracting notice to herself.

Dravenwood gazed down at his sister-in-law, his expression once again inscrutable. "Are you going to give me another well-deserved slap before you go as you did at our last meeting? Sometimes I fancy I can still feel the sting of it."

The woman reached up to touch her gloved fingertips to his cheek, then stood on tiptoe and pressed a gentle kiss to the exact same spot. "That's all in the past now, Max," she murmured. "All I wish for you is the same happiness I have found. I'll never forget all you've done for me. Or why you did it."

She was turning away from him when she spotted Anne standing awkwardly off to the side. Giving her brother-in-law a sly sideways glance, she crossed to Anne and whispered in her ear, "Look after him, won't you, Mrs. Spencer? He's always been too proud to admit it, but he needs it very badly."

Stunned by the woman's candor and keenly aware of her employer's scrutiny, Anne could only nod.

As Dravenwood watched Clarinda Burke turn and walk away to join her husband and child, Anne felt her own heart wrench. She would almost have sworn she had seen that look in his eyes before.

Off for adventures unknown, the handsome young family crowded into the coach, leaving their host standing stiffly in the middle of the drive. As the coach began to jolt its way down the rutted drive, his niece leaned out the window, frantically waving her little, white-gloved hand. "G'bye, Unca Max! G'bye!"

Dravenwood lifted a hand. He didn't lower it again until the coach rolled out of sight, swallowed by the sweeping grasses of the moor. He stood there staring after them for a long time after they'd gone, his dark hair dancing in the wind.

Emboldened by her unspoken promise to Mrs. Burke, Anne drew closer to him and gently touched the back of his coat sleeve. He turned to give her a narrow look. "Just what did my sister-in-law say to you?"

Anne's hand fell back to her side. She briefly considered lying, but the challenge in his gaze stopped her. "She asked me to look after you."

"How very charitable of her. But I'm afraid I don't require looking after. I'm quite capable of looking after myself." Without another word, he went stalking toward the weed-clotted breezeway separating the main section of the house from the east wing, heading for the cliffs.

"Then why did you command me to stay in the study last night while you were speaking to your brother?" she called after him.

He hesitated for the briefest second, then kept walking as if she hadn't even spoken.

He was her employer. She was obligated to respect his wishes. Her duty was to meekly return to the house and find something to sweep or dust or polish so he could brood in privacy and continue to mourn his lost fiancée and punish himself for whatever terrible transgression he believed he had committed against his brother and sister-in-law.

Anne lifted her chin, feeling her temper start to rise. For the first time in a long while, she had no intention of doing what she *should* do. Contrary to what she'd let everyone believe for the past several years, she was not a woman who would so easily be dismissed.

# ⤚ Chapter Twenty

W HEN ANNE EMERGED AT the back of the house, it wasn't the spectacular view from the cliffs that made her steps slow and her breath catch in her throat, but the man standing at their edge.

Dravenwood stood with one boot propped on a large rock, gazing out to sea as if transfixed by what he saw before him. Something about his stance was irresistibly timeless and masculine. He could have been a pirate king, waiting to board a ship so he could sail the high seas to ravish and plunder. Or one of Arthur's knights, dreaming of the lady fair he had left behind in Camelot to pine for his return.

"You might have warned me," he said without turning around as she approached.

Anne would have sworn she hadn't so much as kicked a pebble to betray her presence. She was quickly learning he was a difficult man to catch unawares. She joined him at the cliff's edge. "About what?"

He swept a hand toward the breathtaking vista stretched out before them. "*This.*"

The coastline had undergone a magical transformation beneath the kiss of the autumn sun. Cottony wisps of cloud drifted across an azure sky. The moss furring the broad rocks along the top of the cliffs was no longer cast in drab shades of gray, but was revealed to be a shade of green somewhere between emerald and jade. Beams of sunlight shattered against the diamond-sharp crests of the waves, brightening the water to a blue-green intense enough to make a man—or woman—dream of Barbados and tropical breezes and swaying palms. Far below them at the foot of the cliffs, the sand of the cove shimmered like gold dust.

"It does rather take one's breath away, doesn't it?" Anne couldn't completely hide her pride as she surveyed the view.

He slanted her a mocking glance. "There was no need for you to follow me out here, you know. I have no intention of flinging myself off the cliffs in a fit of pique like your impulsive Miss Cadgwyck."

"Well, that's certainly a relief." She seated herself on the opposite side of the rock, ignoring her first inclination to hug one knee to her chest as she might have done when she was a girl. "I suspect you would make a very intolerable ghost, always slamming doors and groaning and rattling your chains. I daresay we'd never get another decent night's rest." As the wind tugged her shawl from her shoulders, she tilted her face to the sun, wishing she could pull the pinching pins from her hair and let it ripple free as well.

"You wound me with your dour assessment of my character. It would no doubt surprise you to learn that for a very long time I was considered the most eligible catch in all of England."

Anne remembered the words of the women in the village: *He was the perfect gent till his fiancée threw him over.* "And why should that surprise me? What woman could resist a gentleman with such a delightful temperament and affable wit?"

He snorted. "As you've probably already guessed, I was pursued more for my title and my fortune than my charms."

Stealing a glance at the rugged purity of his profile and the shadows his long, sooty lashes cast on his beautifully sculpted cheekbones, Anne doubted that was entirely true. "It's been my experience that charming men tend to think even more highly of themselves than they want others to do. I've never cared for them myself."

"Then you should be *very* fond of me."

May God help her if she was, Anne thought. She

dragged her gaze away from his profile and returned it to the sea, feeling suddenly dizzy in a way that had little to do with the height of their perch. "You certainly weren't very charming to your brother and his wife. Especially not after they came all this way just to bid you farewell."

The distant look in his frosty gray eyes deepened, as if he were staring at something far beyond the sea. "I shall have to beg your forbearance for my ill manners. Their visit came as something of an unwelcome shock. I hadn't seen Clarinda since our wedding day."

Anne frowned in bewilderment. "Don't you mean *her* wedding day?"

He gave her an arch look.

"Oh!" Anne breathed, thankful she was already sitting down. So Clarinda Burke was the woman who had jilted him at the altar, the woman who had broken his heart and given his lips their cynical curl. She remembered the look she'd glimpsed in his eyes as he had watched his brother's wife walk away from him, possibly for the last time. Now she knew *exactly* where she had seen that look before— whenever he gazed up at Angelica's portrait.

"Needless to say, it came as quite a shock to society when my bride tossed me over at the altar so she could marry my brother. All of London was abuzz with the gossip. I'm surprised it didn't travel as far as Cadgwyck."

Not wanting him to know that it finally had, Anne forced herself to say lightly, "Ah, but you forget—we have our own scandals to gossip about in Cadgwyck. Why did she toss you over? Did you do something to earn the slap the two of you spoke of?"

His laughter was edged with bitterness. "I was fortunate it was no more than a slap. Had there been a pistol handy that day, she might have very well shot me."

"Were you unfaithful to her?"

"Once she agreed to wed me? Never." Dravenwood swung around to face Anne, the frost in his eyes extinguished by a fierce fire. "Not in word or in deed. Not with my body or in my heart."

Mesmerized by the passion in his eyes, Anne felt her own heart skip a beat. She had always dreamed of having a man look at her that way.

But not while he was thinking of another woman.

He returned his gaze to the sea, his jaw set in a rigid line. "Clarinda and my brother fell in love when they were very young. They had a rather . . . *tempestuous* relationship, and when Ash went off to seek his fortune, leaving her behind, it broke her heart."

"And you were there to pick up the pieces?"

"I tried. After she was forced to accept that Ash wasn't coming back for her, she collapsed and became very ill. I"—he hesitated—"I helped to look after her for several months. Until she was well enough to manage on her own."

While a wealth of information was in that simple explanation, Anne sensed he was leaving out large chunks of the story, not to protect himself, but to protect his sister-in-law. Anne had become quite adept at doing that herself.

"Once Clarinda recovered, I offered for her. But she refused me. Since I was Ash's brother, she was afraid she would never see me as anything more than a reminder of the love she had lost. It took me nine years to finally convince her we would suit."

"Nine years?" Anne echoed in disbelief. "Well, no one can accuse you of being fickle, can they?"

"You don't know how many times I wished they could! Wished I was the sort of man who could tumble a different woman into my bed every night without ever once stopping to count the cost to their hearts or mine."

His frank confession made Anne feel oddly breathless. "After finally agreeing to marry you, what made her change her mind?"

A sardonic smile curved his lips. "Since I was the one fool enough to save Ash from a firing squad and bring him back into her life, I have only myself to blame. On the day we were supposed to be wed, she found out that all those years ago I'd had a hand in keeping them apart because I didn't believe Ash was good enough for her. So she slapped me across the face and walked right back into his arms. She got the man she had always loved while I got exactly what I deserved—a lifetime of regrets and a crumbling manor haunted by a spiteful White Lady."

Anne pondered his confession for a moment. "Just how old were you when you committed this terrible crime of the heart?"

He shrugged. "Two-and-twenty, I suppose."

A ripple of laughter escaped her, earning a puzzled scowl from him. She rose to face him. "You say your brother and Clarinda were very young when they fell in love, but you were little more than a babe yourself—a young man in the first flush of passion. You lashed out because your heart was wounded. Because you couldn't accept that the woman you loved might never come to love you back. But now you seek to condemn that impulsive young fool with the wisdom and experience of a man full grown. Tell me—would you be so merciless and unbending toward any other soul who made such an error in judgment?"

Dravenwood drew closer, glowering down at her. "Are you mad, woman? I don't deserve any mercy. I robbed my own brother and the woman he loved of ten years they might have spent in each other's arms!"

"Perhaps you did them an unintended service. You said yourself their young relationship was very tempestuous. Their love might have needed time to season and gain in maturity so they could truly embrace the happiness they've found today."

"What I did was unforgivable!"

"It might have been wrong—even wicked perhaps—but was it truly unforgivable? Is any sin unforgivable if the heart is genuinely repentant?"

There was no way for Anne to let him know how desperately she needed him to agree with her. Especially while standing at the edge of those cliffs where another life had ended because a young girl had been too foolish and proud to forgive herself. A pleading note softened her voice. "There's a difference in being sorry for what you did and throwing away the rest of your life because you feel sorry for yourself."

He took a swift step toward her, his hands closing over her upper arms. Even through her shawl she could feel their fierce strength, their irresistible heat as he drew her toward him. He gave her a sharp, little shake, his scowl a fearsome thing to behold. "I didn't come to this place looking for absolution. And I certainly don't need *your* absolution, Mrs. Spencer."

"What do you need, my lord?" she asked, feeling

her breath quicken, her moist lips part in reckless challenge.

His smoldering gaze strayed to her lips, giving her a dangerous glimpse of exactly what he needed. Not forgiveness, but forgetfulness, if only for a night or perhaps even just a few hours. What he needed was the chance to be the sort of fickle man who could tumble a woman into his bed just because he desired her, not because he had loved her for half his life.

She could almost see the effort it took for him to drag his gaze from her lips, to gentle his grip and firmly set her away from him. Instead of the relief she should have felt, her heart ached with disappointment.

"I need the same thing Angelica needs," he said hoarsely, unable to completely purge the passion from his voice. "To be left the bloody hell alone."

With that, he turned and went stalking away from her, skirting dangerously close to the edge of the cliffs as he followed them around to the promontory.

Anne hugged her shawl around her as she watched him go. The wind snatched the sigh from her lips as she whispered, "As you wish, my lord."

THE ROGUE HAD DARED *to put his hands on her.*

Hodges stood at the corner of the window in the second-floor study, his temple pulsing with fury as he watched Cadgwyck's new master turn his back on Annie and stride away. She stood there gazing after him, hugging herself through the flimsy protection of her shawl.

She looked so small standing there at the edge of those towering cliffs, so terribly vulnerable—as if it would take little more than a gust of wind to blow her right over them.

Hodges touched his fingertips to the windowpane, his face drooping in a mask of sorrow. He never could bear it when she was sad. All he wanted to do was coax a smile back to her lips, to hear her merry laughter ringing through the halls of the manor once again.

The butler's eyes narrowed as they followed the rogue's path along the cliffs. *He* was the one who had stolen her smile. The one who had left her there all alone to be buffeted by the winds of fate.

The man was a fraud, an impostor, a shameless seducer of all that was pure and virtuous. Hodges drew his shoulders back, standing so straight and true that few who had known him in recent years would have recognized him.

There could only be one true master of Cadgwyck. Once the impostor was banished, that master could return to take his rightful place.

Hearing the door behind him creak open, Hodges

whirled around, tucking both hands behind his back like a guilty child.

Dickon's freckled face appeared in the crack between frame and door. "Pardon me, sir, but have you seen the good shovel? I thought I'd head down to the caves and do some more excavating while the earl's out on the cliffs."

"Haven't seen it, lad," Hodges replied, his shoulders settling back into their natural slump. "But you might ask Nana."

"Will do. Thanks!" Dickon set off on his errand, his cheerful whistle drifting back to Hodges's ears.

Hodges drew his hands out from behind his back. He stood there for a long time, gazing down at the brass-handled letter opener gripped in his trembling fist. For the life of him, he could not remember how it had gotten there.

# Chapter Twenty-one

For the first time in their brief acquaintance, Mrs. Spencer did precisely what Max had ordered her to do. She performed her duties and supervised the other servants without so much as a hint of impropriety in her actions or her words.

Max was surprised by how much he missed being flayed by her sharp tongue or being offered some opinion he had not solicited and did not welcome. His every request, no matter how trifling, was met with polite subservience. After a few days of this, he began to have wicked fantasies about requesting her to do something utterly outrageous. Every time she asked, "Will there be anything else, my lord?" he had to bite his tongue to keep from blurting out "Take down your hair" or "Lift the hem of your skirt so I can steal a peek at your garters." He was no longer sure of what he would do if she responded with a dutiful "As you wish, my lord" while slowly raising her hem to tease him with a glimpse of a trim ankle or a shapely calf.

Even brooding about Clarinda would have been a welcome distraction from his growing obsession with his housekeeper. But his brother's wife seemed to occupy his thoughts less with each passing day. It was almost as if Clarinda's kiss and her benediction had finally broken the spell she had cast over him when he had been little more than a boy. When his hikes along the cliffs no longer relieved the peculiar tension gathering like a storm in him, he took to walking to the village each afternoon, hoping to receive a reply from his inquiry into Angelica's precious artist. But as his housekeeper had warned him, the post was notoriously slow in reaching Cadgwyck. Although it had been nearly a month since he had posted the inquiry, there was still no word.

The villagers had begun to eye him as if something were suspect about any man who could survive sharing a house with a ghost.

He supposed his ferocious demeanor and barked requests didn't help. Before long, they were crossing both themselves and the street whenever he came stalking down it.

His patience—or lack thereof—was finally rewarded on a sunny Thursday afternoon. As the squat postmistress handed over the thick package tied in string with his name neatly inscribed on the front, she seemed as relieved as he was.

Max tore open the package and began to scan the first page. He'd read only a few lines when a grim smile began to spread across his face. This was one discovery even his unflappable housekeeper would not be able to ignore.

ANNE WAS IN THE kitchen, chatting with Nana and nursing a copper kettle of crab stew over the fire, when one of the bells strung over the door began to jingle. Ignoring the treacherous leap of her heart, Anne glanced up to discover it was the bell for the master's study.

She was tempted to ignore it or to send Hodges or Dickon to answer the summons purely out of spite. But after a morning spent scouring every inch of the attic for what had to feel like the millionth time, Dickon had gone out for a well-deserved romp on the moors. And the last time she'd seen Hodges, he had been merrily waltzing through the ballroom with an invisible partner on his arm and a tea cozy on his head.

Anne traded her gravy-stained apron for a clean one, then leaned down to bellow into Nana's ear, "I don't suppose I could talk *you* into going to see what his lordship wants?"

Nana grinned up at Anne from her rocking chair, baring her toothless gums. "If I was but a few years younger, I'd be more than happy to give that man whatever he wanted."

Anne recoiled in mock horror. "Why, Nana! I had no idea you were such a shameless little hoyden!"

Nana cackled. "The right man can turn any woman into a shameless hoyden."

Anne sobered, remembering the dangerous desire she had glimpsed in Dravenwood's eyes before he had set her away from him on the cliffs. "What about the wrong man, Nana? What can he do?"

Nana caught Anne's sleeve in one of her bony claws, urging her down so the old woman could whisper in her ear, "Give her what *she* wants."

"YOU RANG, MY LORD?"

Anne stood stiffly in the doorway of the study, trying not to think about Nana's words or how beguiling Lord Dravenwood looked as he sat behind the desk, his coat draped carelessly over the back of his chair while he worked in a waistcoat of copper-colored silk and dazzling-white shirtsleeves.

This time he did not leave her waiting while he tended to his ledgers, but immediately rose and came around the desk. "I just returned from the village. I received something in the post that I thought might be of interest to you."

"Have you been summoned back to London?" she inquired hopefully, blinking at him with all of the innocence she could muster.

He leveled a reproachful look at her before nodding toward the leather chair in front of the desk. "There's no need to hover there in the doorway like a raven portending doom. Do sit."

"Is that a request or an order?"

"It's an invitation. Please?" The husky note in his voice gave her a jarring glimpse of just how dangerous he could be to her resolve when he wasn't ordering her about in that high-handed manner of his.

Anne approached the desk and gingerly sat, clasping her hands primly in her lap.

Dravenwood propped one lean hip on a corner of the desk, an ember of excitement flaring in his smoky eyes. "I've always believed every mystery is nothing more than a mathematical equation that can be solved if you find the right variables and apply them in the correct order. The one variable we already have in Angelica Cadgwyck's mystery is the name of the artist who seduced her. So I decided if I wanted to find out what *really* happened on the night of her birthday ball, I needed to learn more about the man."

Anne kept her face expressionless with tremendous effort. She could only pray he hadn't noticed the blood drain from it.

"While I was perusing Miss Cadgwyck's portrait, it occurred to me that any man who could paint with such undeniable skill must have left *some* mark on society. So I enlisted the help of a certain investigator the Company has done business with in the past—an extremely tenacious Scot named Andrew Murray. Mr. Murray has a gift for ferreting out the one grain of truth in even the most sordid and convoluted nugget of gossip." Dravenwood stopped abruptly, tilting his head to study her. "Aren't you going to scold me for prying into matters that are none of my concern?"

"I wouldn't dare to be so presumptuous. As you so aptly reminded me, *you* are master of Cadgwyck now. It's your house. Your painting." She hesitated for the briefest instant. "Your ghost."

Nodding his approval, he retrieved a thick sheaf of papers from the desk behind him and shook them open with a crisp snap. "As you probably already noted from the signature on the portrait, the artist's name was Laurence Timberlake."

"Laurie," Anne whispered before she could stop herself.

Dravenwood frowned at her. "What was that?"

"Oh, nothing. I once had a childhood friend named Laurence."

He went back to scanning the papers. "Murray was able to locate several of Timberlake's paintings scattered throughout London and the surrounding countryside and agreed he was a most remarkable talent. Murray was as surprised as I that the man hadn't attracted the attention of some wealthy patron and achieved greater fame."

"Perhaps being shot to death curtailed his career opportunities," Anne offered drily.

"On the contrary, meeting a tragic end at such a young age should have only enhanced his reputation and made the artwork he left behind that much more valuable to a collector. There's nothing society adores more than a love affair gone wrong. Trust me . . . I should know," he added, flicking a wry glance in her direction.

"So why does this Murray fellow believe Timberlake's talents were overlooked?"

"When he was tracking down the portraits, he noticed something peculiar. All of the paintings were of young women, and very few of them had remained with the families who had commissioned them. Most had been sold or wound up stored in an attic somewhere."

"But why?" Anne was thankful she didn't have to hide her growing bewilderment. "Why would anyone wish to bury such treasures?"

"That question wasn't answered until Murray was

able to track down a young woman from one of the paintings. She's a marchioness now and the mother of three small children. She agreed to speak to him only if he promised her his utmost discretion. She was the one who revealed that the majority of Timberlake's income wasn't derived from his art, but from something far more sinister—blackmail."

# ❧ *Chapter Twenty-two*

"*B*LACKMAIL?" ANNE ECHOED THROUGH lips that had gone suddenly numb.

Tossing the papers on the desk behind him, Dravenwood nodded. "The scoundrel would choose his victims with care—usually some beautiful young girl with a promising future about to make her debut." Anne could tell he was thinking of Angelica by the distant look in his eye. "He would deliberately seek out girls who came from wealthy and prominent families whose continuing fortunes and good names might depend on her making a first-rate match. He would accept the commission to paint her portrait, then worm his way into her family's home and her affections. From what I understand, it was no great challenge for him. He was young, handsome, charming, well-spoken."

"Everything a naïve young girl might desire," Anne said softly. "Especially after he immortalized her on canvas, making her believe she was every-thing she wanted others to see in her."

"Precisely. After the painting was finished, he would complete his seduction. Then he would go to her father and threaten to expose their sordid little affair to all the world unless her father paid him a handsome sum to buy his silence."

Anne's growing agitation made it impossible for her to sit still any longer. She rose and paced over to the window, drawing back the drape to gaze blindly out over the churning waves of the sea. "How can you prove any of this is true? For all you know, the woman your man spoke to might have simply been a scorned lover, out to destroy what was left of Tim-berlake's reputation."

"With her help, Murray was able to track down two more of the women in the portraits. One of them had been cast out in the streets by her fam-ily after Timberlake ruined her and was plying her wares on the streets of Whitechapel." They both knew there was only one sort of ware a woman might be plying on the streets of Whitechapel. The grim note in Dravenwood's voice deepened. "When Timberlake painted her portrait, she was only thir-teen."

Anne turned to face him, her voice a ragged whisper she barely recognized. "*Thirteen?*"

"She was the one who told Murray that when

Timberlake's seduction failed, he would sometimes resort to more"—Dravenwood's brow darkened—"*forceful* measures."

Anne slowly drifted back across the room, tugged toward him by the fierce emotion in his eyes and the unmistakable ring of conviction in his words.

"It's awkward to speak of such an unspeakable failing of my own sex to a woman. Men are supposed to cherish women, protect them, even at the cost of their own lives. The thought of a man using brute strength to overpower any woman—especially an innocent girl—in such a way makes me ill. If you ask me, shooting was too good for him." Dravenwood curled his powerful hands into fists, his eyes narrowing to smoky slits. "I'd like nothing more than the chance to beat the bastard to a bloody pulp myself."

Anne might be able to shield her overflowing heart from him, but she could do nothing to hide the warm rush of tears in her eyes.

Dravenwood straightened, gazing down at her with a mixture of alarm and dismay. "Forgive me. I shouldn't have spoken of such things to you. Since you'd expressed an interest in Angelica, I thought you'd want to know that whatever happened to her that night might not have been through any fault of her own."

What Anne wanted in that moment was to bring one of his clenched fists to her lips and soften it with a kiss, if for no other reason than that he was everything Laurence Timberlake had never been. But all she could do was whisper a heartfelt "Thank you."

He retrieved the sheaf of papers from the desk, thrusting them toward her as if they were a handkerchief to dry her tears. "Would you care to take the report to your room and look over it?"

"Yes, my lord. I do believe I would." She accepted the document from his hand, handling it as if it were a pardon from the hand of the king himself. Although she was desperate to escape his scrutiny, she could not resist pausing at the door to give him one last look. "For a man so reluctant to accept absolution for his own sins, you certainly seem eager enough to dole it out to others."

"Perhaps I simply believe others are more deserving of it."

"Isn't that the point of absolution? That we sometimes receive it even when we don't deserve it?"

Leaving him with that to ponder, she gently drew the door shut behind her.

ANNE STOOD ON THE landing gazing up at Angelica's portrait, Murray's report still clutched in her hand. It had been a long time since the two of them had talked.

"He's determined to prove you didn't deserve what

happened to you," Anne said softly. "But you and I know differently, don't we?"

Angelica gazed down at Anne, her enigmatic half smile hiding secrets even the most tenacious investigator would never unearth.

"He's half in love with you, you know. Perhaps more than half. But you could never truly appreciate a man like him. You'd rather squander your affections on some glib charlatan who would steal a child's innocence just to line his own pockets with gold. All the earl did was prove you were even more of a fool than anyone will ever know."

Was that a pout she detected playing around Angelica's full lips?

"You needn't waste your pretty sulks on me," Anne warned her. "Save it for some starry-eyed swain who will appreciate it. I don't feel sorry for you. Not one whit."

Anne wasn't being completely truthful. Like the hands of the longcase clock in the entrance hall, Angelica was frozen in time, unable to travel back to the past to undo what had been done or move forward to embrace the future.

Just like her.

As Max started down the stairs the next morning, he was still thinking about his housekeeper. He was beginning to wonder if this house was driving him well and truly mad. He'd never even flirted with a pretty parlor maid as a young man. He had always felt it would be unsporting of him to prey on women who depended on him and his family for their livelihood. Yet now all he could think about was his housekeeper and what might lie beneath her starched apron and staid skirts.

She'd jarred him even more when he had shown her the investigator's report. Her unexpected compassion for Angelica and all the other young women Timberlake had betrayed had caught him off guard. When he had seen the tears well up in her luminous hazel eyes, he'd nearly been overwhelmed by the urge to draw her into his arms and kiss them away.

As he reached the turn in the landing between the third and second floors, he braced a hand on the newel as he always did to slow his momentum. The ball snapped off in his hand, sending him hurtling toward the banister.

Thanks to reflexes honed while sailing some of the roughest seas in the world, he ended up teetering on the edge of the next step instead of pitching forward over the banister in a tumble that would have left him lying broken and bleeding in the entrance hall below.

Or dead.

His heart was thundering against his rib cage just

as it had in the moments after the shelf of rock had crumbled beneath his feet on the promontory. He turned the ball over to examine it. Far too much rot was in the wood to determine what had caused the break.

If the ball had deliberately been severed from the post, this was no harmless bit of mischief like a closed chimney flue or ghostly giggles in the night.

He frowned down at the jagged edges of the post. What if something more sinister than a ghost was at work at Cadgwyck? He'd been so intent upon solving the mysteries of the dead that he'd been ignoring the secrets of the living. He was reasonably sure Mrs. Spencer was hiding something. He hadn't forgotten the desperate conversation he'd overheard between her and Hodges in the drawing room or the untimely death of Cadgwyck's previous master.

Not wanting anyone else to fall into the trap that might have been set for him, Max slipped the ball into the pocket of his coat. Since he didn't have Mr. Murray's resources to reply upon, perhaps it was time he did a little sleuthing of his own.

He was not trespassing.

That's what Max told himself that afternoon as he climbed the back staircase leading up to the fourth-floor servants' quarters. The manor belonged to him. He was free to roam wherever he liked. And besides, if someone should spot him, he had a perfectly valid excuse for bearding his housekeeper in her den. She wasn't in any of her usual haunts, and he wanted to take her up on her offer to go over the household accounts with him. For some reason, spending the afternoon closeted in his study with her in front of a cozy fire wasn't the unpleasant prospect it had once been.

Of course, he could simply have rung for her, but then he wouldn't have had any excuse to . . . well . . . not trespass.

He emerged at the top of the stairs in an uncarpeted corridor flanked with doors. He could still remember his horror as a boy when his father had drolly informed him servants were always to be housed on the highest floor so they would be the first to burn to death in the event of a fire while the family made their escape. The observation might have been more amusing if his father had been joking.

Since all the doors were standing wide open, Max didn't even have to feel guilty about stealing a look inside each room as he passed. It didn't require any detective work on his part to deduce who slept in the first room. Books pilfered from *his* library were scattered all over the room in untidy piles. Although it was the middle of the day, he wouldn't have been surprised to see Pippa sprawled across the bed, munching on an apple with her nose buried in a book.

The occupant of the next room was just as easily identified. An ancient hornets' nest dangled from the ceiling, and the table beside the bed sported a collection of interesting rocks and something that looked suspiciously like a mummified toad. They were exactly the sort of treasures Max might have collected as a lad had he been allowed to roam the woods and meadows as Ash had been instead of attending to his lessons.

The next room was slightly larger and looked quite cozy with its neatly made bed and faded leather chair drawn up in front of the coal stove. Max assumed it must belong to his butler.

The last chamber off the corridor was a long dormer room with five beds where the Elizabeths must sleep. Mrs. Spencer had claimed Max had heard their giggles on the night he had left his bed to chase a ghost. He still didn't believe her. Angelica might not have paid him any more visits, but the echo of her laughter continued to haunt his dreams.

He had reached the end of the corridor. Baffled, he turned in a circle, but there was still no sign of his housekeeper's room. He was about to give up on his quest and retreat before someone discovered him when he noticed the steep staircase tucked into the corner.

The narrow stairs were more forbidding than inviting, yet Max could not seem to resist them. Shadows enveloped him as he climbed, the risers creaking beneath his boots with each step. At the top of the stairs was a plain wooden door.

He gave it a soft rap. "Mrs. Spencer?"

When there was no response, he tested the knob. The door was fitted with a lock, but it opened easily beneath his hand. Max might have believed he was still in the wrong place if he hadn't recognized the plain black shawl draped over the foot of the bed. After stealing a furtive glance over his shoulder, he slipped into the room and closed the door behind him.

*Now* he was trespassing.

The first thing he noticed was the cold.

The weather had turned on them during the night, almost as if the coming winter sought to punish them for enjoying those all-too-brief sunny autumn days. The wind was whistling around the eaves of the attic room, its perch at the peak of the house providing little defense against drafts.

His original mission forgotten, Max wandered deeper into the room, growing more dismayed with every step. A single window set into a recessed dormer let in just enough daylight to reveal how Spartan the room was. It seemed to have been stripped of even the most basic of human comforts. The rooms on the floor below had all been fitted with coal stoves, but this room had only a bare hearth with no hint of recent ash. The other servants' beds were outfitted with feather ticks and piled high with thick, colorful quilts, but the bed in the attic was little more than a narrow cot with a thin mattress covered by a single worn wool blanket.

Aside from the bed, the furniture consisted of a washstand topped by a chipped porcelain pitcher and basin, a side table, and a battered wardrobe that was obviously the castoff of some distant Cadgwyck ancestor. It wasn't difficult to imagine the water in the basin icing over on frigid winter mornings.

A pewter candlestick with a nub of a tallow candle, a tinderbox, and a book rested on the table next to the bed. Max picked up the book, shaking his head as he read the title on the clothbound spine— *Pilgrim's Progress*. Why should that surprise him? If this room was anything, it was the cell of a penitent.

Max tossed the book back down in disgust, then strode over to the window, half-expecting to find iron bars fixed over it. The window overlooked a desolate sea of moorland with endless waves of gorse and grass swaying in the wind. He shoved it open and leaned out, struck by a dizzying rush of vertigo as the flagstones of the courtyard below seemed to rise up to meet him.

He jerked his head back into the room and

slammed the window. As he turned to sweep a despairing look over the bleak little chamber his housekeeper called home, he could not help but compare it to Angelica's tower with all of the lavish luxuries it must have once afforded a pampered child.

A burst of girlish laughter drifted to his ears. There was nothing spectral about those giggles. His despair shifting into anger, Max hastened down the stairs, his bootheels clattering against the wood.

Two of the young maids had just emerged from the back staircase and were heading for their dormer room, their heads together as they tittered over some private jest.

"Elizabeth!" he snapped.

Both girls jerked to attention, visibly shocked to discover their master had invaded their humble domain. Max could only imagine how thunderous his brow must have looked in that moment.

"Where is Mrs. Spencer?" he demanded.

The maids exchanged a furtive look that made Max want to grind his teeth in frustration. Why did everyone in this house always look so bloody guilty?

"It's Friday, yer lordship," one of them finally provided. "She goes to market every Friday. She won't be back until it's time to prepare supper."

He pondered the girl's words for a moment. "Good. Then I need to set you both to a task. But first you have to promise me something."

"What, m'lord?" asked the other girl, looking even more apprehensive.

"That you know how to keep a secret." With that, Max drew the two wide-eyed girls into the circle of his arms and began to murmur his instructions.

ANNE TRUDGED UP THE back staircase, bleary-eyed with exhaustion. She could hardly wait to sink down on the edge of her bed and tug the boots from her aching feet. She'd been up on them since before dawn, and the long walk to the village and back had spread the ache from her feet to her calves.

She had returned from her errands to find Dickon on hands and knees desperately trying to coax Hodges out from the cabinet in the dining-room cupboard before Lord Dravenwood discovered him. Hodges had crawled into the cabinet shortly after lunch and had been cowering there ever since, wild-eyed with fright because he believed the authorities were coming to cart him off to the asylum. It had taken Anne so long to lure him out that she'd had to prepare supper in a terrible rush. She'd been so frazzled she'd inadvertently stomped on Sir Fluffytoes's tail, nearly broken her neck tripping over Nana's never-ending scarf, and snapped so sharply at Pippa for leaving a strip of peel on a potato that the usually unflappable girl had burst into tears.

Then she had been forced to play the role of perfect housekeeper as she had helped the maids serve Lord Dravenwood his supper. It might have been her imagination, but he had seemed even more smug than usual. She had turned more than once to catch him watching her from beneath those ridiculously long lashes of his, a speculative gleam in his smoky gray eyes.

Performing her final duties of the day had sapped the last of her strength. She'd helped the maids clean up the kitchen, then sent them off to bed while she prepared the dough for the next morning's bread. Leaving the loaves to rise beneath a clean cloth, she'd made one last circuit of the downstairs to make sure every candle and lamp had been extinguished.

As she passed through the servants' quarters, the sound of bellicose snoring drifted out of Hodges's room. When he had refused to come out from the cabinet earlier, she had wanted nothing more than to strangle him with her bare hands. But as she peeked into his room to find him tucked safely in his nest of quilts with just a tuft of white hair visible, she was flooded with a rush of helpless tenderness.

By the time she reached the steep stairs that led to her own attic room, her eyelids were already drooping. On nights like this, it seemed as if she could climb forever and the staircase would never end. The wind was moaning mournfully around the eaves, and the chill hanging in the air seemed to deepen with each step she took. Hoping to lessen the time it would take to wash up and crawl beneath her blanket, she unbuttoned the first three buttons of her bodice, tugged the net from her hair, and began to pull out her hairpins, dropping them into the pocket of her apron.

Just as she pushed open the door, an enormous yawn seized her. She covered her mouth and closed her eyes. When she opened them, she was standing on the threshold of a dream.

# Chapter Twenty-three

ANNE BLINKED IN WONDER, thinking for a dazed instant that she must somehow have stumbled into the wrong room. But there was no room like this in Cadgwyck Manor.

There hadn't been for a long time.

A cheerful fire crackled on the grate, sending out waves of warmth to envelop her and draw her deeper into the attic. The wooden bedstead was the same as it had been that morning when she had stiffly climbed out of it, but her ancient mattress had been replaced with a fluffy feather tick draped in a plush down comforter. The pewter candlestick on the side table had been shoved aside to make room for an oil lamp. The lamp's cut-glass, ruby-hued shade cast a rosy glow over the room. A stack of handsome, leatherbound books with gilt-edged pages now accompanied her worn copy of *Pilgrim's Progress*.

A luxurious Turkish rug had been laid beside the bed, as if to protect her feet from the cold when she first arose, while a pair of green velvet drapes had been hung over the window to keep the worst of the drafts at bay. A small, round table fitted with a single chair sat in front of the hearth—the perfect place to enjoy a private supper after a long day of work. There was even a plump ottoman where she might prop her aching feet.

Anne recognized almost every item in the room. They had all been pilfered from other chambers in the house. The attic now looked more like a lady's sitting room than a housekeeper's quarters.

But she was no lady.

She drifted toward the washstand, bewitched by the tendrils of steam she could see wending their way into the air. As if in a trance, she lifted the ceramic pitcher and poured a stream of heated water into the basin. She would have liked nothing more than to splash the water on her face, to surrender to the tantalizing temptation of having someone look after her after so many years of looking after herself and everyone around her.

But as she lifted her eyes from the basin, she realized one thing in the room had not changed. The oval looking glass still hung behind the washstand. Steam misted the looking glass, softening her reflection, turning back the clock and erasing all of the lonely years until the only features she recognized were the eyes gazing back at her.

And the helpless longing within them. A longing only intensified by the spicy, masculine scent of bayberry soap still lingering in the air.

WHEN ANNE REACHED HER employer's bedchamber, she didn't even bother to knock. She simply shoved open the door and stormed inside. Fortunately, Lord Dravenwood's bed curtains had been tied back with gold cords to welcome in the heat from the fire crackling on his grate. She didn't even have to whisk them aside or rip them clear off the canopy to find him.

He was propped up on the pillows reading by candlelight, a pair of incongruous wire-framed spectacles perched low on his nose. He glanced up, his gaze mildly curious, as she closed the door behind her so as not to rouse the rest of the house.

She marched across the chamber and halted at the foot of the four-poster. "How *dare* you go into my room without my leave?" she demanded, her chest heaving with fury. "I suppose it wasn't enough for you to paw through the belongings of some poor dead girl. You had to go and poke your aristocratic nose into *my* business as well. Tell me—are you so very arrogant, so very presumptuous, so very convinced of your own natural-born superiority, that you believe those in your employ aren't entitled to even a dollop of privacy? Some humble space they can call their own?" He opened his mouth, but closed it again when he realized she had only paused to suck in an outraged breath. "If that's what you believe, you are sorely mistaken. You may own this house, my lord. *But you do not own me!*"

He cocked one eyebrow, calmly surveying her over the top of the spectacles. "Are you quite through, Mrs. Spencer?"

An icy-hot wave of horror and despair washed over Anne as she realized what she had done. She had allowed herself to fly into a full-blown tantrum, losing the temper she'd fought so hard to keep for so long.

And now everyone she loved would suffer for her failings.

"I suppose I am," she said stiffly, her voice stripped of all emotion except for regret. "There's no need for you to dismiss me, my lord. I shall tender my resignation first thing in the morning."

Dravenwood drew off the spectacles and laid them aside, along with his book. "Had I wanted to be rid of you, I'd have continued to let you sleep in that inhospitable crypt you insist upon calling a bedchamber. I'm sure it would have only been a matter of time before you succumbed to consumption or a fatal ague. Then you and Miss Cadgwyck could have taken turns haunting me."

Anne's ire had subsided just enough for her to realize she was standing in a gentleman's bedchamber in the middle of the night. A gentleman who didn't appear to be wearing anything but the sheet drawn up to the taut planes of his abdomen. A silk dressing gown was draped over the foot of the bed, confirming her worst suspicions.

With his naked chest hers for the ogling, there didn't seem to be anywhere else to look. Anne had heard some gentlemen were forced to pad their coats and wear a corset of sorts to achieve the broad-shouldered, narrow-waisted look so favored by fashion these days. Lord Dravenwood was *not* one of those men. His chest was well muscled and lightly furred with the same dark hair that dusted the back of his hands. Anne's hands itched with the pagan desire to rake her fingertips through it, to see if it felt as soft, yet crisp, as it looked.

He cleared his throat. She jerked her gaze back up to his face, her cheeks heating with mortification to have been caught gawking.

He might be a guarded man, but there was no mistaking the gleam of amusement in his eyes. "I'm afraid you have me at a disadvantage, Mrs. Spencer. Had I known I would be receiving a female caller who hadn't been dead for a decade, I would have dressed—or undressed—with more care."

He was eyeing her with frank appreciation. She had forgotten all about yanking the pins from her hair and unbuttoning the first few buttons of her bodice as she climbed the stairs to her room.

Her hair was half-up and half-down, a thick, curling rope of it hanging over one shoulder. Her gown was no longer buttoned up to her chin, but was gaping open to reveal the worn lace of her chemise and a creamy slice of cleavage. She probably looked as if she'd just crawled out of a man's bed.

Or was about to crawl into one.

She snatched her collar closed at the throat with one hand, hoping to hide the silver locket nestled between her breasts from his piercing gaze. "I should have knocked. But then again," she added sweetly, "I'm sure you can understand just how much easier it is to barge in where you haven't been invited and aren't welcome."

"Just so you know, I did knock when I came to your room."

"When no one answers, it's customary to go away and return at another time, not refurbish their abode to your own tastes."

A dangerous glitter dawned in his eyes. "I would have refurbished it to your tastes, but I was fresh out of sackcloth and ashes."

Anne swallowed. If she hadn't let her anger get the best of her, she would have recognized coming here would be a terrible mistake. "Some of us are not so easily seduced by creature comforts."

"You have a lot of nerve reproaching me for wallowing in my self-condemnation when you've confined yourself to a cell like some sort of criminal or penitent nun. Tell me, Mrs. Spencer, just what terrible sins have you committed that would require such sacrifice? Are you hoping to atone for them by freezing yourself to death?"

Stung by the sharp lash of truth in his words, she snapped, "My sins are of no more concern to you than where I sleep at night. You had no right to meddle. I was perfectly content with things the way they were."

"Is that all you believe you deserve from life? Contentment? What about satisfaction? Joy?" Dravenwood tilted his head to survey her, his voice deepening on a husky note that sent a treacherous little shiver cascading through her. "Passion? Pleasure?"

"All luxuries reserved for those of your class, my lord. We humble servants are expected to find our satisfaction in duty, loyalty, sacrifice, obedience."

"Obedience?" A skeptical bark of laughter escaped him. "No wonder you seem so dissatisfied."

Anne could feel her temper rising again. "You're

a fine one to lecture me on the benefits of joy and pleasure. I'd wager you can't remember the last time you experienced either one. You squandered your youth loving a woman who could never love you back just so you could keep your heart safely walled behind the blocks of ice you've built to protect it. All Angelica did was replace that golden idol in your heart. You'd rather pine for a ghost than risk loving a woman fashioned from flesh and blood."

*A woman such as her.*

Shaken by that treacherous whisper of her heart, Anne spun around and retraced her steps to the door. "I should have never come here. I should have known reasoning with you would prove to be impossible."

The rustle of Dravenwood tossing back the sheets and yanking on his dressing gown was Anne's only warning. Before she could open the door more than a crack, he had crossed the chamber with the same predatory grace he had used to capture her on the night he'd gone ghost hunting. He slammed both palms against the door on either side of her head, shoving the door closed and leaving her with no choice but to stand there trembling in the circle of his arms as he embraced her without laying so much as a finger on her.

"You have every right to berate me for invading your privacy." His mouth was so close to her ear the warmth of his breath stirred the invisible dusting of hair along its lobe. "But you were wrong about one thing."

"And what would that be, my lord?" she whispered tautly, thankful he couldn't see her face in that moment.

"As long as I am master at Cadgwyck, you do belong to me." His bold claim sent a wicked little thrill shooting through her. "Your welfare is my concern and my responsibility. If you want to spend your nights lying in your lonely bed reading *Pilgrim's Progress* by candlelight until your eyesight fails, then by God you'll at least do it in warmth and comfort. Do we understand each other?"

Mustering every last ounce of her courage, Anne turned to face him. Still held captive by those muscular forearms and the imposing wall of his chest, she gazed up into the passion-darkened planes of his face. "Yes, my lord. I think we understand each other very well."

She didn't realize just how well until he cupped her face in his hands and brought his mouth down on hers. Hard. Her lips melted beneath his, softening the punishing force of his kiss with the aching tenderness of her surrender. His tongue accepted the invitation of her parted lips, licking into her with a sinuous hunger that coaxed a helpless little whimper from her lips.

Her hands drifted upward to clutch at his upper arms, sliding over the silk sleeves of his dressing gown to explore the firm swell of muscle beneath. She knew she should push him away, but all she wanted to do was tug him closer. To be enveloped in the heat radiating from every unyielding, masculine inch of him.

As his lips blazed a searing path from the corner of her mouth to the pulse beating madly at the side of her throat, she whispered, "Maximillian," cursing and blessing him in the same breath. If he had never come to Cadgwyck, she would never have known how lonely she'd been. How desperately she'd been craving a man's kiss, a man's touch. But not just any touch, she realized with a mingled thrill of joy and despair.

*His* touch.

"Anne." Her own name was a shuddering growl against the satiny skin of her throat. "My sweet, stubborn Anne."

Then his mouth was on hers again, the rough velvet of his tongue coaxing hers into joining the pagan dance until their mouths were as one. He wrapped an arm around her waist while his other hand combed the remaining pins from her hair, sending it tumbling around her shoulders in decadent disarray.

"You don't know how long I've wanted to do

that," he muttered against her lips before seizing her mouth once more for a deep, drugging kiss that seemed to have no end.

Anne might have slid right into a puddle of desire at his feet if he hadn't used his hips to bear her back against the door. She could feel the rigid outline of his arousal pressed against the softness of her belly even through her skirts and petticoats, showing her just how desperately he wanted her. She felt her womb clench at the primal power of it.

This had to stop. *She* had to stop.

But instead she lifted a hand to his hair, sliding her fingers through his thick, dark locks just as she had longed to do for so long. His hand drifted downward, tracing the graceful curve of her throat and the delicate arch of her collarbone before finally dipping into her unbuttoned bodice to claim the softness of one breast.

Anne gasped into his mouth. She had accused him of denying himself pleasure, but he certainly knew how to give it. That much was evident in the deft brush of his fingertips against the throbbing little bud of her nipple. He gently tugged, knowing just how much pressure to apply to keep pleasure from turning into pain.

That irresistible surge of delight shocked Anne back to her senses. She'd been fool enough to trust herself to a man's hands once before. She could not afford to do it again. Not when so much was at stake.

"I have to go, my lord," she murmured against his lips. "Coming here was a terrible mistake."

Dravenwood's hand went still against her breast, his long, masculine fingers still cupping its weight ever so gently. "I've made far more damning mistakes in my life. With far less reward."

She leaned back to peer up into his face. "What would you have me do? Sneak into your bed each night after the others are asleep? Slip away in the morning before the sun rises?"

He lifted both hands to smooth her hair back from her face, his quicksilver eyes heavy-lidded with passion, his voice hoarse with need. "At the moment I can think of nothing in all the world that I'd like more."

"I'm sorry, my lord. I'm not that woman. I can't be that woman." She closed her eyes and pressed her cheek to his chest to block out the sight of his hopeful face before whispering, "Not even for you."

His arms tightened around her, binding her to his heart with a fierce tenderness. For one bittersweet moment, it was enough to pretend that would be enough for them. That a simple embrace would satisfy the craving in both of their souls.

Even when they both knew it would never be enough.

"Are you certain this is what you want?" he asked, burying his mouth in the softness of her hair.

Anne nodded, her throat too tight with longing and regret for speech. For a breathless moment, she was torn between fearing he wasn't going to let her go and praying he wouldn't.

But then he stepped away from the door and her, setting her free to flee back to the cozy comforts of her lonely room.

FROM THAT DAY FORWARD, Anne would return to her attic each night to find a cheery fire crackling on the grate and a pitcher of hot water steaming on the washstand. Other treasures began to appear as well: a thick pair of new woolen stockings; some little cakes of French soap carved into the shapes of seashells; all three volumes of *Sense and Sensibility*, one of the novels she had adored as a young girl.

Had Dravenwood been any other man, she would have suspected him of trying to seduce her. But she had grown to know him well enough in the past few weeks to recognize that his gifts were given freely, without a price attached. He would never know how high their cost was to her yearning heart.

Anne's only satisfaction came when she would catch Beth or Betsy scurrying guiltily down the attic stairs as she trudged up them so she could mutter, "*Et tu, Brute*," at them beneath her breath. Unfortunately, neither of them spoke Latin. There was no need for a translator to interpret her accusing glare.

"We're never going to be rid of His Gracelessness, are we?" Pippa said darkly as they all gathered in the kitchen to prepare supper late one afternoon.

With every lamp and candle lit, the kitchen was even more cozy than usual. Clouds had been rolling in from the sea all day, bringing with them an early twilight and a gusty breeze scented with the threat of rain.

Pippa was wielding the pestle she was using to grind up some fresh parsley as if it were a cudgel. "He's going to die of old age right here in his bed. A bed whose linens I was forced to change."

"Oh, I don't know," Dickon said, an amiable grin lighting his freckled face. He was perched on the edge of the kitchen hearth, an iron kettle propped between his knees. He was in such good spirits he hadn't even complained about being tasked to scour out the kettle with handfuls of sand. "I'm starting to think he's not such a bad sort after all. Why, just yesterday he asked if I'd take him down to the cove and show him the sea caves. And he's talking about having the stable repaired and bringing in one of them fancy phaetons and some horses. *Real* horses, not just wild moor ponies."

Anne kept her attention studiously fixed on the plate she was preparing. "I wouldn't grow too attached to him if I were you, Dickon. Even without our *encouragement,* he'll doubtlessly tire of the provincial country life soon enough and long to return to the excitement of London."

Pippa shot her a resentful look. "Angelica certainly hasn't been of much help lately. I'm beginning to think she fancies him for herself."

"Angelica has had ten long years to learn patience," Anne replied tartly. "She simply knows how to bide her time."

What Anne couldn't tell Pippa was that she didn't think they would even need Angelica to drive Dravenwood away. She was perfectly capable of doing that all on her own. By denying him the thing he most wanted, she had made it nearly impossible for him to stay at Cadgwyck.

She could not quite squelch a thrill of pride as she gazed down upon her creation. She'd given up trying to starve Dravenwood out of Cadgwyck and started feeding him the same dishes she prepared for the rest of them. Tonight's meal consisted of a miniature hen Dickon had snared in one of his traps, its succulent skin browned and crisped to perfection, roasted potatoes swimming in a sea of butter, and a salad of greens she'd grown herself in the manor garden.

"Have you finished filling up the saltcellar?" she asked Hodges.

"Almost!" he sang out. He was hunched over the end of the long table, pouring a stream of salt into a chipped crystal bowl. His childlike smile made Anne's heart clench.

There was no denying his condition was deteriorating. Rapidly. Anne had learned that assigning him some simple task served the twofold purpose of making him feel useful and keeping him out of mischief.

Bess and Lisbeth came bustling into the kitchen. "The master's at table," Lisbeth informed Anne, while Bess fetched a silver tray from the cupboard and set it in front of Anne.

Anne placed the china plate on the tray, then arranged some freshly polished cutlery and a snowy-white linen serviette to compliment it. The last addition was a loaf of bread fresh from the oven.

"Just a minute!" she cried as Lisbeth held open the door so Bess could carry the heavy tray through it. Anne hurried over to whisk the saltcellar out from under Hodges's nose, then plunked it down on the tray.

As the maids disappeared through the door with their burden, Anne sank down on one of the benches flanking the table, wondering what Dravenwood would make of her meal.

For reasons she didn't care to examine, it was a pleasure to imagine him eating the food she had prepared—his strong, white teeth sinking into the crisp, juicy skin of the hen, his tongue curling around the buttery goodness of the potatoes.

She was still lost in that agreeable image when Hodges said, "I've always heard there's only one way to rid one's home of vermin."

Distracted by her wayward thoughts, Anne murmured, "Hmm? What was that, dear?"

"Won't be any rats dying in their beds of old age in *my* house."

Pippa's pestle froze in midmotion. Dickon slowly stood, his grin fading. Anne turned to look down the length of the table. Hodges was dusting off his hands, looking extremely pleased with himself.

Only then did Anne spot the glass bottle sitting in front of him—a brown medicine bottle with a black skull and scarlet crossbones emblazoned on its label.

"Dear God," she whispered, horror chilling her blood to ice. "It's not salt."

# *Chapter Twenty-four*

*D*ICKON TOOK OFF FOR the door at a dead run, but Anne still beat him to it. Lifting the hem of her heavy skirts to keep them from tripping her, she went pelting down the endless corridors of the basement and up the stairs to the main floor of the manor. In her mind's eye, she could already see Dravenwood slumped over his plate, his mighty heart laboring harder with each sluggish beat, his piercing gray eyes slowly losing their focus. By the time she finally reached the dining room, her own heart was on the verge of imploding in her chest.

Lisbeth and Bess were just returning through the dining-room door with empty hands, laughing and talking among themselves. Ignoring their startled cries, Anne shoved her way past them and into the dining room.

Dravenwood was gazing down at his meal with obvious pleasure, his fingers poised to add a generous pinch of salt to it. As the crystals rained down from his fingers to dust his food, Anne lunged across the room and used one arm to sweep everything in front of him off the table.

It hit the floor with an explosion of china and crockery, spattering food everywhere, including over the freshly polished leather of his boots.

Silence descended over the room. Lisbeth and Bess stood frozen in the doorway, gawking at Anne as if she'd gone stark raving mad.

Dravenwood slowly lifted his gaze from the carnage on the floor to her face. "Is there something I should know, Mrs. Spencer?" he inquired, the gentleness of his tone belied by the suspicious gleam in his eyes.

Fighting to steady her breathing, Anne tucked a fallen tendril of hair behind her ear, then wiped her sweat-dampened palms on her apron. "Nothing of any import, my lord. Dickon just realized there was a chance the hen might be rancid."

"Indeed."

Anne hadn't even known it was possible for a single word to convey such withering skepticism. Fixing a shaky smile on her lips, she frantically beckoned the maids back into the room. "Don't mind the mess. Lisbeth and Bess will get it all cleaned up while I fix you a nice mutton sandwich."

Although he didn't utter another word, Anne

could feel the steady weight of his gaze following her from the room, as inescapable as the coming storm.

IT WASN'T HIS HOUSEKEEPER who visited Max in his bedchamber that night, but his ghost.

Max had almost given up on her. He had been on the verge of being forced to accept Angelica Cadgwyck was no more real than the naughty nymphs and big-bosomed mermaids who had haunted his boyhood fantasies.

But that was before he felt her lips gently brush his brow, then drift lower to graze the corner of his mouth with bewitching tenderness. He turned his head to fully capture her kiss. He had no intention of letting her escape him this time.

Wrapping his arms around her, he tumbled her into his embrace and his bed. Rolling over, he trapped her beneath him, breathing in the sweetness of her sigh in the heartbeat before his lips descended on hers. She tasted like warm, ripe berries on a hot summer day. Like cool rain watering the parched sands of the Moroccan desert.

He tangled his fingers in the silky skein of her curls, thrusting his tongue deep into the lush sweetness of her mouth. His hips were already moving against hers in an ancient rhythm. The heat roiling off his naked flesh melted away the gauzy skein of silk she was wearing until nothing was left to keep them apart. Not fear. Not time.

Not even death. He entered her in one smooth thrust, his soul singing in tune with his body.

She was here. She was real.

And she was his.

Until a gunshot rang out, snatching her away.

Max sat straight up in the bed, biting off a savage oath to find himself alone. He had been dreaming again. A dream so real it had left his body hard and aching for a woman who had died a decade ago.

He shoved aside the bed curtains and swung his legs over the side of the bed. Ever since he had learned about Timberlake's treachery, he had been haunted by another image of Angelica as well—Timberlake shoving her down on the window seat of the tower, his cruel fingers biting into her tender flesh. Timberlake's sneering mouth descending on hers to smother her screams for help.

He had wanted answers, but those weren't the answers he had wanted. He would rather continue to believe Angelica had simply succumbed to the artist's seduction, that she had stepped off the edge of that cliff still believing Timberlake was a romantic hero who had died adoring her.

Max dropped his aching head into his hands. He supposed he ought to be grateful he had slept long enough to dream. Ever since Anne had come barging into his bedchamber, he had spent most of his nights tossing and turning until the wee hours of the morning. His sulking body still hadn't forgiven him for letting her go. His body didn't seem to care that she was his housekeeper, only that she was warm and alive and had more substance than a wisp of mist.

He had previously discovered she was capable of delivering a fine scold, but he hadn't realized until that night that she could work herself into such a magnificent fury. Her ire had brought a most becoming sparkle to her hazel eyes and a healthy flush of color into her alabaster cheeks. With the soft swell of her breasts straining to overflow the confines of her bodice and that provocative curl tumbling out of its pins and over one shoulder, she had borne little resemblance to the prim and proper housekeeper with starch in her spine and vinegar running through her veins. He might have been able to dismiss her dramatic transformation if he hadn't been fool enough to leave his bed and corner her at the door.

He was still unsettled by her peculiar behavior in the dining room. Angelica might not be real, but the panicked guilt in Anne's eyes most definitely was.

Perhaps the time had come for him to admit he didn't belong in this place. There was nothing to hold him here, nothing to stop him from packing his valise and slipping away before daybreak. Wouldn't it be better to let the villagers mock him as a coward driven from his own house by a ghost than to waste another minute of his life being haunted by not one, but *two* women, neither of whom he could ever have? Somehow Anne and Angelica had become inextricably bound in his imagination.

And his heart.

He could send for the rest of his things in the morning, then return to London and his position with the Company. He could allow his parents to choose a suitable bride for him and settle down to produce an heir and the requisite spare. He could sleep soundly through the night, never again troubled by mysterious laughter or dreams that left him aching for a passion he would never know.

How would Anne feel when she found his bed empty and his things gone? he wondered. Would she rejoice? Would she gather the other servants around her to celebrate vanquishing another unwanted master? Or would she miss him just the tiniest bit? Would she lie in her narrow bed with the cold winter winds moaning around the eaves of her attic and remember the man who had wanted only to warm her?

A sullen rumble rattled the house. Max slowly lifted his head. It wasn't the ghostly echo of a pistol being fired that had robbed him of his dream lover after all, but a sharp crack of thunder heralding the arrival of the storm that had been brooding over the manor all day. Fat drops of rain began to pelt the French windows. A flash of lightning illuminated the room.

Max's breath froze in his throat. Angelica hadn't abandoned him after all.

Although the French windows remained closed and latched, a sinuous ribbon of mist was twining its way through the room. Max watched in open-mouthed fascination as it drifted this way and that before rising to coalesce beside the bed.

As he waited for the lithe female curves to gain shape and substance, he drew in an uneven breath, expecting it to be perfumed with the sultry aroma of jasmine. Instead, a choking cloud filled his lungs with the acrid stench of gunpowder and brimstone.

A wracking cough doubled him over. He blinked away a stinging rush of tears, realizing it wasn't mist seeping steadily beneath his bedchamber door, but deadly ribbons of smoke.

# Chapter Twenty-five

$\mathcal{M}$ AX SPRANG OUT OF the bed and rushed across the room to snatch a shirt and a pair of trousers out of the armoire. There was no time to seek out the source of the fire and try to extinguish it. As ancient and as full of rotting wood as the manor was, it could go up like a tinderbox in minutes. He grabbed a monogrammed handkerchief from his dressing table. He dipped it into his washbasin to soak up as much water as it could hold, then pressed it over his mouth and nose before yanking open the door.

Billowing clouds of smoke crowded the corridor. A flickering glow emanated from the direction of the entrance hall. Ignoring his instinctive urge to sprint down the two flights of stairs and straight out the front door, Max took off in the opposite direction, heading for the back staircase leading up to the servants' quarters. The smoke made the darkness even more impenetrable, but the fitful flashes of lightning striking the windows guided his steps. Perhaps a bolt of it had struck the house and ignited the fire.

He shot up the steps, his father's smug voice echoing in his ears: *Servants should always be quartered on the highest floor. Should the house catch fire, they won't be underfoot while you're trying to collect your valuables and escape.*

In his mind's eye, all could see was Anne nestled beneath her cozy down comforter, enjoying a blissful slumber with no idea her attic room was about to be engulfed by a raging inferno from which there would be no escape.

By the time Max reached the fourth floor, the smoke had thinned out a little. He shoved the damp handkerchief in the pocket of his trousers. The steady drumming of the rain on the slate shingles could easily drown out the sound of crackling flames from below.

He made a beeline for Dickon's room. He snatched the boy up by his shoulders, yanking him out of the bed and clear off his feet. "Listen to me, lad! There's a fire downstairs. I need you to get the girls up and out of the house. I'll meet you by the back gate to help you with Nana. And Tinkles. And Mr. Furryboots," he added, thinking how displeased Anne would be with him if he let her precious pets perish.

Dickon's head bobbed up and down like a rag doll's, his eyes as wide as saucers. "Yes, s-s-sir . . . I mean, His Graciousness . . . I mean . . ."

"Go!" Max shouted, lowering Dickon to his feet and shoving him in the direction of the door.

Dickon took off for Pippa's room while Max strode toward the steep stairs at the far end of the corridor. As he passed the other rooms, he noted that the Elizabeths had already began to stir, but Hodges's rumpled bed was empty.

Max took the attic stairs two at a time. He gave the door at the top of the stairs an impatient push, expecting it to swing open at his touch as it had before.

The door was locked.

Swearing out loud, he lifted one bare foot and kicked the door clean off its bottom hinge. As it listed crazily, Anne bolted upright in the bed.

Max crossed the room in two long strides and scooped her into his arms, comforter and all.

Still half-asleep, she blinked up at him, her tousled braids making her look even younger than Pippa. "Forgive me, my lord. I didn't hear you ring."

He gave her a brief, but fierce, squeeze, cherishing the solid feel of her weight in his arms. "The manor is on fire. I need to get you downstairs."

"Fire?" Panic flared in her eyes as she came fully awake. "What about Dickon? Pippa? Hodges? Put me down this instant! I have to warn the others!" She began to struggle against his embrace, fighting to get to her feet.

"They're all safe," he promised, feeling a twinge of conscience as he remembered Hodges's empty bed. "Just hang on to me, damn it all, and you will be, too! Please . . ." When she continued to struggle, he added fiercely, "Anne."

She stilled, blinking up at him in obvious surprise. He expected her to argue, as was her nature, but after a brief hesitation, she looped her arms around his neck, holding on for dear life. Her trust in him gave his heart a curious little wrench.

They were halfway down the stairs when she cried, "Wait! My locket!" When he glared at her in disbelief, she gave him a beseeching look. "Please . . . Maximillian."

"Where is it?" he growled, infuriated to discover he had no defenses against that look or the sound of his name on her lips.

"Back of the door."

Max snatched the locket from the peg on the back of the dangling door, dropped its chain over her head, then carried her swiftly down the attic stairs. His confidence in Dickon had not been misplaced. The servants' quarters were deserted, the doors standing open to reveal scattered bedclothes abandoned in desperate haste.

They descended the back stairs to the third floor to find the smoke much thicker and blacker than when Max had climbed them. A fit of coughing wracked Anne's slender body.

Bracing her weight against the wall with one arm, Max tugged the handkerchief from his pocket and shoved it into her hand. "Press it over your mouth and nose."

"What about you?"

"I'll be fine," he promised her grimly, hoping he was right.

Since he didn't care for the idea of hauling her blindly down that narrow back staircase into a potential inferno, he started across the third floor, heading for the main stairs. If he could get a clear look at the entrance hall, at least he would know what they were up against.

Thunder cracked and lightning flashed as Max sprinted across the length of the house. The smoke seemed to pursue them, snaking through the corridors and down the stairs to the second-floor gallery like a dragon's tail looking for an ankle to seize. Time seemed to swell until it felt as if it had been hours instead of only minutes since Max had bolted up the stairs to rescue Anne.

The view from the gallery brought Max up short. There could be no mistaking the hellish glow or the hungry crackle of flames coming from the drawing room. Smoke was billowing through the arched doorway and into the entrance hall, but a clear path from the foot of the main staircase to the front door still remained. When Anne lowered the handkerchief and tried to peer over the banister, Max cradled the back of her head in his hand, gently urging her face into his chest, and took off at a dead run.

The second-floor gallery seemed to grow longer with each jarring step, but they finally reached the landing. From her gilt frame Angelica watched them fly past her and down the steps, her gaze as coolly amused as ever. Max felt a sharp stab of regret at the thought of leaving her to perish in the flames. But all that truly mattered to him now was the woman clinging to his neck.

They were almost across the entrance hall when a tremendous crash of glass sounded from the drawing room, followed by a rousing cheer.

"What the hell?" Max muttered.

He swept open the front door just in time to see a heap of flaming draperies go sailing through the drawing-room window to land in the overgrown courtyard. They lay there, hissing and steaming as the pouring rain quickly squelched the worst of the flames.

Max and Anne exchanged a baffled glance. Since the smoke had ceased its billowing with no sign of any fresh flames leaping through the window, Max slowly retraced his steps until they stood in the doorway of the drawing room.

Dickon and Pippa were hanging half out the window, admiring the results of their handiwork, while the maids hugged one another in the corner behind the settee, their faces wreathed in smiles of relief.

Max cleared his throat.

Dickon and Pippa swung around to face him, the soot blacking their faces making their triumphant grins seem that much more dazzling. Stray embers had scorched holes in their nightclothes. They looked like a pair of cheeky chimney sweeps.

Max glared at Dickon. "What in the bloody hell did you do, boy? I thought I told you to get the women out of the house."

Dickon's grin lost none of its cockiness. "We were running past the drawing room when I saw it was the drapes all ablaze. We thought if we could get them out the window, the rain would douse the flames. So Pippa hurled a coal bucket through the glass, then I used a poker to drag down the drapes and stuff them through the hole."

Max surveyed the carnage through the lingering haze of smoke hanging over the room. The window frame had already began to buckle from the heat. The flames had shot up the wall above the drapery rod, blistering the paint and blackening the crown molding and a large section of ceiling. Another few minutes and the entire room would have gone up in flames, taking the rest of the manor with it.

Anne began to wriggle in earnest. This time there was no stopping her and she slid out of his arms and went rushing across the room to Dickon and Pippa, leaving Max holding the empty comforter. "You fools! You silly, brave little fools! Why, I ought to box both your ears and send you to bed without supper!"

Dickon and Pippa exchanged a glance before saying in unison, "We've already had supper."

"Then I ought to send you to bed without breakfast!"

Max watched in fascination as Anne burst into tears, threw her arms around them both, and took turns smothering their ash-flaked hair with kisses. He'd never seen a housekeeper quite so devoted to her staff.

When Anne finally lifted her face, it was streaked with both tears and ashes. She gazed up at the charred ceiling, shaking her head in disbelief. "I don't understand. How could such a thing have happened?"

Dickon crouched down, using the poker to sift through the still-smoking debris beneath the window. With a dull clang the poker struck something heavy. A blackened silver candlestick came rolling slowly across the floor toward Max's feet.

The bewilderment in Anne's expression deepened, mingled with burgeoning horror. "But I snuffed all the candles before going up to bed. I swear I did! Checking the lamps and candles is the last duty I do each night before I retire."

"I left it burning for her." They all turned as Hodges came drifting through the door that led to the shadowy dining room, looking like a ghost himself with his unfocused eyes and long, white nightshirt. His snowy hair was standing straight up around his head in a disheveled halo. "I told her not to go walking along the cliffs on such a night, but she wouldn't listen. She was always so headstrong. I thought if I left a candle burning in the window, she'd be able to find her way back. I've been waiting so long for her to return. So very long . . ." His voice trailed off in a mournful sigh and he began to hum.

Max's nape prickled as he recognized the off-key notes of the melody from the music box in the tower.

"Oh, darling," Anne whispered, her face crumpling into a mask of pity and pain. She went to the old man, gently folding him into her arms. He buried his face in the crook of her neck, his slumped shoulders beginning to heave with silent sobs. "There, there," she murmured, patting him on the back. "It was just an oversight. I know you didn't mean to hurt anyone."

Struck by the full enormity of what might have happened if the thunder hadn't awakened him from his dreams of Angelica, Max felt his compassion ebbing and his anger rising. Tossing the comforter aside, he said, "I want that man out of here."

Hodges lifted his head. He and Anne both stared at Max as if he had just suggested they sacrifice a kitten on the front lawn.

"You can't mean it," she said. "It was nothing but a simple mistake. I'm sure he had no intention of—"

"*He almost killed you!*" Max's shout echoed through the drawing room, louder than any clap of thunder. "Us," he amended, feeling the curious gazes of the others settle on him. "He almost burned us all to death in our beds. He's a danger to himself and to everyone around him. I want him out of this house first thing in the morning."

Hodges cowered in Anne's arms, his quivering lower lip making Max feel like the worst sort of bully. But he wasn't about to relent this time. Not when so much was at stake, Max thought, his gaze straying to Anne's pale, ash-streaked face.

She gently extracted herself from Hodges's grip and stepped in front of the butler, drawing herself up as if she were armored in far more than just a soot-stained nightdress and a disheveled pair of braids. She lifted her chin, her gaze openly defiant. "If he goes, I go."

Max knew exactly what was expected of him then. It had been ingrained into his character from the day he'd been born. He was master of this house. He might be able to tolerate a bit of teasing insubordination, but a full-out mutiny—especially in front of the other servants—was grounds for immediate dismissal. His housekeeper had left him with no choice but to send her packing along with his butler and without so much as a letter of recommendation to guarantee her a chance at another position.

He opened his mouth, then closed it again, glowering at her for a long moment before snapping, "In my study. *Now.*"

# Chapter Twenty-six

*L*ORD DRAVENWOOD TURNED ON his heel and strode from the room, the beautifully carved planes of his face making him look positively demonic in the flicker of the lightning dancing through the broken window. Anne could already feel her courage starting to falter.

She gave Hodges a gentle shove in Pippa's direction, her eyes silently pleading with the girl. "Look after him."

Pippa nodded, looking far more worried about Anne's fate than the butler's.

Anne followed Dravenwood up the stairs, each measured step making her feel more as if she were following a black-hooded executioner to the gallows. Her alarm mounted when he didn't even waste a yearning glance on Angelica as he strode past her portrait.

When they reached the door of the study, he stood aside to let her pass, still every inch the gentleman despite his bare feet, sleep-tousled hair, and murderous expression. His ivory shirt was unfastened at the throat, and Anne felt her cheeks heat as she brushed past him and noted that the top two buttons of his trousers were also undone.

He followed her into the room. She expected him to slam the door behind them, but he closed it with such deliberate care it sent a delicate shiver of foreboding down her spine.

She stood awkwardly in the middle of the room while he lit the lamp sitting on the corner of his desk. The drapes were drawn, giving them a cozy reprieve from the jagged bursts of lightning and pouring rain.

Anne was halfway hoping he would retreat to his favorite sanctuary behind the desk, placing an impenetrable shield between them. Instead, he leaned against the front of it, folding his arms over his chest and crossing his feet at the ankles. The cool and composed Mrs. Spencer seemed to have deserted Anne, leaving her standing before this powerful man in nothing but her nightdress, her hair escaping from her braids in untidy brown wisps.

She forced herself to meet his level gaze. "Perhaps it would be best if we spoke of this in the morning after tempers—and passions—have cooled."

"Ah, but I think we both know there's not much chance of that, now is there, Mrs. Spencer?" he drawled.

So she was back to being Mrs. Spencer again, was she? When he had begged her to remain in his arms, her Christian name had sounded like a promise on his lips.

"I'm certain Hodges didn't mean any harm," she began, choosing her words with care. "It was nothing but an accident."

"It was the careless act of a maniac. If you're not worried about your own well-being—or mine— then perhaps you should stop and think about what would have happened had that fire cut off escape from the servants' quarters. Or if Pippa and Dickon had failed in their foolish efforts to extinguish it and set themselves ablaze instead."

Anne could feel her face blanch. She'd never seen Dravenwood's striking features set in such pitiless lines. "I'll give Hodges a stern talking-to first thing in the morning," she vowed. "We'll all be more vigilant in the future when it comes to keeping an eye on—"

"Just who was keeping an eye on him tonight when my supper was being prepared?"

A blade of ice pierced Anne's heart as she relived that terrible moment when she had seen the skull and crossbones on the bottle and feared it might be too late to save Dravenwood. "How did you know it was poison?" she whispered.

The corner of his mouth curled in a victorious little smile. "I didn't. Until just now."

Infuriated by his trickery, she glared at him. "It was an honest mistake on Hodges's part. He thought we'd charged him with ridding the manor of rats."

"How do I know it was all Hodges's doing? If you hadn't knocked my supper off the table in such a timely manner, I might suspect you were willing to let the poor deranged fellow do your dirty work for you. For all I know, you simply suffered a belated qualm of conscience. Or didn't want to risk your pretty little neck being stretched on the gallows."

She was so caught off guard by the unexpected compliment it took a minute for his words to sink in. "Are you accusing me of trying to *murder* you?"

"Don't try to tell me the thought hasn't crossed your mind."

Exasperated beyond bearing, she snapped, "I'm sure the thought has crossed the mind of everyone who has ever made your acquaintance!"

A muscle in his jaw twitched, although whether from fury or amusement she could not tell. "I'm growing weary of your secrets and lies, Mrs. Spencer. While I'm deciding whether or not to fetch the constable, perhaps you'd like to share if it was you or Hodges who shoved your former master out the window? Or did Angelica do it in a fit of the sulks?"

Anne's mouth fell open as he continued.

"I've never given much credence to rumors, having been the subject of them more often than not. But after suffering so many near-death experiences since my arrival at Cadgwyck, I'm beginning to think the villagers might be either more or less superstitious than I first believed."

Tearing her guilty gaze away from his accusing one, Anne sank down in the chair in front of the desk. She was fully prepared to offer up some easily digested lie, but to her own surprise, when she opened her mouth, the truth emerged. She'd become such an accomplished liar that her voice sounded rusty and unconvincing, even to her own ears. "I'm afraid Lord Drysdale fancied himself quite the lothario. Apparently, a doting mama had convinced him at a very young age that no woman in her right mind could resist the charms of a bandy-legged, overgrown toad. From the moment he arrived at the manor, he was a bit . . . how shall I say it? . . . overly *friendly* with his hands. He was always patting Lizzie on the rump when she bent over to add a log to the fire or peeping up Bess's skirts when she climbed on a stool to dust the top of a bookshelf."

Anne stole a look at Dravenwood from beneath

her lashes. He was watching her intently, his face revealing nothing.

"One night after indulging in a few too many after-dinner cordials, he climbed the stairs to the servants' quarters after everyone was abed and decided to creep into my room. I awoke with the stench of his breath in my face and shot up out of the bed, screaming at the top of my lungs. Startled out of his not particularly considerable wits by my less than welcoming response to his advances, he went stumbling backward, bleating like a stuck sheep. Unfortunately—for Lord Drysdale, that is—it was a warm spring night and my bedchamber window was standing wide open. We all agreed it was best just to tell the constable he rose in the middle of the night to use the convenience and took a wrong turn."

Rubbing her chilled arms through the thin sleeves of her nightdress, Anne gazed into her lap and waited for Lord Dravenwood's response. And waited. And waited. She was beginning to wonder if he had dozed off on his feet when she heard a strange sound.

She had expected him to express shock, horror, outrage, perhaps even sympathy, but the last sound she had expected was a deep rumble of a chuckle.

Her gaze flew to his face. He was openly laughing now, his grin making his eyes crinkle at the corners just as his brother's had done and erasing a world of care from his face. Anne's heart did a helpless little somersault. If the man believed women were only after him for his fortune and title, he was madder than Hodges.

When his mirth showed no sign of waning, she surged to her feet with an indignant sniff. "I'm glad you found my sordid little story so amusing."

"I'm not laughing at you. I'm laughing because the poor fool had the audacity to try to crawl into *your* bed."

That only made Anne feel *more* insulted. "You needn't mock me, my lord. I'm perfectly aware I'm no legendary beauty like Angelica Cadgwyck or your precious sister-in-law."

"Oh, I wasn't mocking you." His grin faded, the sparkle in his eyes deepening to a thoughtful glint that almost made her regret her indignation. "I was mocking him for being so foolish as to try to storm the bastion of our Mrs. Spencer's unassailable virtue." Dravenwood pushed himself off the corner of the desk, bringing them entirely too close to one another. "I've already learned what an impossible feat that is."

Anne knew it was her responsibility to put a more proper distance between them, but her feet seemed to be rooted to the floor. As he reached down to gently swipe a smudge of soot from her cheek with the broad pad of his thumb, she drew in a shuddering breath.

His palm lingered against her cheek while his thumb strayed into far more dangerous territory, grazing her parted lips, testing their softness. She gasped against the firmness of his flesh, unable to hide the devastating effect his touch had on her. He was a most difficult man. Yet he caressed her with an irresistible ease, as if he had been born to the task.

His sooty fringe of lashes swept down to shutter his eyes as he leaned forward and touched his cheek to her hair. "Mrs. Spencer?" The smoke had left his smooth baritone even deeper and more husky than usual.

"Anne," she corrected, her voice a tremulous sigh.

"If you're going to shove me out the window, you'd best do it now."

Anne's hands closed over his upper arms as if to push him away. But her hands were no more cooperative than her feet had been. All they would do was cling to him. "I didn't shove Lord Drysdale. He tumbled out quite of his own accord."

Dravenwood nuzzled her temple with his nose, breathing deeply of her scent as if she didn't smell of ash, but of some potent aphrodisiac he'd been seeking all his life. "I'm afraid I haven't the strength left to tumble out of my own accord. You'll have to do it for me."

Anne was tired of being the strong one. In that moment all she wanted to do was surrender to a strength and a will greater than her own. She wanted to be weak and wanton and foolish enough to make deplorable mistakes that would haunt her for the rest of her life.

And she wanted to do all of those things in this man's arms.

"I forgot to open the window, my lord."

"Max," he breathed into her mouth in the heartbeat before he touched his lips to hers.

That gentle, grazing caress was nearly her undoing. If she hadn't been able to dig her fingertips into the bunched muscles of his upper arms, she might have slid to her knees at his feet. Sipping softly at her lips only seemed to whet his thirst. He deftly deepened his kiss, coaxing the pliant petals of her lips apart with a tender, insistent mastery. She gasped as the warm, sleek velvet of his tongue swept through her mouth, claiming the nectar he found there for his own.

Without warning, the study door came crashing open. The two of them sprang apart. Anne could only pray she didn't look as flushed and guilty as she felt.

Pippa stood in the doorway, her agitation so great she probably wouldn't have noticed if Anne and the earl had been rolling about naked on the desk.

"What is it?" Anne demanded, her chagrin replaced by alarm.

Pippa's entire body was trembling and her dark eyes were brimming with tears. "It's Hodges. He's gone."

# *Chapter Twenty-seven*

RAVENWOOD SWORE.

"Gone?" Anne echoed frantically. "What do you mean he's *gone*? I told you to look after him."

Pippa drew in a shuddering breath. "He slipped away while I was helping Betsy roll up the drawing-room carpet. I only took my eyes off him for a moment. I swear it! I had no idea he would bolt the second I turned my back."

Anne struggled to digest the information, her mind racing. "How do you know he's not hiding somewhere in the house? Have you checked the dining-room cupboard?"

"He left the front door standing wide open."

Anne flinched as a violent clap of thunder shook the house, as if to remind them all that a storm still raged outside.

"Oh, dear God, the cliffs," she whispered. She

didn't realize she had swayed on her feet until Dravenwood cupped her elbow to steady her.

Pippa shook her head. "He didn't head for the cliffs. Dickon is almost positive he saw him running toward the moors during a flash of lightning. He's getting ready to go looking for him now."

"Like hell he is," Dravenwood growled, striding toward the door.

Pippa glared at the earl through her tears. She was crying in earnest now, her chest hitching with ragged sobs, her pretty face splotched with red. "This is all your fault! You're the one who said you wanted him gone! How could you be so heartless and cruel? Did you think he was deaf as well as daft?"

"You'll have ample time to berate me for my heartlessness later, child," Dravenwood said grimly, taking Pippa by the shoulders and setting her gently out of his path. "At the moment we have more important matters to attend to."

BY THE TIME THE three of them reached the entrance hall, Dickon was fully dressed and seated on the bench of the coat tree. He was tugging on a pair of careworn boots with a jagged hole in one toe, his lean face taut with determination.

The storm had only just begun to unleash the full force of its fury.

The rain had deepened to a torrential downpour while the wind hurtled rattling fistfuls of hail at the arched window above the door.

It made Anne's heart twist with helpless terror to imagine Hodges out there somewhere, wandering lost and alone.

"Fetch my overcoat and boots," Dravenwood commanded Betsy when he spotted the white-faced maids and Nana huddled in the doorway of the drawing room. When she hesitated, casting Anne a questioning look, he shouted, "Now!"

Betsy scurried past them and up the stairs to do his bidding.

Dickon rose to face them, squaring his thin shoulders and giving them all a fleeting glimpse of the man he would become. "Don't blame Pippa for letting him go. He was mine to watch as well. That's why I'm going to fetch him."

"Don't be ridiculous." Anne rushed to his side. "I can't bear to lose the both of you. He's my responsibility. I'll go."

Pippa sniffled. "I'm the one who lost him. I should be the one to go."

Dravenwood's voice cracked louder than the thunder. "In case all of you have forgotten, I am the master of this house. If anyone is going out in this hell's spawn of a night to look for Hodges, it's me."

"But I know the moors like the back of my own hand," Dickon protested. "I might even be able to catch one of the wild ponies and—"

"The only thing you're going to catch in this weather is your death of a cold," Dravenwood said.

Betsy came rushing back down the stairs with the earl's boots in hand and his overcoat draped over her arm.

"Dickon is right," Anne said, her heart swelling with panic. "You don't know the moors. They can be deadly during a storm."

Dravenwood sank down on the second stair to tug on his boots. "I survived a cholera outbreak in Burma, a sandstorm in the Tunisian desert, being jilted by my bride for my brother at the altar, and nearly being poisoned and burned to death in my bed by you and your motley little crew of minions. I have no intention of letting a little thunder and lightning or your blasted moor finish me off."

Dickon said, "But I—"

"*You* are not setting foot outside this house, young man." Max rose to yank on his overcoat. "You're going to stay right here and look after the women. *That's an order.*" Max turned to Anne. "If he tries to slip out after I'm gone, use those keys of yours to lock him in the pantry. Or the dungeon."

Dickon flung himself back down on the bench, returning the earl's glare with one of his own. Pippa moved to stand beside the boy, placing a hand on his shoulder in a rare show of solidarity.

By the time Max reached the door, Anne was waiting for him there.

Since she didn't dare touch him in front of the others, all she could do was reach up to correct the angle of his shoulder cape. "Take care, my lord. *Please.*"

He gazed down at her, the dangerous gleam in his eye warning her he was on the verge of doing something completely mad. Like drawing her into his arms in front of them all for a long, passionate kiss. "I'll bring him back to you. I swear it."

Leaving her with that vow, he swept open the door and ducked out into the storm.


ANNE PERCHED ON THE sill of the attic window, straining to see through the inky curtain of rain lashing the windowpanes. She had retreated to her bedchamber when she could no longer bear the stillness of the longcase clock in the entrance hall or the way everyone looked at her expectantly at every brief lull in the storm or noise from outside the manor. Noises that inevitably turned out to be the banging of a loose shutter or a splintered branch slamming into the side of the house.

The storm's rage was even more virulent up here. The attic shuddered and groaned beneath the battering fists of the wind. Anne could clearly hear each time a slate tile gave up the fight and went skittering off the roof.

But her window also provided the best view of the moor. As she watched, a jagged bolt of lightning rent the sky, illuminating the landscape for a precious fraction of a second. She pressed her nose to the glass, her pulse quickening with excitement. She would almost have sworn she had seen two figures in the far distance, grappling against the storm. But by the next flicker of lightning they were gone, leaving only the gnarled corpse of a tree and a standing stone where they had been.

Anne sank back against the window frame and gazed down at the candle flickering on the windowsill. Her eyelids were growing heavier, but every time she closed her eyes, she saw Dravenwood or Hodges lying facedown in some overflowing brook or flooded gully. She had ordered the maids to set a lamp in every window of the manor to serve as beacons, all the while knowing that anyone bold or foolish enough to brave the moor on a night such as this probably couldn't see more than a hand's length in front of their face.

She had briefly occupied her trembling hands by exchanging her soot-streaked nightdress for a plain gray gown and pinning up her hair, almost as if those commonplace rituals could help to temper the capricious nature of the storm. She lifted a hand to her throat, instinctively seeking comfort from her locket. She almost wished she had pressed it into Lord Dravenwood's hand before he had disappeared into the storm. He could have carried it as a knight would carry his lady's favor, using it as a talisman to guide him and Hodges back to Cadgwyck.

And back to her.

ANNE AWOKE WITH A guilty start and a painful crick in her neck. She must have dozed off without meaning to. The candle on the windowsill next to her had burned down to a stub. Its wick was on the verge of drowning in a pool of melted wax.

It took her a dazed moment to recognize the sound that had awakened her—silence.

Rubbing the crook between her neck and shoulder, she lifted her gaze to the window. The rain had departed with the night, taking the howling winds with it, but not the towering banks of clouds. Her mouth opened in a silent gasp. The destruction the storm had left behind was almost more terrifying than the storm itself. The somber dawn light revealed that one of the crumbling gateposts had tumbled the rest of the way over to block the drive.

The drive itself was almost completely washed away, reduced to muddy ruts overflowing with rushing water. Roof tiles were scattered everywhere she looked, and a window shutter torn clean away from the house lay splintered on the ground. Even the veils of ivy had been ripped away from the tower windows.

It was hard to imagine how anything—or anyone—could have survived such a night.

Refusing to surrender to such grim thoughts, Anne scrambled off the windowsill to fetch her cloak so she could go out hunting for Hodges and the earl herself. If she had to, she would throw herself on the mercy of the villagers and beg them to send out a search party. But then she caught a flicker of movement out of the corner of her eye.

She turned slowly back to the window, afraid to breathe, afraid to hope.

At first she thought it was a lone figure staggering toward the house. But then she realized it wasn't one man, but two. The taller of the pair had his arm braced beneath the shoulders of the second man and was all but carrying him. The taller man's tousled dark head hung between his broad shoulders. The visible effort it was taking for him to plant one foot in front of the other warned that any step could be his last.

Anne's heart leapt into her throat. Casting a

silent yet fervent prayer of thanksgiving heaven-ward, she blew out the candle and headed down the stairs.

THE DISTANCE BETWEEN THE attic and the entrance hall had never seemed so great. By the time Anne reached the front door, Dickon was already sweep-ing it open. They all poured down the portico steps, through the courtyard, and onto the front lawn. Even a beaming Nana joined them, Bess supporting the old woman's lumbering steps.

The thick mud sucked at Anne's half boots as she lifted the hem of her gown and went sprinting past Dickon, reaching the two men lurching their way up the remains of the drive before anyone else.

Dravenwood lifted his head to give her a weary but triumphant smile. Mud smudged his face, and a rapidly purpling bruise marred his temple. "I couldn't catch a pony but I did manage to catch a butler."

"Where in the name of God was he?" Anne asked, torn between laughter and tears.

"I searched for most of the night and finally found him near dawn curled up in a hollow tree less than a stone's throw from here, none the worse for wear."

Hodges was half-asleep on his feet and mumbling beneath his breath. As Dravenwood staggered beneath the butler's weight, Anne rushed forward to relieve him of his burden. She cradled Hodges in her arms while the rest of the servants gathered around them, laughing and chattering and slapping the bewildered butler on his shoulders and back.

All but forgotten by the others, Dravenwood stood there, still swaying on his feet. Anne hadn't realized just how much he had been depending on Hodges's stout form to balance him. Handing Hodges off into the waiting arms of Lizzie and Lisbeth, Anne gave Dickon a frantic hand signal. To her surprise, the earl didn't even protest when Dickon wrapped one lanky arm around him, supporting Dravenwood's weight much as Dravenwood had supported Hodges's.

Hodges might be none the worse for wear, but she couldn't say the same for the earl. He was soaked through to the skin. His hair was curled into sooty ringlets by the rainwater still dripping from its ends. The expensive doeskin of his trousers was torn to reveal a nasty gash on one shin. Although he was doing his best not to shiver in the dawn chill, the blue cast of his lips matched the shadows beneath his eyes.

Anne wanted nothing more than to wrap her arms around him and tuck him into a warm, dry bed herself, but instead she forced herself to briskly say, "Betsy, Beth, help Lord Dravenwood up to his bedchamber immediately. See that he gets a hot bath and some dry things before retiring."

"No," Dickon said resolutely, standing even taller than usual. "His lordship needs a manservant right now. I'll look after him."

Anne nodded. She had never before been quite so proud of the boy.

As he guided Dravenwood past her, she could not resist reaching out and catching the earl's hand in hers. His usually heated flesh felt cold and clammy to the touch. "Thank you for everything . . . my lord."

He nodded down at her, the ghost of a mocking smile playing around his lips. "Happy to be of service . . . Mrs. Spencer."

As the others drifted back toward the house, she stood there gazing after him. Her every breath seemed to draw her deeper into his debt. It was growing more and more difficult to convince herself the emotion she felt swelling in her heart every time she looked at him was simply gratitude.

SINCE THEY WERE ALL exhausted by the excitement of the fire and the storm and from keeping vigil through the long hours of the night, Anne gave the rest of the servants leave to sleep the morning away. As soon as Hodges and the earl were safely tucked in their beds, she stumbled up to her attic to do the same.

By afternoon, all of them except Lord Dravenwood were up and gathered around the table in the kitchen to enjoy some warm cocoa and discuss the storm. Humbled by his misadventure, Hodges seemed perfectly content to sit with Nana beside the fire, holding a skein of yarn wrapped around his hands while the old woman added another foot to her knitting.

Darkness was falling when Anne ordered Bess to take a tray of sandwiches up to Lord Dravenwood's bedchamber. When Bess returned to report that her knock on the earl's door had received no answer, Anne felt a wave of tenderness wash over her. "Leave him be, then," she told the girl. "It won't do any harm to let him sleep through the night."

Taking his new duties as the earl's manservant seriously, Dickon marched up the stairs first thing the next morning to see if his master would require any assistance with bathing and dressing.

He returned to the kitchen a short while later, looking somewhat nonplussed. "I knocked and knocked and he didn't answer for the longest time, but then he finally groaned and shouted at me to go away."

Anne frowned, her concern growing. She was tempted to look in on him herself, but ever since the night when she had stormed into his chamber only to end up in his arms, she had done all she could to avoid being alone with him in any room that contained a bed. "Perhaps he just needs a bit more time to recover. I'm sure he'll ring when he's ready to rejoin the world."

That evening, after a long day spent helping the maids scrub the ash from the drawing-room walls and supervising Dickon and Pippa while they cleaned up the debris from the yard, she sent Betsy up with another tray, this one topped with the one thing she knew Dravenwood couldn't resist—a steaming loaf of her freshly baked bread.

Anne turned around a short while later to find Betsy standing in the kitchen doorway, still holding the untouched tray. The look on the girl's kind, broad face made Anne's heart cringe with dread. "It's the master, ma'am," Betsy said reluctantly. "When he didn't answer my knock, I looked in on him to see if he'd be wantin' any supper, just like you said, but I couldn't rouse him."

"What do you mean you couldn't rouse him? Was he still sleeping?"

"At first I thought he was just sleepin'. But he was moanin' something fierce. And when I touched his arm, it was burnin' up."

Before Betsy could even finish speaking, Anne was through the doorway. She didn't even realize she had knocked the tray from the girl's hands until she heard it clatter to the floor behind her.

ANNE YANKED BACK THE bed curtains of Lord Dravenwood's bed to find him caught in the grips of a full-blown chill. She touched the back of her hand to his brow. Despite the audible chattering of his teeth, her worst fears were confirmed. He was burning with fever.

His breathing had deepened to a painful rasp. He'd probably inhaled far more of the smoke than he'd realized when rescuing her from the attic, then compounded that insult to his lungs by spending the night in the cold, pouring rain.

Betsy hovered in the doorway, anxiously wringing her apron in her hands and looking nearly as helpless as Anne felt. "What should I do, ma'am? Should I run to the village and fetch someone?"

"Who would you fetch?" Anne asked grimly. "There's no doctor there, and even if there were, you'd never be able to convince him to come here." She glanced out the window at the gathering shadows, fighting a bitter surge of despair. "Especially not after nightfall."

Eyeing the earl's shivering form, Betsy asked, "Shall I fetch some more blankets, then?"

"No." Shaking away the paralysis of her fear, Anne

briskly tore the bed curtains clean from their moorings, then whipped away his down comforter, leaving only the thin sheet draped across his waist. "He doesn't need to be warmed. He needs to be cooled." She marched over to the French windows and swept them open, welcoming in a rush of chill evening air, before returning to the bed. "Go to the kitchen and tell Nana to brew me up a pot of yarrow tea. Then find Lisbeth and Bess and bring me as much cool water as the three of you can carry."

"Should I fetch Dickon to tend to him?"

Anne shook her head, her heart contracting with helpless tenderness as she gazed down upon the earl's violently trembling form. "Not this time. This time I'll be the one tending to him."

# ❦ *Chapter Twenty-eight*

ANNE DID NOT HAVE to keep her vigil alone. As night melted into day and day into night and one day into another, the other servants took turns finding some excuse to join her at Lord Dravenwood's bedside.

Dickon was there to brace his shoulders while Anne tried to spoon some warm broth between his lips, spilling more of the stuff down his chest than down his throat. Bess and Lisbeth were there to lend their efforts to hers when his delirium deepened and Anne had to throw herself across his chest to keep him from harming himself as he thrashed about, shouting in a language none of them recognized until both his strength and his voice gave out. Lizzie was there to witness Anne's relieved tears at finding him alive after she'd woken from a brief nap in the chair beside his bed to discover him so still and waxen she'd thought he had died while she slept. Beth and Betsy were there to painstakingly arrange the sheets to protect Anne's modesty as she bathed him, her hands tenderly trailing the soapy cloth over the muscled planes of his chest.

On the third day of her vigil, Anne looked up from reading the same passage from *Pilgrim's Progress* for the tenth time to find Nana hobbling into the room.

Secretly relieved to be rescued from her own Slough of Despond, Anne leapt up from her chair, dislodging a disgruntled Sir Fluffytoes from her lap. She rushed over to assist the old woman, speaking directly into her ear. "Nana! However did you manage the stairs?"

"The same way I been managin' 'em for the last fifty years, girl. By puttin' one foot in front o' the other."

Nana shuffled over to the bed, shaking her head as she gazed down at Lord Dravenwood's prostate form. "There's nothin' worse for a woman than to see such a powerful man laid so low."

"I despise feeling so helpless," Anne confessed, swallowing around the tightness in her throat.

Nana slanted her a chiding look. "Don't give up on him yet, girl. And don't give up on yourself. If there's anythin' you've always excelled at, it's gettin' your own way. I'm guessin' you could still wrap fate 'round your little finger if you set your mind to it."

"At the moment it feels more like fate has its fingers wrapped around my throat." Anne noticed the colorful garment draped over the old woman's arm. "Why, Nana, did you finally finish your . . ." Anne hesitated, at a loss as to what to call the voluminous creation.

"These old knuckles of mine are gettin' too stiff to work the needles, and half the time I can't see what color I've picked out. Someone might as well get some use out of it while I'm still here to see it." The old woman carefully unfolded her gift and draped it across Lord Dravenwood's chest.

"Oh, Nana, it's beautiful!" Anne breathed. The garment's rainbow of hues did brighten the room considerably, even giving the illusion of color to Dravenwood's pallid cheeks.

"There's a bit o' love woven into every strand." Offering Anne a toothless smile, Nana tenderly stroked the knotted yarn with her gnarled fingers. "Never forget, girl. Love is still the most powerful medicine of all."

"IF HE DIES, THE constable will swear we murdered him," Pippa said glumly from her rocking chair on the other side of the bed, peering over the top of her much-read copy of *The Mysteries of Udolpho* at Anne.

Anne leaned forward in her chair to smooth the earl's sweat-dampened hair away from his brow. He had been drifting in and out of delirium for most of the day. "Perhaps we did."

"You mustn't blame yourself. It was his choice to go after Hodges. We didn't force him to play knight in shining armor."

Anne remembered how Dravenwood had told her about saving his brother from a firing squad, how he had looked after Clarinda when she had fallen ill, his determination to prove Angelica had no part in her own downfall, how he'd charged up the attic stairs to rescue Anne from the fire without giving a thought to his own welfare. "I don't think he had any other choice. He may be loathe to admit it, but I suspect it's the role he was born to play." A rueful laugh escaped her. "He even rescued Dickon from that ridiculous wig." Anne's smile faded, her fingers lingering against the hot, dry skin of his cheek. "He just hasn't figured out yet that he can't save everyone. Perhaps not even himself."

LATE THAT NIGHT ANNE found herself alone with Dravenwood at last. After watching Pippa nod off into her book not once, but three times, Anne had finally coaxed the girl into going to bed by promising to don a nightdress and curl up on the divan for a nap once she was gone.

Anne had slipped into Dravenwood's dressing room to change into the nightdress and tug the pins from her hair, but instead of curling up on the divan, she had claimed the rocking chair Pippa had vacated and drawn it even closer to the bed.

At some point in the past few days, she had stopped worrying about the impropriety of spending the night in a gentleman's bedchamber, much less spending the night in a gentleman's bedchamber in her nightdress.

She glanced at the French lyre clock on the mantel. It was just after midnight. Even though she knew its voice had been silenced forever, sometimes she still caught herself listening for the hollow bong of the longcase clock in the entrance hall.

Sleep held little attraction for her. Every time she drifted off, she would feel herself slipping beneath the surface of the waves, feel the strangling cords of silk tightening around her ankles, making it impossible for her to kick her way toward freedom. Then she would begin to sink . . . down . . . down . . . down into the darkness of utter oblivion before yanking herself awake with a start.

She couldn't sleep and Dravenwood couldn't seem to wake up. His fever had finally broken, but except for the shallow rise and fall of his chest, he was as still and pale as a carved marble effigy on a tomb. Anne would almost have preferred delirium to this. At least when he was raving and thrashing, she didn't have to touch her ear to his lips just to hear the whisper of his breathing.

If he didn't survive, she would have to gather pen and paper and write to inform his parents of his death.

Would they mourn the man he had been or would his father grieve because he'd lost his precious heir? How long would it take for word to travel across the distant seas to reach his brother? Would Ashton Burke remember the difficult man Dravenwood had become or would he fondly recall the boys they had once been together—the boys who had played at toy soldiers and fought mock naval battles in the bath? Would Clarinda shed a tear for the man who had loved her so long and so faithfully? Would she regret scorning a loyal heart another woman might have cherished? Would little Charlotte even remember her "Unca Max," the man who had scooped her up in his big, strong arms and held her so tenderly, no doubt thinking that she might have been his if circumstances had been different?

Anne hugged her woolen shawl tighter around her shoulders. None of Nana's medicinal teas or poultices seemed to be working. They hadn't been able to get so much as a drop of broth down his throat since dawn. All she could do was bathe him, shave his jaw, keep his sheets fresh, gently polish his teeth with her own tooth powder, and accept that he was probably never going to wake up. She would never again see his brow furrow in one of his infuriating scowls or hear him snap out some order she had no intention of obeying.

His face blurred before her eyes as she caught his hand in a fierce grip. "Damn you, Dravenwood! You survived cholera in Burma, a sandstorm in the Tunisian desert, and a broken heart! How dare you let a little rain finish you off? If you're planning on dying just so you can spend eternity flitting hand in hand around the manor with your precious Angelica, then you're wasting your last breath. She won't have you! I'll see to it!"

The irony wasn't wasted on Anne. If he died, she would be the one haunted until her dying day. She would be the one who would awaken in the middle of the night, aching for a touch she would never know, craving a kiss she would never taste again.

Still clutching his hand in both of hers, she glared at him through her tears. "Pippa was right, you know. You're probably just doing this out of spite. If you die, they'll swear I murdered you. Is that what you want, you stubborn, arrogant fool? Do you want me to hang because you were so foolhardy as to rush out in the storm after I tried to warn you it could kill you?" Her voice broke on a raw sob. She doubled over and buried her brow against their entwined hands, watering his flesh with her tears.

She was so distraught it took her several seconds to feel the hand gently skimming over her unbound hair. Trembling with disbelief, she slowly lifted her head.

Dravenwood was looking right at her, his eyes alight with a tender regard that stole the breath right out of her throat. "There you are, angel," he said, disuse deepening the husky note in his voice. A half smile curved one corner of his mouth. "I always knew you'd come back to me."

# ❖ *Chapter Twenty-nine*

*A*NNE GAZED INTO DRAVENWOOD'S eyes, mesmerized by their crystalline clarity. It was as if he was seeing her—*truly* seeing her—for the first time. His regard was like the most rare and costly of gifts, giving her back something she had believed to be forever lost.

*Herself.*

He slid his hand through her hair, his fingers toying with the velvety locks, then curled his palm around her nape and gently drew her mouth down to his. His fever might have faded, but he was probably still under the sway of his illness. He couldn't possibly be thinking clearly, if at all. Anne knew she should pull away, should ease him back to the bed and urge him to rest, but she had neither the will nor the desire to resist him. As he tenderly molded her lips to his, she breathed in his breath as if it held her only chance of survival after being submerged beneath the water for a lifetime. His breath was no longer scented of sickness, but of peppermint and hope.

She felt her shawl skitter from her shoulders to the floor, but didn't care. She was too lost in the tantalizing flick of his tongue against hers as he breached the seam of her lips and tenderly ravished her mouth.

When her tongue responded with a bold foray of its own, he wrapped both of his arms around her, groaning deep in his throat. This was no groan of pain but of a pleasure sharper and more dangerous than pain.

The two of them might never meet on a ballroom floor to share a waltz, but he swept her into his bed in a dizzying turn until she was lying beneath him. Even as his mouth continued to work its dark and delicious wonders, one of his hands slid down her side, lingering ever so briefly against the fullness of her breast before tracing the graceful dip of her waist, the flare of her hip, then slipping beneath her thigh to lift one leg so he could wedge himself in the cradle of her hips.

Anne gasped, her hips arching off the bed of their own accord to embrace the evidence of his desire. There was no cure for this delirium. The fever was contagious and had infected them both. She could feel its flames licking higher as his hand slid around and up the silken skin of her thigh, easing her night-dress up with it.

The cold, distant man she had once believed him to be had vanished, leaving a hot-blooded stranger in his place. There was no time for thought. No time for caution. No time for regrets. There was only the warmth of his tongue stroking the velvety recesses of her mouth in a rhythm that was unmistakably and irresistibly carnal. The heat of his hand as he slid it to the side and pressed its heel against the tender mound between her thighs, urging her to ride him to some extraordinary place where pleasure was not only possible but inevitable.

A shuddering sigh trembled on her lips as his fingers followed the path his palm had forged. She buried her face against his shoulder to hide her burning cheeks as his long, elegantly tapered fingers slid through the softness of her nether curls and began to have their way with the silky flesh they found beneath—stroking, gliding, caressing until her sighs turned into breathless, little gasps. When the callused pad of his thumb brushed the throbbing little bud at the crux of those curls, her womb responded with a shiver of delight and a pulse of pure liquid pleasure that made her ache to clench her thighs together.

But his hand was still there, urging them apart, urging her to cede dominion of all that she was—

all that she would ever be—to his desperate hunger. Even then, he was not content to simply seize the prize he had won. He continued to toy with her, each deft flick of his nimble fingertips threatening to incinerate her in a consuming fire.

"You came to me, angel," he whispered hoarsely, the scorching heat of his lips tracing the column of her throat until they settled against the pulse beating wildly beneath her skin. "Now come for me."

He was her master. She had no choice but to obey his command.

The waves of pleasure broke over her in a blinding torrent. But instead of dragging her down as she had feared, they sent her shooting up out of the darkness and into the light.

Anne was still quaking with delectable little aftershocks when he covered her again. She clung to his shoulders, torn between drawing him closer and pushing him away. He suddenly seemed very large, very overpowering, very . . . male.

His mouth closed over hers once more, sampling the honeyed sweetness of her lips with a tender ferocity that soothed her panic, gave her the courage to open her thighs for him when he sought to nudge them apart with his knee. She felt the heavy weight of his arousal settle against the part of her still throbbing from his touch. He rubbed himself in the creamy pearls of nectar he'd coaxed from her melting core, then entered her with one long, smooth stroke, sheathing his rigid length deep within her.

Rent asunder by both the agony and the wonder of it all, Anne dug her fingernails into his back and sank her teeth into his shoulder to muffle a helpless wail. She had been foolish enough to believe she had known passion before, but that had been only a pale shadow compared to this, a frivolous little ghost of pleasures to come. A guttural groan tore from Dravenwood's throat as he rocked hard against her, deepening both the pace and the intensity of his thrusts until her wordless pleas swelled into shuddering moans she could no longer contain.

Still he did not relent, making it clear he wouldn't be satisfied until those delicious shivers of ecstasy began to wrack her womb once again. The second they did, he stiffened and surged within her, an even deeper groan tearing from his throat as he was swept away by the same relentless tide of rapture he had sent spilling through her.

ANNE'S EYES FLUTTERED OPEN to find the misty light of dawn breaking through the French windows of Dravenwood's bedchamber. She sighed, her limbs weighted with a delicious languor that made her feel as if she had somehow melted during the night, then been reformed into something finer. Unlike Pippa, who whined and groaned and buried her head beneath the pillow when required to rise before ten o'clock, Anne had always been a cheerful riser. She would bound out of bed and dress quickly, eager to face the challenges of the day. But on this day, she would have been perfectly content to lie abed until noon, her every muscle a little sore, but still tingling with satisfaction.

She stretched with all of the languid grace of Sir Fluffytoes as she rolled over to seek the source of that satisfaction.

Dravenwood was lying on his back, one muscular forearm flung over his head. She sat up on one elbow to study his rugged chest and beautifully sculpted profile at her leisure. He looked so incredibly peaceful.

Her eyes widened in alarm. Dear Lord, what if his heart had been too weak to withstand their exertions? What if she had inadvertently finished him off?

She touched a hand to his chest. She could feel it rise and fall with each even breath, could count each steady beat of his heart beneath her palm.

She collapsed back on the pillow, grateful tears springing to her eyes.

*Love is still the most powerful medicine of all.*

As Nana's voice echoed through Anne's mind, a smile touched her lips. She had somehow accomplished what all of the poultices and medicinal teas had failed to do—she had saved him.

She was still feeling rather pleased with herself when he reached over without opening his eyes and drew her into his arms. She settled against him, her back pressed to his broad chest. When she felt his arousal nudging the softness of her rump, she couldn't resist giving her hips a taunting little wiggle. His immediate response made her grin. Yes, he was most definitely showing signs of life.

He tugged her even closer, his possessive embrace making her feel warm and safe and cherished for the first time in a very long while.

"Maximillian," she murmured, savoring the taste of his name on her lips.

A husky groan escaped him. "Hmmm . . . my angel . . . my sweet . . . my Angelica . . ."

# ✣ Chapter Thirty

ANNE FROZE, GLARING BLINDLY at the French windows. One of Dravenwood's hands closed around the softness of her breast, gently squeezing. Anne hesitated a moment, then reached down and flung his hand off her. As she struggled out of his embrace, he grunted in protest, then rolled to his opposite side and began gently snoring.

Anne slid out of the bed and snatched her discarded nightdress from the floor, determined to make her escape before he could discover he had taken the wrong woman to bed.

WHEN ANNE CAME MARCHING across the gallery a short while later, bathed, dressed, and starched to within an inch of her life, Angelica was lying in wait for her on the landing. Anne was determined to ignore her, but as she started down the stairs to the entrance hall, she could feel the legendary beauty's taunting gaze boring into her back.

She swung around, pointing an accusing finger at the portrait. "If you don't stop smirking at me like that, you conceited cow, I'm going to draw a pair of mustaches, some bushy eyebrows, and a wart or two on your disgustingly perfect nose. And then we'll see just how fetching your precious Lord Dravenwood finds you!"

Angelica continued to gaze down her disgustingly perfect nose at Anne, her amusement at Anne's expense undaunted by the threat.

From the entrance hall below came the sound of someone clearing his or her throat. Anne jerked around to find Pippa standing at the bottom of the stairs.

The girl was eyeing Anne cautiously, the same way they all tended to eye Hodges whenever they caught him jousting with the chickens or scampering through the gardens at twilight trying to catch a gnome. "Just who were you talking to?"

"No one," Anne snapped, casting Angelica one last baleful look before descending the rest of the stairs at a brisk clip. "No one at all."

MAX AWOKE TO FIND himself alone for the first time in days. He struggled to sit up. His head spun and his stiff muscles throbbed in protest, forcing him to flop back to the pillows with a groan. He lay gazing up at the canopy, waiting for his muzzy head to clear.

Despite his lingering weakness, he was flooded with an undeniable sense of well-being. For as long as he could remember, he had felt as if he were suffering from some ravening hunger that made him snarl and snap at everyone around him. But now he felt deliciously sated, like a giant jungle cat that had just devoured a nice juicy gazelle.

Closing his eyes, he lifted his balled fists above his head and stretched, his rusty muscles rippling with exhilaration. He'd never felt quite so happy just to be alive. Ironic considering his last visitor had been a ghost. His eyes flew open, his memory honing in on the source of his satisfaction.

*Angelica.*

She had come to him in a dream, just as she had before. Only this time when he had reached for her, she had melted into his arms instead of back into the night.

Max sat up, his confusion growing. Pale, early-afternoon sunlight streamed through the French windows, shining on the empty rocking chair that had been drawn up to the very edge of the bed.

He would almost swear the woman in his arms last night hadn't been a vapor of mist, but flesh and blood. She had been warm and responsive, her

mouth a living flame beneath his. Surely no halluci-
nation could be *that* vivid.

He raked a hand through his tousled hair, scouring the blurred edges of his memory. If he concen-
trated hard, he could almost hear a voice gently
coaxing him to part his parched lips so the cool
metal of a spoon could be slipped between them.
Could feel the scrape of a straight razor wielded by
steady fingers against the bristles of his beard. Could
feel a cool hand on his brow, gently testing the temperature of his fevered flesh.

He could see a woman bending over him, her
skin as fine and pale as alabaster, exhaustion shadowing her hazel eyes. Her hair had escaped its unraveling chignon to hang in limp strands around her
worried face. A face that suddenly came into focus
with brutal clarity.

It was the face of his housekeeper, Mrs. Spencer.

Not Angelica, but Anne.

A wave of horror washed over him. Dear God,
what had he done? Had he dragged the woman into
his bed and forced himself upon her in his delirium?

That scenario didn't fit the tantalizing glimpses
stealing through his memory—the softness of her
lips flowering beneath his to welcome his kiss; the
trusting warmth of her hand twining through his
hair to caress his nape; the enticing way her hips had
arched off the bed in an invitation no man could

resist; the throaty little cry she had tried to bury in his throat when his fingertips had coaxed her over the precipice of pleasure into ecstasy.

As the memories came flooding back one by one, Max could feel himself growing hard all over again. He swore beneath his breath.

There was only one way to prove the *memories* were nothing but the ravings of his feverish brain. He would seek out his housekeeper and no doubt find her calmly going about her duties, proving nothing untoward had transpired between them.

He had no intention of ever telling her about his lurid fantasies. If he did, she would probably either recoil in horror, slap him silly, or laugh in his face.

Max slid out of the bed, taking the comforter with him to wrap around his waist just in case anyone should come barging into the bedchamber before he could reach his dressing room. When the blanket's hem snagged on the edge of the bedpost, he turned around to give it a yank.

That was when he saw the rusty stains marring the silk sheets.

Max gazed down at them, his disbelief slowly hardening into certainty. He had been right all along. The woman who had spent the night in his arms and his bed had not been a vapor of mist. She had been flesh.

And blood.

\*   \*   \*

WHEN MAX DESCENDED THE stairs that afternoon, no tantalizing aroma of baking bread greeted him.

Lisbeth, however, was passing through the entrance hall, feather duster in hand. "M'lord!" she exclaimed, a snaggletoothed smile lighting up her freckled face. "So glad to see you up and about. Mrs. Spencer told us your fever had finally broken."

"Oh, she did, did she?" He supposed the deceitful woman hadn't bothered to tell them it had been replaced by another sort of fever altogether.

"She said you'd had a *very* hard night and we were to let you sleep as late as you wanted." Lisbeth frowned at the heap of bedclothes in his arms. "There was no need for you to strip the bed, m'lord. All you had to do was ring. One of us Elizabeths would have run right up to fetch the sheets for the laundry."

"I don't want them laundered. I want them burned. We need to make sure no one else in the household falls ill."

"I don't believe what you had was catchin', m'lord. Why, none of us has had so much as a sniffle!"

"You can never be too careful about that sort of thing." He loomed over her. "Carelessness can cost lives. Just look at what happened to poor Mr. Spencer."

Clearly alarmed by his ominous leer, she backed up a step before reluctantly reaching for the sheets. "Very well, m'lord. I'll see that they're burned."

Max yanked them out of her reach. "I'd prefer to see to it myself. Unless, of course, Hodges is available. I've heard he excels at that sort of thing." Without another word, Max went striding toward the kitchen, leaving Lisbeth gaping after him and no doubt wondering if the fever had boiled his brain.

MAX'S DETERMINATION TO CONFRONT his house-keeper right away was doomed to be thwarted. Everyone he questioned insisted she was in a different location.

Pippa and Dickon were convinced they'd seen her heading for the chicken coop to gather some fresh eggs, while Nana swore Anne was in the drawing room helping Bess swab the remaining soot from the ceiling. Bess claimed she had spotted the housekeeper from the drawing-room window just a short while ago "thtrolling toward the orchard with a bathket over her arm." When Max arrived at the orchard, his muscles screaming from the effort after so many days spent languishing in bed, he found Beth and Betsy halfway up an apple tree with their skirts tied up to their knees, but no

Mrs. Spencer. Lizzie informed him Anne was last seen in the dining room helping Hodges polish the silver. Hodges insisted she was in London having tea with the king.

Max would have suspected them all of deliberately trying to confound him if their own bewilderment hadn't been so convincing.

As the afternoon melted away and his housekeeper continued to stay one step ahead of him, Max's frustration deepened to anger. He was as angry with himself as he was with her. After Clarinda had left him, he had sworn he would never allow himself to feel this way again. Would never abandon reason for the madness that only love—or lust—could inflict.

Growing weary of the chase, he finally retreated to his study, leaving explicit instructions that Mrs. Spencer was to report to him the very *instant* she was spotted by one of the others. The infernal woman couldn't elude him forever.

He was rewarded for his persistence by a crisp rap on the door just after sunset.

"Enter," he commanded, caught off guard by the heavy thud of his heart. Perhaps he'd overtaxed himself with his exertions. Perhaps he was on the verge of a relapse. Or death.

The door slipped open and Mrs. Spencer came

gliding into the room. Max wasn't sure what he had expected from her—an accusing glare or tearful recriminations perhaps? But she looked as calm and unruffled as she had on the night he'd arrived at Cadgwyck Manor.

Except for her snowy-white apron and that provocative bit of lace at her throat, she was garbed in black from throat to toe. Her hair was sleeked back from her face and confined to its usual net. Her lips were pursed as if they'd never softened beneath a man's kiss. Her expression couldn't have been any more bland.

Max scowled, finding her cool aplomb somehow more infuriating than a foot-stomping tantrum might have been. She could have had the common decency to look more . . . well . . . *ravished.*

He wanted to see her with her cheeks flushed and her hair tumbled around her shoulders. He wanted her lips parted and trembling beneath his. He wanted to see some evidence of the pleasure she had found in his arms and the pleasure she had given him. Seeing her look so untouched—and untouchable—only made him want to see what he could do to rectify that situation.

She arched one eyebrow at him. "You sent for me, my lord?"

"Sit." He nodded toward the chair in front of the desk.

As she obeyed, he watched her face carefully for any sign of strain. Was it his imagination or did he detect a faint wince as she settled her pert little bottom in the chair?

"I'm glad to see you looking so well," she said after every fold in her skirt was arranged to her satisfaction. "Would you care to review the household accounts or discuss the repairs to the drawing room?"

Max's mouth fell open. Lisbeth had been wrong. His fever must have been contagious after all. The woman was obviously delirious.

"Oh, I don't know," he drawled. "I thought we might review what happened between the two of us in my bedchamber last night."

She was silent for a gratifying moment. "I was rather hoping you wouldn't remember that."

He didn't bother to hide his incredulity. "Did you truly believe I could forget something like that?"

"I must confess the thought did cross my mind." She leaned forward in the chair, studying him intently. "Just how much *do* you remember?"

Leaning back in his chair, he propped his ankle on the opposite knee and met her gaze squarely. "*Everything.*"

Every kiss. Every caress. The sharp dig of her fingernails into his back as he had slid deep within her and made her his own.

Her slender throat bobbed as she swallowed. He

had finally succeeded in ruffling her composure. "I hope you don't think I intend to blame you for what transpired between us. You'd been half out of your head with fever for days."

"Only half?" he said drily.

She blinked at him. "What are you implying, my lord? That a man would have to be completely out of his head to take me to his bed?"

"No, Mrs. Spencer, you know damn well that is *not* what I was implying!" He surged to his feet and paced over to the window. He gazed out into the deepening shadows of twilight, struggling to gain control over his temper. "You'll have to forgive me. This is all new to me. I'm not in the habit of debauching the help."

"That's fortunate. Nana will be ever so relieved."

Max swung around to give her a reproachful glare. "Yes, do assure the Elizabeths it should still be safe to bend over to scoop the ashes from the hearth if I'm anywhere in the vicinity. I'll try to resist the temptation to toss their skirts up over their heads and have my way with them."

A becoming blush crept into her cheeks. "I fear you're making far too much of this. You're a man. I'm a woman. We've probably both suffered more than our share of loneliness in recent years." She shrugged, lowering her gaze to her lap. "Was it any wonder that we reached out to each other during a difficult time? You needn't trouble yourself any further, my lord. As far as I'm concerned, last night never happened."

While most men might have been relieved, Max was shocked to discover that was the one thing he would not allow. He leaned against the windowsill, folding his arms over his chest. "Perhaps you're right, Mrs. Spencer. After all, you are a widow. I'm sure you were accustomed to welcoming your husband's attentions with equal . . . enthusiasm." She yanked up her head to stare at him. "Why, one might even consider your Mr. Spencer a lucky man were it not for his being crushed to death in such an untimely manner by . . . what was it again?" Max tapped his lips with his forefinger. "A runaway team of horses?"

"A wagon," she bit off, giving him a stony look. "He was crushed by a wagon."

"Every gentleman in London knows there's very little challenge involved in tumbling a widow into his bed. He doesn't have to squander his time or effort on all of that tiresome wooing—the compliments, the flowers, the endless round of balls and operas and rides through Hyde Park." He sighed, as if savoring some particularly salacious memory. "Widows are always so eager to please . . . and almost pathetically grateful for any scrap of male attention. Why, I remember hearing about the widow of a certain Lord Langley who could do the most extraordinary trick with her tongue—"

Anne surged to her feet, her blush replaced by a flush of anger. "I'll have you know I am neither eager to please nor pathetically grateful!"

"Nor are you a widow, Mrs. Spencer," he thundered. "Or should I say *Miss* Spencer."

She paled. "How did you know?"

"Let's just say you left behind certain . . . clues."

"Oh, God . . . the sheets," she whispered, realization dawning in her eyes. "I was in such a hurry to make my escape, I forgot all about the sheets. If one of the maids sees them . . . or Dickon!" She started for the door.

"There's no need," he said quietly. "I've already destroyed them."

She collapsed with her back against the door, eyeing him with grudging admiration. "A gentleman to the bitter end, aren't you?"

"One wouldn't know it from my behavior last night." He tilted his head to study her. "So why did you lie to me? Why have you been pretending to be a widow for all these years?"

"I don't expect a man of your rank and privilege to understand. It's difficult enough for a woman to find employment in a reputable household, but it becomes nearly impossible when everyone around her equates being unmarried with weakness and inexperience."

He leveled a mocking look at her. "Ah, yes, and you are a woman of *vast* experience."

"I learned very quickly that most ladies aren't willing to hire a young, unmarried woman to manage their households. They're too afraid their husbands might . . ." She trailed off, lowering her eyes.

"Do precisely what I did last night?" He took a few steps toward her, unable to help himself. "Did it not occur to you that had I known you'd never been . . . married, I might have at least shown you more consideration?"

"Married?" Her rueful little laugh mocked them both. "You didn't even know I was alive. You called me Angelica."

Max winced. Apparently, he hadn't remembered everything about last night after all.

"Don't be so hard on yourself, my lord. At least you didn't call me Clarinda."

Max was surprised by how little her gibe stung. Loving and losing Clarinda was no longer a searing wound in his heart, but a bittersweet ache that was already fading.

Retreating behind the desk, he sank back into his chair. He'd successfully negotiated treaties between countries that had been warring for centuries, yet this one hardheaded woman continued to confound him. "It was one thing to steal a kiss. Quite another to rob you of your innocence. If you don't wish to remain in my employ after my deplorable behavior toward you, I wouldn't blame you. If you choose to go, I'll make sure you receive the compensation you're due." He watched her face, holding his breath without realizing it.

"And what's the going rate for that sort of thing?"

He felt himself color. "That's not what I meant! I meant that you were deserving of a handsome severance sum. With my name and connections, I could secure a position for you in one of the most desirable households in all of England. You'd be free of this accursed place forever."

She lifted her chin. Max would almost have sworn he saw a faint quiver in it. "Cadgwyck is my home."

Max nodded, feeling a curious kinship with her. The rattletrap, old manor had somehow become his home, too. "Then I suppose there's no help for it, is there?"

"For what?"

"If you won't let me atone for my sins by sending you away, then you'll simply have to stay and punish me for them."

"Punish you? How?"

"By agreeing to become my wife."

# ❧ Chapter Thirty-one

"**Y**OUR WIFE?" ANNE CROAKED. If she hadn't had the door to support her, she might well have slid to the floor in a heap of skirts. "You'll have to forgive me, my lord. I was under the mistaken impression that you had recovered from your fever. I'll ring for Dickon at once so he can help you back to bed."

Dravenwood gave her a chiding look. "I don't mind if you make me grovel a bit just to placate your pride, but you should know I've no intention of squandering nine years of my life wooing you."

"You can't possibly marry me! Why would you even suggest such a ridiculous thing?"

"It's what a gentleman does when he compromises a lady," he patiently explained. "And as you just pointed out, I am a gentleman to the bitter end."

"But I'm no lady! I'm ... well ... I'm your inferior!"

Dravenwood rose to his feet, looking as dangerous as she had ever seen him. "You are inferior to no man. Or woman, for that matter."

"But . . . but you can't just take your housekeeper and make her your countess. Why, you'd be the laughingstock of all society!"

"It wouldn't be the first time, now would it? Do you honestly believe their scornful glances and cruel gibes have any power left to hurt me?"

"It's not just society who would scorn you. You have your family to consider as well."

Instead of looking alarmed, he looked rather delighted by the prospect. "When I offered for Clarinda, my father threw an enormous tantrum and my mother took to her bed for a fortnight. And all because Clarinda's father was a 'commoner' who had made his considerable fortune in trade. Can you imagine what they'll say when I write to tell them I'm marrying my housekeeper? Why, they might even go so far as to disinherit me and drag Ash back from his adventures to take my place!" His smile deepened into a bloodthirsty grin that made him look more like a pirate than an earl. "Perhaps we should travel to London and give them the news in person. It would almost be worth it just to see the look on their faces."

Despite all of her noble intentions, Anne's heart had begun to lurch with reckless hope. But his words dashed that hope. She could never travel to

London. She could never become his countess. She could never be his wife.

"I'm sorry, my lord," she said softly. "I appreciate your single-minded devotion to propriety, but I'm afraid I shall have to refuse your offer."

He scowled, pondering her words. "Then it's not an offer. It's an order."

She gaped at him in disbelief. "Why, of all the high-handed, arrogant, presumptuous . . ." She briefly sputtered into incoherence before blurting out, "You can't just order me to marry you!"

"And why not? You're still in my employ, aren't you? I can order you to serve fresh pheasant for supper or bring me a cup of tea. Why can't I order you to marry me?"

"Because I have no intention of continuing to work for a madman. I quit!"

"Marvelous. Now that you're no longer my housekeeper, we'll be free to marry."

Anne threw up her hands with a strangled little shriek of frustration.

He came around the desk, the coaxing look in his eye far more dangerous to her resolve than his bullying. "The two of us aren't so different, are we? We're both bound by duty and the expectations of others. There's no need for you to spend the rest of your life attending to the needs of others until you're as stiff and dried-up as you're pretending to be." Her mouth fell open in outrage, but before she could speak, he continued, "As for me, I have no choice but to marry someday to provide an heir to carry on the family line. And I'd already made up my mind I'd never be foolish enough to do it for love."

Hoping to hide the fresh blow his words dealt her heart, Anne said crisply, "I'm so glad you decided to spare me the tiresome wooing."

"All I'm saying is that in my world men and women marry for convenience every day. There's no reason you and I can't do the same."

"It won't work. We don't suit."

"Are you so sure about that? From what I do recall about last night, we seemed to suit very well." The silky note in his voice deepened, sending a reckless little shiver through her womb. "If we marry, we can do that whenever we like, you know. It's not only legal and condoned by the church, but encouraged."

Anne had once heard that when a person was drowning, the person's entire past could flash before his or her eyes. But in that moment, as she felt herself bobbing beneath the waves of his persistence, it was her future that flashed before hers: waking in the warmth of his arms on a chill winter morning, her cheek laid against the crisp fur of his chest; watching him heft their daughter in the air just as he had hefted little Charlotte, twirling her about until she collapsed in helpless giggles; seeing the silvery frost at his temples slowly melt through his sooty locks; spending the years softening all of his scowls into smiles until their children's children danced around them, making the halls of Cadgwyck ring once more with the music of love and laughter and hope.

But it was a future that could never be. She'd surrendered her future in the same moment she'd surrendered her past.

"You make a compelling case," she said. "But I'll need some time to consider your . . . proposition."

"I believe I can afford to grant you that much."

She straightened, smoothing her apron and donning Mrs. Spencer's bland mask. "Will that be all, my lord?"

He scowled. "No, Mrs. . . . *Miss* Spencer. I don't believe it will." She stood frozen in place as he came sauntering toward her, a predatory glint in his eye.

Her mask slipped as he framed her face in his hands and brought his mouth down on hers. This was a kiss no woman could resist. He crushed his mouth against hers, the harsh demand of his lips tempered by the sweeping mastery of his tongue. He raked his fingers through her hair, loosening the silky tendrils from their net until they tumbled around her face in wild disarray. By the time he stepped away from her, she was limp and breathless and aching with want. Her cheeks were flushed with heat and her lips were parted and trembling in anticipation of another kiss.

He surveyed her, his satisfaction with what he saw evident. "*That* will be all. For now." His passion-darkened eyes and roguish grin promised her his kiss was only a taste of the delights to come should she be sensible enough to accept his suit.

ANGELICA CADGWYCK STOOD OVER Maximillian Burke's bed. It wasn't the first time she had slipped into his chamber just to watch him sleep. But it would be the last.

Moonlight drifted through the open French doors, bathing his handsome features in its silvery glow. His lips were slightly parted, the stern lines of his face relaxed in boyish repose. The sheet had slipped down to his hip bones, exposing the impressive expanse of his chest and the chiseled planes of his abdomen. She had always found it fascinating that despite his fondness for propriety, he didn't sleep in a nightshirt or nightcap like other men, but was content to wrap himself in nothing more substantial than a moonbeam.

He was a greater mystery to her than she would ever be to him. She was still searching for clues as to what manner of man he might have become had he not been prone to such hopeless affairs of the heart. If the two of them had met at a ball in some other lifetime, would he have asked her to dance? Would he have scrawled his name on her dance card and waltzed her out the nearest terrace door into the moonlight so he could steal a kiss? Would he have wooed her with pretty words and bouquets of roses and trips to the opera and rides in Hyde Park?

She had promised herself she wouldn't touch him this time. But the rebellious lock of hair that persisted in tumbling over his brow posed too great a temptation. She reached to gently brush it back, her fingertips grazing the satiny warmth of his skin.

He stirred. She froze. What would she do if he reached for her? Would she be able to resist him if he sought to tug her into his bed and into his arms? After a moment, he simply nestled deeper into the pillow, murmuring a name in his sleep—a plain name that sounded like a sigh on his lips. A name that sent a wistful lance of yearning through her heart.

Not *Angelica,* but *Anne.*

It seemed his destiny would always lie in loving the right woman at the wrong time.

She withdrew her hand, holding it up to the moonlight. She could already feel herself fading. For all these years she had been nothing but a shadow, flitting through the corridors of life. But then he had come along and done everything in his considerable power to give her substance again.

She couldn't afford to let that happen. A ghost couldn't be hurt by the sharp edges of life. A ghost couldn't bleed from a broken heart or dream a dream that could never come true.

A ghost couldn't fall in love.

She pressed a tender kiss to his brow, then turned away from him and drifted across the room. She cast one last longing look over her shoulder at the bed before melting back into the wall and the past.

MAX AWOKE ENVELOPED IN the sultry scent of jasmine. He sat up abruptly, his nostrils flaring. His heart was pounding wildly in his chest, but he couldn't remember what he had been dreaming. For some reason, that deeply disturbed him. He didn't want to go back to being the man he had been before he came to this place—a man who didn't dream at all.

Whatever he had been dreaming, it had left him with a nearly inconsolable sense of loss. This was different from what he had felt when Clarinda had tossed him over—deeper and more piercing to the heart. It was as if something had gone terribly awry that could never be put right again. He'd had the exact same feeling when he had ruffled through the blank pages at the end of Angelica Cadgwyck's journal.

He glanced at the empty bed beside him, surprised by how fiercely he wanted to find Anne there, wrapped up in those rumpled sheets. He wanted to pull her into his arms just as he had last night and bury his doubts and fears in the lush sweetness of her warm and willing body.

The ethereal aroma of the jasmine hadn't dissipated along with his dream, but had only gotten sweeter and more overpowering. He slowly turned to find the French windows standing wide open, just as they had been on his first night at Cadgwyck. He was no more able to resist their invitation now than he had been then.

He tossed back the blankets and reached for his dressing gown in the same motion, compelled by a peculiar sense of destiny. It was almost as if his every choice since coming to Cadgwyck had somehow brought him to this moment.

Slipping into the dressing gown, he padded across the room and out onto the balcony. Lacy tatters of clouds drifted across a luminous opal of a moon. He closed his hands over the cool iron of the balustrade, his gaze instinctively seeking the tower on the far side of the manor.

At first glance the tower appeared to be shrouded in shadows, the blank eyes of its windows still jealously guarding its secrets. But when Max squinted against the darkness, he saw something else—a faint glimmer that could have been a trick of the moonlight ... or the flickering flame of a single candle, the exact sort of beacon a man might light to guide the girl he was seeking to seduce to a secret rendezvous.

Although it still made the tiny hairs on his nape prickle, Max wasn't even startled when the first tinkling notes from the music box came wafting across the courtyard to his ears.

Perhaps he had always known the night would come when Angelica Cadgwyck would be ready to dance with him again.

# Chapter Thirty-two

MAX COULD STILL REMEMBER the weight of the silver music box in his hands, the way its wistful notes had tugged at his heart like the echo of a waltz danced in the arms of a phantom lover. It could have been his imagination, but on this night the notes sounded even more off-key than usual, giving their song a sinister cast.

He already knew what would come next. But this time he wasn't going to allow himself to be seduced by that tantalizing ripple of feminine laughter. He wouldn't be lured into the darkness by a promise that could never be fulfilled. He'd had his fill of chasing ghosts. He was ready to trust his heart to the hands of a warm, living woman—one strong and sensible enough to keep all of his ghosts at bay, even the ones he'd created himself.

He straightened, loosening his hands from the

balustrade. "I'm sorry, sweetheart," he whispered. "I would have saved you if I could have."

The music abruptly stopped.

He was turning away from the balcony railing when a woman's scream, ripe with anguish, tore through the night, followed by the sharp report of a single gunshot.

HAUNTED BY THAT HEART-WRENCHING scream, Max raced across the second-floor gallery, dragging on his shirt as he ran. He rounded the landing and headed down the stairs without sparing Angelica's portrait a single glance.

Unwilling to waste precious minutes crashing his way through the darkened house, he wrenched open the front door and went pelting across the weed-choked flagstones of the courtyard. Except for the wispy clouds and a misty scattering of stars, the sky was clear. On this night there could be no mistaking a crack of thunder for the report of a pistol.

The tower loomed up out of the darkness. Max had to circle it twice before he finally located an outer door. At first he feared it was bolted, but when he set his shoulder to it and shoved with all of his might, it gave way with a full-throated groan of protest. He found himself on the first floor. Shafts of moonlight pierced the arrow slits, illuminating the winding steps leading up to the top floor.

As he started up the stairs, he could hear Anne's brisk, no-nonsense voice warning him away from this place: *The stairs are crumbling and are quite dangerous to anyone not familiar with them.*

He hadn't taken the time to yank on his boots, but he was moving too fast to feel the bite of the crumbling stone beneath his bare feet. Centuries ago he might have had a sword in his hand as he made the dizzying charge up the stairs to storm the keep. Now he had nothing but his wits and the instinctive urge to help whoever had let out that terrible cry.

The iron-banded door at the top of the stairs was closed, a flickering ribbon of light visible beneath it. Max's steps slowed. What if he was running straight into some sort of ambush? What if his suspicions were founded after all and someone in this house wanted him dead? What if someone was waiting on the other side of that door with a pistol that had not yet been fired?

His mouth set in a grim line, he shoved open the door, sending it crashing against the opposite wall.

This time there was no egret to greet him. The tower was deserted. As he padded across the room, the vacant eyes of Angelica's dolls watched him from their shelf.

A single candle was burning in a silver candlestick on the edge of the dressing table, its dancing flame casting a warm glow over the tower. In that forgiving light it was almost possible to imagine the chamber exactly as it had been on the night Timberlake had died.

The report Max had received from Andrew Murray had brought the events of that night into crisp focus. As Max turned in a slow circle, the room seemed to revolve around him, the present melting into the past. Instead of a brisk autumn wind, he could feel a warm spring breeze drifting through windows that weren't shattered, but propped open, their diamond-paned glass fracturing the candle's glow into a thousand tiny flames. The lace draped over the half-tester's canopy drifted in a snowy-white fall over the shiny brass bed. The keys of the harpsichord weren't cracked and yellow, but white and even. The trailing ivy painted on the freshly whitewashed walls was verdant and green.

Several silk and satin bolsters had been removed from the cream-colored coverlet adorning the bed and piled on the velvet cushions of the window seat. It was a stage set for seduction.

Angelica would have had to wait for the perfect moment to slip away from her own birthday fete so she could meet Timberlake for their rendezvous. They would have already publicly celebrated

the triumph of her portrait's unveiling together—
Timberlake basking in the delighted gasps and applause of the guests, Angelica stunned to see herself
through his adoring eyes for the first time.

Hearing the ghostly tap of a woman's slippers on
the stairs, Max whirled around to face the door.

As she hurried up the winding stairs, Angelica
could probably still hear the muted laughter, the clink
of champagne glasses, and the music of the string
orchestra drifting into the night through the open
French windows of the ballroom. She would have appeared in the doorway, breathless from ascending the
stairs so fast, the color high in her cheeks, her sherry-
colored eyes sparkling with both nerves and anticipation.

Timberlake would have been standing just *there*,
Max decided, where the candlelight would show
him off to his best advantage. He would have given
her that teasing smile she loved so well, his hair
gleaming like spun gold. He would have looked so
handsome, so dashing—like a young prince who
had scaled the walls of her tower to steal a kiss. How
could she resist him? How could any woman resist
him?

Max closed his eyes, inhaling a phantom breath
of jasmine as Angelica rushed right through him
and into Timberlake's waiting arms. Had he wooed
her with a private waltz around the tower before

claiming the softness of her trembling lips as his prize? How long had it taken for his embrace to become too tight, his kisses too forceful, his groping hands too free? How long before he'd shattered all of her hopes and dreams by shoving her down on the window seat and falling on top of her, his greedy hands tearing at the finery she had chosen just to please him?

Was that when she had screamed? Was that when her brother had come rushing up those stairs and burst into the tower, pistol in hand, and put an end to Timberlake and his wicked schemes forever?

Max opened his eyes. A darkened stain was on the timber floor next to the window seat overlooking the sea—a stain that hadn't been there the last time he had visited the tower.

He crossed the floor and crouched beside it, touching two fingertips to the dark blot to find it still warm and sticky. As he lifted his fingers to his nose and inhaled, there was no mistaking the coppery tang of fresh blood.

He slowly stood, wiping his fingertips on his trousers. A gust of wind soared through the tower, extinguishing both the candle and his glimpse into the past. Moonlight revealed the chamber for the ruin it was. A jagged crack divided the looking glass in two. Rotting lace drifted from the canopy of the half-tester like a shroud for a body that would never be found. The window seat was a gaping mouth, its rotted wooden teeth lying in wait to devour anyone who ventured too near.

Without the candle to hold the darkness at bay, the night beyond the window came into sharper focus. Max sucked in a harsh breath as he spotted the woman standing on the very tip of the promontory.

He must not have forgotten how to dream after all. Hadn't he seen her just like this once before in his dreams? Standing on the edge of those cliffs with her buttercup-colored skirts billowing around her?

He wanted to shout her name, but he knew she would never hear him over the bullying voice of the wind and the roar of the waves crashing against the cliffs.

Max took off down the stairs at a dead run. He slipped on a crumbling step and almost fell, but didn't slow, not even when he reached the foot of the stairs. He burst out of the tower, emerging from its shadow to find the wind had scattered the clouds, but left the stars hanging like shards of ice against a field of black velvet.

He sprinted through the breezeway and went racing along the edge of the cliffs toward the promontory. He might be dreaming, but the sharp stones tearing at the soles of his feet felt painfully real.

As he drew closer to the promontory, he half-expected to find it as deserted as the tower. But she was still there, a slender figure standing all alone on the fragile shelf of rock that jutted out over the water.

The White Lady of Cadgwyck.

Moonlight silvered the crests of the waves behind her and limned her in its loving light, making her look less than solid. Max stumbled to a halt, his chest heaving with ragged breaths. He was terrified that if he drew even one step closer to her, he would startle her right over the edge of the cliff. The wind buffeted him with the force of a fist, as if trying to keep them apart.

She slowly turned to look over her shoulder at him, her long, dark hair whipping across her face until all he could see was the wistful regret in her eyes. Then she turned back to the sea, spread her arms as if they were wings, and vanished over the edge of the cliff.

"*No!*"

The hoarse echo of Max's shout was still ringing in his ears when he lunged forward and went diving over the edge of the cliff after her.

# Chapter Thirty-three

MAX WAS SINKING.

The darkness enveloped him in its seductive embrace as if it had always been waiting for him. He could hear its sibilant whisper through the roaring in his ears, promising him that all he had to do was close his eyes and open his mouth and he could sleep, never to be troubled by dreams again. He wondered if it was the same voice Angelica had heard all those years ago.

Fighting to resist both the voice and the pressure swelling in his lungs, he kicked frantically toward the undulating orb of the moon. He broke through the surface of the water just in time to catch a salty wave square in the mouth. He coughed and sputtered, then dragged in a desperate breath and dove again, ignoring the painful scrape of thigh against rock as another wave sought to hurl him to his death.

Trying to peer through the murk was futile. Closing his eyes, he raked his arm through the water, seeking any evidence that he was not alone.

That he was not too late.

His groping hands closed on emptiness again and again until he could feel both his breath and his strength begin to flag. It seemed his White Lady was going to have the last laugh after all. He could almost see Anne rolling her eyes over his foolishness as she was marched before the constable to explain how their latest master had drowned after plunging over the edge of a cliff to rescue a ghost.

Then he felt it—the silky ribbons of a woman's hair drifting through his splayed fingers. He lunged forward, half-afraid his arms were going to close around the rotting bones of a corpse that had been trapped beneath the sea for a decade. But living flesh filled his arms, its squirming softness undeniably feminine.

Triumph coursed through his veins, fueling his determination. He was not going to be too late. Not this time.

Anchoring his arm around his prize, he used the last of his strength on a mighty kick, sending them both shooting toward the surface. They broke through the churning water, gasping for breath. The outgoing tide tried to suck them out to sea, but Max's powerful kicks drove them away from the deadly rocks and toward the gentle curve of the cove, where the surf murmured instead of roared and the sand shimmered like crushed diamonds in the moonlight.

The waves continued to batter them from behind until they washed up on the shore and collapsed in the wet sand, still sputtering and coughing.

Max was too exhausted to protest when his companion struggled her way out of his arms. She crawled a few feet away from him, then staggered to her feet.

Still panting with exertion, she swung around to glare at him through the strings of sodden hair plastered to her face. "Damn you, Maximillian Burke! *Would you stop rescuing me?*"

Even with its crisp tones softened by fear, it was impossible not to recognize that no-nonsense voice. Max sat up, tossing his wet hair out of his eyes. If he hadn't looked like a beached herring before, he most certainly did now. Especially with his mouth hanging open in shock.

His housekeeper was standing before him, the yellow dress from the portrait clinging to her every luscious curve and revealing *exactly* what she'd been hiding beneath her staid gowns and aprons for all these weeks. Without the restricting net to confine it, her hair hung nearly to her waist. The weight of the water couldn't completely dampen its natural exuberance. It was already beginning to curl into charming little ringlets in the moist sea air.

"You *idiot*!" she shouted. "What in the bloody hell did you think you were doing?"

Rising slowly to his feet to face her, he said evenly, "Don't you think I should be the one asking you what in the bloody hell *you* were doing?"

"Oh, I was just in the mood for a little midnight swim," she said, sarcasm ripening in her voice.

"Perhaps you should consider swimming in a place where you aren't in danger of being dashed to death on the rocks."

"I know exactly where all the rocks are! You don't! You could have landed on one and cracked your fool skull wide open. Of course as hard as your head is, it probably would have cracked the rock instead! And I wouldn't have been in any danger of being dashed to death on the rocks if I hadn't had to jump back in the water to try and save you."

"If you didn't want me to dive in after you, then just what did you want me to do?" he thundered, his temper mounting along with his confusion.

"I wanted you to go away, you silly, stubborn, dear man," she wailed, tears welling up in her eyes. "I wanted you to be just like all the rest of them and tuck your expensive tailcoat between your legs and go running bàck to London!"

Max pondered her words for a moment. "If you

didn't want to marry me, you could have just said so. There was no need for you to throw yourself over a cliff."

A strangled sound between a sob and a shriek tore from her throat. Still swaying on her feet, she bent to scoop up a gout of wet sand and hurled it at his head.

He dodged it easily. "It was you all along, wasn't it?" he asked, the pieces of the puzzle finally beginning to click into place. "The mysterious lights, the music box, the ghostly laughter. *You're* the White Lady of Cadgwyck Manor." He drifted across the sand toward her, no more able to resist her now than when she had been standing on the edge of the cliff. "But why, Anne? What would you stand to gain by perpetrating such a dangerous hoax?"

"It wasn't what I stood to gain! It's what I stood to lose!"

Before she could elaborate, Dickon and Pippa came spilling out of the shadows at the base of the cliffs, all five of the Elizabeths fast on their heels. Max stared as they came pelting across the sand toward them, Dickon in the lead. Even if a path had been carved into the rocks, they could not possibly have climbed down the steep face of the cliffs that quickly.

*The sea caves,* he thought. The ones Dickon had promised to show him before the fire. The coast had been rife with smugglers only a few decades ago. Why should it surprise him to learn the caves were hiding passages leading up to the house? Hell, why should anything he discovered on this night surprise him?

Dickon and the others stumbled to a halt. As Pippa bent over to rest her hands on her knees so she could catch her breath, Dickon jumped into the air, pumping his fist in Max's direction. "I can't believe you're still alive!" The boy flashed Anne a delighted grin. "You should have seen the way he went flying off that cliff after you. He didn't hesitate for even a heartbeat. It was magnificent!"

"It was insane!" Anne shouted at him before rounding on Max once more. "I was a ghost! I was supposed to already be dead. What was your brilliant plan? To join me?"

"I didn't really have a plan." Max eyed the others through narrowed eyes. "Although obviously the rest of you did. What was your part in all this, lad?" he asked Dickon, hoping to take advantage of the boy's exhilaration to ferret the truth out of him.

Dickon cast Anne a questioning look. When she responded with a weary nod, his grin widened. "It was my job to light the candle and open the music box when Annie gave me the signal."

"And I was the one who provided the scream," Pippa added eagerly, plainly tired of hiding her light beneath a bushel. "Bloodcurdling, wasn't it? I do believe I might have an affinity for the stage. I'm thinking of going to London to tread the boards. I could very well be the next Sarah Siddons!"

Max shifted his darkening gaze to the wide-eyed huddle of Elizabeths. "And you?"

The maids briefly conferred among themselves before nudging Lisbeth forward. Eyeing him shyly, she bobbed an awkward curtsy. "We was to clean up the tower before you returned, m'lord. You know . . . so you'd think you'd gone all squirrelly in the head and catch the next coach back to London like them others did."

"Why didn't you just throw a sheet over poor Nana's head and make her shuffle up and down the lawn, clanking chains?" Max asked.

"Nana strangled the chicken we used for the blood," Dickon cheerfully offered. "We're having stewed chicken for supper tomorrow, you know."

"Which one of you had the job of sneaking into my bedchamber in the dead of night?" Max suspected he already knew the answer to that question.

"That would be me." Anne folded her arms over her chest, looking decidedly unrepentant. "Your armoire has a false back that leads to a secret passage, one that was once used to hide Cadgwyck's priest when the soldiers of Henry VIII came looking for him. It was a simple enough feat to slip into your bedchamber, open your balcony doors, wave a bottle of perfume around."

Max glared at her, wondering if it had been her on every occasion he had felt Angelica's presence hovering near his bed. "I ought to have the lot of you hauled off to jail. But, unfortunately, I don't think impersonating a dead woman is a hanging offense." He started toward her, trying to figure out how a woman could look like a drowned rat and yet so beguiling all at the same time. "I may just save the constable the trouble and strangle you myself."

She took a wary step backward, but before he could reach her, another shape came melting out of the cliff face. Max shook his head in disgust. "And I suppose it was *his* job to fire the pistol?"

They all turned to find Hodges crossing the sand in the moonlight, an ivory-plated dueling pistol gripped in his hand.

"No." Dickon's grin faded. "That was my job, too."

"Dickon," Anne said softly.

Heeding her unspoken command, the boy immediately wrapped his arms around Pippa and the maids, shepherding them out of harm's way.

Max rolled his eyes. "I don't know what you're so worried about. The pistol has already been fired."

"They're a matched pair of dueling pistols," Anne murmured calmly, as if a maniac with murder on his mind weren't marching across the sand toward them. "They were both loaded and I have no way of knowing which one he has."

Max lunged forward, determined to put himself between her and the weapon. Before he could succeed, Hodges raised the pistol, his hand surprisingly steady, and pointed it right at Max's chest. Max froze, afraid to make any sudden movements. He might accidentally goad the butler into firing, and if the man's aim was off, he could still easily hit Anne.

Hodges's voice rang with a confidence Max had never before heard. "Step away from her, you scoundrel! Or I'll blow you straight to hell!"

"Put down the pistol, Hodges," Max said gently, inching away from Anne instead of toward her. "Then we can discuss this man-to-man."

"You're no man! A man wouldn't try to force himself on an innocent girl! You're a monster!" Hodges raked back the hammer of the pistol.

"No!" Anne cried, stepping toward him with hand outstretched. "He's not the one who tried to hurt me. He's the one who tried to save me." She forced a tremulous smile, a coaxing note creeping into her voice. "Why, just look at him! He's all wet because he jumped into the water after me! Isn't he such a silly goose?"

Hodges cocked his head, still eyeing Max with

open suspicion. "But I would have sworn I heard you scream."

"That was me," Pippa said desperately. "I . . . I saw a spider. A very *large*, very hairy spider."

Hodges's hand had began to waver.

"There now, darling," Anne said soothingly. "Why don't you hand over that nasty pistol and let Dickon take you up to bed? You must be ever so tired."

The butler shook his head. "It's all my fault. I'm the one who brought him here. I won't leave you alone with him. I should have never left you alone with him."

"Hodges!" Max snapped, imbuing his voice with all of the authority at his command. "I'm your master and I order you to give Dickon that pistol! Right now!"

It was almost painful to watch Hodges's shoulders slump, to see his features soften back into a mask of bewilderment. "Aye, my lord," he whispered. "As you wish."

His hand fell to his side, leaving the pistol dangling from his fingertips. As Dickon rushed forward to gently remove it from his grip, Anne closed her eyes, breathing a shuddering sigh of relief.

"You're right," the old man mumbled, reaching up to ruffle his hair. "I'm ever so tired. Not accustomed to staying up so late . . . the ball . . . so many guests to look after . . . such a dreadful fuss . . ."

"Come now, sir," Dickon said, taking him by the elbow. "I'll see you to your bed."

Before Dickon could steer him back toward the caves, Hodges turned to look at Anne. "I'm so glad you decided to wear that gown to the ball. You look absolutely stunning in it. It was your mother's, you know. That's why I wanted you painted in it. She would have been so proud of you."

Anne took a step toward him, her face constricted with some painful emotion. "Do you know who I am?"

"Of course I know who you are." Hodges beamed at her, all the love in the world shining from his eyes. "You're my darling little girl—my angel . . . my Angelica."

"Dear God," Max breathed as he realized his butler was no butler at all, but mad old Lord Cadgwyck himself.

Anne went to him, then. Cupping his ruddy face in her hands, she touched her lips to his brow, then drew back and whispered, "Good night, Papa."

He gently smoothed her wet hair away from her face, gazing tenderly at her. "There now, don't cry, poppet. You know I can't bear it when you cry. You're my good girl, aren't you? You've always been my good girl. I'm so glad you came back. I've been waiting for ever so long."

He was still beaming at her over his shoulder as

Dickon led him away. Avoiding Max's eyes, the others trailed after them, leaving Max and Anne all alone on the beach.

Still standing with her back to him, Anne wrapped her arms around herself, shivering in the cool night air.

Max shook his head, stunned by what he had just witnessed. "That poor devil. No wonder he's so confused. He actually believes you're his daughter. After all this time, who would have ever thought . . ." Max trailed off as she turned to look over her shoulder at him, the beseeching look in her eyes more devastating than a blow.

He should have seen it before. It had been there, right before his eyes the entire time—in the proud tilt of her head, the sparkle of mischief in her eyes, the mocking smile that always seemed to be poised on her lips even when she wasn't smiling. She might never live up to the absurdly idealized vision of herself in the portrait, but she was beautiful in her own right—even more beautiful in Max's eyes because of the very flaws the artist had chosen to conceal.

He was haunted by his own smug words: *I've always believed every mystery is nothing more than a mathematical equation that can be solved if you find the right variables and apply them in the correct order.* How had he managed to find all of the wrong variables, then applied them in no particular order whatso-ever?

As the girl from the portrait and the woman standing before him merged into one, Max sank down on the nearest rock, gazing up at her in speech-less wonder.

# ❧ *Chapter Thirty-four*

*S*URPRISED BY HOW GOOD it felt to finally have substance and form again, Angelica turned to face Max, tossing her wet hair out of her eyes. "You needn't berate yourself for not seeing the resemblance sooner. Laurie's gift was to flatter his subjects until they were all but unrecognizable, even to themselves. And I am ten years older than when the portrait was painted. I lost my baby fat a long time ago. Of course, in my vainer moments I still like to think I bear some passing resemblance to that spectacular creature. But my hair was never quite that glossy, my nose so perfect, or my cheek so rosy. And Timberlake did insist on painting me with my mouth closed to hide that unsightly gap between my teeth."

"I adore the gap between your teeth," Max growled. "But why? Why on earth would you fake your own death?"

Unable to bear the weight of his searching gaze, Angelica turned toward the sea, watching the moonlight dance across the crests of the waves. "When I stepped off the cliff that night, I had every intention of ending my life. But it seems God, with his infinite wit and wisdom, had other ideas. I missed the rocks entirely, and when the current started to drag me beneath the water and out to sea, I discovered I was just as selfish and strong willed as I'd always been. It wasn't in me to just give up and sink into the sea and meet the tragic end I deserved. So I took a deep breath and struck out for the cove. I had always been a strong swimmer, you see." A faint smile touched her lips as she remembered warmer days, summer idylls with her laughing, freckle-faced brother by her side. "When we were little, Theo and I used to sneak down through the caves and swim here whenever Papa was otherwise occupied. It took every ounce of strength I had, but I finally managed to haul myself up on this very beach." She turned to look at Max, meeting his fierce gaze with one of her own. "A girl went into the sea that night. A woman came out. A woman who would fight to survive and win back everything she'd lost."

"Anne Spencer," he said softly.

She nodded. "They would have never let Angelica Cadgwyck back into the manor. But with patience and planning, I knew Anne Spencer just might be able to sneak in through the servants' entrance. So I tossed my shawl back into the water, slipped back up to the house through the caves, packed a bag, and ran away."

Max rose to his feet, his face a study in frustration and rage. "I still can't understand why you were driven to such a desperate act. Was there no one to help you?"

"Theo was already on a ship bound for Australia in chains, and they'd come and taken Papa away to the asylum in Falmouth. It was to be my last night in the only home I'd ever known. Papa's solicitor had paid a call earlier in the day. He was kind enough to point out that there might be certain *opportunities* for a young woman of my looks and breeding who was considered to be 'soiled goods.' He even very generously offered to take me to London himself and set me up in a small apartment he could visit whenever the fancy struck him."

"Give me the man's name," Max said flatly. "I'll see him ruined within the fortnight ... if I don't kill him first. How in the name of God did you survive after you *died* that night?"

She shrugged away all the years of drudgery and loneliness. "I went into service. I became exactly who I was pretending to be. I learned all there was to know about managing a household so I could come back here someday and mismanage Cadgwyck." A rueful little smile played around her lips. "If Papa had his wits about him, I've often thought how it would have made him laugh to imagine his pampered little princess changing linens and scrubbing baseboards."

Max didn't look the least bit amused. "Why come back to this place at all? Why take such a risk? Is it because Cadgwyck was your home?"

She lifted her gaze to the top of the cliffs, where the uneven roofline and crumbling chimneys of the manor were just barely visible. "My home and my prison. There have been days when I think I'd like nothing more than to set a match to it myself and watch it burn." She drew closer to him, desperate to make him understand. "But from the time Theo and I were very small children, Papa told us tales of a mysterious and fantastic treasure that had been brought back from Jerusalem by one of our ancestors after the last Crusade. Papa never worried about his creditors or his mounting debts because he told us that if things ever became too dire, we would simply sell the treasure and be so fabulously rich we'd never lack for anything." She sighed. "But he never would tell us what the treasure was, just that it was hidden somewhere within the walls of the manor."

Max's words would have been less painful if he hadn't taken such care to gentle his gruff tones.

"What if this treasure never existed? What if it was just some fanciful tale concocted from legend and wishful thinking to amuse his children?"

"I couldn't afford to believe that. I knew if I could find it, I would be able to hire a solicitor to clear Theo's name and an investigator to locate him and bring him back from Australia. We could buy a new home somewhere far away from this place and be a family again."

"Your father looked very comfortable with that pistol in his hand. It wasn't Theo who pulled the trigger that night, was it?"

Angelica closed her eyes briefly, haunted by images she had spent the last ten years trying to forget. "They both heard me scream, but it was Papa who made it up the stairs first and found me with my dress half torn off and Timberlake on top of me, trying to . . ." She swallowed, surprised by how fresh the memory of that night still was. "I went there believing he was going to offer for me, to ask Papa for my hand. Or perhaps even try to coax me into eloping with him. What a ridiculous little fool I was to fall for that charlatan's tricks! And my folly cost my family everything."

"You might have been young and innocent and naïve," Max said softly, "but you were no fool."

"Papa shot Timberlake, but the strain was too much for him. He collapsed to the floor, clutching his head. Theo and I both knew he would never survive prison, especially not in that condition. So we made a pact never to tell anyone what really happened. When the first guests came rushing over from the ballroom and up the stairs, it was to find Theo standing over Timberlake's body with the gun." She lifted her chin and met Max's gaze squarely, no longer forced to hide the bloodthirsty glint in her eye. "I wish it had been me who shot him."

Max slowly nodded. "And I wish it had been me. Just how long did it take you to make your way back here?"

"Six years. After five years, I managed to collect Papa from the asylum by pretending to be a long-lost cousin. He'd been there so long no one remembered he had once been a powerful lord. His *keepers* thought it was just another delusion. I found him living in squalor in a dirty cell that was little more than a stall." She lowered her eyes and bit her lip, reluctant to reveal such a private pain. "He didn't remember me. He talked about Angelica all the time, but never seemed to realize that I was her."

"Until tonight," Max said softly, reminding her of the tender adoration in her father's eyes as he had smoothed her hair away from her face. "What about Pippa and Dickon? Where did you manage to collect them?"

She dragged the chain of her locket over her head

and handed it to him. He snapped the locket open, a puzzled frown furrowing his brow as he studied the two miniatures nestled within. "I recognize you and the boy who must be Theo. But who are the two children on the other side?"

Angelica leaned over, pointing at the little girl with the riotous dark curls holding a scowling baby boy in a long, white gown in her chubby arms. "The girl is Pippa and the boy is Dickon. They're my half brother and sister."

Max looked nearly as stunned as he had when he'd discovered she was Angelica.

"Please don't judge Papa too harshly. To honor my mother's memory, he chose never to remarry. But he had been a widower for a *very* long time, which resulted in a certain *friendship* with a pretty, young seamstress in Falmouth. When she died during a cholera outbreak, he brought Pippa and Dickon into our household and passed them off as distant cousins. He was determined to provide for them in every way, both emotionally and financially."

"What happened to them after your father's collapse?"

Angelica felt her face harden again. "Papa's oh-so-helpful solicitor managed to find homes for them—at a workhouse in London. It took me almost five years to track them down. Pippa had been adopted by a wealthy tradesman and had grown accustomed to lolling about in the lap of luxury, and Dickon had run away from the workhouse and was living on the streets, picking pockets to earn his bread." She couldn't help laughing at the memory. "Although they both came with me of their own accord, you've never met two more surly brats. Pippa still fancies herself quite the little lady of the manor, but Dickon began to blossom after I brought him here and turned him loose to run on the moors."

Max arched an eyebrow at her. "And just who might the Elizabeths be? Long-lost cousins?"

"Just girls who had lost their way in this world. I found most of them on the streets of London, half-starved and abandoned by the men they had believed would take care of them."

"And Nana?"

"My former nurse. Since my mother died in childbirth, Nana all but raised me. She was staying with her son and his brood in a nearby village when I came back to Cornwall, but leapt at the chance to return to Cadgwyck and live out her final years. Everyone I brought to this place had one thing in common: they understood the power of secrets and knew how to keep them."

"Aren't you forgetting the most important member of your cozy little household?"

"Who?"

"The White Lady."

Anne lifted her chin to a haughty angle. "Nobody around these parts had ever forgotten Angelica Cadgwyck and her tragic end. We started spreading fresh rumors about the ghost long before we arrived. As you've already discovered, the locals are a superstitious lot, only too willing to attribute a will-o'-the-wisp or a banging shutter to some restless spirit. Before long Cadgwyck's new owners couldn't find anyone brave enough to spend the night here, much less staff the manor."

"And that's when the ever-practical Anne Spencer stepped in to save the day," Max said, irony lacing his tone.

Anne Spencer's dutiful smile appeared on Angelica's lips. "Who could resist a reputable housekeeper with an entire staff of servants at her disposal? Once we were in residence, it became even easier to keep the legend of the White Lady alive. With each new master, the manor became a little less hospitable, a little more haunted."

"How did you keep the villagers from recognizing you all?"

"Dickon does bear a striking resemblance to Theo, but he and Pippa were only small children when they were taken away. And we never let Hodges—I mean Papa—go into the village."

"What about you? You go into the village every

week. How on earth could they fail to recognize you?"

"Even without the portrait to confuse them, I bear little resemblance to the pampered child they knew. People see what they expect to see. And most people don't see servants at all. They're nearly as invisible to the rest of the world as ghosts."

Max shook his head. "When I think of your poor father reduced to living as a servant in his own home . . ." He frowned. "Wait a minute. You told me it was a stipulation of his that Angelica's portrait never leave the house."

"There was no stipulation. *I* was the one who dragged the portrait down from the attic and hung it on the landing to keep the legend of the White Lady alive. And to remind myself of the girl I had once been . . . and who I never wanted to be again. Then you had to come along and ruin everything! To prove I was still the same romantic fool who would give my heart to a man for the price of a kiss."

Dangerous storm clouds had began to gather in his eyes. "*You're* a romantic fool? I just flung myself over a cliff for you."

She shook her head sadly. "Not for me. For *her*. For Angelica."

"You *are* Angelica," he growled. "My head wouldn't let me admit it, but somewhere deep in my heart, I think I always knew."

They stood there glaring at each other in the moonlight for a long moment before Angelica said quietly, "If you're not going to send for the constable and have me hauled off to jail, I suppose I should start looking for another position."

"Yes. I think that would be best. For the both of us." He drew himself up, every inch the cold, forbidding master who had come to Cadgwyck Manor all those weeks ago. "I'd be more than happy to write you a letter of recommendation."

"Considering the circumstances," she said stiffly, "that would be incredibly gracious of you."

"It will probably read something like this: 'Angelica Cadgwyck, also known as Anne Spencer and any other number of unknown aliases, is the very model of everything a gentleman would seek in a housekeeper—sharp-tongued, bossy, deceitful, proud, sneaky, conniving, unscrupulous, utterly ruthless when it comes to achieving her aims—'"

Although his words flayed her tender heart like a barbed whip, Angelica held her tongue, knowing she had earned every acerbic syllable of his rebuke.

"'—clever, courageous, honorable, sensible, determined, patient, generous, kind, devoted, an outstanding cook, marvelous with children, the elderly, the mentally infirm, and small, annoying pets, loyal to a fault, and by far the finest kisser I have *ever* had the pleasure of taking to my bed. Any man would be blessed to welcome her to his household, not as a housekeeper, but as a wife. Which is why I pray she'll do me the honor of becoming mine.'"

Angelica turned her back on him, not wanting him to see the fresh tears welling up in her eyes. "I know what you're trying to do, Maximillian Burke, and I won't have it! I'm not some damsel in distress anymore, and I don't require rescuing by the likes of you!"

His hands closed over her upper arms, warming her chilled flesh with their irresistible heat. He touched his lips to her hair, the smoky rasp of his voice making her shiver with a need deeper than longing. "I'm the one who needs rescuing. Save me, Anne . . . Angelica . . . sweetheart. Save me from going back to being the man I was before I came here. Save me from all the years of loneliness I'll have to endure without you in my arms. Save me from spending the rest of my life longing for a woman I can never have."

Angelica turned in his arms. His dear, handsome face blurred before her eyes as she reached up to touch her fingertip to the furrow between his brows, smoothing out the scowl she loved so well. "Beneath that fearsome mask you wear, you're nothing but a hopeless romantic. It's what I've always adored the most about you."

He gazed down at her, his gray eyes no longer

cold, but smoldering with a fierce heat. "I don't want to be hopeless anymore. Will you give me hope?"

"I'll give you more than hope," she vowed, smiling up at him through a shimmering veil of tears. "I'll give you my heart, my body, and my love for as long as we both shall live."

He shook his head, his expression solemn. "That's not long enough. If you should die before I do, God forbid, you have to promise to come back and haunt me until we can be reunited again."

"Have no fear. I promise to wail and clank my chains so loudly you'll never get another decent night's rest. Especially if you're foolish enough to re-marry and bring your new bride back to Cadgwyck."

Max's lips curled in a wicked grin. "If I have anything to say about it, you'll never get another decent night's rest after we're wed."

As a joyous peal of laughter burst from her lips, he swept her up into his arms and off her feet, swinging her in a wide circle. He had finally succeeded in catching his ghost, and there on the same beach where Angelica Cadgwyck's life had ended, it began again.

## ⁂ *Epilogue*

MAXIMILLIAN BURKE'S COACH ROLLED through the imposing wrought-iron gates and up the long, winding drive of crushed shells. He stuck his head out the window of the elegant vehicle, eager for his first glimpse of home. As the steep gables and soaring brick chimneys of the house came into view, his heart leapt with an undeniable mixture of satisfaction and pride.

Cadgwyck Manor was one of the shining gems of the Cornwall coast. No one could say it had seen better days because these were undoubtedly its best. A gleaming cherrywood door had been set in the mouth of the ancient gatehouse that served as both entrance hall and the heart of the house. Graceful Elizabethan wings flanked the gatehouse. The leering gargoyles that doubled as rainspouts had been replaced with chubby stone cherubs.

The manor looked not only well cared for, but well

loved, as if its sturdy walls might well stand guardian on the edge of the cliffs for another five centuries.

A tower right out of a fairy tale crowned the far corner of the west wing, capped by a pretty little red-tiled turret. The autumn sunshine winked off its diamond-paned windows, and just enough ivy had been left creeping up its stone walls to give it an enchanted air. Max felt a roguish smile curve his lips. The tower now served as the master bedchamber of the house, and he had every intention of making some magic there on this very night.

As the coach rolled to a stop in the courtyard, its handsome team of matched grays still prancing restlessly, a footman in blue-and-gold livery came rushing forward to whisk open its lacquered door.

"Welcome home, m'lord," Derrick Hammett said, his ginger hair and good-natured grin a welcome sight indeed. The lad's cheeks were no longer sunken. His broad shoulders filled out his livery so nicely that the Elizabeths all blushed and stammered and had to fan themselves with their feather dusters whenever he sauntered by.

"Hammett." Max greeted the young man with a nod and a smile as he descended from the carriage. "I hope your mother and sister are well."

"Indeed they are, m'lord! Indeed they are!"

Max had no reason to doubt Hammett's words, especially now that the young man's mother and sister were working in the Cadgwyck kitchens. There seemed to be no shortage of help at Cadgwyck these days. The generosity of its master and mistress toward their staff was becoming something of a legend around these parts. Just last December, they had hosted a Christmas ball for the servants featuring bowls of warm, spiced punch, individual flaming puddings, and a bonus of two pounds apiece. Each servant had also received a colorful wool muffler knit by Nana herself to ease them through the cold winter months.

Max handed his hat and walking stick to Hammett and turned toward the house, breathing deeply of the scent of the sea, which had come to mean home to him.

The front door of the manor came flying open.

He had once imagined returning home from a long journey only to have a loving wife run out to greet him, trailed by a moppet or two, all eager to leap into his arms and smother his face with kisses.

That face split into a huge grin as Angelica came running down the steps of the portico and across the courtyard, her lovely face alight with joy and her arms already outstretched toward him.

Dickon was right behind her. At fourteen, he was finally on the verge of growing into his lanky legs and arms. Pippa strolled behind her brother, twirling the parasol she carried everywhere to protect her fair skin from the sun. She was far too dignified and elegant a young lady to be caught sprinting across a courtyard.

Max opened his arms and Angelica flew right into them, smothering his throat and jaw with eager kisses. He wrapped his arms around her, burying his face in hair that still smelled of freshly baked bread and cherishing the solid warmth of her in his arms. He supposed he would always secretly fear he might reach for her only to have her vanish into a wisp of jasmine-scented vapor.

She tipped back her head and he claimed her smiling lips for a tender kiss. He could feel the firm swell of her growing belly pressing against his groin. Soon he would have a moppet of his very own to run out and greet him when he returned from a journey. Not that he intended to make many more journeys without Angelica by his side.

For now he would have to content himself with Piddles, who capered around their merry little group on his stout legs, barking in staccato bursts designed solely for the purpose of piercing the human eardrum.

"We missed you so much!" Angelica exclaimed. "I can't believe you let that nasty old Company drag you away from us again."

"I'm sorry, darling. I told them I wouldn't come back to the Court of Directors, but there was a very important matter that required my attention."

She gave him a haughty look. "I am a very important matter that requires your attention."

"And I can promise you now that I'm home, I have absolutely no intention of neglecting my duties." He gave her a wicked leer, then seized her mouth for another long, fierce kiss that made Dickon groan and Pippa duck behind her parasol, rolling her eyes.

"How was your voyage?" Dickon asked, always eager to hear about adventure and exotic climes.

"Far too long," Max replied.

"Did you bring me a present?" Pippa inquired, peering hopefully toward the coach.

"I most certainly did, poppet. But I couldn't bring it with me. I'm afraid you'll have to be patient until it arrives." Max could hardly wait for her to meet the stout, balding, seventy-three-year-old artist who would be arriving within the fortnight to paint her portrait as a surprise for her eighteenth birthday.

Angelica patted the pocket of her apron. She still had a habit of wearing a plain white apron over the exquisite gowns Max had ordered from the finest modistes in London for her extensive wardrobe. "I received another letter from Clarinda while you were gone."

Since he and Angelica had wed, she and Clarinda had struck up quite a correspondence, a rather unnerving prospect for any man who had ever loved two women at different times in his life.

"She and Ash are coming home in November for

a few months and she wants to know if they can bring Charlotte and spend Christmas here with us at Cadgwyck."

Max heaved a long-suffering sigh. "If I'm never going to be rid of that ne'er-do-well brother of mine, I suppose I might as well get used to having him around. Perhaps I can drag out the toy soldiers and best him in a mock battle."

"They'd also like to bring Farouk and Poppy and their brood. If you don't mind, of course."

"Why would I mind? Wait a minute," he added, warned by the mischievous sparkle dancing in her eyes. "Just how large is Farouk's brood?"

She blinked up at him, all innocence. "At last count, I believe they had twenty children."

"Twenty?"

"Well, they only have one son of their own so far, but Farouk did have a harem before he fell in love with Poppy."

Max shook his head in dazed disbelief. "Dear God, and to think I was willing to be content with an even dozen."

"Ha!" Angelica said, resting a hand on her belly. "You'll be content with two if I have anything to say about it. Or maybe three, if you don't scowl and growl at me too much."

Max leaned down to nuzzle her throat, murmuring, "I thought you liked it when I growled."

She giggled like a girl, then leaned away from him to peer into his face. "Was there any word this time?"

Max hesitated. Every time he'd been to London in the past two years to meet with his team of investigators—the finest money could hire, including Andrew Murray, the man who had ferreted out the truth about Laurence Timberlake—Max had returned to Angelica only to quench the hope in her beautiful hazel eyes.

"There was no word," he said softly, watching her face fall. "But I did bring you something that might be of interest."

Max crooked a finger toward the coach. A man slowly emerged from the shadows of the vehicle. If his tawny hair hadn't been bleached pale gold by the sun and his freckles buried beneath a deep-bronze tan, it would have been like seeing an image of Dickon as he might look twenty years from now.

The man stood beside the carriage, clutching his hat in his hands and hanging back as if uncertain of his welcome.

"*Theo?*" Angelica whispered, a mixture of wonder and disbelief dawning in her eyes.

"Annie?" The man's throat bobbed as he swallowed back a visible rush of emotion.

Max felt his own throat tighten as Angelica ran to her brother and flung her arms around his neck, a sob of pure joy spilling from her lips. When Pippa and Dickon would have joined her, Max held them back, wanting to give Angelica and Theo time to savor their reunion. After a few minutes of laughing and crying and murmuring among themselves, Angelica beckoned Pippa and Dickon over to greet their half brother.

Dickon immediately began to tug Theo toward the house. "I want to hear all about Australia! Are there really little bears that live in trees and eat leaves and jackrabbits as tall as a man who can knock a bloke out with a single punch?"

Pippa followed, still twirling her parasol. "Are there lots of handsome convicts in Australia? Are very many of them looking for brides?"

Angelica linked her arm through Max's, resting her head against his shoulder as they followed the others to the house. "I can't believe you did this for me."

He patted the hand she'd wrapped around his arm. "I would do anything for you. Even fling myself off a cliff."

"If you'll meet me in the tower tonight after everyone else is abed, I'll show you everything I would do for you."

"Everything?" he echoed hopefully, cocking one eyebrow.

"Everything," she promised, smiling up at him.

They climbed the stairs of the portico and entered the house to find the others had already headed for the kitchen, no doubt following the irresistible aroma of the freshly baked bread Angelica had taken from the oven shortly before Max's coach arrived. At first they thought the entrance hall was deserted, but then they heard a peculiar melody of clanging and cursing.

The door to the longcase clock at the foot of the stairs was standing open. Angelica's papa had crawled half inside the thing. All that was visible of him was his black-clad rump.

"He spends most of his time dodging the nurses you've hired to take care of him," Angelica whispered. "Since the clock will probably never work again anyway, we decided it wouldn't do any harm to let him poke around in the works. It keeps him out of trouble."

Her papa emerged from the clock, his snowy-white hair standing on end and his nose smudged with grease. "You there, lad," he said, pointing a wooden wrench at Max. "Fetch me a cup of tea right away."

As he disappeared back into the clock, Angelica explained apologetically, "He thinks he's master of the house and you're a footman."

"Then I'd best fetch him some tea so he doesn't sack me."

Max was drawing her toward the kitchen when the first majestic bong echoed through the entrance hall. The two of them exchanged a disbelieving look as the clock continued to chime, finding its voice for the first time since the night of Angelica's eighteenth birthday ball. The clock didn't fall silent until it had chimed exactly twelve times.

They turned as one to find Angelica's papa triumphantly holding up a glowing ruby the size of his fist. "I thought it would be the safest place to hide it with all those fools traipsing through the house for your ball. How was I to know the damn thing would get stuck in the works?"

Max and Angelica exchanged a wondering look, then burst out laughing. Now that they no longer needed it, the Cadgwyck treasure had been found. They were wise enough now to know that the only true treasure lay in the love they had found in each other's arms.

As Max swept Angelica off her feet, still laughing with delight, the girl she had been gazed down at them from the portrait on the landing, her cheek finally dimpling in the smile she'd been holding back for all those years. Max winked at her over his wife's shoulder.

It seemed Maximillian Burke was a man who dreamed after all.

And she was the woman who had made all of his dreams come true.

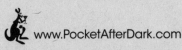

# Develop a passion
## for the past...
**Bestselling Historical Romances
from Pocket Books!**

**Pick up or download your copies today!**
PocketAfterDark.com

32660